AGENT OF DARKNESS

C.N. CRAWFORD

ALEX RIVERS

Agent of Darkness

Book 3 of the Dark Fae FBI Series.

Copyright © 2017 by C. N. Crawford and Alex Rivers.

All rights reserved.

❀ Created with Vellum

CHAPTER 1

I sat on Roan's floor, bathed in the orange light that licked along the length of a charred log in the fireplace. I pulled the rough wool blanket tighter around my naked skin. Exhaustion had seeped into my muscles like a toxin, eating at my tendons. The last few days had taken their toll on my body, and my legs wouldn't stop shaking. I felt like the last time I'd actually slept well had been in Roan's arms, listening to his heart beat, enveloped in his warmth.

But it wasn't just the physical effects of my journey through the woods that made me shiver. My thoughts churned in my mind like unquiet spirits. In the past few weeks, I'd discovered that the people who'd raised me weren't my birth parents. I was a fae changeling, swapped at birth. My biological father had been a sadistic monster known as the Rix—and I'd killed him. I'd trapped my human counterpart, Siofra, in a reflection. As far as I knew, she lingered there still.

Unable to get warm, I trembled under the coarse blanket, trying to block out the look in Siofra's eyes when she had realized what was happening to her.

1

With a sudden snap, the log in the fireplace broke into two, its pieces tumbling into the glowing embers. A stream of sparks shot up from the flames, the fire crackling. I took a shuddering breath.

Footsteps sounded behind me, and I turned to see Roan, clutching a pile of clothes. He dropped them next to my bag on the floor. "I found you something to wear."

Golden firelight danced over the beautiful planes of his face, and his emerald eyes burned into me. I forced my breathing to slow down, taking in the vicious tattoos that whorled over his thickly-corded forearms. He could feel my inner turmoil, the thoughts that roiled in my skull. I knew he could feel my emotions whirling out of control, though his expression remained stony, his jaw rigid with disapproval. I'd disappointed him by arriving days later than I'd promised, and he was not in a sympathetic mood. I could almost feel his anger washing over me.

Slowly, I rose. "Thanks." I had meant for it to sound grateful, but instead it sounded bitter, acidic.

Shadows darkened his eyes. "The king's men are canvasing the woods, looking for me. You can't stay here long. They'll sense your pixie energy."

I arched an eyebrow. "Your aura shields mine."

He folded his arms, glaring at me.

"Look, I came here," I said. "As I promised."

"We needed you days ago, at the Council—as I said. Your presence serves no purpose now."

I was not getting into that argument again. I couldn't have come at that point, not while my changeling twin had been slaughtering humans across the city. "You said that war is coming to the fae realm. Maybe we can still stop it. You said I was the key. Tell me what I need to—"

"I no longer need your help, and this war is none of your concern."

I took a deep breath. I'd traveled here past a frozen forest of fae monsters, and I didn't want to believe it served no purpose. "Tell me about the war," I said, hoping to stall, to distract him. "What was so important about this council meeting that I missed?"

He simply stared at me, his otherworldly stillness raising the hair on the back of my neck. Only the shadows moved over his golden skin. After a moment, he spoke again. "Tell me why you're really here."

"Because I made a promise, and I'm here to keep it."

"Lie." The air grew colder, the fire waning in the fireplace.

I frowned. "It's not a lie. I made a promise to you, and I intended to keep it. I'm true to my word." I didn't add the obvious second part of the sentence. Breaking a promise to a fae tended to end really badly, as I'd painfully learned.

"You're not telling me the whole truth." His low growl wrapped around me, tingling up my spine. His voice alone threw me off guard, and I found it hard to concentrate.

I sucked in a sharp breath, clearing my thoughts. Not telling him the whole truth. He was right—there was more than just the promise. After everything that had happened in London, my head had been a complete mess. I'd just needed to do *something*. "I didn't feel right just going back to America, just carrying on at the FBI like none of this had ever happened. Like the magical world didn't exist. I'm involved in the fae world now."

"Lie." Shadows darkened his eyes, and a chill whispered over my skin. "You're still not telling me the whole truth."

I swallowed hard. When I'd found myself alone and in quiet moments after defeating Siofra, I'd felt lost at sea with my own thoughts. I needed to escape them. As long as I kept moving, maybe I could stay one step ahead of the memories that threatened to drag me under the surface. I could forget the sounds of my mother's life slipping away from her, and

3

the toxic feel of the Rix's twisted soul just before I'd killed him. I craved distraction from those dark thoughts the way sunflowers craved the light. "I also needed an escape."

"And you thought I could help."

I nodded. If Roan kicked me out of here, I had nothing to return to. I couldn't just go back to my old life, haunted by these memories.

"And that's it? Those are all your reasons?"

"Yes."

For just a moment, I thought I saw a flicker of pain flash in his eyes. The air seemed to thin, cooling around me.

Really, I'd still only given him part of the answer. As I looked at him, I knew he'd drawn me here too, his beauty so exquisite that it actually *hurt* to look at him. And beyond the muscled body and golden skin, his eyes shone with a deep sadness. I couldn't escape the sense that grief seemed to hang over him like a funeral shroud, and right now, I had the strongest urge to cross to him and lay my hand against his chest, to feel his heart. I wanted to drop the blanket from my body and press myself against him, to feel the warmth of his naked skin against mine. I wanted to escape my own pain, and to pull him from his, too. But I knew if I tried anything like that, he'd just rebuff me. He didn't seem the type to forgive easily. "I'm sorry I disappointed you. I want to help. Maybe I still can."

"The timing mattered," he began. "The Callach said I needed to bring you to the Council when it was meeting." He cocked his head almost imperceptibly. "The Callach said you were the key." Something about his tone suggested he no longer entirely believed this claim.

"Why was the timing so important?"

"The fae High King—King Ogmios—had been fighting the Elder Fae in the Hawkwood Forest for centuries. After the council meeting, he defeated them, broke their forces, chased them away from their homes. Most of their warriors are dead, and those remaining are in hiding with Ebor, their king. This changes everything."

Dread whispered over my skin. "Why?"

"Because now King Ogmios is free to do what he's always wanted to do. To wage a war with his true enemies—the fae who drove him from his lands, who forced him to carve out his own kingdom from the lands of the Elder Fae. Now that he has vanquished his enemies here, he no longer fights two battlefronts. He is free to press with all his might and attack the Seelie."

My stomach lurched, and I held tighter to the blanket. "So let's find a way to stop him. If I'm the key, maybe I can still help."

He stared at me, the shadows seeming to thicken around him. "Since when do *you* care about our politics? About King Ogmios?"

"I don't want a war."

He moved closer, his muscles tightly coiled, like a snake about to strike. He peered down into my eyes, and I could feel the heat radiating from his powerful body. "What does an FBI agent care about a fae war?"

"I know that the casualties will be immense."

His eyes narrowed. "You are worried about the humans."

I stared right back at him. "Humans raised me. Of course I care about them."

"You think you belong among them? Among humans like your friend Gabriel—is that where you intend to live out your life?"

I shrugged. "I guess. I certainly don't get the sense I belong here."

For just an instant, a look of intense pain flashed in Roan's eyes. "And yet they don't accept you, do they? What would the CIA do with you, if they knew the truth about you?" He cocked his head. "I understand where your loyalty lies, and it means you are of no use to me. You're a liability. I needed you a week ago, before the slaughter of the Elder Fae tribes, but you failed me because of your loyalty to your humans. You have no place here. And moreover, you're not capable of fighting among the fae. As you said, you grew up among the humans."

The insult stung. Without thinking, I said, "I can fight as well as any fae. You've already seen me do it."

A muscle twitched in his jaw. "Cassandra. Go home. As far as I am concerned, you are worthless."

My heart hammered in my chest, and a heavy silence hung in the air. Maybe it was my fatigue, but tears pricked my eyes, and his words hit me like a punch to the gut. "Is that right?"

"You should return to your people," he said at last. "You have no business here. Get dressed, and I will take you to the portal."

* * *

ROAN'S white horse towered over me, and I stared up at it. I'd never ridden a horse, and this one seemed much larger and angrier than anything I'd seen before. Its black eyes locked on me, and it snorted, emitting a cloud of steam from its nostrils.

Roan leapt on the horse's back in one swift movement, grasping its reins. He peered down at me, waiting for me to climb on.

"What's his name?"

"Oberon. Aren't you joining us?" He failed to offer me any help.

"He's a bit tall."

He arched an eyebrow. "Of course. I should have expected as much."

I gritted my teeth, resolved to climb that horse even if it killed me. I knew nothing about horses, but I had done my share of wall climbing back in the Academy. That's what this was—a wall of muscle, skin, and hair

I walked back a few steps, then ran forward and leaped up, grabbing on to the horse's hair. As I did, the damn wall moved away. Still, ungracefully, I managed to hook my leg over its rump. I steadied myself by grabbing hold of Roan's enormous torso.

"Graceful," he said.

"I made it, didn't I?"

He shrugged, and kicked the horse into motion. The first step nearly made me tumble backward, and I tightened my grip, clinging tightly to Roan's chest. Under his dark wool sweater, I could feel his powerful muscles shifting slightly as he spurred his horse.

I wasn't ready for the horse's speed, for the lurches as he galloped. My legs tightened, and against my better judgment, I clenched my hands around Roan's body. He seemed completely at ease, his body moving as one with his steed. I somehow managed to do the exact opposite. When the horse would go down, my body would lift above it. Then the horse would rise up just as I came crashing down, my ass jolting against its body. I considered asking Roan to slow down, but pride stopped me. Surely he was unnerving me on purpose?

The horse jolted me hard, and my teeth snapped shut, nearly biting my tongue in half. As we rode, I took pleasure in digging my fingernails into Roan. He gave no indication that he minded, or that he enjoyed it. In fact, he gave no indication that he noticed my presence at all.

After a while, I figured out how to move in tune with the

horse, and the ride became more bearable. Exhaustion gripped my mind, and I found myself relaxing as I watched the cedars and pines from the corner of my vision. Milky sunlight sparked off icicles hanging from their boughs and flecked the snowy earth with sparks of light. The air smelled thickly of moss and soil, and the ancient wisdom of oaks. Slowly, the horse's rhythmic gallop began lulling me to sleep. For the first time in ages, my mind felt quiet, and beautiful images flickered in my mind—a sun-dappled river sparkling in the sunlight beneath the oaks, wild strawberries growing on its banks. I rested my head against Roan's back as the images claimed my mind.

"Damn it." Roan's voice suddenly jolted me awake.

"What is it?" I asked.

"The king's men."

My pulse began to race, and I searched the quiet, snow-laden oaks as we went past. "I don't see anyone."

"You will."

I hugged him tighter. "Why are they after you?"

"After the battle with the Elder Fae, they know for certain I'm working against them. But they can track me out here in the Hawkwood Forest."

He leaned forward, kicking up Oberon's speed into a proper gallop. The wind tore at my hair, and my breath left my lungs as we picked up speed, the trees moving past us in a blur. It seemed impossible that the horse could keep up this pace without slamming into a tree, but Roan navigated the woods seamlessly.

With a sound like a boom of thunder, the foliage behind us broke and a flock of large, copper-red birds burst between the branches, their wings shimmering. Oberon sped up, moving at breakneck speed, and I turned to look back at the birds. Then, from the shrubs, a rider emerged, snow spraying under his horse's feet, sparkling in the light, and the sight of him nearly stopped my heart. He had three bird-like heads, each covered in a dark hood. Long, curved beaks protruded from the hoods, their dark eyes glinting. And on his cloak, he wore a familiar insignia—a skull under water.

One of the heads opened a dark beak, unleashing a shrill battle cry that froze my heart. He drew a sword from his cloak, and spurred his horse.

Oberon huffed and snorted, his pace too fast to maintain, and the three-headed fae galloped closer. My mind scrambled for options. In the bag on my back, I had a gun loaded with iron bullets, but it was an awkward angle, and I doubted I'd hit him.

The mirrors in my bag… It would be good to have one on hand. Perhaps if I disappeared, Oberon could gallop faster, shake the pursuit. Gripping Roan with one hand, I fumbled in my bag with the other.

"Hold tight!" Roan snarled. "Let me lose him."

He suddenly twisted the reins, and I hugged him tighter. Behind us, the rider unleashed a shriek that echoed off the forest's oaks.

Off the trail, tree branches whipped at my body as we raced through the forest. Roan leaned down, and I followed suit, trying to shield my face. Several times, leaves and nettles lashed at my cheeks, and a large branch hit my back, tearing into my shirt and skin.

But the branches slowed the rider, too, ever so slightly. His flock of coppery birds swooped overhead.

"Hang on tight!" Roan pulled at the reins, and Oberon reared on his hind legs. I clung onto Roan for dear life, just managing to stay on. By the time Oberon's front hooves landed in the snow, Roan had unsheathed his sword.

The rider charged for us, his cries nearly unintelligible, but one word ringing out clearly. *Traitor!*

Roan swung his sword, striking it clean through one of

the rider's necks. The head tumbled off, and a hot arc of crimson blood stained the snow.

The rider turned sharply, still gripping his own sword. He charged us again, his shrieks piercing the quiet woodland. As he swung, Roan moved, quick as lightning, parrying his blow. He swung again, striking off another head, and blood spurted into the air. With a final shriek, the rider galloped off into the forest. I let out a long breath.

"Damn!" Roan snapped.

"What?"

"He'll get his men to block the trail to the portal. We won't be able to get through."

My heart thundered against my ribs. "Do we need to hunt him down and kill him?"

Roan shook his head. "He could be leading us into a trap. I don't want to risk being outnumbered. There's another way."

In the next moment, we were galloping again, leaving the severed heads behind us. I wiped at my cheek, my fingers coming away sticky with blood.

The wind whipped at my hair as Roan guided his horse over the rocky terrain. Slowly, a low roar began to drown out the sounds of the horse's footfalls in the snow. At last, the forest began to thin, and we approached a rolling river. Water rushed over sharp rocks, breaking in angry white foam. As I clung to Roan's body, he guided his horse directly to the most turbulent part of the river, where the water churned violently over rocks. What the hell was he doing?

"Roan?"

He ignored me, and my stomach lurched. But as Oberon's hoofs plunged into the water, the surface shimmered. A cool energy whispered over my skin, and the waters around me calmed, the rocks growing smaller and rounder.

"Ancient glamour," Roan said. "Created by the Elder Fae,

and recently used by the king's opposition. A secret rebel path, known only to a few."

I stared down at the water, mesmerized by the illusion. Wherever the horse stepped in the turbulent river, the waters calmed, growing shallow and clear. Darting away from the horse's hooves, small, emerald-green fish swam.

After a few minutes, the towering oaks began to look more familiar. The portal was nearby.

The adrenaline began to leave my body, and fatigue replaced it. My eyelids felt heavy, and I had the strongest urge to lean against his back and fall asleep.

"There." Roan pointed to an oak—the towering tree that would take me back to London.

Reluctantly, I climbed off Oberon. Away from Roan's warmth, a shiver overtook my body, and hollowness filled my ribs. I looked up at him. "Thanks for the ride."

He stared down at me. "Just returning you to where you belong."

A lump rose in my throat, and I walked to the portal, emptiness gnawing at my chest. I felt unmoored, I guess, completely untethered. I'd hoped Roan would be some kind of an answer for me—a goal, a mission. I needed to serve a purpose now. And maybe I wanted to feel his powerful arms around me again, so I could feel that sense of peace, sleeping against his beating heart. It seemed that in Roan's presence, the raging chaos on my mind went quiet.

Worthless. His word rang in my mind like a curse.

I could feel his eyes on me, as if to make sure he'd finally rid me from his life. I walked into the snug crevice of the oak, surrounded by the scents of the forest. While Roan stared at me, I thought of losing myself in London's crowded and winding streets, and the magic of the fae oak transported me.

CHAPTER 2

I stepped into the dingy reception area of the St.
Paul's Youth Hostel, the ground floor of an old
Victorian building. A white-haired man behind the desk
glared at me over the rims of his glasses. Yellow fluorescent
light flickered off his thick lenses.

I crossed to the desk. "Hi. I need a room." I frowned,
thinking of the youth hostels I'd been in before—the
cramped rooms with bunkbeds, people coming and going at
all hours. "Are there any single rooms?"

"Forty pounds a night." He looked me slowly up and
down, with the disgusted look you might give an old bit of
cheese in your fridge.

I was running seriously low on cash at this point, but I'd
pay whatever I had for my own room. "Great. Fine."

"How many nights?" Somehow, his tone conveyed that
zero was the preferred answer.

"I don't know. At least one. Maybe a few more."

"You pay in advance. Cash."

I nodded. Slung on my shoulder was the bag I'd stashed in
a locker at Liverpool Street Station for the past week. I'd

stashed in it all the things I couldn't use in the fae realm—a phone, my wallet, keys, some clothes, and a laptop. I shoved my hand into the bag and yanked out my wallet, divesting myself of two of my twenty-pound notes. The man snatched them up, narrowing his eyes as he examined the notes for signs of fraud. At last, he slid a room key across the desk.

When I climbed the narrow stairwell to the second floor, I found a dark hall covered in a faded blue carpet. Room twenty-seven was at the end of the hall, a white door with cracked paint. It creaked open into a small space that managed to seem both drab and garish at the same time: cracked, green walls and a gray carpet—what Scarlett would have called a *crapet*. And then on the bed, as if to try and battle with the horror of the green walls, butterflies and flowers of neon pink and purple covered the duvet. A large brown smudge on the carpet left me playing my favorite game, *Guess the Stain*. Coke? Blood? Vomit?

Still, the room was a perfect match for the dark, hollow feeling in my chest. Might as well run with the misery.

I dropped the bags near the door, my magic senses already attuning to reflections in the room. A body-length mirror hung on the wall beside the closet. Just down the hall, I could feel the reflections of the mirrors in the communal bathroom. Fainter reflections glowed from the single window pane, and the dull metal of the bed frame.

I approached the mirror, staring at myself. No wonder the receptionist had given me a chilly welcome. My clothing dripped into the rug. Brambles and horse hair covered my clothes. My hair was a mess—dirty and bedraggled, its pink tint fading. Purple smudges darkened my eyes. I stroked my fingers over the soft wool sweater Roan had given to me, now spattered in mud. If I lifted the fabric to my face, I could almost smell him—the faint scent of moss and musk. I'd fallen asleep on him once—in Trinovantum, curled in his lap, with my head on his chest. His warm arms around me, the sound of his beating heart had calmed me until I'd fallen into a deep sleep. I ached for that feeling of safety now.

Still, that wasn't an option. I let out a shuddering sigh, and felt for the reflection, merging with it. I tried to imagine the old Cassandra into it, the Cassandra who thought she was human, the FBI agent who helped catch serial killers and would scoff at the idea of magic. But I couldn't seem to control my thoughts. Instead, an image of my parents shimmered in the reflection. My mom and dad, as I wanted to remember them: sitting in the backyard in the afternoon sun, my father grilling burgers and awkwardly shimmying to "Hungry Like the Wolf" while he worked, my mom setting up citronella candles to keep the bugs away.

For just a moment, my chest unclenched. I wanted to step right into those entrancing images. But just as I shifted closer to the mirror, my treacherous mind cast the Rix into the reflection, standing by my father's grill, a cruel smile twitching on his face behind the smoke. I snarled, severing my connection to the mirror.

Horace and Martha Liddell had never known who I really was, that their daughter had been kidnapped, switched with a monster. What would they have thought of me if they'd known?

I tried to shove those thoughts to the back of my mind. The damn silence in this place would drive me crazy. My mind reeling, I pulled my phone from my bag and plugged it in to charge it. Then I snatched a change of clothes from my bag.

I hadn't brought a towel with me, which would make a shower interesting, but I headed down the hall anyway, pushing through a door into a beige-tiled room. In one of the stalls, I pulled off my clothes, shivering from the cold, then turned on a tepid stream of water.

In the quiet of the bathroom, with the sad stream of water running over my body, I couldn't ignore some basic questions.

Namely, what the fuck was I doing with my life at this point? I should have gone from the portal straight to the airport—should have bought the first available ticket back to the US, and tried to get my life back on track. I should have been heading back to the FBI like I was supposed to a week ago, moving on with my life.

As I soaped the forest grime from my body, I tried to think about what I could say to the chief. The FBI didn't know the fae existed. I couldn't tell him I'd stayed in London to fight my changeling twin, to prevent her from destroying the city. Maybe I could just beg forgiveness. He was a tough old man, but I suspected that somewhere inside he had a soft heart. I'd always been a favorite of his. Maybe I could even piece together some semblance of a normal life, with a nice, wholesome boyfriend I'd meet online.

I turned off the shower, stepping into the changing stall. I pulled my clothes onto my wet body without drying off, my underwear sticking to my thighs on the way up. At least the sweater I pulled on would keep me somewhat warm.

Back in my room, I threw myself down on the butterfly-flower duvet of horror. I stared at the ceiling, scanning the cracks. My mind churned relentlessly with the memories of the past few weeks, and somehow, the thought of returning to the States felt *wrong*.

The past week, I felt as if I'd been skimming over a chaotic bubble, a delicate sphere that protected me from the raging waters under its surface. And only one thing could keep me from plummeting into those chaotic depths: movement. I had to keep going, rushing along into the world of the fae, or my delicate bubble would burst.

I grabbed my phone off the bed. It still had less than

twenty percent battery. Leaving it plugged, I called Scarlett's number.

"Hello?" she answered almost immediately, her voice alert and sharp. "Cass?"

"Hey Scarlett." I tried to keep my voice steady.

"Cass, are you okay? What's wrong?" Apparently I had failed miserably at my attempts to hide the truth from my best friend.

I swallowed hard. "Scarlett, I'm so tired."

"Cass, where are you?"

"A hostel. In London."

"Back from your vacation already?" she asked, her voice soft, but carrying an undercurrent of tension. The line wasn't secure, I knew. Talking about my recent visit to Trinovantum wouldn't be a good idea.

"Yeah." I sniffed. "The, uh... guy I was visiting wasn't interested to see me after all."

"It wasn't a good idea, Cass. You need to come back to the States."

Come back. I realized what she was saying, and another pang of loneliness hit me. "You've left the UK already?"

She let out a sigh. "Yeah. I flew back two days ago. I'm back in the States."

"Oh."

"Cass, you should *really* come home. We have a lot to talk about. Face to face. And I think your guys are getting kind of impatient with your disappearing act."

"Yeah." My voice sounded hollow. "You're right."

"Cass, you sound terrible."

"I'm just tired. I haven't slept for..." I thought back. "For days. I'm worn out."

"So you said." Worry tinged her voice.

I suddenly regretted calling her. I should have known we

wouldn't be able to talk properly on the phone. "I wish you were here."

"Me too, sweetie. You want me to buy you a ticket home? All you need to do is show up at Heathrow."

"Thanks, but it's okay. I'll do it."

"Get some sleep," she said. "I can buy you a ticket, and you can pay me back later. They need you here."

"I'm not convinced I still have a job, Scarlett."

"Cass…"

That image flashed in my mind again—my parents, with the Rix looming behind them. "Did you know that my parents weren't my real parents?" I asked. "Did it say that in my file?"

"We can't talk about your file right now."

A sudden realization struck me like a punch to the gut. "Cassandra Liddell isn't even my name. The name belonged to another baby, one stolen by the fae." I could almost see her eyes—the horrified look on Siofra's face when I'd trapped her in the void between reflections.

"Cass," Scarlett said firmly. "This isn't a secure line, and I think you really need to sleep—"

"It's not my name, It's a… a… stolen name. I trapped its owner…"

I heard a click as she hung up the line, obviously trying to cut short my indiscretions.

Right. Not a secure line.

I was barely hanging on, I knew. Exhaustion and the oedipal horror of killing my own dad were causing an emotional meltdown. Not to mention the deep sting of Roan's rejection. Scarlett was right. I should sleep, and in the morning, I'd buy a ticket and go back home, forget this whole disaster of a trip.

I slid my legs under the sheets, flicked off the bedside lamp, and pulled the blankets tight around my shoulder.

My mind whirling, I rolled to my stomach and closed my eyes, willing sleep to come. But instead, memories echoed in my skull. My mother's voice: *Such a chubby-faced baby. Everyone in the maternity ward fell in love with you instantly.* Then, the sound of my mother's dying breath the day she'd been murdered. I'd hid under the bed, staring at my discarded sweatshirt on the floor, listening to my world fall apart. Then the images flickered faster in my mind: My first day of school; my seventh birthday, a roller-skating party with arcade games; the day I got the ballerina doll for Christmas.

How would it have all turned out if I hadn't been swapped? If I'd grown up in Trinovantum with the Rix and… and…

And who?

If the Rix was my father, who was my birth mother?

Distraction. I had been desperate for something to take me away from these memories, and now that this tantalizing question dangled in front of me, I clung to it desperately. I might have a mom out there. If I could find her, maybe I had a chance at getting a family back. Maybe she *wanted* to see me.

I couldn't go back to the US just yet. I still had a bit of my past to uncover. I needed to know my identity. I was a pixie; I had a human mother whose name I didn't know.

I rose from the bed, completely giving up on sleep, and pulled on my shoes.

* * *

As I WALKED down the creaking stairs to Leroy's Wine Bar, a sad jazz tune wound over the low hum of conversation. Over the sound of a trumpet and sax, a woman sang forlornly about a lost love who'd abandoned her by the seashore.

At the bottom of the stairs, I scanned the room for just a moment, taking in the familiar decor—the tunnels that branched off from the main room, the barrels of aged wine, and the old heraldic emblems hung on the walls: a raven, a dove, a skull under water, foxglove, a phoenix. But the emblem that most drew my eye was the one that had been defaced, its surface smashed. The six kingdoms of Trinovantum, one of them ruined. Once, I'd asked Roan about the smashed emblem, and he'd simply changed the subject.

At the thought of him, and that look in his face when he'd kicked me out of his house, an ache gripped my chest. I hugged myself, looking at Leroy's patrons for the first time. That was when I noticed the dozens of suspicious eyes, staring directly at me.

Since I'd walked in, all conversation had ceased. A woman whose blue hair cascaded down to her hips gaped at me through milky white eyes; another with mahogany skin, dressed in a white velvet doublet, had paused mid-wine-sip to stare in my direction. A man with a pointed beard and black lace collar narrowed his eyes at me. Even the sax player stared.

That's right. Last time I'd been here, I'd brought Scarlett with me, and she'd threatened everyone with an iron-bullet gun. Apparently that didn't go over well with the fae crowd.

Still, they didn't look like they were about to attack. The only person *not* staring at me right now was the woman singing into the microphone, her long, silver hair draped over a crimson gown, seemingly lost in the pain of her own song. I listened to the music for several seconds, meeting the glares around me, trying to appear casual, relaxed. Slowly, the faces turned away, and the muttered conversations resumed.

I heaved a sigh, spotting a narrow-framed figure hunched

over a barstool, his shaggy blond hair hanging in his eyes. *Alvin.* Just who I'd wanted to find.

Keeping my head down, I crossed to him. As I walked, I couldn't help but notice that the bar patrons seemed to visibly recoil from me as I walked past them.

As I approached Alvin, a haze of marijuana smoke greeted me, and he turned to smile lazily at me, his eyes bloodshot. "All right, boss?"

"Yeah," I lied. "How are you?"

"Leroy!" he called out. "Claret for my friend, here! And one for me, while you're at it."

Leroy pushed through a door by the bar, frowning at me. "You want two clarets?"

I nodded, my body tight with nervous energy. "A generous pour, please." I tapped the faded wooden bar, my chest aching with a familiar hollowness. "In fact, can you just bring us a bottle?"

He nodded and turned to the rack behind him. I swiveled my stool, turning to face Alvin. He wore a black jacket over a shirt that read, *If we can't make it, we'll fake it—NASA, 1969.*

He stared at me, his eyes glazed. "You sure you're all right?"

I nodded. "Yeah, thanks. How are you? Everything okay with your... acquaintances?"

Last time we'd met, Alvin had told me he'd been acting as a double agent for the CIA Fae Unit. If the king had found out, Alvin would be dead right now. So I'd helped him out, deleting his name from the CIA database.

"Yeah. It's all cool now. Cheers for that."

I smoothed my wrinkled shirt, casting another nervous glance around the bar. "Everyone here seems on edge."

"Yeah?"

"Yeah." I leaned in, whispering. "I guess they're still pissed off about the gun thing."

He snorted. "Come on, Cass. No one gives a fuck about that."

"They don't? Then why am I getting all the death stares?"

"Can't you even feel what you're projecting?" He swirled his glass of water. "You're a storm on the horizon, Cass. You feel like a hurricane of anger and pain."

I blinked. "Oh. You don't seem to mind."

"I'm lean."

"What?"

"I'm stoned. It helps."

Leroy slid two large wine glasses across the bar, then filled them up slowly, and I watched, transfixed, as the amber liquid caught in the pale candlelight of his bar. He left the bottle and slunk into the shadows, then leaned in the corner, arms folded, looking half asleep.

Light glinted through the dark green glass of the bottle— the color of Roan's eyes. I took a sip of the claret, letting the sweet liquid linger on my tongue before swallowing it. Maybe if I drank enough of this stuff, I could finally relax.

I nodded at the singer. "She's good."

Alvin shrugged. "She's been singing these sad songs for a few hundred years. I've heard them all before."

"Is she particularly sad about something?"

He swiveled in his chair, watching the singer. "Her fella left her for his soulmate three hundred years ago, and she never got over it."

I took another sip of claret. "His soulmate?"

"Yeah. Some fae have soulmates. People talk about it like it's a gift from the gods, but it's mostly something that ruins everyone's lives. Like Roxanne here." He lifted a glass to the singer, a tribute. "Her life is ruined."

"So, what—people are predestined to love others, and there's nothing anyone can do about it? You have to leave the person you've been with for centuries, just because fate says so?"

"Yeah. It's some bullshit, if you ask me."

"No arguments here."

He turned to face me. "I'm surprised to see you here. I heard you went to Trinovantum."

"How did you hear that? Who told you?"

"I know things, Cass. That's what I do."

I sipped my wine. "Well, I'm back. And I need some information."

"Really?" His eyes flickered with an orange glow. "What about?"

"My birth mother."

"Oh? What about her?"

I took a long sip before answering. "You know what I am."

"A nice girl," Alvin said. "A Fed. A pixie—"

"A changeling."

"Yeah. That too."

"You knew all along. You even told me, when I asked about Siofra." I felt the tears stinging my eyes.

He lifted his bony shoulders in a shrug. "I knew… some of it."

"You could have saved me a lot of trouble if you'd just told me from the start. Maybe you would have saved some lives."

"I deal in secrets, Cassandra. You know what makes a secret valuable?"

I drained the last of my glass, not responding.

"Of course you do. Secrets are valuable when not many people know them."

"Is that all you care about? The value of your wares?"

"What do you need, Cass?"

I refilled my glass. "I want to know who gave birth to me —who my real mother is."

"I haven't got a clue."

My spirits sank. It had been a flimsy hope to begin with, but now that it was shattered, I felt the emptiness starting to eat at me again.

He took a deep breath. "But I have something that could help you find out."

My eyes met his, trying to appear calm. "What is it?"

"What do you have to trade for it?"

"What do you need?"

"You can always… owe me a favor."

"No. Never again." Last time, it nearly got me killed. "Name another price. How about dinner?"

"Nah, that won't even come close to covering it. But you should get it for me anyway. It's a good way to start the bargaining process, know what I mean? Leroy recently got a wheel of Vacherin Mont d'Or that's mad good. Let's start with that, shall we?"

I sighed and glanced at Leroy. "Can we have a plate of… what he wants, and some bread?"

"And make sure it's the Vacherin. Don't give me that American knock-off shit and think I won't know, Leroy. I always know." He stared at Leroy, muttering, "I always know."

Leroy grunted, pushing past the kitchen door.

I knocked back a long slug of claret, then met Alvin's gaze. "So, how do I find my mother?"

"First, let's talk about what you can give me."

With my next sip of wine, I finally felt what I needed—that gentle slowing and dulling of my thoughts. At last, the tension in my shoulders began to relax. So what did Alvin value? "How about some information?"

He nodded. "What do you have?"

Leroy returned, placing a round, wooden tray with a slab of bread and cheese on the bar. Steam curled off the bread.

Alvin snatched a piece, spreading some cheese on its surface. He took a deep bite, and shut his eyes in pleasure.

I grabbed a piece of the warm bread. "The previous mayor of London was a changeling."

"Come on, Cass. *Everyone* knows that. That has no value."

I thought hard. "War is coming. The king is planning to attack the Seelie."

"Do you really need me to explain again what makes a secret valuable?" Alvin sucked a smudge of cheese off his thumb.

"Fine!" I gritted my teeth, considering leaving. I closed my eyes, searching my mind for a piece of intel this infuriating fae might want. And as I thought, an image burned in my mind. Siofra's eyes, after I'd trapped her in the reflection. "Siofra," I said slowly.

"What about her?"

"She's gone." I took a sip of wine. "But she isn't dead."

His chewing slowed down, his eyes glimmering with that uncanny orange color. "Isn't she, now? Talk softly. I have good ears."

I lowered my voice. "She's trapped. Trapped between mirrors. Still alive."

He stared at me, his body taking on that eerie fae stillness. "You've changed, Cass. It feels as if only weeks ago you blundered in here to ask me how magic works."

My mind had taken on a happy buzz, and I poured myself another glass. "It *was* only weeks ago."

"And now look at you."

"Only *I* know this," I said. After a moment I added, "And maybe Scarlett. I told her part of it."

"Still. A good secret."

"So how can I find my mother?"

He put down his bread and reached into the fold of his jacket, then pulled out a round, tarnished brass object. It looked like an old pocket watch. He handed it to me, and I clicked it open, revealing a compass. The needle swiveled round and round, never stopping.

"What do I do with this?" I asked.

"You think of the person you're looking for, while holding it to your right cheek. It'll start pointing toward that person's aura."

"What if the person is dead?"

"It'll point to where her essence is strongest. A home she lived in for many years, or a place she used to visit often. Possibly her grave."

"What if she's two thousand miles away?"

"It'll still point to the right way, but you'd have a hell of time finding her."

For the first time in days, my mind felt at ease. "How do I think of her if I don't know the first thing about her?"

"All you need is an idea. You are talking about the woman who gave birth to you. That's an idea."

"Okay." I pocketed the compass, smiling. "Thanks."

"Sure." He sliced another piece of the cheese. "I hope finding her makes you whole, Cass."

CHAPTER 3

I stood outside Leroy's, shivering in the chilly night air, dwarfed by the towering spires of Guildhall. For once, the memories that had been plaguing me over the past week, that word *worthless* that had been rolling in my mind relentlessly, had all gone quiet. Probably something to do with the half-bottle of wine I'd chugged, and the ground tilting beneath my feet. *Obviously,* I thought, *I should go back to the hostel, sleep it off, and try to use the compass tomorrow when I'm sober.* But I had to see how this thing worked first.

I pulled the compass out of my pocket and flipped it open. Its needle whirled, occasionally shuddering to a halt for a second, and then moving again, searching. I took a deep breath, and held the compass to my cheek, thinking of what my birth must have been like, of a biological connection to a woman I had never known. What was she like? Did she look anything like me? Had she given me up for adoption, or had the fae abducted me?

In the back of my mind, a silhouette formed of my mother, a hollow form, made of questions.

The metal on my cheek began pulsing with warmth.

When I pulled it away, the tarnished compass metal pulsed with a gentle silver light. The needle pointed southeast, completely unwavering. I crossed down Guildhall Yard, following the arrow.

With my eyes glued to the metal circle, I began to walk along the quiet city streets, staring at the needle. For all I knew, it could be pointing to Italy, or the United States, or a location in the middle of the ocean. Nevertheless, I walked, following the needle's signal, my mind and gaze focused on it completely.

When I got near Walbrook—the site of the underground river, where I could sometimes hear tormented screams—the needle suddenly jumped a fraction, and my heart leaped. I took a few steps back, then walked forward again. It was no accident. It moved with me.

If the target were far away, it wouldn't move. It would point stubbornly the same way, just like most compasses point toward the north pole, never shifting. I was homing in on her, moving past the wide streets around Bank Station, following the needle south. The way the needle moved, it sure seemed like my mom was in *London*—not far at all. My pulse began to race. Was it really possible?

I turned onto an old, narrow road—St. Swithin's Lane, an alley, really. Modern buildings towered over the passage. The needle led me onward until some of the architecture began to look older; Victorian buildings with ornate stone cornices. I watched as the needle slowly edged along, until it reached a fixed point. At the end of the alley, I stepped into a larger, shop-lined road, with a few black taxi cabs rolling along. The needle pointed sharply to the right.

I turned onto the wide sidewalk, and the needle now aligned almost completely with the direction I faced. I was heading the right way. As I walked, the needle vibrated, until at last it stopped, pointing right again. My heart thudding, I raised my eyes, staring at a building's façade.

I knew where I was, and my heart began to sink.

Roan had taken me here weeks ago, when he'd first told me about the fae. It was where I'd caught my first glimpse of Trinovantum—the building that housed the London Stone.

Slowly, I crouched next to the ornate iron grill in the wall beside me. Beyond it, protected behind dull glass, yellow light glowed over the London Stone. I moved the compass left and right next to the Stone, watching the needle. It followed the limestone, constantly pointing to its center. This was where it had fucking led me?

Sadness bloomed in my chest, and before I knew it, a hot tear trickled down my cheek. I'd honestly thought the compass was leading me to my mom—a flesh and blood woman who could finally give me some answers. But it hadn't. It led me to this stone—a lifeless thing—and that meant my mother had died. Here, perhaps.

I took a deep breath, trying to think clearly. If Alvin had been speaking the truth, my mother's essence lingered here. What did that mean? When Roan had first taken me here, he'd used the Stone to show me a vision of Trinovantum. He'd treated the rock with a reverence I hadn't seen from him since. What the hell *was* this Stone, exactly? A connection to the fae realm. Maybe a portal?

I looked between the bars and the glass that protected it. It was difficult to see into the room beyond the glass, but through the darkness, I could see racks of clothing. A sports store, perhaps.

I let my magic seep into the building, searching. As if pulled by a magnetic tug, my magic homed in on the reflections inside, on metal and glass. I rummaged in my bag, took out one of my hand mirrors, and stared at it, merging with a mirror on one of the shop walls. My mind clicked as I bonded with it, and I felt the cool rush of magic wash over my skin as I jumped into the reflection.

I stepped out into the darkened shop, turning around until I spotted the Stone in the window. I wove between the racks of clothing to get to the Stone, staring at the glass smudged with fingerprints and dust. This ancient, powerful relic had obviously seen better times.

I knelt in front of it, wondering how Roan had managed to use it. I tried to *feel* for the Stone, like I felt for reflections. I pressed my hand against the dingy glass, but felt nothing. Closing my eyes, I thought of Trinovantum. Nothing. When I took out the compass, I found that it still pointed at the Stone. This was definitely the right place. Cold sweat broke out on my skin.

I thought of my mother, of a woman holding me as a newborn. Questions roiled in my mind like a storm, breaking through the haze of my wine buzz. Had my mom gotten to hold me? Had it hurt her when they took me away? The questions echoed in my skull, amplified by my loneliness. My heart raced, hammering hard against my ribs. My vision went dark, until an image of rushing water pooled in my mind, the currents surrounding my skin, moving higher up my body. Terrified screams pierced my mind, the cries of the sacrifices…

My eyes snapped open again, and I stared, pain lancing my knuckles. Consumed by the hallucination, I'd punched my damn fist through the glass. Blood dripped down my fingertips, staining the dusty shelf. And yet the Stone seemed to pull me closer.

As if drawn in by a gravitational pull, I touched its rough surface. The instant my fingers made contact, a wave of noise slammed over me. It felt like plunging into a river of voices, my own voice a mere drop among the cacophony, inter-twining with the rest. There was no *me* anymore. No

Cassandra—no Rix's daughter, worthless terror leech. Just the river of tormented screams in a void of darkness.

In the shadows, whirling eddies of fearful, sorrowful, tormented voices churned together, clamoring against each other. The sounds of Hell filled my body with a dark thrill, intense power that vibrated along my skin, ran up my spine. Maybe it horrified me, but I *needed* it—a release from my own thoughts.

A powerful charge of horror enveloped me, pulling me under, until nothing existed but me and the black rush of the screams. And then, just for a fragment of a moment, I recalled a name: *Cassandra*. I forced myself to roll this idea around in my mind, slowly collecting bits and pieces of myself from the river. I was an FBI agent. I liked Oreos, hip-hop, and I couldn't tell expensive wine from the cheap stuff which meant I liked all of it. I liked watching dance videos and binge-reading historical romances about brawny Scottish lairds. I used to keep a diary in high school with cutouts of old movie stars I wanted to look like—Audrey Hepburn, Grace Kelley. I was a pixie, a half-fae. I'd been stung by bees three times and had an allergy to bananas. I was a profiler. My first crush was a boy nicknamed Blaze who wore eyeliner and played guitar. I was a terror leech. And a changeling.

I'd come to find the woman who'd brought me into the world.

Where was I? Had I moved *inside* the Stone somehow? The space around me pulsed with life, and the Stone seemed to connect me to the rest of the city—and not just London as it existed now, but ancient London, the layers of its history. I was mainlining centuries of London's terror. I began to drown in the din of the disembodied wails.

I unleashed a shriek into the river, "Mom!", but the screams drowned out my voice. I sought her, sought a connection with a woman who'd been separated from her daughter. I felt for that sense of loss.

Somewhere in the torrent, a soft keening rose above the rest and I could feel a link, something shared. A genetic link? Shared loss? I only knew it was a bond. I tried to touch the voice, to tell her I wanted to help, to ask how I could get her out of there. But the cry just kept going, radiating sorrow and fear.

The next thing I knew, I was lying flat on the gray carpet, breathing hard, tears streaming down my face. Pain seared my hand where I'd punched the glass. When I pushed myself up to look at it, I felt nauseated at the sight of the gashes running down my forearm. At least one of them was deep, running with blood. Stumbling to my feet, I snatched a sports jersey off the rack to staunch the bleeding. I glanced at the broken display case, at my blood streaming over the jagged edges of glass. Even though I was no longer touching the Stone, voices still clamored in my head. The screams of tortured souls, and one that keened above the rest—the one connected to me. What had *happened* to her? I needed to know.

Stumbling to one of the shiny, metallic clothing racks, I stared into the reflection, searching for somewhere safe.

CHAPTER 4

I lay on the bed in the hostel, yearning for sleep, but
the voices echoing in my mind kept snapping me
awake. Every time I drifted off for a few minutes, the
screams turned into nightmares. Images rose in my mind—
men and women standing by a riverside, dressed in white
robes, their cries piercing the air. Old Cassandra would have
diagnosed herself with auditory hallucinations and a stress-
induced psychotic break, but Old Cassandra hadn't known
the truth. She hadn't known about magic. After a few
seconds of sleep, my eyes would snap open again, and I'd pull
the blanket tightly around me.

Slowly, a theory grew about the Stone. It had felt *alive,* a
pulsing nexus in a living city. Not its heart, but part of its
brain—a conscious entity. The London Stone was like the
city's amygdala—the ancient part of the brain that told us if
we should fight or run. And somehow, by mainlining
London's terror, I'd screwed up my own brain. How? I didn't
know. I guess I'd skipped the *Magical Stones and Their Effect
on the Brain* class in grad school.

After several hours of rolling around in bed, I grabbed my

phone, glancing at the time. Half past three. How long had I been in the Stone? Minutes? Hours? It had felt like days.

I threw off my covers and rose from my bed, my mind reeling. How long had I been awake? Too long.

Even if I didn't know what the Stone had done to my brain, I knew what insomnia did. My thalamus—the central switching station of the brain—would burn out. All the functions of the prefrontal cortex—emotional regulation, planning ability, reality-testing—it would all go to shit. Then my brain would feed on its own neurons and synaptic connections while my emotions completely took over.

Basically, I had to sleep, or I'd finish my descent into insanity pretty fast. Blinking, I pulled on my jacket. Obviously, I needed more wine to quiet the fucking screaming in my head. Just enough that I could pass out.

I quickly pulled on my jeans and my leather jacket, then snuck through the darkened hostel's lobby into the cool night air. Silence fell over the city at this time of night, which disturbed me. Without distractions, I had nothing to listen to but the echoes of screams in my mind. What the hell had that thing *done* to me? I felt as if toxins from the Stone had seeped into my mind, poisoning me. But of course, that didn't make a lot of sense.

I hurried across the street to a twenty-four hour Tesco. When the doors slid open, the fluorescent lights of the supermarket felt blinding. My head pounded, and shapes clouded my vision. I blinked to clear my mind.

A maze of consumer products lay before me—beans, white bread, frozen foods. I wandered between the shelves for what felt like hours, lost. And then I found what I was looking for. The booze section. I scanned it until I got to the cheapest bottle I could find—something simply called *French Wine* for £2.99. Perfect. All I needed was something to dull the screams, to ease me to sleep. It didn't need to be good.

I pulled two bottles from the shelf, then crossed to the checkout line.

The young woman at the counter frowned at me. I knew what she saw: a disheveled woman who looked half-insane buying cheap wine at close to four a.m. I didn't care. If she could hear the screams in my head, and if she knew what I knew, she might be indulging in a tipple, too.

I swiped my card. When it beeped, I snatched the plastic bag from the counter. As I hurried back to the hostel, pulling out my key card, I tried to block out the voices that rolled around my skull in waves.

As soon as I got back into the hostel room, I unscrewed the cap of the first bottle. I took a swig. Then another, trying to chug down as much cheap wine as I could. Lucky for me, I wasn't a wine connoisseur, so the £2.99 French Wine seemed good enough—though when I drank it, it became clear that it paled in comparison to Leroy's claret, and the generic label was starting to bother me. Maybe I should have sprung for something fancier even if I couldn't taste the difference, just so I didn't feel like a total wino. Still, the cheap stuff did the job.

When I'd drained half the bottle, the voices began to quiet in my mind. The dingy hostel room tipped and turned, my mind emptying, dulling. I rummaged in my bag, pulled out a pen, and scrawled the word *Fancy* over the wine's label.

As the sharp cries dulled to a low roar, nothing remained in my mind but a dim sense of misery. And with that, I finally fell asleep in my clothes.

* * *

"Can I help you?" The young blond woman stared at me from behind the counter at the sports shop, her eyes betraying her thoughts. The main thought being *you look like shit.*

I glanced down at myself, taking in the jeans with the zipper down, the T-shirt covered in mustard stains... *When the hell did I eat mustard? Please don't tell me I ate a sausage from a street vendor.*

I tried to discreetly zip up my fly, my eyes already trailing back to the display case. A white cloth covered half of it, draped over the jagged hole in the glass. The bottom half of the London Stone still showed under the cloth, humming with a strange power that drew me in. I *needed* to touch it again, to hear that one scream.

Maybe I could just tell this woman that my mother's essence lingered in that rock, trapped and alone. As I stepped nearer to the Stone, the screams grew deafening.

Peering around the corner of a small glass fridge of sports drinks, the shop clerk narrowed her eyes. Probably wondering if she should call the police at this point. Did she suspect that I'd smashed the glass? A mixture of blood and mustard stained the bandage on my wrist.

I met her gaze. "Just looking for a bottle of water." I opened the fridge and pulled out a bottle. "Got it."

My hands trembled as I dropped it on the countertop, the screams still echoing in my mind. The clamoring emotions overwhelmed my own thoughts.

I forced a smile. "I like to stay hydrated." Did that sound normal?

No. That most definitely did not sound normal.

* * *

LATE THAT NIGHT, I shimmered into the shop again, shivering, sickness climbing up my throat. When had I last eaten?

As soon as I left the shop, I'd get some food. Anything but a street sausage.

The London Stone loomed in the display case, drawing me closer. I couldn't explain why I'd come. The thing *terrified* me, filled my skull with these terrible screams. And yet, I yearned to feel that dark thrill that had surged over my body when I'd touched it, the power so intense it had drowned out my own thoughts. I just needed the screams to be *loud* enough. Pure terror, not the memories that haunted my mind. When I'd touched the Stone, for just a few moments, I'd lost myself in the rushing torrents of screams. It had felt like freedom—a dark, Dionysian ecstasy. The ancients had known the importance of this feeling, this freedom from the thoughts that haunted us.

More than that, it connected me to my mother. I'd heard her voice there, wailing above the rest. I couldn't tell what compelled me to the Stone more: the need for that release, or the desperation to connect with my mom.

Haltingly, I moved closer, until I stood before the cloth-covered glass. I reached out, lifting the fabric, staring at the rough limestone surface, and I felt it tug on my body. My fingers trembled as I reached into the jagged hole.

Of course I *shouldn't* touch the rock, but I wanted to lose myself in the screams again. As if hearing my doubts, the rock's power flowed into my mind, a river of wails. For just a moment, I melded with the Stone—and through it, with another presence: a masculine spirit. From its smooth surface, visions arose: a powerful hand, gripping a sword, the blade slicing through a woman's neck by a riverside. Those same hands, dripping red wax onto a folded parchment, and sealing it with the symbol of a cypress tree. Then, the same powerful hands, picking up a blade, driving it into the soft flesh below a woman's ribs; I felt the stranger's murderous thrill lighting up my body with power. Then, an apple orchard, fruit hanging from a bough, red and tempting until the skin blackened and rotted before my eyes.

My hand shook harder, and the glass pierced the skin on my wrist. The shock of pain brought me to my senses, and I snatched my hand back, forcing myself to step away.

Fuck. I needed to stop this. I didn't know what was going on at this point, but this wasn't good.

I scrambled back, my blood dripping onto the floor. The screams that had lured me to the mirror called me back, begging me for mercy. And in their cries, three words rang out: *Mistress of Dread.*

* * *

I BLINKED in Tesco's blindingly bright lights. The clerk glared at my feet, and as I swayed before the counter, it took me a moment to realize why. I'd stumbled out of the hostel wearing a pair of slippers, paired with a gold cocktail dress. Crumbs littered my dress, and what I could only assume was wine stained the front. I *really* needed to look in the mirror before venturing out or they'd stop selling me wine and whiskey, but the damn screams in my mind kept distracting me.

"They're comfortable," I said. "The slippers."

Glaring at me, the woman behind the counter took my second bottle of whiskey, scanning it.

I'd already prepared the pound notes as she scanned the third bottle, and I thrust them at her. I yearned to get back to my hotel room, dim the echoes in my mind, to sleep deeply.

Maybe I'd just visit the Stone one more time before going to bed, hear my mom again. Maybe this time she wouldn't be screaming.

* * *

I STOOD in the hostel bathroom, staring at the mirror. The Stone looked back at me, visible in the reflection of the display glass. If I reached into the reflection, I could touch it. Would I hear my mother's voice again? Could I free her? That would be an interesting experiment: most of my body in a dirty communal bathroom, my hand on the London Stone more than a mile away, my soul merging with it. I raised the whiskey to my lips, took a swig, relishing the delicious burn in my throat.

What time was it? Near three a.m. maybe? But then, ruddy daylight lit the limestone surface, staining it rose. It must be dawn already. Somewhere in another dimension, a mentally functioning Cassandra jogged in a park, eating grapefruit for breakfast, feeling good to be alive.

My phone buzzed—probably Scarlett again. I ignored it, staring at the Stone. My mind felt heavy, sluggish with the whiskey.

I resisted touching the Stone again, letting its image shimmer away, and my reflection returned, staring at me. My pale pink hair hung lank over my shoulders, and purple bags darkened the skin below my bloodshot eyes. I looked like absolute shit. *Worthless.*

Somewhere inside, my mind screamed at me to get out of that city, away from that terrible rock before it was too late. Before Cassandra Liddell disappeared forever.

* * *

"CASS, PLEASE," said Scarlett. "What are you talking about?"

Lying flat on my back, I held the phone to my ear, frustrated that she wasn't getting this. "I said I found my mother. What's left of her. She's in the city's amygdala." I tried to mask the trembling in my voice, the slurring of my words. Maybe I should have called *after* the whiskey had worn off. But then again, if I sobered up, the screams would return.

"The what now?" she asked.

"The amygdala, where the fear lives. I heard my mother's voice in the Stone." What was so complicated about this?

"Cass, sweetie. Your mother is dead. What do you—"

"Not *that* mother! Not the woman who raised me. I'm talking about my birth mother. I found *her*. She's in the London Stone, or at least her spirit is. And when I touch it… I feel power. Terror and power. It means something. It's like… like a reservoir of terrible things. Fear and horror, like the ancient part of the brain. Right?"

Silence greeted me for a few long moments. "Cass, I'm buying you a plane ticket right now. I want you to get back here. Whatever you're talking about, we'll get this sorted."

"I'm not coming back! Not until I figure out how my mom is connected to the Stone, and what it's for. I can hear her screaming, like she was there. Or her spirit is trapped there. You know what I mean? But I need your help, Scarlett, I need everything the CIA has on the London Stone. It's some sort of fae artifact, or a tool. It's important."

"Cass, this line isn't secure."

I waved my hand. "Who do you think is listening to us? The fae? They don't even have phones, let alone wiretaps. Their technology ends in the Iron Age. Trust me. And anyway, they've got bigger things to worry about than us."

"I'm about three seconds from hanging up on you," she said. "I know you've been through some shit, but you're endangering national security interests. Not to mention my job. You need to get some coffee, sober up, and get a flight back to the States. And then maybe you should see a thera-pist or something. I don't know. You're better with all the touchy-feely stuff than I am, but I feel like if I were babbling incoherently to you, you would tell me to see a therapist."

Anger ignited. "Incoherent? I've just given you a crucial piece of intel—the rock is full of tormented spirits. And you're telling me I need therapy? You don't trust me anymore?"

"Maybe if you were sober it would make more sense, but as it is, no, I don't really trust your judgment. The only reason I haven't hung up already is that it's so nonsensical, you're not leaking anything useful. I'd go to London to bring you home myself if I could, but I've got a crisis here, and two dead agents. So I need you to get some sleep and some coffee, and get the hell out of London."

"I might be drunk, yes, but that's because of the screams. My work is here. In London. The Stone is a seat of ancient power."

"You're clearly not working effectively right now, Cass, or you wouldn't be slurring your words."

"I'm not coming back, Scarlett. And if you're not going to help me, you're worthless to me." I hung up, my body shaking, then threw the phone out the window. I watched it as it tumbled through the air, smashing on the dark street below. I'd switched a lot of phones in this city. Maybe I should stop buying new ones.

* * *

I sat in my underwear at the edge of my bed, staring at the Stone's reflection in my last hand mirror. I watched it with bloodshot eyes, trying to tear myself away. I fumbled for the whiskey, but the damn bottle lay empty. How many bottles had I gone through in the past few days?

Blinking blearily, I scanned the room until I spotted the shopping bag with a single bottle still in it. I let out a breath of relief. Still one to go. I returned my gaze to the Stone, mesmerized. Where had it come from?

The reflection shimmered, changed, and I blinked as it solidified, revealing an image of a towering limestone, standing in a field of tall grasses, white anemones, bluebells, and dandelions. The stone looked different—larger, but I recognized it all the same. The London Stone.

The image shimmered again, giving way to an image of an ancient city: the London Stone towered over a dirty street, and white timber-framed buildings with ruddy tiled roofs lined the road. A crow landed on the stone surface, puffing its wings. Women in white dresses, their curling locks piled up high, walked past the Stone.

I was watching the Stone through time, centuries ago. How could this be possible?

The image flickered, the buildings growing taller and darker—but engulfed in flames. The great city burned. Fire roared above the cityscape, the air full of smoke and ash. People ran along the muddy streets, eyes wide with terror. It was the Great Fire of London, the Stone at its center, its surface glowing with a silvery power.

And that was when I started to understand why I felt so connected to the rock.

Like me, the Stone was a terror leech.

* * *

THE CASHIER at Tesco eyed me cautiously as I slowly emptied my shopping cart onto the counter. This time, I'd worn shoes *and* had my fly zipped up, so the woman had no cause to give me the stink-eye, but she was doing it anyway.

Six, eight, ten, fourteen... mirrors upon mirrors, in various shapes and sizes.

"What's all this for, then?" she asked. "Some sort of party?"

"Yeah. I'm having a mirror party." Okay, so the screams

and alcohol were making me a bit cranky.

One of the mirrors flickered on the counter, the London Stone flashing on the surface. I clenched my jaw tightly, severing the connection with the reflection. The woman didn't seem to notice.

I read the smudged name tag on her T-shirt.

"Julia, can we do this really quickly? It's important."

* * *

I'D SPREAD the mirrors around me, images flickering on them. The Stone under the night sky, the houses around it more shabby and poor. The Stone in the middle of a busy street, and oxen dragging a cart. The Stone in a storm, lightning setting the street alight, rain hammering the ground. The Stone inside a church, then in a green pasture. In each image it looked different, its size changing, its surface growing worn with age. But its essence remained the same.

I sat in the middle of the mirrors, gazing at the flickering glass around me. I cradled the nearly-empty bottle, no longer sure what I was looking for. A glimmer caught my eye, and I turned my head.

Fae, standing around the Stone. Some with wings, others with ivory or metallic horns. Mist whirled around them, and I couldn't see their faces. Just brief flashes of teeth and hands —males *red in tooth and claw*, blood dripping from their mouths and fingertips.

At their feet lay a young fae, her face streaked with tears and blood. A man's hands—were they the same powerful hands I'd seen in the reflections?—held a torch before her terrified face. He shoved the flames at the girl's body, igniting her dress. My heart clenched as she writhed, mouth wide in a wordless cry. Tears stung my eyes, and I swear her screams filtered through the reflection.

Bile climbed up my throat. Stumbling back, I flung the mirror against the wall, watched it shatter to pieces.

Around me, the reflections shimmered, showing the room, showing my wild eyes, my dirty face.

In others, my reflection smiled, her eyes dark with pleasure. Cassandra, the Mistress of Dread.

* * *

I STOOD on the dimly-lit Cannon Street, staring at the London Stone between the iron latticework. Safer to stay on this side of the Stone. I didn't want to feel compelled to touch it, to feed off those centuries of horror. Somewhere, from London's dark and winding streets, a man's song floated on the breeze. A drunk man singing. A happy drunk.

Footsteps sounded behind me, but I didn't bother turning my head until a man's voice broke my concentration.

"You all right there, love?"

I turned, frowning at the portly man in a Millwall T-shirt, a pint sloshing in his hand. "I'm fine. It's just that the fae have stored my mom's soul in the rock, and it's calling to me. I don't think she's happy."

His forehead crinkled, and he sipped his beer contemplatively before wiping the back of his hand across his mouth. "I think I had that happen once. The thing with the rock."

"Right."

I raised my bottle in mock salute to the man and took the final swig of the whiskey, feeling the drops of the soothing liquid touching my tongue, running down my throat, my mind dulling just a bit more. I let the bottle drop to the pavement, and it rolled away. Ignoring the man, I crouched down, touching the metal grating, following the curving lines. I didn't know what I felt anymore.

CHAPTER 5

"Cassandra? Cassandra, talk to me!" A deep voice penetrated my dreamless sleep, and I felt a strong hand on my shoulder.

I lay on my back—on the floor, maybe. As soon as I opened my eyes a crack, letting in a thin haze of pearly light, my brain began to pound. I think it was struggling to flee my skull. I tried to say something, but I only managed a soft moan.

"Thank God." The voice was tinged with relief, and it took me a moment to recognize it as Gabriel's.

My eyes fluttered open, and I immediately regretted it. The glaring morning light pierced my skull like a hot poker. "The light," I whimpered.

He muttered soft curses as he rose, then he pulled the curtains closed.

I looked around myself, finding myself lying next to an empty bottle of whiskey and my discarded clothes. If I hadn't felt near death, I might have mustered up some embarrassment at the crumpled black underwear on the floor. With the curtains closed, shadows darkened the room. Gabriel walked past my inert body, and I heard him leave the room, closing the door behind him. After a minute, he was back, crouching by my side and holding a glass of water.

His brow furrowed, and concern shone in his hazel eyes. "Can you sit up?"

"I'm fine." Slowly, fighting the nausea climbing up my gut, I managed to sit up and reached for the glass. When I grabbed it, I nearly dropped it on the floor, my fingers trembling. Clutching it harder, I took a small sip. The water in it felt sublime on my parched throat, but a moment later, the nausea intensified. I handed him the glass and lay back on the floor, hoping that he would now leave and let me die. To my horror, I realized I'd been sleeping in a pile of discarded Cheesy Wotsits, some of which had become embedded in my hair. An orange film covered my fingers, and a new cell phone lay among the garbage. When the hell had I bought a cell phone? I didn't remember that, but trashing and buying cell phones had become something of a habit in London.

He stared at me. "You're fine, you say."

I swallowed hard, my mouth tasting of death. "I often sleep in processed cheese products. They ward away nightmares. An old fae superstition."

Apparently, my death would wait, because Gabriel seemed determined to revive me. He crossed to my suitcase, and I listened to him rummaging around for a minute, cringing slightly at the thought of him riffling through my tampons and lip-plumping gloss.

He turned to me a few moments later with two white pills in the palm of his hand. "Lucky for you, I found some paracetamol." He dropped them in my palm. "The trick is to take them *before* you go to bed. Staves off the hangover."

I swallowed the pills. "Thanks. At least I didn't puke." God forbid I lose my dignity. I brushed a mashed cheese puff from my hair.

"You'd probably be feeling better if you did throw up."

I nodded weakly. "True. Can you help me up?"

Crouching next to me, he slipped his arm around my back, his other one cradling my back. Slowly and carefully, he helped me get up to my feet. I wobbled, the world still tipping gently. Nausea rose in my throat, and I swallowed it down again. It was bad enough that Gabriel had found me passed out on the floor next to my discarded panties and neon orange snacks; I didn't want to bathe him in vomit.

I sat on the edge of the bed, looking around the room. "Fuck."

"Yeah. I've had my share of benders, but you took this one to the next level. You've made drunken binges into some kind of art form."

Jagged shards of mirror littered the carpet, along with a few plastic bags, and piles of dirty clothes. I could spot only one or two mirrors left whole. I vaguely remembered buying them, but not breaking them. What had I seen in them?

I swallowed hard, trying to think through the fog in my brain. I definitely remembered breaking a mirror after seeing...

My mind shied away from the memory. Not yet.

I breathed in deeply, for the first time realizing how bad I smelled. Just another entry in my ledger of complete humiliation. "I should probably shower."

"Do that," he agreed. "I'll get you something to eat."

I groaned, as if he had just threatened me with horrendous torture, but said nothing. I was in no position to argue. Instead, I stumbled out the door to the communal bathroom, crunching over the broken glass on my way out.

* * *

AFTER A SHOWER, I brushed my teeth in the steamy bathroom,

for the first time realizing what was missing. The screams. I couldn't hear them anymore, and I nearly broke down and wept in relief at the realization. Their memory still whispered in the hollows of my mind, and I was pretty sure I'd never forget it. But they no longer seemed to reverberate in my skull. Maybe the whiskey had purified my brain.

Freshly cleaned, I wrapped a white terrycloth bathrobe around myself, and opened the door to my disastrous hostel room. Gabriel sat in a chair in the corner of the room, a plastic bag of groceries by his feet. On the rickety table next to him, he'd laid out a plate with two croissants and a Starbucks cup.

"You look better," he said.

"Yeah. I think some of the alcohol escaped my pores through the steam." Already, the painkillers were getting to work on the throbbing in my skull.

He frowned. "I found three empty bottles of whiskey. How long, exactly, did this bender last?"

"Not even sure I can answer that," I muttered, preferring not to mention the three other bottles that he hadn't found.

"What happened, Cassandra? I understand going out on the lash for a night, maybe two, but this is a bit much."

I squinted, struggling to find a way and explain it all. "Let me have some coffee first." I sat on the corner of the bed and he handed me a cup of black coffee. I took a sip, wincing slightly at the strong taste. "This is helping."

He held out the paper plate with croissants, and I nibbled at the edge of one of them. As soon as the buttery, flaky taste hit my tongue, my stomach roared with hunger. I chomped into the croissant, flakes dropping all over my bathrobe. It only took another thirty seconds for me to get the second one.

A sudden wave of nausea nearly made me spew the entire thing back out, but I took a few shallow breaths, clutching the side of the bed, until the sickness subsided. I slowly drank the rest of the coffee, feeling my mind slowly sharpening, the mists clearing from my skull. As they did, a memory rose in my mind—something I'd seen in the reflections. A woman burning to death at the base of the London Stone.

I swallowed hard. "How did you know where to find me?"

"I didn't. Scarlett called me two days ago, worried sick. She said something was wrong with you. That you sounded drunk, and that she wasn't a psychologist but you also... sounded confused."

"She said I'd lost my fucking mind."

"Basically, yeah. She asked if I could find you, and for the past two days, that's what I've been doing." He arched an eyebrow. "Would have been helpful if you used your credit card."

"Force of habit after living as a fugitive."

"I found you eventually by following up on police reports. Some reports of a drunk and disorderly pink-haired woman on Cannon Street and near Walbrook. A break-in at a sports shop on Cannon Street, blood all over the glass. Seems someone wanted to get at the London Stone. Can you believe that? And a series of weird calls to dispatch about mirrors flickering strangely. Almost all those reports were less than a mile from here. So I checked all the nearby hotels, flashing my handy detective badge, searching for a woman with pink hair. For someone used to being a fugitive, you're not exactly blending in with that look you've got going."

I nodded, and instantly regretted the gesture. "You raise a good point."

He sipped his own coffee. "Last time I saw you, you had a rude raven on your shoulder, and you said you were heading back to America. What happened?"

"Odin is in an animal shelter, I believe."

He raised one eyebrow. Clearly, he wasn't interested in the raven.

"I thought Roan needed my help." I ignored Gabriel's frown. "I gave him my word. But I was too late, and he wasn't interested. So I came back."

"Okay." He leaned back in his chair, then nodded at the shattered mirrors and chaotic state of the room. "And all this? Why did you spend a week getting trollied and punching windows?"

I loosed a long sigh. "I was looking for my mom. My birth mother, I mean. I had a magic trinket that led me to the London Stone, and then I just felt it pulling me closer. It's magical, Gabriel. And it's full of horror. When I touched it, I could hear these screams, and they…" *And they thrilled me.* "As long as I touched it, it blocked out my own thoughts. But when I left, they just echoed in my mind. Gabriel, I don't think I can explain. It's like being in a room with a thousand people, all crying in pain. Except that room is your brain, and the screaming is drowning your thoughts. And you can't leave, can't shut your ears. I couldn't sleep. I think the Stone is some kind of terror leech, like me. It soaks up fear, but it also doles it out again."

"And when you drank?"

"I needed something to dull the screams, and that's where the whiskey came in. And I kept returning to that Stone." I clenched my hands together. "But there's more. I heard a voice there, keening above the rest. I can't explain why, but I think it was my mother. I mean, the woman who gave birth to me. I just felt it. I need to understand her connection to the Stone."

"I don't understand. Is she alive?"

I shook my head. "No, I don't think so. I think it's a memory of her. Or some of her essence, her terror, stored in the Stone."

"Maybe it's one you're better off leaving buried."

"No. I need to know who my mother was." My voice cracked.

He said nothing.

"Do you think I'm nuts?"

He shrugged. "You've told me some crazy things since I met you, and they all turned out to be true. You can walk into other dimensions through mirrors, so I don't see why a spirit-filled rock can't be real. But I have a better question for you. Why does it matter? You've told me that you don't think it matters who gave birth to you. Lineage doesn't matter, just whether you were raised with love. Nature and nurture and all that."

"I know."

"The London Stone is possibly a powerful relic. Just touching this Stone sent you on a week-long drinking binge that could have ended with you choking on your own vomit. I've never seen you look worse, and I've seen you in some pretty awful states."

"You know how to make a girl feel nice."

"You came here to find a killer. You did that. Now it's time to move on. Your birth mother is gone, and there's nothing you can do."

A lump rose in my throat. "I have no family left. The people who raised me are dead. I murdered my biological father. I know what I said, that lineage doesn't matter…" I took a deep breath. "I'm not so sure it's easy to believe that anymore. Not when I can feel myself feeding off other people's terror. And it's more than that. I felt like the Stone was… alive, or conscious. What if my mom's consciousness is still trapped in there?" I rubbed my throbbing temple. "I don't know. I have no idea how it works."

"And let me guess. This involves going deeper into the fae realm, even though it seems like it's killing you, and to be honest, it's ruining your life. How can you really be so sure it was your mom's voice? You've never heard her voice before. Like you said—you have no family left. And I know that hurts but… is there a chance this could be wishful thinking? You're a psychologist. How would you interpret it if someone told you they heard their mother's voice in a rock?"

"You don't understand!" I gritted my teeth in frustration. "I could feel that we were connected somehow. I can't explain it. I just felt it."

As soon as the words were out of my mouth, I hated myself for saying them. I'd never operated on gut instincts before. I always thought everything through, and here I was clinging to something just because of a feeling.

"Let me just pose another explanation. The most obvious one is that you haven't slept for days, and you were drunk, and you're yearning for a family. And I don't blame you, Cassandra, I really don't. Being lost and alone isn't a great feeling. And you've been struggling with it for how long now?"

"My parents died when I was fourteen. I've been alone since then. But this time it just feels… different." Hollowness ate at my chest, and I stared at the floor. "I know I felt a connection. I know it was her."

"Look, Cassandra." He softened his tone. "You found out some shocking things about yourself, about your origins. Maybe I don't know exactly what you're going through, but I think you're desperate for a purpose right now, for an easy answer to make yourself feel better. That's why you went to help Roan, right? What better way to avoid your own problems than trotting off to dive into the problems of the fae? You're quite literally trying to escape to another world."

A wave of exhaustion hit me. "Okay. You've stated your opinion at this point. It's noted. You want me to let it go. I think you're wrong. I don't need your help." My head throbbed. "I need to find out what happened to my mom. I don't have anyone else."

"You have Scarlett. You have me. And you look like you need my help right now." As if to punctuate his point, he shot a sharp look at the wine bottle I'd left on the floor—the one with the word FANCY scrawled across the label in my hand-writing.

"Don't patronize me." The ice in my voice surprised me. "If you're not going to help me learn about the Stone, you're just getting in the way. And let's be honest: You don't know a lot about the fae to begin with."

Slowly, he rose to his feet. "Yeah, you're doing a bang-up job on your own, Cassandra."

I said nothing. He crossed the room and left, closing the door silently behind him.

CHAPTER 6

ive minutes later and I was hurrying down the stairs after Gabriel, hastily dressed in jeans and a T-shirt. I moved as fast as my throbbing muscles would allow. I flung the hostel's front door open, desperately searching the narrow street for him in the glaring sunlight. Since when had London gotten so damn sunny?

Not catching any sign of him, I hurried down Carter Lane, taking a guess that he'd headed for St. Paul's.

As soon as Gabriel had left, I'd regretted turning him away. Maybe Gabriel was right—I wasn't completely alone. What did it matter if they were blood relatives? Your family were the people who looked after you, who you cared about. Family was whoever was willing to show up in your shitty hostel room and get you through a brutal hangover. Who knows what my biological mom was like? I knew what Gabriel was like. Since I'd met him, he'd been there for me.

When I got near St. Paul's, the Restoration-era cathedral that towered over the churchyard, I surveyed the streets, searching for him. I scanned past the exhausted woman pushing a child in a stroller, and two men holding hands. No Gabriel.

I hurried to the closest office building, across from St. Paul's, and stared into one of the windows, feeling for its reflection, searching for Gabriel. The glass shimmered, and Gabriel appeared, his jaw clenched tight. I almost jumped into the reflection, but I felt too weak, and I couldn't risk getting stuck. Instead I looked carefully, identifying his whereabouts by his surroundings. He was already striding down Cheapside, heading for the tube.

I broke into a jog, each step firing sharp pain through my throbbing skull. A punishment well deserved. I didn't slow down, ignoring the nausea and the dizziness.

Every once in a while I'd stop, glancing in a shop's window or a car's side mirror, making sure I could still track Gabriel. This city, which had seemed so alien weeks ago, now felt like a familiar friend. I was starting to learn its curves and twists.

Glimpsing him in the window of a coffee shop, I saw him turn onto Old Jewry, a narrow lane in the center of the city. So he wasn't heading for the tube, and he was only a minute away. I picked up my pace, fighting past my body's objections. As nausea welled in my stomach, I turned into the alley and ran, its stony walls seeming to close in on me.

I reviewed the past week in my mind. As an agent who had gone AWOL after an investigation, I probably no longer had a job with the Bureau. I'd pissed off Roan, Gabriel, *and* Scarlett. I'd broken my promise to Roan, told Gabriel he knew nothing and that I didn't need him, and... I couldn't entirely remember what I'd said to Scarlett, but I was pretty sure it hadn't been nice. I wasn't isolated because my family was dead. It had something to do with the fact that I'd been pushing everyone away, hiding out in a shithole with my whiskey bottles and dirty laundry.

Catching my breath, I slowed down to a walk, then stopped altogether, resting my hands on my knees, my gut twisting. I wasn't sure if it was the hangover, but a tear was sliding down my cheek. I should go back to my hostel, and I could find a way to call Gabriel later. I needed some hair of the dog to get through the damn day.

As I was catching my breath, a horrible screech pierced the air, and I raised my eyes to the skies. Three large, silvery cranes circled the skies. Slowly, they glided lower. As I stared at them, a chill shuddered up my spine. They were too large to be simple birds, and something about their presence had cleared most of the people off the street, as if the passersby had begun to sense an otherworldly threat.

Then, one after the other, they dove onto the street, landing on the pavement around me. Two in front of me, one behind. Death glinted in their eyes, dark as coal, and an icy chill fell over the air, raising goosebumps on my skin.

The largest one quirked its head, then burst into a large form, cloaked in mist. When some of the fog cleared, a bony woman stood before me, draped in a crimson cloak. Tangled silver hair tumbled over her shoulders, and she glowed with a greenish-gray light. Her enormous black eyes transfixed me, and I hardly noticed the other cranes transforming. Waves of frigid air rolled off their bodies, and my teeth chattered.

"Poor child." She ran a bony finger over my cheek, her touch pure ice, and a chill rippled over my body. Her voice seemed to echo from the inside of my mind. "So lonely. It wasn't your fault."

My heart hammered against my ribs.

"You were just a baby. Your mother abandoning you like that. You couldn't help growing into a monster like you did."

I took a step back, transfixed by her eyes, but wanting to get away from the stench of death.

C.N. CRAWFORD & ALEX RIVERS

"And now, all alone. Humans turning their backs on you. The fae folk treating you like a mongrel. Poor child. So much suffering." She opened her gaunt arms wide. "Time to rest. Come to me. Let me take your pain away."

As the fog thickened, I felt a strange tug urging me to move closer to her, but I clamped down on it hard. From the corner of my eye, I saw another figure emerge from the fog— a man this time—but I kept my gaze locked on the hag. I couldn't let her touch me again, or I'd sink into her spell. When she reached for me again, I was ready. I smacked her hand away, and the crunch of bone echoed off the buildings. I was in no mood for fae manipulation.

"You need to back away from me." Ice laced my voice, and my gaze darted to a reflection in the mirror.

But as it did, I glimpsed another figure moving closer— Gabriel's broad form, moving toward us through the mist.

He lifted a gun—the one I'd given him—to the crone's chest. "Get away from her, demon."

Slowly, the hag's head swiveled to face him. "Gabriel. It's been so long since I've seen you."

For just a moment, surprise flickered in his eyes. "This is called a gun, demon. It shoots bullets. Iron bullets."

The crone smiled sadly at him. "Violence? Is that really the answer? A man like you, who has lost so much to violence. You should know better. Don't you remember me, Gabriel? Didn't you hear my cry before your wife died?"

His hand began to shake. I'd never seen him look so unnerved before, and my stomach churned. "Violence has its uses."

"Your poor wife. Killed so suddenly. Do you know what killed her?"

"A demon."

"No." The crone clutched her chest. "It was a terror wraith, a fear-spirit with no body. One who could slip into humans, take control of them. The wraith fae passed into a man's body—a lonely nobody. Wrapped in human flesh, the wraith thrust a knife into your wife's heart, then fed as you held her dying body, terrified for her safety. I watched it all. I knew it was coming, and I showed up for the thrill. We feed on sorrow. We foretell despair. And then we scream." She reached out, stroking his gun, and Gabriel seemed to freeze. "When you hear a banshee wail, death always follows."

Gabriel fired the gun, but the banshee's body clouded into mist, the bullet flying right through her, shattering the glass behind her. It only took a moment for her body to solidify again, and the sound she emitted next would haunt me for the rest of my life. She flung back her head, shrieking to the skies, her voice like a thousand tormented souls, piercing me to the marrow. The other banshees howled with her, their cries deafening, and I clamped my hands over my ears.

The three of them launched themselves forward, claws lengthening, sharp teeth bared. As the largest one lunged, slashing for Gabriel with long, sharp talons, I grabbed her by the hood, yanking her neck back hard.

When she whirled to face me, I slammed my forehead into her nose, cracking the bone. Pain flashed in my skull, still throbbing from before. She let out a shriek as her nose crunched, broken. Dazed, with colored spots dancing in my vision, I reared back for another punch. This one I landed on her temple.

The three of them had unveiled, their fingers tapering into talons, silvery feathers sprouting on their skin.

The tallest of them slashed at me with her claws, and red-hot pain lanced my cheek as she tore into the flesh. I punched her again, her head snapping back. Before I could land another blow, one of the banshees slammed into me, knocking me to the ground, a maddened grin on her face.

She slashed at me, but I grabbed one of her talons,

twisting it backward. Blood ran down my arm as the talon pierced my skin. Nevertheless, I snapped the talon, her screams sending a dark thrill sparking through my blood. As she fell off me, I scrambled to my feet.

And that's when I saw what had happened to Gabriel, and my world tilted.

He lay flat on his back, blood pooling around his body in a glistening puddle. One of the banshees gnawed at his neck, and my heart stopped. So much blood on the pavement. Grief slammed me in the chest with the force of a freight train. I couldn't breathe.

"No!" I yelled, my mind echoing with tormented screams. I rushed for the fae, slamming my foot into her head. She tumbled off Gabriel, but I couldn't quite bring myself to look at him.

Endless cries of agony, drowning me in a river of sorrow. I let it block out my own pain, my own sorrow, just submerged myself in the torment of others.

Time slowed to a crawl, the droplets of blood seeming to fall from the fae's teeth in slow motion, suspended in the air. A silver feather, frozen above us, unmoving.

In the misty air, tendrils of fear whirled around me. *Fae fear.* Somehow, as if by instinct, I knew exactly what I needed to do. I arched my back, letting the banshees' fear flow into me, feeding from it. Then, with a snarl no longer quite human, I blasted it back at them.

As time resumed its pace, the banshees' eyes widened, their jaws slackening, hands freezing in place. One of them jerked and scrambled backward, desperate to flee from me.

In the depths of my mind, I could feel their screams, interweaving with thousands of tormented souls, clamoring in terror. Their horror filled my body with power.

The fae all scrambled to their feet, screeching, turning

away, fleeing, but I wasn't going to let them go. They'd killed my friend, and I wanted them to suffer.

I let the terror flow from my body into theirs, paralyzing them with dread. One after another, they crumpled on the sidewalk. Dark fury raged, and I crossed to the first—the one who had feasted on Gabriel. Power flooded my bones as she looked up at me, shaking. Her terror only spurred me on.

Defensively, she held up her hands. "Please."

I reached down, snapping her neck, the crack echoing off the walls. Her body slumped to the ground.

With rage poisoning my blood, I stalked to the next one, who whimpered, staring at me with her eerie, black eyes, her fear paralyzing her. I picked up a large shard of glass from where the bullet had smashed the window, not caring that it cut into my fingers.

The banshee tried to form a word, but she emitted only a garbled string of sounds. I pulled back her tangled silver hair, exposing her icy throat, and stabbed the shard of glass into her jugular. Blood sprayed into the air.

Nearby, the last banshee emitted a strangled sound. Drenched in fae blood, I crossed to her, gripping the shard of glass.

She lay huddled against the wall, gaping at me, and I held the glass to her throat.

"Why me?" I snarled. "Why did you come after me?"

She stammered something incomprehensible, and I pressed the tip of the shard to her throat.

"Why me?" I roared.

"Mistress... of... Dread..." she stammered. "Must... die..."

Mistress of Dread. Ice frosted my mind. "Why?"

"He... commanded it."

"Who?" While she trembled, I brought the shard of glass up to her black eye, threatening to carve it out. "Who, damn it? Who sent you?"

"The… king…"

The sound of police sirens sliced the air.

"The fae High King? He sent you to kill me? Why?"

Her jaw opened and closed again, and I pressed the shard just under her eye. "I… don't know!" she shrieked.

I believed her. But in the next moment, she was frantically reaching for my throat, desperate to save her own life. Her frigid talons tightened around my neck.

I reared back my hand, then slammed the shard into her throat, severing her arteries. Soaked in her blood, I rose, my entire body shaking.

Mistress of Dread.

As the police sirens drew closer, I hurried to Gabriel's side, really looking at him for the first time, barely able to breathe. His neck had been ripped out, and his beautiful hazel eyes stared at the sky. Grief threatened to suffocate me, to pull me under. His blood stained the street in a wide pool.

"Gabriel," I whispered. The banshee had screamed for him.

He lay dead, well beyond saving. The weight of my sorrow knocked the wind out of me.

CHAPTER 7

I slipped back into my room through one of my mirrors, my chest aching with sorrow. Tears flowed down my cheeks, and blood soaked my clothes—banshee blood, my blood, Gabriel's blood—the metallic scent turning my stomach. I quickly stripped off my jeans, the fabric drenched. I looked down at my legs, at the blood that had seeped into the fabric, creating a strange, sickly red pattern on my skin. So much blood. I couldn't breathe.

I slumped onto my bed, wiping the tears off on the back of my hand. Gabriel had died trying to help me. He'd been a better friend than I deserved.

I stared at the room's floor, still littered with fragments of glass. A sob escaped my throat, and then another. I tried to contain them, to tell myself that I had to keep moving, that the fae were out to kill me and that I needed to act, but sorrow washed over me.

I thought of the first time I'd met Gabriel at the crime scene in Mitre Square, first glimpsing his hazel eyes. Of the time I'd had a nightmare and woke up screaming in his home, and he came in to talk to me. Of all the times I'd asked for help and he didn't even hesitate, and the way he'd taken care of me, humming gently as he scrambled eggs for me.

I couldn't let those memories be forever marred by the image of him lying on his back in an alley, eyes vacant, throat torn, a grimace of pain on his face. Would I ever be able to think of him without conjuring that horrible moment? Without wondering how his life would have turned out if he'd never met me?

I clutched the edge of my dirty bedsheets, wishing Gabriel had never come here to check up on me. Tears blinded my vision, flowing down my face.

Finally, there were no tears left—just a hollowness in my ribs. I didn't know how long I'd sat on that bed, staring at the floor, but it could have been hours. When my back began to ache, I rose and stared around me. A honeyed ray of sunlight shone between the blinds, glinting off a shard of mirror. I crossed to the corner of the room, picking up a plastic bag from the floor.

Carefully, I began collecting the shards one by one, dropping them in the plastic bag. I did it carefully, gently, avoiding the sharp edges, trying to keep my mind focused on the task. Something that got me moving. The shrieks in my head had faded slightly, becoming bearable. I pushed my grief and rage under the surface, letting my mind ice over until a chilling sense of calm overtook me.

As I tidied up the room, my mind roamed over the attack. What exactly had happened to me? Somehow, I'd sucked up fear from the banshees and thrown it back at them, paralyzing them with terror. I'd never felt fae fear before. If only I'd discovered that strange power *before* they'd torn Gabriel's throat out.

Under the ice floes of my mind, a voice keened, *The Mistress of Dread must die.*

It was the second time someone had called me the

Mistress of Dread. What did it mean? I stared at my reflection in a large shard in my hand. Red nose, swollen eyes. Not especially frightening, and yet the fae king wanted me dead.

I could only guess it had something to do with that terror I'd managed to instill into the banshees.

The king. The king had sent the banshees after me, and they'd slaughtered Gabriel while they were at it.

A cold rage spread through my body, replacing the initial shock. It wasn't my fault that Gabriel had died. The fae High King was responsible. He had sent those assassins to kill me, and my friend had paid the price for it.

My fingers tightened into fists. The king had killed my friend, and he would pay for it with his life.

I was the goddamn Mistress of Dread, and he'd better fear me.

* * *

ICE. I let my mind become pure ice, just focusing on what I needed to do next. Freshly showered, I pulled on the last of my clean clothes—a pair of leather leggings, a black shirt. I collected all my possessions, sorting through them, concentrating on the task at hand. I pushed away the dark thoughts that prodded the back of my mind, just focusing on sorting out my clothes, picking out the ones covered in mustard, wine, and blood. The sweatshirt with a mysterious hole burnt in the elbow, the bra that smelled of whiskey—I threw them all out. Anything good got shoved into my backpack, along with the gun I'd pulled off Gabriel's body, loaded with bullets, plus my own gun, covered in pond muck. I wrapped my laptop in its leather case, then jammed it in with the rest of my things. I left the compass on the bedside table. It had done its job.

I put some cash on the bed, a large tip for whoever

cleaned up the mess I left behind. I wouldn't need the money where I was going. Then I pulled on my backpack, trying to formulate exactly what I was going to do next, what I would say.

My body shaking, I crossed to the bathroom, gripping my backpack tight.

Lucky for me, no one was in the bathroom, giving me uninterrupted access to the mirror. Burying my grief, my anger, I stared at the reflection, hardly recognizing myself. Gone was the blubbering mess with the screams in her head. Gone was the profiler who got to work early in the morning, bright-eyed and sipping coffee. I stared at the reflection, my own hard, steely eyes gazing back at me. An ugly red scratch marred my neck, and my bloodshot eyes spoke of weeks of disrupted sleep. I clenched my jaw, needing to feel in control again before I left on my next mission. I let my mind ice over, a glacier of calm.

I dropped my backpack on the floor, then pulled out my makeup bag. I smeared concealer under my eyes, hiding the deep bags, then blended pearly blush on my cheeks until I nearly looked like a functioning human.

Once I'd finished, I stared at the mirror again. I felt for the reflection, letting my mind bond with it. I merged with the mirror until I felt that satisfying connection in my mind, and I searched until I found what I wanted.

There: sitting by the fireplace, bathed in warm light in a mahogany-walled room. Not a room I recognized; this one was grand, the walls finely carved with wood sculptures, the oak floors polished. And there he was, bathed in warm fire-light, the man whose goals now aligned starkly with my own. My heart skipped a beat at the sight of him.

I let myself fall into the reflection, feeling its frigid, liquid surface wash over my skin, chilling me to the bone. I landed in the corner of the room, beneath a window.

And that's when Roan charged for me, fury burning in his golden eyes.

* * *

I HELD up my hands defensively. "Roan. It's just me."

He froze a foot away from me, eyes glimmering with gold, teeth lengthening into sharp fangs. Firelight wavered over his powerful body. Snarling, he sniffed the air, and the temperature around us dropped sharply. Ivory horns sprouted from his head. He was about to unveil completely.

A primal fear stopped my heart. "Roan?"

"Cassandra." He closed his eyes, growling softly, and I watched as he gained control of himself, the fangs and horns disappearing. Still, the threat lingered, and tension thickened the air. The room felt freezing, and my breath clouded in front of my face.

Shivering, I hugged myself. He'd stopped unveiling, but I could find not a hint of warmth in his features. "I need to talk to you."

A smile curled his lips. "What a coincidence. I need to talk to you as well." He frowned, eyes scanning the room. "Not here, though. I can take you someplace more comfortable."

"Sure. Whatever." My heart still thundered from the sight of him nearly unveiling.

He turned to the door. "Nerius?"

A hulking man with dark eyes and olive skin swooped through the doorway, and the sight of him sent a chill over my skin. His long brown hair hung over leather fighting gear, and a scar marred his handsome face. He glared at me. "*That's* what I was feeling." Venom laced his voice. "The pixie. How clever of you to get her back here."

Roan shoved his hands into his pockets. "I think she

missed me. Cassandra, my friend Nerius will take your things."

I clutched my bag harder. At the strange welcome I was receiving, the sorrow I'd trapped under the surface threatened to break free. I blinked, clearing the tears from my eyes. "I'll keep my bags, thanks."

Nerius crossed to me, shadows sliding through his eyes. His lip curled in a snarl, and the ghost of dark wings cascaded from behind his shoulders.

My gut swooped, and I scanned the room for reflections, catching sight of a mirror in the corner.

Nerius held out his hand. "He *said* I'll take your things."

I folded my arms. "What the hell, Roan?"

Roan merely shrugged. "What can I say? The House of Taranis is known for its hospitality."

Fuck it. I'd come here for a reason, and right now I had nowhere else to go. I'd have to play along—and maybe I didn't need guns to protect myself anymore. I pulled off my shoulder bag and my backpack, handing them over to the asshole with the wings. He turned abruptly, crossing to Roan. Then, he leaned closer to Roan, while the golden-haired fae whispered something into his ear.

When Nerius left the room, I stared at Roan, trying to ignore the hollow ache in my chest. "Gabriel is dead. The king's minions had him killed."

Shock registered on Roan's face, and the atmosphere in the room thinned. "What?"

"They tried to assassinate me. Gabriel..." My throat tightened. "He tried to help."

Roan frowned, glancing at the mirror I'd stepped through. "I'm sorry to hear that, Cassandra."

"Thanks. I want vengeance. I want—"

"Let's talk in the Morgen Apartments. We can sit there

more comfortably, and discuss this at length." He turned, crossing to the door.

I clenched my jaw and followed him into an oak-walled hall, the dark ceilings arched high above us. Tall windows looked out over a grassy courtyard dappled with blue and yellow wildflowers. If it weren't for the stark London buildings towering over the other side of the building, I'd have thought we were in Trinovantum.

"What is this place?" I asked.

He didn't answer, and I kept studying the walls, carved with images of forests and stags. A heraldic emblem hung on the mahogany—one I'd never seen before. A stag's head. *The House of Taranis.* Did Roan come from one of the six noble houses? In Leroy's, a defaced heraldic shield hung on the wall. Maybe this was it.

We reached an arched doorway, just as Nerius walked out, arms full of vases and metal candlesticks. He dumped them unceremoniously in the hall, and one of the vases shattered. My mouth went dry. They were taking all the reflective surfaces out of the room. Roan didn't want me to go anywhere.

"You don't have to bother," I said. "I came here willingly."

"It's done," said Nerius, his body exuding dark magic.

Roan gestured into the dimly-lit room, indicating I should enter.

I stepped inside the room, the walls a deep blue, a bed in the center of the room. No windows, no metal. Not a single reflective surface, and nothing to light the space. As I surveyed the room, straining my eyes in the dim light, I heard the door slam behind me, the lock clicking shut.

Roan, the bastard, had locked me inside.

CHAPTER 8

With the door shut, I could hardly see a thing. From under the door, a faint stream of sunlight pierced the darkness—but that was it. Darkness muted reflections, so even if Nerius had missed something, I'm not sure I could have used it. Nevertheless, I turned in a slow circle, feeling for reflections. I felt the faint tug of a few reflections, like an invisible cord pulling at my chest, but they were so subtle they must have been in other rooms. I needed to actually see a reflection to use it. In this room, a rug covered the floor. Would the floor under it be shiny enough to use? Doubtful.

More to the point, I'd come here for a reason—to find out why the king wanted me dead. For one reason or another, he saw me as a powerful threat to him—and maybe I was. If I could join the rebellion against the king, maybe I could make a difference.

Just as soon as I got out of the room they'd locked me in. An image of Gabriel flashed in my mind—lying on the pavement, mouth agape. Blood pooling behind his head. I curled my fingers into fists, my fingernails digging into my skin.

Closing my eyes, the ice in my mind began to crack, threatening to let the sorrow out, to unleash the dam of grief.

Nausea climbed up my throat and I clutched my stomach, dropping down to the bed. *Not now.* I couldn't let grief overwhelm me now.

I still had to keep my wits about me. Taking a deep breath, I summoned the ice in my mind again, the glacier of calm. *Distraction.* I focused on my full bladder. I had to pee like a racehorse, and I let the discomfort pull me from my pain.

But I still had no idea what was going on. As soon as Roan had seen me, he'd nearly unveiled. Somehow, *Roan* saw me as a threat.

Why?

Maybe he saw me as the *Mistress of Dread* too. Had I unleashed some new power when I'd touched the Stone? The Stone was powerful, I was sure. I just didn't know how.

After a few more minutes, the door clicked open. Roan stood in the doorway, holding a candle—no candleholder, of course. That would be too shiny. He closed the door behind him, crossed to a bureau, and dripped some wax onto the surface. Then, he wedged the candlestick into the wax, so it stood upright.

He crossed to sit next to me on the bed, depressing the mattress with his weight. I could feel the warmth radiating off his body, and the scent of moss and oaks curled off him. His deep green eyes met mine, and he studied my face.

I tightened my grip on the bedsheets. "Are you going to explain why I'm suddenly your prisoner?"

"Sorry about that."

"That's not much of an explanation."

"I need to ask you some questions, and I don't want you running off when you learn what I know."

I swallowed hard. "And what do you think you know?"

The candle guttered. "That I can't trust you."

Join the club. "Why? Does this have to do with the Mistress of Dread thing, by any chance?"

Genuine confusion flickered across his features. "The *what*? No. Look, Abellio and I have some questions for you."

"Who?"

As if on cue, the door opened again and another man came in. His brown hair contrasted with his pale skin, and kindness shone in his pale blue eyes. In the pocket of his midnight-blue shirt, the top of a silver pen glinted in the candlelight. Tall as hell, though still not as tall as Roan. I'd take him over Nerius in a second.

He closed the door, locking it behind him, then turned to me. "I'm Abellio." He leaned down, gazing into my eyes. "And you're Cassandra. I've heard a lot about you."

I stared back at him. "Is that so?" I asked dryly.

"Well, you know Roan. A talkative fellow, can't stop sharing, am I right?" There was an amused glint in his eye. "So… what are you doing here, Cassandra?"

"I came here to join forces with you and destroy the king," I said.

Silence fell as they both stared at me with bemused looks.

"I can give you information," I added defensively.

"Can you?" asked Roan in a tone that suggested he didn't believe me at all.

With his arms crossed, Abellio backed away, leaning against the bureau, watching me with fascination.

I bit my lip, trying to think of information I could barter with. I knew the London Stone was important, but all my attempts to explain it to other people had been disastrous so far. My mother seemed to be in the Stone, screaming. What else? Oh, I thought it might be a reservoir of terror, through which I could see another fae's visions. It sounded like a stream of insanity even to me.

Roan leaned in closer to me, and he brushed my damp hair off my neck, the gesture surprisingly gentle. Sliding his hand down to my back, he leaned in, smelling my neck.

Instinctively, I tilted my head back.

Roan pulled away, shadows darkening his eyes. He looked furious. "Where did you go once you returned to London, five days ago?"

"I checked into a hotel. Why did you just smell me?"

Roan cocked his head. "You're lying," he said softly.

"I'm not. Okay, first, I went to get my stuff back. I'd left some in a locker at the metro station. Then I checked into a hotel. Well, not a hotel, really. A shitty hostel, because I was low on cash." And then I spent a week getting drunk and obsessing over a stone. Maybe I'd skip over that part.

"Who did you meet since then? Who did you talk to?"

"I'm not telling you another thing until you explain to me what's going on." My urge to pee was out of control, and it was only making me more annoyed.

Roan's face darkened. "You're not in a position to—"

Abellio stepped forward, laying a hand on Roan's shoulder. "Cassandra. Don't worry. We don't want to hurt you. But the faster you answer our questions, the quicker we can resolve this. We really need to know who you talked to since you returned."

"Fine," I said coldly. I had nothing to hide from them. Might as well be honest. "Since I last saw Roan, I met with a young fae I know named Alvin. I wanted to know where I could find my mom. My birth mother, I mean. I talked to Scarlett on the phone." I shook my head, trying to grasp onto clear images from that lost week. "Strangers. I talked to human strangers, people in shops, nothing significant. And then Gabriel came to see me this morning." My voice broke, and I trailed off, the ice cracking just a little.

Roan nodded slowly. "That doesn't explain why you smell like banshees."

The memory of Gabriel's body blazed in my mind, and the breath left my lungs. "They're the ones who attacked me —three of them." Sadness welled, threatening to pull me under, and a hot tear slid down my cheek.

I felt Roan's palm on my back. "What happened?"

I stared at the floor, tears now sliding down my cheeks. "He was trying to protect me. The banshees came for me. They said the king had sent them. They said I was the Mistress of Dread."

"You?" Roan asked, disbelieving. "The Mistress of Dread?"

"Apparently."

Roan glanced at Abellio, who nodded.

"Who were the banshees?" asked Roan.

"I didn't get their names, Roan. We were busy trying to slaughter each other. They killed Gabriel."

He stared at me for a long moment, as if trying to read my thoughts. "I understand."

I wiped the tears off on the back of my hand. "That's why I came here. I can help. And now we want the same thing."

He took a deep breath. "First, I need to know about the path. You must have told someone."

"What path?"

"The secret path. Through the river in Trinovantum. The magical route I showed you. Who did you tell? Alvin?"

I shook my head. "No." At least, I was pretty sure I hadn't. I took a deep breath. "Look, I spent a lot of the past week drunk on wine and whiskey, but I'm nearly positive I didn't tell anyone about the path."

Roan breathed in deeply. "What happened to the banshees?"

"I killed them."

He frowned. "*You* killed three banshees?"

"Yes. I..." I hesitated, trying to think how I could explain what had happened. "I used their own fear against them. I'm not sure how; it just happened."

"Your story makes little sense. You can't use fae emotion, Cassandra."

"I'm telling you, that's what happened." Exhaustion began to seep in. They clearly didn't believe me.

Roan glanced at Abellio, who gave him a slight nod. He turned back to look at me. "This Alvin. Describe him."

"He's young, shaggy blond hair, constantly stoned, hangs around in Leroy's. He definitely knows you. He's mentioned you several times—"

"Alvin Taranis?" Roan's lip curled slightly.

"He never gave me his last name." I shook my head. "Are you related?"

Roan gritted his teeth. "He's a *distant* relative."

Abellio smiled, his cheek dimpling. "Surely not *that* distant?"

"Distant enough. Did you tell him about the path? I wouldn't trust him with anything."

"Like I said, I'm nearly positive I didn't."

Roan's emerald gaze pierced me. "You don't quite remember. How convenient."

"It's actually really inconvenient."

Roan glanced at Abellio again.

Abellio stroked his jawline, frowning. "Not sure. There's so much emotion here, and so much hidden emotion as well. It's like reading the ocean."

"What are you?" I asked. "Some kind of lie detector?"

Abellio nodded. "That's a very good definition. But being in your presence is... confusing. There's a lot of pain. A lot of anger. It's hard to distinguish the truth from the lies. Even harder to see if the lies are aimed at us, or at yourself."

"Oh great. A fae therapist."

"Why don't we start again?" he continued. "You came back to London after Roan took you to the portal. Please recount your story. Slowly this time."

I wanted to pee, but I also knew that if I told them that, they would have even more leverage over me. How many times had I told a suspect he could go to the bathroom after he answered just one more question? No. I wouldn't give them the satisfaction.

"Like I told you, I went to see Alvin after returning to London."

"Why?"

"I hoped he could help me find my birth mother. I know my biological father was the Rix. I don't know who my birth mother was. I wanted to find out."

If either of them were surprised or interested in the answer, it didn't show. "And did he know who she was?"

"No." It wasn't the whole truth, but it wasn't a lie either.

"Did you tell him anything about your trip to Trinovantum?"

"No. I wasn't drunk then. I remember." They weren't good interviewers. They led the interview, enabling me to skip over details, to avoid mentioning my visits to the London Stone, the screams in my head. All the things that would make me sound unhinged. They didn't even ask why I'd spent a week drunk. "Now can you tell me what happened?"

Roan stared at the floor. "Two days after I showed you our secret path, three rebels were ambushed by the king's men while crossing it. One died, and one was captured."

"She's telling the truth, Roan," Abellio said. "The king must have found it on his own. Or perhaps there is another traitor among us."

"Of course I'm telling the truth. Why would I lie?"

"You have no other way out," Roan suggested. "And you hope to get more information from us."

I crossed my arms. "Roan. I can always find a way out."

"How?"

I pointed to the silver pen in Abellio's shirt, the reflection gleaming in the dim candlelight. "You can tell your friend that next time he should keep his pretty stationery supplies away from me."

Abellio looked down at his shirt pocket, then burst out laughing. Roan glanced at him in irritation and then turned back to me, studying my face as if trying to memorize every feature. "I need to know the truth for myself."

"You'll just have to trust me and Abellio," I said. "Can someone point the way to the bathroom, or do I have to jump there through Abellio's chest?"

Abellio raised his eyebrows quizzically. "I must admit I want to know what that feels like. Is that weird?"

Roan nodded at him. "Take her to the bathroom, but bring her back. I have a few more things I want to ask her. Alone."

CHAPTER 9

When I got back to the Morgen Apartments, no longer distracted by my full bladder, Roan was waiting for me on the edge of the bed, exactly where I'd left him.

I closed the door behind me and sat by his side. "Why do I get the feeling that I still need to convince you?"

His green eyes pierced me. "It's hard to believe that one of our own passed along the information. I'd trust them all with my life."

"And you don't trust me."

He narrowed his eyes. "Your lineage is the same as the Rix's, and the same as the king's. The House of Weala Broc. The Court of Terror."

My throat tightened. "Is this what this is about? Me being a terror leech? After everything I've done?"

"We have no one among the rebels who belongs to that house."

"I don't *belong* to that house. It's just genetics. It means nothing." At least, that's what I was trying to convince myself.

"The other rebels will have a hard time believing your story. A Weala Broc fae whom they don't know found out about our secret path, and the king's banshees just happened to ambush our men there two days later. And then you—the very same terror-fae we already suspect—just happened to break into my home a week later, reeking of banshee magic. What a coincidence."

Okay. So it looked bad. *Very* bad. "It *is* a coincidence." I frowned. "So this is your home? I thought you lived in that cabin in the woods, but apparently you're the Lord of Taranis, with your own palace and family crest. One of the six kingdoms of Trinovantum, is that right?"

"This was my family's London residence. I haven't been here in centuries."

"Why? What happened?"

A hint of gold flashed in his eyes, but he didn't answer me. He was so close to me, I could feel the warmth coming off his skin, could smell the scent of moss and pine. It smelled like... *home.* He smelled like coming home.

The glacier in my mind began to crack again, and loneliness gnawed at my ribs. "You still don't trust me. And it will be particularly hard for you to convince your friends if you don't actually believe it yourself."

"Maybe there's a way to prove to me you're telling me the truth."

"How?"

He rose, towering over me. "Stand up."

I did as instructed, gazing up at him. He simply stared at me, as if trying to read my thoughts. *Could* he read my thoughts? The way he was looking at me, I felt as if he was laying me bare, exposing each of my secrets. And yet I couldn't tear my eyes away. Electricity seemed to charge the air between us, raising the hair on the back of my neck, and I felt acutely aware of every inch of my skin.

If he could truly see into my mind, he would have found two Cassandras at war with each other. One Cassandra stood entranced by the shock of his beauty, acutely aware of every detail: his thick black eyelashes, the golden hair, the sensual curve of his lips. The other Cassandra lay submerged under the ice floes of my mind, frozen in grief. The other Cassandra could die of the cold.

I craved his heat, wanted to hear his heartbeat and feel his warm lips against mine. And yet somehow I knew if I closed the distance between us, all that ice would crack and a river of sorrow would drown me. It was all I had keeping me together.

So I kept my distance from him, resisting the magnetic pull I felt toward his body, my mind glacial. Hollowness welled in my chest—but it was controlled. I had it under control.

And yet as he gazed at me, it was almost as if he pierced through my armor, stripping me down and claiming me. This close to him, I could feel the power of his ancient magic curling around my body, a sensual caress, dangerously close to penetrating my defenses.

His brow furrowed. "You're not happy. You're devastated. That's real. I can feel that. Your emotions are seeping into me." He reached out, tracing his fingertips over my cheek. "I need to see what's happened to you."

The feel of his fingertips on my skin sent a shiver through my body, and I closed my eyes, my loneliness just now hitting me like a tsunami. "I'm not lying to you. I told you the truth." Taking a deep breath, I opened my eyes again.

"I need to see everything. Okay?"

"Okay." I had no idea what I was agreeing to, but he cupped his hand around my neck, pulling me closer. He seemed to drink me in with his gaze. Instinctively, I reached up, wrapping my arms around him, no longer sure what we were doing. I only knew I needed his heat, or the cold would consume me.

As if in a trance, I stared into his eyes, that deep green flecked with gold that spoke of ancient forests, of fingers curling into the mossy earth, arched backs, the thrill of the hunt. Footfalls hammering over the earth like heartbeats, the rush of blood, hands and knees in the dirt. This close to Roan, the world seemed to fall away around me—no ice, no gaping eyes, no death. No Mistress of Dread.

For just this moment, the rest of the world did not exist—just me, and the man before me. Slowly, his powerful hands stroked down my back, sending molten heat racing into my core. He gripped under my ass, then hoisted me up until my face was level with his. I locked my legs around him, arching my back.

Roan's golden skin entranced me, and he tilted back his head, giving me a view of his alluring throat. When we'd been in the woods that day, our minds clouded by magic, Roan had bit my neck. And right now, I could think of nothing else but closing my teeth on his throat, piercing the skin just a little. I needed to make this perfect creature *mine.*

Wait—what? Why was I thinking about that?

I didn't know. And yet—drawn in by his scent and his warmth—I lowered my mouth to his neck, brushing my tongue against his skin. Driven by a primal need, I let my teeth graze over his throat. As I did, an ancient power claimed my body, pooling in my ribs, my belly. Euphoria surged, and I moaned, arching my back to grind my hips at him, no longer in control. I felt him harden against me, and with a groan, he ran a clawed finger down the front of my shirt, ripping it open. As I felt the air over my bare breasts, I was consumed by an overpowering urge to claim him. I needed to sink my teeth into his skin, to taste him. *Mine.* Why? I'd never wanted to bite anyone before, and yet the thought overwhelmed me, until one word alone screamed in my skull. *Mine.*

I rocked my hips against him, my teeth pressing harder against his throat, wanting to feel my bare skin against his. And that's when I felt my canines *lengthen.* Without realizing what I was doing, I pushed them deeper, piercing his skin just the way I'd needed to. *Perfect ecstasy.* A wave of power lit up my body. *This is where I belong. This is where he belongs. Mine.*

My senses heightened, and I could smell everything around me—the leather on the chairs, the oak in the walls. Roan's deep, mossy scent. The smells overwhelmed me, the powerful sensations strangely familiar, like a long-lost power I'd just reclaimed.

I flicked my tongue against his neck, soothing the place where I'd bit him, tasting copper and salt. A low moan escaped him, and my mind whirled with images, memories— but not from my life. A girl with cheeks like shiny apples, laughing, trying to skip rocks across the river. Somehow, I knew her name was Morgana, and that she'd look after me. Here, the air smelled of wild strawberries, and the sunlight pierced the canopies of oak leaves, dappling the ground with flecks of amber. A tall woman walked along a forest path, her blond hair tumbling over a honey-gold gown. Gossamer wings cascaded from her back, catching in the sunlight. She turned to look at me, her eyes shining with love. Then, night-fall, when the Sluagh crawled from the shadows and swooped from the darkening skies. There were men coming for us, men who wanted to flay the skin from our bodies, and my heart pounded like a war drum...

My eyes snapped open, my heart thundering. I'd dragged my claws down Roan's back, piercing his skin through his clothes—

Hang on. *Claws?*

Horrified, I unhooked my legs from his body and stepped away from him, shaking. I gaped as my claws slowly retracted into my skin, their tips red with blood. The metallic taste of blood stained my tongue. "What the fuck was that?" I pulled the front of my ripped shirt together.

Roan's eyes had turned gold, his horns gleaming on his head, ears pointed. His long, pale blond hair flowed over his shoulders, body glowing with golden light—he'd dropped his glamour and completely unveiled. And yet, for the first time, the sight of him unveiled didn't terrify me or make me want to run screaming from him in horror. I looked at Roan, the *real* Roan, and felt instead a strange surge of warmth. I could almost see him in his natural element, among the towering oaks of Trinovantum, the sunlight flecking his hair with gold, or racing through the woods after his prey, moving like the wind.

"You were discovering your fae form. You were unveiling." Slowly, he transformed before me, his hair darkening and shortening, eyes returning to that deep green.

He reached for my cheek, brushing his thumb over my skin, his green eyes burning with intensity. I reached up to touch his hand. What had just happened?

My legs trembled, and I tried to regain control of myself. I'd lost myself there, drawn in by his memories, lured in by that powerful need to bite him. "I don't understand what just happened. I lost control."

He pulled me close, holding me against his body. The slow, rhythmic beating of his heart calmed me, my chest pressed against him. "I just needed to see for myself. I needed to see some of your memories. And you saw mine."

I felt... different now, as if a strange, warm glow had sparked in my chest, a tiny flame that burned within me. "Who is Morgana?"

He took a deep, shuddering breath, as if trying to master himself. "She was my sister."

"And the beautiful woman with the wings?"

Before he could answer, a knock sounded on the door, then Nerius's voice boomed through the oak door. "Are you still interrogating the prisoner?"

Roan's body tensed against me. He tightened his powerful arms around me, one hand protectively around the back of my head. "She's no longer a prisoner, Nerius. Abellio cleared her."

"You've got to be fucking kidding me."

"Go speak to Abellio," Roan barked.

I looked up at him. "Why didn't you mention your little mind-reading excursion?"

"He doesn't need to know that," he said, his voice softer now. Something seemed *different* about him now. "He just needs to do what I say. The important thing is that I know you were telling me the truth, and we need to discover why the king wants you dead."

An image of Gabriel's body came unbidden into my mind. I should never have gotten him involved in the world of the fae. "We need to find out why the king wants me dead, and then I would like to personally deliver *his* death."

"Ambitious. I like it."

"With your help, of course." I stepped away from him, still clutching the pieces of my shirt together. "It seemed like you've heard of the Mistress of Dread."

"I have heard of something similar several times. Lately, I've been hearing about it from Gormal. He was obsessed with the Masters of Dread, though none of us believed they were real. It's just an old fae legend"

"Who's Gormal?"

"The Lord of Balor. He is working with us, against the

king. He has been researching the Masters of Dread. He knows more about them than anyone else."

My pulse raced. We were on the right track. "Where do we find him?"

"He's nearly impossible to find, for a number of reasons. For one, he is very secretive, and no one knows where he lives. I see him only at the meeting of the Council." He frowned, biting his lip. "Of course. The key."

"Right. I'm the key. The Mistress of Dread is the key."

"That must be why I was supposed to take you to the Council. It was a guarantee that you'd meet Gormal."

I crossed my arms in front of my chest. "Can't we find him now?"

"No. He was one of the men ambushed while traversing the secret path."

My stomach dropped. "Oh. I see. Was he killed?"

Roan shook his head. "Captured. The banshees took him."

Banshees took the man who knew most about the Masters of Dread, and then, a few days later, banshees tried to kill me. This was feeling less and less like a coincidence.

Roan cleared his throat. "There was one other place I've seen a mention of the Masters of Dread. In my own library. I'll take you there."

I nodded, looking down at myself. "Maybe I can get a shirt first? You've ripped mine. For the second time, I might add."

He let his gaze rake slowly up and down my body. A sly smile curled his lips. A *smile?* On Roan? "Sorry about that. It's hard to control myself around you."

"You'll have to try or I'll be sending you my shopping bills."

* * *

DRESSED in one of Roan's shirts, I followed him through a hallway on the upper level, half-distracted by the strange warmth in my chest. As I walked down the hall, I glanced out the lattice windows. Storm clouds had gathered on the horizon, and a few rays of sunlight pierced the gloom, illuminating the ruddy brick walls of Roan's mansion. Four wings enclosed a courtyard dappled with flowers. Over the other side of the building, the turrets of the Tower of London loomed, and to the right, the modern, glassy façade of the Gerkin building towered over the city.

I moved on, hurrying to keep pace with Roan. "How is this entire castle in the center of London, near the Tower, and I've never even heard of it?" As soon as the words were out of my mouth, I knew the answer. "It's glamoured."

"Exactly. This was once my family's London home, but the fae homes in the human realm are always hidden."

"What happened to your family?"

He took a sharp breath. "My parents were accused and convicted of treason. My entire family was imprisoned or killed. I'm the only one who remains."

My heart tightened. "I'm so sorry, Roan."

He led me to a mahogany door, carved with images of stags' antlers entwined with hemlock boughs. "It was a long time ago. Hundreds of years. And now, I have finally returned." With one hand on the door, he met my gaze. "The house is hidden from the king as well. For now."

He pulled open the door into a towering library, with wooden ladders connecting one level after another of books. Leafy vines grew between the center of the shelves, and a rowan tree grew from the center of the room. Light from an oculus high above streamed into the library, illuminating the tree's red berries and the dust motes floating around the hall. Cobwebs hung between the shelves.

"I haven't had this room cleaned yet." Roan walked into

the room, running his fingertip along a dusty row of books. "I spent a lot of time in here as a boy, reading about the ancient fae wars."

I quirked an eyebrow. I could almost imagine him as a golden-haired boy, huddled under the tree, lost in a book.

An ornate rug covered the floor, its surface embroidered with a forest scene—a beautiful woman in a white dress, standing by a stag in the woods.

I crossed further into the hall, inspecting some of the books on the shelves, all bound in leather, their spines faded.

Roan stared at a shelf, narrowing his eyes at the titles. As he searched for the right book, he said, "Tell me what it felt like."

"When I bit you?"

He turned to me, eyes flickering with surprise. "No. When you reflected the fae terror back at them."

I closed my eyes, my mind whirling with that terrible attack. Why hadn't I seen them attacking Gabriel? If only I'd turned my head earlier, or if I'd found my power sooner, instead of after he was dead... A wave of sorrow washed over me. His hazel eyes, staring blankly at the sky...

I took a slow breath, trying to focus on the banshees, what I'd felt. "It felt like I was amplifying their fear."

"What do you mean?"

"I could feel their fear and I..." I searched for a way to put it. "I threw it back in their faces. I drenched them in their own terror."

"That shouldn't be possible," he muttered, returning to the shelf.

As he searched the titles, the door creaked open, and Elrine strode in. Or perhaps I should say she flowed in.

When I'd first met Roan's oldest friend, she'd been imprisoned, starved, and tortured. Watching her now was like watching a gazelle running in the woods, a being possessed of complete grace and composure. She walked with complete certainty, as if she derived a sensual pleasure from every sway of her hips or movement of her arms. Her long, cherry-red hair draped over a silver gown, the neckline low enough to expose her creamy-white skin. She gazed at both of us as she approached a tall mahogany chair. She sat in it languidly, making the dark hard wood seem somehow comfortable. A soft scent of wood anemone and grass followed her.

"Hello, Cassandra," she said lightly. "This needs to stop."

I blinked. "Uh... hi. What does?"

"Your emotions. You have to get them under control. You'll bring any fae within a mile to our door, and we're kinda trying to lay low here. I understand Abellio has cleared you, and you are no longer our prisoner. I must admit, it surprised me. But Abellio is never wrong. So you can relax now, okay?" She shot a sharp glance at Roan. "What's going on with you? You're glowing."

He didn't answer, and I felt that flame glow brighter in my chest. Yet still, that undercurrent of sorrow and guilt washed over it, and I had no idea how to get it under control. I glanced at Roan.

Roan looked at me, his expression uncharacteristically soft. "Elrine is right. I can't hide such a torrent. I'm doing my best, but it feels like I'm trying to dam a river with a few sticks."

I bit my lip. "Give me a moment." I shut my eyes, trying to clear my mind. I was a psychologist. I knew you couldn't just freeze over your emotions and expect them to melt away. I had to live with the grief, to let it in. I had to sit with the knowledge I would never see Gabriel again. With my last memory of him, lying in a pool of his own blood. I had to live with the question of whether or not I could have stopped it...

Elrine cleared her throat, and I opened my eyes. Okay,

these feelings were not going away anytime soon. Bring on the mental prison of ice.

I imagined an empty riverbed, and I collected all the sadness and guilt, laying it across the rocky floor. The corpses I needed to bury—my mother and father, the birth mother in the London Stone, Gabriel's corpse... I lay them all down and flooded the river with icy water, then let it freeze over with a bone-deep chill.

I shivered, opening my eyes. I wasn't happy, but I'd contained my emotions. A bottled vessel full of roiling feelings frozen beneath the surface. With my emotions under control, Roan visibly relaxed, and I realized for the first time how much effort he'd probably been putting into trying to mask my presence.

"Well done." Elrine nodded. "I'm impressed with your control. I understand why you were so devastated. I heard about Gabriel. I'm sorry."

"Thanks." My voice sounded hollow.

"He helped you find me and Scarlett when Siofra held us. I will always be thankful for that. To him, and to you."

I tightened my jaw, keeping my control, and kept silent.

"What are you both doing in here?" asked Elrine.

"Learning about the Masters of Dread," said Roan. "I'm sure I saw something in here once."

Elrine folded her arms. "Dread. Surely it has something to do with Weala Broc."

I raised my eyebrows. "That's the king's house, yes? The Court of Terror. And my lineage, apparently."

"Exactly," said Elrine. "One of the Unseelie courts. King Ogmios of Weala Broc is the head."

"And the Rix, and all the other terror leeches like me, right?" I asked. "I've seen the emblem. The skull under water."

"The Drowned Man," said Elrine.

I pressed my finger on my lips. "The king sent banshees to kill me because I'm supposedly the Mistress of Dread. Why would one of the king's own kind be a threat to him?"

Elrine shrugged. "I couldn't tell you that."

I frowned, trying to piece together how this had all started. I'd never been able to feel fae terror so clearly until that one moment with Gabriel. Why then? I'd been in life-or-death situations before then, even after I'd discovered my magic. But this had never happened before.

The Stone.

It had all started after I touched the London Stone.

The Stone had either given me those powers, or ignited them within me. I just didn't know how to explain any of this —the lost week, the screams that had rung in my skull, the visions I'd seen of another fae's life.

"What do you know about the London Stone?" I asked.

Roan had pulled a book from a shelf, and he frowned at the open pages. "There. The Masters of Dread." He pointed at the book's page emphatically. "It's very vague. There's a mention of them as possessing the power to take and give fae fear. Something about a rumored Master of Dread twelve centuries ago who bathed the fae village of Oxendon in nightmares for a fortnight."

"Yeah, but that's impossible," Elrine said.

"Why?" I asked.

"Because you can't use fae emotions with magic, Cassandra. Only human emotions."

"But I *did* that. I used the banshees' fear against them."

Elrine raised a skeptical brow, and said nothing.

Roan shut the book in disgust. "There's nothing else here. We need more information."

"What are the chances we can find this Gormal person?" I asked. "The Lord of Balor?"

Roan studied me. "We know banshees are from the House

of Arawn, the Court of Sorrow, but there are so many factions of banshees, we don't know where to look. But the banshees who took him are likely to be the same ones that attacked you."

"Right," I said. "They must have gotten something from him that led them to me. But they're dead. I killed them."

Elrine stared at the floor, and I could almost see the wheels turning in her mind. "You killed them? Please tell me you drew blood."

"Of course I did."

Her lips curled in a sharp, predatory smile. "Perfect, because I can follow blood. We have everything we need."

CHAPTER 10

*J*ust as we were discussing the exact logistics of breaking into one of the banshee mansions, a knock interrupted us, and Abellio peered into the library. "The twins cooked dinner."

"I'm starving," Elrine said.

"Will our guest be staying for dinner?" asked Abellio.

"Yes." I clutched my rumbling stomach. "We have a lot to discuss, I think."

"Perfect." Abellio's blue eyes glinted in the candlelight. "We've set up in the dining room."

Roan nodded at the door, and I followed him back into the hall. Outside, the sun had begun to set, hanging just over the opposite wall of Roan's mansion, in a livid sky streaked with honey and rose. The day had begun with me sleeping on the floor in the pile of Cheesy Wotsits, my head throbbing. It seemed impossible that mere hours ago, Gabriel leaned over me, helping me up, fetching me painkillers for my hangover. And now he was gone, and I was hiding in a mansion full of fae rebels, planning the downfall of a king who wanted me dead. Elrine shot me sharp look, and I realized my emotions were threatening to pierce the surface again. I summoned my inner ice.

Flanked by Elrine and Roan, I crossed into the curving stone stairwell, and into a cavernous dining room at the bottom of the stairs.

Here the walls were made of stone, and open to the courtyard. Flowering vines crawled up to the high ceiling, winding around the tall windows, and a heavy summer breeze filtered into the open air.

Two fae already sat at the candlelit table—Nerius, and next to him, a woman whose dark hair flowed over one shoulder. Dressed in a crimson gown, she had the same dark, almond eyes as Nerius, the same olive skin. These were the aforementioned twins, I presumed.

Nerius's lip curled. "Is the fortal really—"

A low growl from Roan silenced him.

I surveyed the table setting, the eight chairs lining the table, and six place settings—each with its own silver-domed tray. A green wine bottle stood on the table between two candelabras. Was this like a family dinner, each of the diners with his own spot?

Abellio apparently noticed my hesitancy, because he pulled out an empty chair across from the twins, catching my gaze. "Cassandra, will you give me the pleasure of sitting by my side?"

I flashed him a grateful smile, then took my seat, stealing a glance outside at the courtyard, now bathed a deep pumpkin in the dying sunlight.

I pulled a napkin onto my lap, trying to ignore the twins' matching death glares.

"Cassandra," Abellio said. "These are the twins, Nerius and Branwen."

I flashed a smile at Branwen, ignoring her twin. "Nice to meet you."

Her crimson lips curled just a bit, and she nodded curtly. She was shorter than the others, her body beautifully curvy. I had yet to meet an unattractive fae. Even Nerius had a certain rough appeal.

By Branwen's side, Elrine's eyes sparkled, the candlelight wavering over her creamy skin. "So, Branwen, what did you prepare this time? Let me guess. Steak pies and mashed potatoes." She lifted the lid on her tray, and steam curled from a plate of pie and mash, covered in dark gravy. The rich scent of meat curled into the air.

"How did you know?" asked Branwen.

Elrine arched an eyebrow. "Because you've made the same meal every night for the past month and a half."

"I didn't see you show up in the kitchen, Elrine. In fact, I'm not sure you know the way."

"The *what*-chen?" Elrine asked, her eyes wide with feigned innocence. "Is that some sort of foreign word for a servant's room?"

Branwen rolled her eyes, pulling off the cover on her own tray. "Eat up, everyone."

Following the others, I pulled the lid off my dish. Instantly, my mouth began to water at the savory scents curling into the air.

"We should make a toast," Nerius said, picking up the green bottle from the table. He unstopped it, and began pouring a tiny measure of clear liquid into each glass. It almost looked like water, except it clung to the glass in a way that made me think of honey.

I noticed a shift of tension in the table. Everyone's eyes were on me. Abellio cleared his throat, looking as if he was about to say something, but Nerius gave him a sharp look and he remained silent. So. This was some sort of test or initiation. Whatever the case, they wanted to see how I reacted to drinking it.

When he'd finished pouring, he lifted his glass, still smirking. "To our guest. And to the utter and complete destruction of the Weala Broc, Court of Terror, of the Drowned Man and everyone who belongs to it."

Roan glared at him, issuing a silent warning, but everyone else lifted their glasses—including me. I wasn't *from* the Court of Terror. Genetics didn't mean anything to me.

Nerius's eyes narrowed at me, a small smile twisting his lips, waiting for me to drink. *Not creepy at all or anything.*

I watched as the others sipped their drinks, and I followed suit. When the sweet, thick liquid hit my tongue, I began to relax. It tasted like walking on a misty morning, breathing in humid spring air. I had expected something bitter or powerfully alcoholic. Instead, it danced over my tongue.

As I took another sip, I felt something warm curl up my spine, as if the liquid were exploring my body. The warmth snaked inside my ribs, creeping up to my skull.

For a moment, I could feel *everything,* knew the histories of everything around me: the texture of the glass I held, its distant history as sand, boiled into liquid, crafted into an intricate goblet. The glassblower who'd created it had been proud of his work. His wife had died the year before, and he devoted himself to his craft to overcome his pain. Now he loved another man's wife, secretly yearning for her from afar.

I closed my eyes, breathing in the myriad scents around me. Suddenly, I knew the chair beneath me had been made of a single oak, which had grown for seventy years before a woodsman sawed it down. The oak had grown from an acorn of another oak, one hundred fifty years old, and that one had grown from another oak... but I opened my eyes, and my attention snagged on another detail, a carving on the table. The daughter of the carpenter who'd made this table had wanted to marry a *knave*. As the carpenter had plied his blade on the hardwood, he'd muttered angrily to himself that she belonged in a nunnery.

And the fae around me. So beautiful, so ethereal, so light —gods among men. I wanted to cry in gratitude that they allowed me to sit and dine with them. I felt the tears sting my eyes, a monologue of broken thanks on the tip of my tongue. The flame I'd felt burning in my chest glowed hotter, warming my ribs with delicious heat.

I turned to Roan, who eyed me with concern, and his beauty took my breath away. Somehow, under the green eyes and short hair, I could see the real Roan, the forest god with golden eyes who blessed me with his presence, enveloping me with his scent.

As his magic seemed to kiss my skin, my pulse raced, and I stared at the perfect planes of his face bathed in golden candlelight. I needed to nestle my face into the crook of his neck, to lick the place where I'd bit him. No—I needed to drag him into another room, tear off my clothes and worship him, beg him to touch me. I clenched my thighs together, my breath catching at the pressure between my legs, body swelling. I could feel my cheeks warm, my body heating, my breasts straining against my shirt—Roan's shirt. My nipples pressed against the soft fabric. I needed to feel Roan kissing them, his tongue flicking over them. As glowing heat poured into my belly, I could think of nothing but stripping down and touching myself. Maybe I could entice his perfect mouth onto my breasts, his fingers between my legs. If I got on all fours... As the flame burned uncontrollably hot in my chest, my fingers found their way to the hem of my shirt, and I began to lift it.

Roan's hand shot out, interrupting me. His eyes glowed bright gold now, his whole body beaming intensely with amber light. A god of sunlight. He was feeding off my pure lust, but keeping a leash on himself. Staying in control.

"Do you like something you see?" It was Nerius's voice.

I turned to look at him, dropping the hem of my shirt, my cheeks burning. Nerius's smile widened. Not ethereal, nor godlike. Amused and cruel. A bully with a helpless victim.

Spots of color danced in front of my eyes. My mind tried to leap everywhere at once, and I actually forgot to breathe. Could I still speak?

I cleared my throat, the sound ringing in my ears. Had I been too loud? Thoughts flitted through my mind. I latched on to the one thing that felt clear and solid in my mind, under the glaciers of sadness. The grief. Gabriel lay dead, underground. A kind and loving friend, murdered because he got too close to me. I pushed everything aside, letting that thought expand in my mind. Slowly, the strange euphoria began to fall away.

I prepared the words beforehand, and prayed that I'd manage to form them without stumbling. Such a complex sentence. So many syllables.

"It's nice." I lowered the timber of my voice to steady it. "A bit sweet. I think I prefer beer."

Branwen and Elrine looked at me with new respect. Nerius's expression darkened, and he frowned at the bottle. Abellio's eyes glinted with mirth.

"It's fae nectar," Roan said. "Most find it very potent the first time they drink it."

Abellio winked at me. "What Roan is trying to say is that it makes people go totally bananas."

Branwen smiled. "Humans often go insane with lust or sensory overload after consuming it. I was hoping we'd see a bit more excitement."

"Good thing I'm only half human, then," I said lightly, concentrating on forming the words. I picked up my fork, trying to ignore where the fork's silver had been mined, and the miner's hopeless infatuation with his fellow miner, and the silversmith who'd crafted the fork when he'd been dying of cancer. I scooped up a forkful of potatoes and let the rich, buttery taste melt in my mouth.

As I ate, the fae around me launched into a discussion, but I couldn't follow it, my mind roaming to the thought of Roan's head between my legs. It wasn't until I'd eaten most of the way through the mashed potatoes and finished the pie that I could feel the effects of the nectar fading, and I started to tune into the conversation again.

"… waste of time," Nerius was saying. "This is nothing but another distraction. The king must be stopped before the attack is launched."

"Yes." Branwen tutted. "You keep saying that like some sort of drunk parrot. But you never give an actual explanation as to *how* we should stop the king."

Nerius glared. "I do, sister, but your soft female mind refuses to listen. Launch an attack on the king's keep."

Branwen let out a long sigh of disgust. "There we go again. Attack the keep. As if it were some sort of afternoon stroll. You'd need a huge army—"

"We have an army!" Nerius interrupted her. "And most of the Elder Fae would join us. And we have incredible powers at hand. Roan could summon a—"

Roan thumped his fist on the table. "I've told you over and over again, do not mention that. *Ever*. This will not happen."

A tense silence fell over the room as Roan and Nerius stared at each other. Finally, Nerius lowered his gaze.

"An attack like that would be suicide," Elrine said, her sharp voice piercing the silence. "You know that well."

Nerius waved his glass as he spoke, the candlelight sparkling in his dark eyes. "All I *know* is that the king *wants* us to think it's impossible. Constantly, we hear tales of how the keep has never fallen, while we know for a fact that it's fallen twice. The Unseelie took it from the Elder Fae, and it fell during the Ulthor rebellion. Gormal—Lord Balor—is a distraction. He's probably dead, and we'll be risking our lives for no reason." He narrowed his eyes at me. "And who's to say this fortal is telling us the truth?"

"*I'm* to say she's telling the truth," said Roan.

Abellio lifted his glass. "And me. I'd tell you if she'd been lying. You know that."

"If we attack the keep," said Roan, a hint of snarl in his voice, "this rebellion will end like the last one."

Another long silence ruled over the room. Roan and Elrine's eyes met, and something silent and heavy passed between them.

Were they fae soulmates?

Roan leaned back in his chair. "I agree with Elrine. If we have a chance to find Lord Balor, we should take it. We need his forces and his knowledge. And on top of that, the king believes Cassandra is important enough to warrant a small horde of banshees. Only Lord Balor can tell us why."

Elrine threw her napkin into her plate. "Good. Let's do it tomorrow. Banshees are most active at night, so we'll have a slight advantage during the day." She rose from her chair, and the others followed, including me.

I felt slightly dizzy from the nectar, and I lingered slightly behind the others. As we reached the doorway, Roan turned to me. "I can bring you to a guest room. Your possessions are already there."

Nerius turned to us from the stairs. "Except for the guns with the iron slugs. She's not getting those back anytime soon."

"Yes. Except for those."

When the others had climbed a little further up the stairs,

Roan grabbed my hand and pulled me closer. He said in a low voice, "If I had intervened with the nectar, the rest would have thought I was coddling you. It would have cost you their respect, and I want you to work with us."

"I know. I figured."

"I would have intervened if you'd done anything I thought you might regret. I was certain that your sanity would survive drinking the nectar."

"You did intervene," I said. "I was ready to..." I let the words die on my tongue. *To strip off and beg you to fuck me on the table? Yeah, let's keep that thought quiet, shall we?* "Anyway."

"I was surprised at how well you took it. You are a woman full of surprises, Cassandra."

Despite everything, I felt a small smile curl my lips. "Thanks, Roan."

CHAPTER 11

I sat in the alcove of a bay window in the guest room, staring at the street below. Rather than facing the courtyard like the other rooms I'd been in, this room overlooked a darkened London street. It was more an alley than a real street, twisting and turning, the cobblestone floor uneven and dimly lit by the yellow streetlights. A man in a long coat skulked through the shadows, and I followed his fluid movements, his steps sharp and certain. He knew exactly where he was going.

He suddenly paused, his attention drawn. He turned around and my heart skipped a beat when I caught a glimpse of those beautiful hazel eyes.

Gabriel.

He began walking back, his manner urgent. I knew where he was going. I thumped the glass.

"Gabriel!" I shouted.

He never even raised his eyes. He just kept going, his eyes intent on the figure in the street. A pink-haired woman, knees on the ground, weeping. Around her, the three banshees. This would end in death. I slammed on the glass again.

"Gabriel, no!"

He didn't hear, but the banshees did, raising their dark eyes to me, smiling, their teeth sharp. Sharp enough to tear a neck open.

"Gabriel! Please!"

He aimed his gun at the banshees, like I knew he would. But I couldn't let it happen again. I just couldn't. I flung my senses to the street, feeling the fear of the three banshees. The gun scared them—but not enough. I drew the dark tendrils of their fear into my body, letting them roil like a maelstrom until they thrummed along my ribs, and I unleashed a storm of pure terror on them.

Their eyes widened, and they fled, Gabriel still aiming his gun at them. Leaping into the air, three banshees transformed into silver cranes, taking off into the dark night sky, leaving behind only Cassandra and Gabriel. I slumped in relief. He would live. Drained, I watched him approach Cassandra, pick her up, wrap his arms around her.

Then I stared as she bit his throat, tearing into it, blood running down her chin, her eyes dead.

"No!"

I sat up in bed, my heart slamming against my ribs, my own screams ringing in my skull. Sweat dampened my nightgown, and my body shook. I hugged my knees, praying for the screaming in my mind to stop.

It didn't.

I clamped my hands over my ears, scanning the room. Silvery moonlight poured through the bay window onto the faded tapestries that hung on the walls. An ancient mahogany cradle lay in the corner of the room, its surface etched with leaves.

There was no way in hell I could fall asleep again with

that shrieking in my mind. I could go to the kitchen and find some alcohol or nectar…

Nope, that was a terrible idea. I had a mission now, and the mission did not include another week of getting wasted.

Flinging off my sheets, I crossed to the door, my bare feet padding over the wood floor. I opened the door, stepping into the dark hallway, the floor covered in a threadbare rug. Only a thin stream of light from a skylight lit the way, and as I passed under it, I gazed up at an uncommonly clear sky, a sliver of a moon gleaming among the stars.

I kept walking, my shadow growing ahead of me as I left the skylight behind. At the end of the hall, I reached a large hall that I hadn't seen before, the walls blood-red. Embers burned in a stone fireplace, and the tiled floor felt cold beneath my feet. Portraits hung on the walls, of beautiful fae with antlers and wings. I recognized one of the paintings—a stunning blond fae with ethereal wings that cascaded down her back. The woman from Roan's memory. That flame in my chest guttered for a moment.

From a shadowy corner, a flicker of movement caught my attention. I tensed, straining my eyes in the dark. When I recognized Abellio, I heaved a sigh of relief. He stood by a window, staring outside. He turned to look at me, his blue eyes shining in the dark. "Nightmares are a terrible thing," he said softly.

I crossed my arms, suddenly self-conscious. "Let me guess. You could feel them?" I crossed to his side, looking out onto the dark London street.

"Yes. I could feel your dreams pulsing through the walls. Roan's room is right next to yours, and he is masking your emotions well. But he can't hide your dreams from me."

"Why is that?"

He grinned mischievously. "Because I eat dreams for breakfast. I'm what the fae call a *bedbug*. I'm a dream fae."

I blinked. "Oh."

"Usually, I just feel the dreams of the humans in the nearby homes. Dreams about their work, or about that time they were late for the math test. Your dreams are a lot more... intense."

"I'm not surprised." I hugged myself. Abellio had seen me at my weakest. He could sense my deepest fears, my embarrassments, my twisted thoughts. Christ, if I had a sex dream about Roan, which was bound to happen at some point...

I cleared my throat. "Can you... uh... turn it off?"

He quirked an eyebrow. "Can you stop feeding on fear?"

"No."

"I can't stop either. But don't worry. Unless you have a sex dream, I can't really see it."

My dread must have been instantly obvious because he burst out laughing. "I'm kidding! I can't see *any* of your dreams; I can only get a very vague taste of what they're about."

I took a deep breath. Okay, so there was nothing I could do about it. I was an open book to all the fae around me. The Rix had enjoyed my terror. Roan could feel my lust, and I'd hit him with a powerful dose of it this evening. Everyone found my pixie emotions interesting, or intense, or exquisite. Now it turned out that even my dreams were an open book. I wondered what the rest of the fae here fed on. "I didn't wake you with my dreams, did I?"

"You probably would have, but that's not why I'm here. I'm staying watch. We always have one fae awake and alert. The king could find out our location at any given moment."

The screams had started to dull in my mind. Something about Abellio's presence soothed me. Must be the dream thing. "You all take shifts?"

"Yes. But I do more than the others. Nighttime is when I feed best."

I couldn't go back to sleep yet, couldn't stand the thought of being left alone with my own thoughts. "So... what do you think about Elrine's idea—breaking into the banshee's home to look for Lord Balor?"

He gazed out the window again. "It's a good idea. We need information, and if we can find Lord Balor, it could help us significantly. Most importantly, we need to find out who our traitor is. *Someone* told the king where to find the path, and if it wasn't you, it was one of our own."

I nodded, and then hesitantly asked, "Abellio... what were they talking about during dinner? Nerius referred to a power that Roan has, and Roan—"

"We really shouldn't talk about it," Abellio said, frowning.

"Talk about what? I don't even know what I'm supposed to avoid. Clearly, everyone here knows about this."

He studied me in silence. Finally, he sighed. "Roan is what we call storm-kissed."

I waited, staying silent.

"Supposedly, fae like Roan can call up a powerful storm. It's a rare talent, and highly volatile and dangerous. A storm is not a power one can control easily."

"And Roan won't use it," I said. "Why?"

"He summoned a lightning storm once, in his past. It... ended badly. Innocents died."

"Who? How did it—"

"Cassandra, you should ask Roan about that, not me."

"Okay," I relented. After a moment, I changed the subject. "They were talking about another rebellion. Something about Ulthor. What was that?"

"You're full of questions, aren't you?"

"Better than being left alone with my nightmares," I muttered.

Abellio nodded, his eyes sympathetic. "The rebellion of Ulthor. What a mess." He traced his fingertips over the age-warped windowpanes, as if scrying into the past. "The house of Taranis and the house of Ernmas conspired to bring down the fae high king. Ulthor Taranis led the revolt—Roan's father. He wanted to restore the old ways—the ancient Unseelie Kingdom used to rule by six courts who made decisions together, with a representative of the Elder Fae to break the tied votes. No one court reigned supreme over the rest. His plan was good. Apart from the Court of Terror, those two courts were the strongest courts—Lust and Mirth. Together, they controlled almost half of the king's army, and they had the element of surprise on their side."

"What happened?"

"They managed to take control of the fortress, but the king fled before they could capture him. Outside the castle walls, he gathered his army and besieged the castle. Weala Broc loyalists who were still inside the keep somehow managed to destroy the keep's stores. And the king announced that he'd grant forgiveness to the first court to surrender."

"Did they surrender?"

"Ulthor Taranis would have starved to death along with all his family before he surrendered. But Leo Ernmas, the head of the Ernmas court, saw his men and women starve. He saw his daughter—Elrine—crying in hunger. He wouldn't let her die. He opened the gate for the king's forces. True to his word, the king pardoned the Ernmas court, executing only Leo. Nearly the entire Taranis court was destroyed, most killed, a few imprisoned for life. Tortured. Roan among them."

My stomach clenched, and tears stung my eyes. A powerful surge of protectiveness overtook me, and I almost wanted to run up to Roan's room and wrap my arms around him. "How did he get out?"

"The Court of Lust was destroyed, and Roan was released

only because he was the single link between the Unseelie and the Elder Fae. The Elder Fae had a long history with his family, and they would negotiate with no one else. The king needed him."

"And the rest of Roan's family is gone now?" My heart ached for him.

Abellio nodded. "Almost all of them. Roan was only fourteen at the time. A babe, by fae reckoning."

My stomach clenched. No wonder he spent so much time alone in the woods—he had no one else.

Abellio frowned at me. "I can feel your emotions running out of control again." He sucked in a breath. "Do you need help managing your dreams?"

"What do you mean?"

"I can soothe your dreams as you sleep."

I frowned. "Can you do that?"

"If you allow it. When you dream, you are not in control. You are at the mercy of your fears, of your lusts, of your guilt. You need someone to help you maintain control over the dream state."

I thought of my nightmare—Gabriel's throat torn by another Cassandra, her eyes dead. "So… what, you stay near me and send me happy thoughts?"

"It's more than that. When you're sleeping, I walk in your dreams and help you maintain control. I can be your ally in the dream. Your friend."

I knew he could already taste my dreams, but I didn't want to let him in any further than I had to. "I think I can manage on my own. But thanks."

"All right." He seemed unperturbed, his eyes locked on the street outside.

"I'm going to try to sleep again. Good night, Abellio."

"Good night, Cassandra. Don't let your dreams fool you. You are not responsible for your friend's death."

I swallowed hard, walking away over the cold tiled floor. I didn't need magic to know he was wrong.

So Elrine was from the Court of Mirth. Too bad for her; she'd be getting none from me.

* * *

BY THE TIME the morning sun stained the sky pale pink, I deeply regretted my decision to decline Abellio's offer. I had slept badly, repeatedly waking up out of breath, my heart beating wildly. A pounding headache throbbed in my skull, even though the screams had faded away completely.

Branwen had loaned me some of her clothes—mostly tight, black leather, and a few short dresses, and I stripped off my nightgown and pulled on a black sundress.

I had a new mission right now. A mission for coffee.

First, I crossed into the open-air dining room, hoping to find someone there, but I found only the morning light sparkling on dust motes in the air. After a few false turns, I found the kitchen—a vast stone hall with enormous brick ovens, copper cauldrons, and an ancient-looking spit for roasting. Nothing, however, that looked like a coffee pot.

Okay. Maybe I could find my way out of this glamoured building to the nearest Starbucks. After all, it's not like I was a prisoner here.

As I crossed through a sandstone corridor, the distinct scent of coffee drew me closer. I paused, glancing inside a room for its source.

There, in the center of a bare room, stood Branwen, dressed in tight leather that hugged her curves. A large mirror covered one wall, and a weapons rack stood against another wall.

Branwen gripped a stiletto knife in each hand. Her eyes were closed, and I stared as she swerved in a graceful arc, the blades whistling in the air around her. Her right hand snaked fast, striking an imaginary opponent, while her left hand rose high as if to deflect an invisible blow.

When she opened her eyes, she turned to look at me. "Good morning. My dress looks awfully good on you."

"Thanks for lending it to me."

"Sleep well?"

"I've had better nights." No use hiding it. The black circles under my eyes gave away the truth, and everyone had probably felt my emotions all night anyway.

"Coffee?" She nodded at the corner of the room. "You can use my cup."

On a small wooden table sat a silver jug, steam curling from its top, and a ceramic mug by its side. I almost gasped in relief. "Yes, thank you." I crossed to it.

Branwen stretched her arms above her head. "It's my one addiction from the human world."

"You have amazing taste." I poured myself a cup of coffee. When I sipped it, I shut my eyes in pleasure. It was sublime.

When I opened my eyes, Branwen was smiling at me in amusement.

"Sorry," I said. "I'm not myself until I drink my first cup."

She lowered her knives. "It's okay. I get it."

A long, uncomfortable silence stretched between us. Our shared interest had run its course, leaving us with nothing to say.

"Training?" I asked. When in doubt, state the obvious.

"Yeah." She sighed. "As much as I can. It's difficult to train without a real opponent." She cocked her head. "Want to spar with me? I want to see what a pixie can do."

"Um." The knives weren't training knives, and I wasn't keen on getting impaled. Also, the pounding in my head didn't exactly stoke my enthusiasm. "I doubt I'd be much good right now. I think your imaginary opponent creates a better challenge than I would."

"Fine." She turned away from me, and I had a feeling I had just lost a measure of respect from her. She pierced the air with one of her stilettos, fast as a biting snake.

"I might be able to help, though," I added.

She glanced at me, looking half-bored. "How?"

I felt for the large mirror's reflection, letting it bond with my mind. Then, I imagined a fae warrior wielding a large sword. Sunlight gleamed off his scaly skin and his dark, reptilian eyes. The image materialized on the mirror, and he lunged, as if about to attack Branwen.

She stared at him before turning to me. "Reflection magic."

I shrugged. "It's kind of my thing."

She nodded, giving me a little smile of renewed appreciation, and turned to the warrior. She attacked, piercing the air, and he moved, as if deflecting her stab. Her other hand swung, slashing at his throat, and I made him pounce back, then lunge forward as if striking. It was just another measure of make-believe. The mirror was flat; Branwen was essentially fighting air, but I did my best to make it look real, embellishing details to distract her: flames in the background, blurry figures fighting each other, a horse galloping across the mirror. A complete fae battleground, harvested from some ancient part of my brain. The entire scene was uncannily silent.

Branwen kept ducking, parrying, stabbing. When she made a particularly clever maneuver with her right blade, I made my warrior's neck bleed, and he toppled over.

"More." She gasped for breath.

Two warriors took his place. One wielded a shield and a sword, the other a long spear. It was engaging, to try and keep the reflections' actions in tune with Branwen's. My mind, completely focused on the task, felt lighter than it had been for days.

"What do you think about breaking into the banshee's house?" I asked.

A spear thrust at her violently, and she whirled to the side. "I agree with my brother," she said, gasping, swinging her left hand at the swordsman. "It's a terrible idea."

He raised his shield. "Why?"

"Dangerous and pointless. Lord Balor is probably dead."

"He might not be. And maybe we can find out information about the spy in your midst."

"There's no spy." She jumped back as both my warriors attacked together.

"How do you know that?

"You're ruining my focus."

I recalled myself sparring with my teacher in the Academy as he kept distracting me with questions about bombs, hostage situations, reading suspects. When the fighting gets real, there's always distraction. And no better time for me to get information that wouldn't be handed out easily otherwise.

"When you actually get to fight, you won't be able to tell everyone around you to shut up and let you concentrate," I pointed out.

"Fine," she snarled, and thrust at the spearman's shoulder. I summoned some blood from his wound.

"Others think that someone told the king about the secret path," I said. "A spy among the rebels. Why don't you believe it?"

"The king has trackers, like Elrine, and even better. They could find that path on their own. I trust our people."

"Perhaps we can find out why the king thinks the Mistress of Dread is a threat, and why he wants me dead."

"I don't care why the king wants you dead."

My swordsman lunged at her with a lightning fast blow. She danced aside, but he would have hit her, and we both knew it.

"Where are the rest of the rebels?" I asked, changing the subject.

"A suspicious person might start to think you're asking too many questions," Branwen said. "Perhaps I should take back my claim that we have no spies among us." Sweat glistened on her neck.

"There are only five of you," I pressed on. "I know there are more. I've met some, they were called—"

"Don't tell me their names!" she barked.

My lips twitched in a small smile. She had stumbled, given me a piece of their strategy. "You're working in cells. That way, if captured, you wouldn't be able to give the details of the others."

She scowled, focusing on the flickering mirror.

"Which court do you belong to?" I asked, changing the subject again.

She sneered. "Why do you ask?"

"Abellio told me about the last rebellion. The courts of Taranis and Ernmas joining together to topple the king. Do you belong to one of those courts or—?"

"Typical royalist fae. Mentioning the courts that took part, but ignoring the rest," she said. Her movements were becoming erratic, angry. She slashed at the mirror.

I pressed on. "What rest? The Elder Fae?"

Slash. "No."

"Another court?"

Slash. "No! It's easy for people like Abellio to forget, but not all fae belong to a court. Most of the people who actually fought in the rebellion were unaligned. Fae who were tired of being trodden on and used by the nobles. They joined Ulthor Taranis because they saw hope for a change. And when the king smashed the rebellion to pieces, most of them paid with their lives."

She thrust at my swordsman, forgetting the spearman, and I had him plunge forward. He would have skewered her.

"Unaligned fae." I recalled the phrase Roan used once. "Is that what people call the... gutter fae?"

She whirled to face me, pointing one of her stilettos at me. "Do you like it when people call you mongrel, or fortal?"

"I'm sorry." I crossed to her, holding up a hand placatingly. "I'm just trying to piece it all together."

"They all call us gutter fae," she snarled, turning to face the mirror, thrusting her stiletto knives with vehemence at the spearman. "Even our allies. We can't own lands, are treated as lesser. A gutter fae will always remain just that—in the *gutter*. When a noble sees a gutter fae, they don't see someone they can really know or love. All they see is—"

She slammed her knife into the mirror with her full force, and, with a loud crack, the mirror broke, pieces falling everywhere. Branwen jumped back, and I grabbed her, steadying her.

"Damn it," she muttered.

We looked at the mess around us. Shards of broken mirror littered the ground.

"Let's clean this up," I suggested softly. I'd obviously set her off.

Silently, we collected the pieces into an old dustbin, and I wondered if Branwen regretted her outburst and her slip of the tongue. I was almost certain that she did. Who was it she loved, who didn't love her back? Abellio? Roan?

As we tidied the room, her breath still seemed labored, even though she was no longer exerting herself. I gave her time to calm herself, saying nothing. Carefully, we piled all the shards into the dustbin, until it was mostly clean. I wondered if the rebels had a vacuum somewhere in this mansion. A large piece of mirror still lay across the floor—six feet tall, and nearly three feet wide.

Branwen bent and picked up the large shard—a piece of glass nearly as tall as her—and placed it against one of the walls. Then she picked up another large shard, and placed it against a different wall. Now, mirrors reflect her from two sides.

"Okay." She raised her knives. "I want to keep training. But no talking."

I nodded, and felt for the reflections in the mirrors. When my mind clicked, I let my thoughts roam, conjuring fae from my past on the mirror. The forked-tongued fae who had assaulted me in Trinovantum; the hoofed woman Scarlett and I had chased into the fire; a silver-skinned fae warrior in the house where Scarlett had been imprisoned.

Branwen whirled and stabbed, dodging and swinging as the enemies around her attacked, faces twisted in angry snarls. Only her grunts and heavy breaths broke the silence as she moved faster and faster, her body a blur of motion. I could hardly follow her attacks anymore, and I let her attackers die, replaced by new fae. The torturer from the king's prison, the fire-winged fae who'd bombed London, the acid-spitting fae who'd attacked me in the alley.

I began to sweat as I let Branwen set her blades on my own terrible memories, her blade slashing the prison's warden. A stiletto plunging into Grendel's throat, his eyes bulging. A flurry of thrusts on the banshee who had attacked Gabriel. I wasn't even looking at Branwen anymore, my own face twisted in a grimace as I conjured all the fae of my nightmares, a bitter taste in my mouth, strangely thrilled at the vengeance before my eyes.

And then the warriors disappeared from the reflections, the mirrors instead blazing with one image—a woman, her mouth twisted in pain, her eyes vacant, hands held up, begging for help. My heart stopped. Siofra.

I let out a scream and severed my connection to all of the mirrors. Siofra disappeared, and the mirror shards showed only Branwen and me, standing alone in the room.

Branwen turned to me and looked at me strangely. "What happened?"

I shook my head. "Nothing. I just need to rest."

I didn't tell her the real reason my heart was beating as wildly as it was.

I hadn't summoned the imaged of Siofra. She'd just appeared.

CHAPTER 12

*A*fter Branwen's training, she led me to the dining room for breakfast, where the rest of the mansion's inhabitants already sat around the table laden with plates of bacon and toast. Nerius was speaking loudly, waving his fork around, and Abellio listened, grinning. On the other side, Roan and Elrine sat next to each other, whispering, their heads nearly touching. Something Roan said made Elrine smile and lick her lower lip. For a moment, a jolt of unbridled jealousy tightened my chest. Of course, they had a lot to whisper about. Their family histories went back literally hundreds of years. If I'd crawled into his room last night like I'd wanted to, would I have found her in his bed?

Anyway, it was nothing to do with me. I was here on a mission, and that mission was revenge. I glanced at Branwen, realizing she was watching them both as well, gritting her teeth. So *that's* who she was in love with.

Nerius continued on with his stupid story. "And the woman, completely naked, got on her knees and—"

Branwen cleared her throat, and the four of them raised

their eyes. "Telling stories of your imaginary exploits again, Nerius?" she said, crossing to him.

"Just teaching Abellio some basic lessons." He glanced at me and his face darkened. "Ah. The mongrel is joining us. Dressed in my sister's clothes. What's that human expression? You can't put fine frocks on a festering corpse?"

I shook my head. "Definitely not a human expression, but nice try."

I pulled out a chair by Roan, my eyes meeting Elrine's for just a moment.

"It's good that you came," Roan said, his eyes briefly lingering over my dress, taking in the short hem. "We need to discuss our next course of action."

Nerius looked like he was ready to crush his ceramic mug. "In front of the terror leech?"

"Yes." Roan's tone brooked no argument, and he stared down Nerius in what I could only imagine was some primal fae display of dominance.

When Nerius's gaze lowered, Roan turned back to the table.

"We now have another reason to think there is a spy among one of the rebel cells. The king's men discovered a stash of our supplies last night. It could be the tracking ability of the king's men, but I think it might be more than that."

"Then maybe it's time to stop hiding," Nerius said, his voice sharp. "The keep is not as protected as it used to be. We still have surprise on our side."

"Not if we have a spy among us," Elrine said. "He'd inform the king."

Roan nodded. "True. We need to capture the spy before an attack can even be considered. In addition, we need Lord Balor. We need his connections to the rebels within the house of Balor. In addition, it is likely that the banshees that took him are the ones in contact with the spy—that's how they knew where to ambush him. We might manage to get information from them regarding that. We will track the banshees down, and see where that leads us. Hopefully, Lord Balor is still alive and can tell us about the Mistress of Dread."

"The Mistress of Dread?" sneered Nerius. "Abellio told me. You can't possibly believe that, can you? A fae can't manipulate fae emotions with magic. Our emotions *are* magic."

Elrine glowered. "We know that. But in any case, we need Lord Balor's forces. Are we agreed? Good."

Roan's face shone with respect as he looked at her, and that unwelcome stab of jealousy pierced my mind again. I shoved the thought away.

Revenge. I was here to get revenge, and vengeance would be mine.

* * *

ON THE NARROW, cobbled street in the city, I led Roan and Elrine toward the place where the banshees had slaughtered my friend. The two fae followed me, eyeing our surroundings warily, looking for signs of an ambush. As we got closer to the spot, bile rose in my throat, the memories of the attack flashing in my mind. Only yesterday, I'd strode the same cobblestones, chasing Gabriel—the living, breathing Gabriel. The Gabriel with a heartbeat, who wanted to help me. I could almost feel the despair that had threatened to consume me that day.

The Court of Sorrow had come for me.

We reached the crimson stain, the one left by Gabriel's blood. The police had already processed the scene and left— just a few shreds of police tape, probably left there to keep away the curious pedestrians until the city could clean the blood from the street.

A torrent of sadness washed over me at the thought of Gabriel's body, left there, alone.

At the sight of blood, Elrine hurried closer to the stain, kneeling by it.

"That's not the banshees' blood." My mouth had gone dry. "That's Gabriel's."

"Oh." She rose. "Where did the banshees die?"

I pointed to the wall where I'd killed one of the banshees. The shattered glass had been swept up, but blotches of maroon still stained the pavement. "Right there."

Elrine frowned, approaching it slowly. "It's very dry."

"Can you use it?" asked Roan.

She crouched, inspecting the blood. To my disgust, she ran her finger across the dark smear and licked it. She frowned, as if deep in concentration.

"Cassandra," she finally said. "I can't fucking concentrate. Your emotions are ringing in my skull."

"Sorry." I shut my eyes and focused, trying to freeze my guilt and grief under the rivers of ice. I summoned the glacier.

The coppery smell of blood curled into my nostrils. *Gabriel's?* No. It couldn't be real—his blood had completely dried. I shoved the scent under the surface, locking it deep under the ice—

A faint buzzing from the alley called my attention, and I opened my eyes. Flies, always drawn to blood. I scanned the scene, catching sight of them. Four, no... five dark specks, crawling over Gabriel's blood, where he had lain after the banshees attacked.

If he hadn't come back to look for me...

If he hadn't been burdened with having to come into my hostel room...

117

If I'd been faster, smarter, stronger...

The ground tilted under my feet, the pounding in my head deafening, bile rising in my throat. My knees buckled and I leaned on the wall, and then bent, throwing up on the cobblestones.

Roan's strong arms grabbed me from behind, steadying me. I coughed, wiping my trembling lips on the back of my hand.

"I have to get out of here," I stuttered. I pulled away from Roan, breaking into a run, eyes blurring with tears as the loss hit me again, harder than before. I reached the high street, and leaned against a glass storefront, trying to control my breathing, to summon the ice.

It only took a moment for Roan to find his way to my side, and his powerful hand warmed my back. "I'm sorry." His soothing voice sparked a flame of warmth between my ribs. "We should have never brought you here."

"It's okay." I took a deep breath. "You're centuries old. I imagine you don't fall to pieces every time one of the rebels dies. But this is new to me."

Roan pulled me close, and once again, with my head just by his heart, I was struck by the certainty that he smelled like home.

Slowly, my racing pulse began to calm, and when my breathing had returned to normal, he said, "It's what the king does. He destroys lives. And we will end him. We will get revenge."

"Yeah," I said hollowly. Vengeance wouldn't bring Gabriel back.

CHAPTER 13

*F*or over two hours, Elrine prowled in front of Roan and me, her hands slightly outstretched, nostrils flared. In her black leather leggings and boots, she moved stealthily, fluidly. It was a strange experience, using an actual person as a blood hound, but she seemed to know what she was doing.

A few times, she stopped and muttered around the ashy ruins of Leadenhall Market—the old Victorian covered market that had been bombed in the fae attack on London. She sniffed the air, mumbling that the traces of blood were fading, lost in the scent of cinders.

At last, she led us to the ancient, crumbling Roman walls that had once enclosed the city, and beyond into a brick courtyard. Here, modern, glassy apartment buildings encircled a stunning pool of green, tree-lined water. Just ahead of us, a small stone church stood in a brick courtyard, surrounded by the glassy water and a curving section of ruins. There was something oddly peaceful about this part of London, this serene blending of the ancient and the modern.

As we drew closer to the church—St. Giles, it said—

Elrine stopped abruptly, looking around her, her crimson hair seeming to snake around her head in the breeze. "Here. The scent is strong here."

I frowned, looking around at the empty expanse of brick around us. "Where, exactly?"

She gestured around her. "Just… here. Underneath us."

I scanned the brick courtyard, looking for a manhole or something that would take us underground, but saw nothing that stood out. "Maybe there's a crypt in the church? It looks medieval."

Elrine nodded. "Right. A crypt. Human burial spaces, yes? Seems appropriate for the Court of Sorrow. They love death, of course."

I crossed to the church's door, glancing at the old wooden sign that read, "City of London – Ward of Cripplegate." Below that, a sign gave notice of a scheduled funeral. I checked the date. It was today, about to start in half an hour.

Elrine folded her arms. "So what's the plan?"

Roan ran his fingertips along the church's stone, as if inspecting an alien object. "How do we find this crypt entrance?"

"There might be dozens of Arawn fae inside," said Elrine. "Whatever we do, we need to remain discreet and blend in with the humans."

"Just ordinary humans," I said, "showing up early to a funeral to search the building for a crypt."

Elrine shrugged. "We could try walking in and pretend to be shopping for a funeral."

"Shopping for a funeral?" I raised an eyebrow.

"Isn't that what people do? Don't they go and choose a fancy corpse-box, and flowers and all that? Pretty makeup to cover the rot? I don't know how you humans work. We just burn our dead in trees like normal people."

I shook my head, quickly getting the sense that we would

not blend in easily among the humans. "Funeral-shopping doesn't happen in a church."

Roan shook his head. "Banshees are sensitive. They will sense that we're fae, and they'll definitely feel your sorrow, even with me close by."

"Okay, hang on." I rummaged through my handbag, pulling out a compact mirror. "We can have a look first."

I gazed into the reflection, letting my mind click with the glass, feeling for other reflections around us. I could sense dozens, and I scanned through them, looking for something crypt-like. I reached for a reflection, using it to gaze into a spacious stone hall, the flagstones covered in an ornate rug. Old church pews lined the room, and portraits of cranes and mourning doves hung on the walls. Three brightly-cloaked women, their locks long and tangled, sat before a burning hearth, silently sipping from black cups. Seemingly trans-fixed, they stared into the flames. Even before the fire, their breath misted in front of their faces, as if they generated cold air. Though all were silver-haired, they ranged in age, from a youthful banshee to an old crone.

I frowned. We'd found what we were looking for, but... Since when did churches have large fireplaces? It must be some sort of banshee lair under the ground. Beyond the crypts, maybe.

"Yeah," I said. "We've found the banshees."

I felt for another reflection, the mirror flickering. Now, it showed me a windowless stone hall, with at least ten banshees, each gripping spears. They were sparring, moving in graceful circles, their cloaks seeming to float on ghostly breezes. How big *was* this underground compound? This was more than just a crypt.

"It's not just a crypt. It's like a whole underground compound, with a lot of armed banshees." I turned the mirror so to give Roan and Elrine a look. "Before we go in, I need to map out exactly what we're walking into. Give me a few minutes to puzzle this out, okay?"

Roan nodded, and I crossed the brick courtyard to a set of stairs that led down to the water. I took a seat on the stairs, then rifled around in my bag for a pen and a piece of paper.

With the compact mirror resting on my knee, I bonded with the reflection and scanned the banshee's compound. After a few minutes, I linked with a reflection in a large brick room full of domed ovens and pots hanging from the ceilings. I flipped through other reflections in the room, trying to estimate the room's size. I finally decided it was a square room, twelve feet wide. I drew a small square labeled *kitchen,* with a door marked on one wall.

Then, I searched for other reflections nearby. After scanning past three of them, I landed on a cavernous dining room with an oblong table. Four banshees sat around the table, eating with their hands, licking their bony fingers clean. I located the door that looked like the door from the kitchen.

Across the room stood a large glass cabinet with plates in it. I felt for the reflection on the glass, and it appeared on the other mirror. I sifted through several reflections until I felt I had a good grip on the room's size and exits, and added it on my paper map. *Dining room.*

On and on, I leaped between reflections, searching rooms for doors and reflections and creating a detailed map of the place on my receipt, my handwriting cramped on the tiny piece of paper.

At one point, I realized in frustration that I had placed the kitchen—my place of origin—too far to the right, and I'd run out of room, needing to flip over the receipt. I scrawled the rest over the front of the receipt. *Training room. Bedroom A. Bedroom B. Bath C* had a tall male fae soaping himself, and I lingered on that reflection just a second longer, to make sure

I got the measurements right. The measurements of the room, that is.

Finally, I felt like I had a reasonable diagram of the place, albeit one that only I would be able to read. I shoved the paper into my pocket and turned to head back to Roan and Elrine. My heart skipped a beat when I couldn't find them, until I found the faint glimmer of tall outlines. Of course— Roan had been glamouring us this whole time to hide us from the banshees.

As I moved closer, their forms became clearer, but I counted five of them. *Five?* Branwen, Nerius, and Abellio had joined us, huddling by the church, their faces clearer as I drew within a few feet of them. Branwen had dressed in a formfitting red dress, cut in a low V that showed off her cleavage, and I couldn't tear my eyes away. Not exactly ideal for a covert mission, but with her dark, wavy hair and dimpled cheeks, she could certainly distract someone if we needed that.

"Hello everyone." I pulled the scrawled map from my handbag. "This is a general outline of the place. There are at least fourteen rooms, not counting the bathrooms."

"At least?" Nerius scowled. "You're not sure?"

"I'm getting to that." I said testily. "I think the entrance is through the church's crypt, and even that is hidden. It's hard to be sure, because I could find no reflections in the actual crypt, but see here?" I pointed at the edge of a corridor, and the fae hunched over my crappy squiggles. "This corridor ends in a large barred door, with a small hatch. I'm pretty sure I could glimpse a low, arched tunnel that leads beyond the crypt."

"How do you propose we get to it?" Nerius asked.

"We probably don't. Two male fae were standing guard there, both with swords."

Nerius huffed a laugh. "Two? We can take two."

"Yes, but we might alert the rest," Branwen said sharply.

"How many are there?" asked Roan.

"Dozens," I said. "Four of the bedrooms look like barracks, with six double beds in each. This is like a small military outpost. An underground fortress for the Court of Sorrow."

I let them digest this for a moment.

"Besides that entrance from the crypt, three doors lead to places without reflections." I pointed at my scrawl. "This one here looks like a door to a pantry, and this one, I think, leads to a bathroom stall. That's the impression I got, anyway. But this one—" I pointed on one I had circled and labeled *mystery door*. "This one hides something. There's a huge padlock on it, and it looked like a heavy door with spikes. *That's* what I meant earlier when I said I wasn't sure how many rooms there were. As far as I know, beyond any of these doors could be an entire section with no reflections."

Elrine smiled, casually sliding her arm around Roan's shoulders. "Good. That's where you should go first."

Branwen was glaring at Elrine, gritting her teeth angrily. Christ, the drama between these fae was distracting as hell.

I blinked, clearing my mind. "Not necessarily. This room here" —I pointed at the one labeled *study*— "has a desk with a bunch of drawers. It's littered with papers. Also, on one of the walls, there's a safe. If it's information about the spy you're looking for, this might be the best place to find it."

Interest sparked in Branwen's dark eyes. "What kind of safe?"

"It looks old and silver, with a dial."

She gripped my arm. "Describe it in detail."

"I can do better than that." I took out a hand mirror, letting my mind click with the reflection. It only took a few seconds for me to find the study, and to bring up the image of the room. I handed the compact mirror to Branwen.

She licked her lips. "Beautiful. I can crack it."

"Are you sure?" Roan asked.

"Branwen can crack any safe," Nerius said. It was the first time I'd heard him say anything nice, and the way he looked at his sister just then heightened my opinion of him.

She cocked her head. "Not *any* safe. But I can crack this one. It's fae-made, and I know just how it works."

"And Lord Balor?" asked Roan.

I shook my head. "If he's in there, he's probably behind that locked door. The room with no reflections."

"Okay." Roan folded his arms. "But there's still just one entrance. So how do we get in there?"

"You don't." I shoved the mirror back in my bag. "I do."

CHAPTER 14

*I*f I had a quarter for every displeased frown around me, I would have been a dollar and twenty-five cents richer just then.

I cocked a hip. "It'll be fine. I can sneak in through the reflection to the study. I can search the desk, get whatever looks important from there."

"And the safe?" asked Elrine.

"Maybe the combination is written down somewhere," I said, though I was doubtful. "And if not, I'm sure I can get something useful in there. We might learn something about your spy."

Abellio's blue eyes bored into me. "I don't like this idea. It's too dangerous for you to go alone."

I shook my head. "You forget how easy it is for me to escape. I know where all the reflections are. I go in with hand mirrors on me."

Roan frowned. "Once you're away from my side, your feelings would be a beacon for any fae in the vicinity. They'd storm inside and grab you."

"We've done it before," I said. "The study is far away from

the crowded rooms. I'll keep my feelings in check, and if I hear anything, I'm gone."

Elrine's forehead crinkled. "No offense, Cassandra, but you haven't convinced us you're capable of something like this. And back in the alley, I wasn't impressed by your ability to contain your emotions."

Nerius rubbed his stubbled chin. "And if there's nothing useful in the desk? You'll return with nothing but a surplus of stationery. The Arawn fae in the complex would discover the break-in, and tighten security. We'd never get a chance to do this again."

"We could storm the complex," Roan said thoughtfully. "I could connect with another cell."

I shook my head. "If these guys are good, they'll have a plan for an assault on their complex. At the very least, they'd probably destroy any useful information before we got our hands on it. That whole study would go up in flames."

Nerius waved a dismissive hand. "They'd never expect a powerful frontal attack. We can take control of the complex before they even consider—"

"I'm not just a pretty face," I said coldly. "I am… I *used* to be an FBI agent. There's *always* a process for eliminating confidential information. We'd lose the intel. If you have a spy, you'll never find out his name."

Abellio shrugged. "Then we take this complex by force and deal a terrible blow to the king's forces. Isn't that enough?"

"No," Roan said. "That's not why we're here."

Branwen raised a hand. "I can get inside to help her." Four frowning fae turned their glares on her. She looked at Roan. "You know I can."

"How?" I asked.

For a moment, silence reigned. I quickly scanned their faces and saw that Elrine and Abellio were as confounded as

I was. Nerius's eyes were wide, his lips a tight line, as if he were silently trying to warn her to shut up.

Branwen looked at the ground, her dark hair falling in front of her eyes, as if she were ashamed. "I can take control of her shadow."

Elrine's breath hitched. Abellio's face twisted for a moment in disgust.

"Shadow magic." Elrine spat the phrase.

Branwen's cheeks reddened. She gritted her teeth and leveled her cold gaze on Elrine. "I didn't go looking for it. I was *born* this way. I didn't want to be a shade. No one does. And you know what? It's actually useful sometimes."

"What does this mean?" I asked, frustrated. I wished there was a "Fae Culture 101" course I could take online.

Abellio was staring at her, his face still shocked. "Shades steal other people's shadows. Without their shadow, a person can slowly wither and die. It takes years, but it always ends the same way. This magic was outlawed over seven hundred years ago."

Branwen met my gaze, shrugging slightly. "Nobility don't have this kind of magic. They never did. It's *gutter* magic." She grimaced. "Of course, no one outlaws mind-fogging, or water control, or any of the other deadly magic that the *nobility* have. Just gutter magic."

I bit my lip. "I see. And are you suggesting that you steal my shadow? I don't understand."

"I don't do that!" Branwen said, her dark eyes shining. She blinked, as if trying to clear the tears from her eyes. "I mean, I'll give it back as soon as you return. You'll never even feel it."

Nerius's expression had darkened. "She never used it to hurt anyone."

Silence fell over us.

Roan rubbed his chin. "I think it can help with the safe,

and of course I trust Branwen. But the banshees will still feel Cassandra's emotions."

As we stood by the side of the church, my gaze drifted to a small crowd of mourners approaching the church, dressed in black—an older woman with a wide-brimmed black hat and a veil, sniffling into a handkerchief, and two men in dark suits flanking her. A few more trailed behind, not noticing us with the magical camouflage Roan had drawn up around us.

Camouflage. Right. "What if I could camouflage my emotions?"

"How?" asked Roan.

I nodded at another small group of funeral goers, approaching the church. "There's a funeral taking place right now in the church. It's the House of Sorrow down there, right? I'm betting they set up shop here centuries ago so they could feed on grief."

Branwen cocked her head. "That, and this was once a leper colony. Hence the charming name *Cripplegate.* Lots of grief around here in the old days."

I nodded at the church. "Still is right now. So what if my sorrow allows me to blend in? Lord knows I have plenty of that. They might not notice me."

Elrine blew a strand of her cherry-red hair from her eyes. "It's a good idea. I doubt they'd be able to find Cassandra's sorrow in the torrent of sadness from above. Worst case scenario, they'd think there's a pixie among the mourners. This will work."

I nodded. "Good. I'll sneak in through the reflection into the study. Once I'm there, Branwen can take control of my shadow."

She held up a hand. "I'll need you to find a way to cast it so it's about your size. If it's too large, or too small, I'll have an awkward time helping out."

"Okay," I said. "I'll be back here as soon as I find something. Or if anyone comes after me."

"What about the locked door?" Elrine pointed at the map. "Will you look for Lord Balor?"

Sunlight sparked in Roan's eyes. "That seems too dangerous."

Shadows seemed to pool around Nerius. "What is the point of having this *pixie* with us, slowing us down and attracting attention, if she's incapable of doing anything useful because you're afraid she might break? You've suddenly got a weak—"

"It's fine," I said, cutting off his monologue. "I can do it."

"Are you sure?" asked Roan.

I sucked in a sharp breath. I *had* to find out what the 'Mistress of Dread' was all about. "Yes. I've got my reflections, and I've got my escape routes. It's worth a shot, at least."

"Fine," said Roan. "I trust you."

"Let's do this." I pulled out the compact mirror, opening it up.

"Wait!" Branwen bit her lower lip. "I can, uh... only control shadows of people I know well."

I blinked. "So... what, do you want me to tell you my life story?"

Nerius was shielding his eyes with his hand, as if he was mortified.

"No." She straightened. "I mean I need to know you intimately."

My cheeks warmed. "You mean we need to... what, exactly?"

With a shy smile, she beckoned me closer, her dark hair tumbling over her red gown. "Just a kiss."

"With a *fortal*," said Nerius vehemently, turning the other way.

I took a deep breath. Okay. Well, I'd never kissed a girl before, but she was certainly beautiful.

I moved closer, standing just a few inches from her, looking into her dark, almond-shaped eyes. She smelled of wildflowers. She reached for me, cupping my face, then pressed her soft lips against mine. My skin began to warm, my nipples tingling, brushing against her breasts. I felt her pull me in closer, one hand around the small of my back, and her tongue gently parting my lips. My back arched, and she let out a low moan—

Roan growled, cutting it short, and her body stiffened. I pulled away from her, shooting a mortified look at Roan. He knew exactly how much I'd enjoyed that.

I cleared my throat, staring at the ground. "So is that... good? Are we good?"

Branwen nodded, a little too eagerly. "That should do it."

My head buzzed and I felt slightly dizzy. I cleared my throat. "Okay. Good enough?"

Roan looked down at me and pulled a stray strand of hair from my face. Flecks of gold shone in his eyes. "Master your emotions before you go in there. You need to feel sorrow only. And right now, I can feel something else altogether."

Mortifying.

"Wait." Branwen reached under her dress, and pulled out a stiletto knife from a sheath strapped to her thigh. "Put this in your purse."

"Thanks." I dropped it in my bag, then closed my eyes, summoning the glaciers, the impenetrable wall of ice.

Then I pulled out my compact mirror and stared at it, scanning the reflections until I found the study. I let myself fall into the mirror, feeling its cool surface wash over my skin in icy, liquid waves, and I tumbled into the study.

In the stony room, the air was colder and stuffier, the room lit only by a dim lantern. Pale orange light wavered over the paper-strewn desk, and the silver safe which was tucked neatly into a stone alcove that looked as if it had been carved for a statue. As I scanned the room, my eyes lingered over a set of shelves lined with what appeared to be human skulls.

I felt a twinge of claustrophobia, realizing that I was deep underground. I pushed that dangerous spark of fear under the surface of my mind. I couldn't afford to feel fear at the moment.

What would Gabriel think if he could see me now? I felt a burning desire to talk to him one last time. Once this was over, I'd go to his grave. Since magic was real, surely I should be able to speak to the dead.

Sorrow. I let it wash over me, thinking of Gabriel's hazel eyes. I crossed into the center of the room, standing in front of the lantern until my shadow spread out over the floor, stopping when it was about my height. When I went still, I stared as my shadow quirked its head and moved its hands.

Branwen seemed to be testing it out, moving the fingers and arms. The shadow then lifted its left foot and detached from my body. I shivered at the strangeness of it.

My shadow instantly turned to look at me, and I could almost feel its reproachful stare.

Right. Sorrow. Not fear.

I summoned the image of Gabriel again, letting the sadness consume my mind. I stared as my shadow skulked over to the alcove, creeping up the stone wall. The dark figure began fiddling with the safe, turning the lock. I looked away, the sight too confusing and distracting. I had to search the desk, anyway.

As I suspected, the papers scattered haphazardly on the desk were written in the fae language, Trinovantum-lish or whatever they called the strange runes that I still didn't know how to read.

I pulled out my cell phone and began snapping photos of the papers, thinking of Gabriel the entire time—his tidy apartment, the delicious meals he'd cooked. His old jazz band.

At one point a tear dropped on one of the papers, spattering on the ink. I wiped my cheeks, realizing that both were wet. Maybe I needed to rein in my sorrow just a tad. It was slowing me down, and I felt like total despair was fast on its heels.

There were about thirty or forty pages on the desk. I'd photographed about half when I suddenly heard a deep voice penetrating the door, slowly growing louder as someone approached. My shadow turned its head as if to look at me. The door handle turned, and my heart thundered.

I quickly raised my phone to my eyes, shutting off the screen. My face appeared in the darkened glass screen, and I jumped into the reflection.

I flickered into an empty bedroom, my heart beating wildly, and forced myself to calm. Quickly, I turned to stare at the mirror, and began searching for the study. It appeared on the glass.

My phone lay discarded on the floor by the desk, full of the photos I'd just taken. I stared at it aghast, and then realized I had used it to jump, leaving it behind. *Stupid!* I scanned the rest of the reflection. I couldn't see a sign of my shadow.

Two male fae dressed in gray robes stood by the door, their voices muted through the reflection. One had scraggly, black hair that fell over his shoulders, and the other was white-blond, closely cropped.

The blond crossed to face the desk, and my heart gave a small jolt as he walked toward it. Would he notice the phone?

Frowning, the dark-haired fae suddenly turned his head as if sensing something. My own fear, I realized. He felt my fear. I quickly shut it away, focusing on Gabriel—his tidy apartment, now left empty.

The blond snatched a paper off the desk and turned away, joining his friend. At last, the two fae crossed out of the room, shutting the door behind them.

Steeling myself, I let out a small breath and jumped back into the study.

Once in the room, I turned around, looking for the shadow. It shimmered out from the desk's shadow, where Branwen had hidden it. I gave it a shaky half-smile. It turned back to the safe, and I crouched down, snatching the phone off the floor.

After five more minutes, I'd managed to snap a photo of every paper on the desk, and I looked up at my shadow. The figure hardly moved, its head against the safe, hand slowly turning the dial. I crouched, slowly pulling open one of the drawers. In the drawer, I found a stack of plain paper, three fountain pens, and a few candles.

In the third drawer, amidst some tiny bottles of dark ink, I spotted a keyring with four keys. *Bingo.* Quietly, I pocketed them.

A creaking noise pierced the silence, and I looked up to find my shadow slowly opening the safe. I hurried, peering over the shadow at the safe's interior.

Three rolled parchments lay inside, two sealed with red wax, the other with a broken seal.

I quickly dropped them into my handbag, and the shadow gently closed the safe's door. It nodded at me once, then crawled back to me, its feet merging with mine.

A light tingle rippled over my skin, and my shadow was mine again. And now, maybe we could find what the Mistress of Dread was all about.

I pulled out a compact mirror, merged with it, and leapt into the icy reflection.

CHAPTER 15

$\mathcal{U}$p close, the locked door seemed even more formidable than it had before, its spiked surface bathed in torchlight. It was built of solid oak and wide metal strips held it in place. The door fitted tightly to the doorway, with no cracks giving a view of the room on the opposite side. An old, rusted padlock held the door closed. I brought up the keyring I had found in the study, and jammed the old keys into the lock. The third key twisted, and it clicked open.

Carefully, I pulled the bar from the metal slots, resting it on the floor. Then, I slowly pulled open the door, cringing as it creaked, revealing a darkened room. The first thing I noticed was the sharp scent of death, warning me away. Another crypt, perhaps?

Only the torchlight in the hallway behind me cast any light, framing my shadow on the dank stone floor. I shut the door carefully behind me, then pulled out my keyring flashlight, clicking the light on.

Tiptoeing, I crossed into the stuffy chamber, straining my eyes in the dim light. I could just about make out furniture covered in white cloth. Something about this room raised the hair on the back of my neck.

I moved the thin beam of light around, quickly establishing that I'd come through the only door. If anyone entered here, it would be from the same door. Given how loudly it had creaked, I didn't worry about anyone sneaking up unannounced.

I frowned at the empty room, a strange sense of unease tingling over my skin. The strange bulges and shapes under the white fabric made no sense. It didn't look like furniture, and the white cloth had a strangely shimmering texture.

I crossed to one of the lumpy objects, tracing my finger over the surface—a silky white substance. The texture felt like thin satin strands that clung to my fingertips in delicate, shimmering fibers.

As soon as I touched the strings, a wave of exhaustion slammed into me, and I felt an overwhelming desire to lie down on the floor. What was the point of any of this? Why had I come here? Gabriel was already dead, and revenge wouldn't change that.

Nerius was right. I was nothing more than a useless fortal, a lilive, a mongrel.

The wave of fatigue hit me so hard, I nearly fell into the white strands. I forced myself back, a gasp of despair escaping from my throat, and quickly crossed to the wall. I rubbed my fingers on the rough stone, scraping off the strands of gleaming white, and some skin along with it. Slowly, the despair subsided, and I took a deep breath.

What the hell was that stuff? It felt like tangible hopelessness. I shone the beam of the light over the room again, suddenly seeing what I should have realized all along. Nausea climbed up my throat. Under the silky strands of fabric were humanoid shapes, completely encased in a thin, shimmering material. My stomach dropped. Christ. There were *people* trapped in here. No wonder the room reeked of death.

As I looked closer, I began noticing the shapes protruding from the silk. A hand jutting out, lifeless and rotting. A half-submerged skull. A long, slender leg, sticking out from a slumped form.

My mouth had gone dry. Nerius had been right. If Lord Balor had been kept in here, he was long gone now. I fumbled in my handbag, searching for a mirror to escape this hell.

A long groan stopped me in my tracks, and I pointed my beam of light toward the source, my heart hammering. A cold sweat beaded over my forehead. Someone in here was still alive.

As I drew closer, my flashlight shone over a man, or what remained of him. His face looked gaunt, his skin gray, and two-thirds of his body lay cocooned in the ghastly material. When I'd touched it with two fingers, I'd wished for death. How did it feel to be wrapped in it? How could he even find the will to groan?

He moved his lips faintly. "Please," he muttered. "Death."

I crouched lower, meeting his gaze. "Who are you?"

He let out a dry sob, his eyes agonized. "No one. Kill me."

"You don't want to die. It's this stuff that's covering you. Hang on, I'll get you out." Easier said than done. I pulled Branwen's stiletto from my bag, and ran it along the man's form, trying to slice through the silk. I managed to slice the material, but it clung to the blade, dulling it. I needed to clean it to try again, but touching the stuff would probably kill me.

"A knife," he croaked. "Here." He tilted back head to expose his neck. "Do it. Please."

Shit shit shit. Even if I somehow managed to pull him out of there, he'd still be covered in the stuff, and if I got any on myself, it was all over. And even then, I had no way to break him out of the complex. He couldn't come through the reflection with me.

"Who are you?" I whispered again.

"My name is Gormal. Please, I beg of you—"

"Gormal? Lord Balor?"

He gave a faint nod.

"What is this place?"

"The end. Please. Do it before she comes back."

"Who?"

"The interrogator."

"What does she want?"

He let out a sob, his head drooping. He began wailing in desperation, ignoring me.

"I'll give you what you want if you talk to me."

He raised his eyes, glimmering with—no, not hope. The opposite of hope. The expectation of death. "You'll kill me?"

I hesitated. "First tell me what I want to know."

His mouth twisted. "Just like the interrogator. She promised to kill me when I told her what she wants to know. And I told her. *Everything.* But still she thinks I'm holding out. I told her everything I know—the fae courts, their bloodlines, the family connections between Seelie and Unseelie, the bloodline of dread—"

"The bloodline of dread?" I pounced on that phrase. "What do you know about that?"

He shut his eyes, lips moving silently as though praying.

"Hey. Hey!" I pressed my stiletto to his throat, and said, "I need to know about the Masters of Dread, the whole bloodline. If you tell me everything you know, I will drive this blade right into your jugular."

His eyes opened at the sound of my twisted threat. "A promise."

I bit my lip. "Yes." There was no hope for him. All I could do for him was put him out of his misery.

"I was a scholar," he said, his words fast and urgent, knowing that death was in his grasp. "Studying fae bloodlines, and I found a peculiar hereditary strand. One that was considered a myth. A family line that held a power over fae emotions."

I tensed. "Some say that magic can't use fae emotions. That fae emotions *are* magic."

"That's almost entirely true. Most fae emotions are just that. Magic in pure form. But there is one emotion that's different. That is more primal, more ancient than any other human emotion."

I swallowed. "Fear."

"Yes," he whispered. "Not love, or happiness, or rage. Fear came before all of that. When Lilith opened her eyes in the Garden of Eden, that was the first thing she felt. A jolt of fear."

"And that family line? What could they do?"

"They could use the fear of fae. Use it for their own powers of magic."

"In what way?"

"Various ways." His voice cracked. "Each one could use it differently. Of course, the ancient fae weren't too happy with this power. They killed any fae that showed a sign of possessing it. But several survived. And they had children. As far as I know, there are still two alive today."

"Who are they?"

"One of them—" A sudden creak made him pause, his eyes widening. "She's coming," he said, his lips trembling. "Kill me, you promised!"

We weren't done yet. There was still that other matter. "Lord Balor—do you have any idea who betrayed you? A spy among the rebels?"

"No," he stammered. "Please. She's here."

My pulse racing, I turned around. An old woman stood in the doorway, peering at me with milky white eyes. Her long, gray hair hung in front of her face, her skin a midnight blue.

"I thought I felt a pixie in my lair," she croaked.

I shuddered.

"Kill me!" the man screamed.

With a lightning-fast move, I jammed the blade into his jugular, and blood sprayed through the air. But as I did, something silky hit the back of my neck, and dizziness clouded my mind, an agonizing emptiness eating at my chest like a cancer. Blinking, I stared down at the man, his lips moving soundlessly. Fatigue was sapping my body. I needed to lie down.

I dropped to the floor, letting the mirror slip from my fingers, emptiness gnawing at my ribs. The jagged void. Why did we put up with all the pain of life? Why didn't mothers break the necks of their babies as soon as they were born? Certainly better than to let them live in this hell.

Something scuttled in the corner of my eyes, and I turned to see the old woman, crawling now, on eight spindly legs, four of them ending in long-fingered hands.

"Well, what do we have here?" she scuttled around me, and as she did so, white strands of string spooled from her mouth. She grabbed them deftly with her hands, circling me, wrapping the strands around my arms. She flattened my arms to my body, then began to cocoon my feet. A powerful maw of despair gripped me, a sense that I was rotting from the inside out—rotting, and completely alone.

She crouched, gazing at me with her milky eyes. When she opened her mouth, I noticed another set of mandibles.

"The Mistress of Dread herself," she whispered, in a voice like a thousand ants crawling on my skin. "The king wants you dead or alive. I wonder which he prefers? Dead? Or alive?"

Dead. Please.

"I can feel your despair, pixie. And it's a glorious banquet."

A tear rolled down my cheek, and I desperately wanted to get to my knife. I could have ended it myself if I had been just slightly quicker.

"But others have underestimated you before, haven't they, little pixie? I'm not the Rix. I'm much older, and much wiser. When I see a threat, I kill it."

I glimpsed a movement in the corner of my eye. A tail, curved and ugly, ending with what appeared to be a large stinger. It twisted closer, and then suddenly whipped and jabbed me in the throat. I gasped in pain.

"You'll die, Dread Mistress," the interrogator rasped above me. "Just like you wanted. It won't be painless. My venom rarely is."

A numbness was spreading through my neck and down my shoulder, a tingling sensation. It wasn't too bad. Just a bit of an itch. And it would bring me the oblivion I craved for. The interrogator scuttled right and left, dropping her threads of despair around me carelessly. Her feet scraped the stone floor unpleasantly. Soon it would be over. The numbness spread to my left arm. Then, my neck began to burn, as if someone had placed a live coal against it. I moaned. Above me, the interrogator cackled.

The pain spread. Shoulder. Arm. Hand. Fingers. Everything began to thrum with agony. I writhed on the floor, groaning, my breath too shallow to scream. The pain pulsed in my skull now. It overcame everything, any coherent thought I had. All I wanted was for it to stop. My eyes fell on an object lying on the floor. The hand mirror I had dropped. And I could glimpse the corner of a reflection. In a desperate twist, I rolled toward it, as I searched for the only person I thought could somehow help me stop the pain.

The world blurred, and I looked up at the cloudy faces of five fae. "Where the fuck did she come from?" barked Nerius.

Roan crouched, scooping me into his arms, his mossy scent enveloping me. "Cassandra? What's happened?"

Even in his embrace, an agonizing sense of isolation consumed my mind, an endless void. "Kill me," I whispered.

An eerie keening pierced the air, cutting me to the marrow. Shrill cries, intermingling in the air.

Then, Elrine's voice. "What's that sound?"

"It's the banshees screaming down in the catacombs," said Abellio. "Foretelling death. They're never wrong."

My death. It was the sting, I knew. My executioner had filled me with venom, and I was about to die. In this gaping void of despair, I welcomed that knowledge.

CHAPTER 16

I gazed into Roan's eyes, hoping he'd end my torment quickly. I was about to die, no matter what, and he could end it fast. My heart fluttered.

Elrine crouched by Roan, reaching for my body. "What's that stuff she's wrapped in?"

Branwen stayed Elrine's hand. "Don't touch it! It feels... wrong."

"I'm removing it," Roan said matter-of-factly.

If he touched the webs, he'd become just like me—rotting from the inside out. Before I could open my mouth to stop him, he grabbed a bunch of the stuff, green eyes widening as the despair hit him.

Then he clenched his jaw, his eyes clearing, and tore the rest off me, pulling it off my arms, my legs. He ripped through the strands, smearing them on the brick to clear them from his hands. He kept going, even though I knew cloying despair must be poisoning his brain, whispering at him that there was no hope.

My heartbeat began to lose its rhythm as the venom streamed into it, poisoning me. As my vision dimmed, my heart skipped a beat, then slowed. My throat clenched, the supply of oxygen dwindling every second. A sharp pain spread down my arm to my fingers, and I felt as if someone was boiling my blood from within. I whimpered. Death lingered around me like a miasma.

As he scraped the last of the despair strands off me, my mind sharpened. Pain splintered my body, but I was desperate to live, to see Roan's eyes again, to run through the forest, to feel my fingers in the dirt, to run my hands over the oaks.

With the last breath left in my body, I whispered, "Sting. Venom. My neck."

Roan cradled my head, leaning in closer to inspect my neck. I heard Elrine gasp. "Roan. She's dying. It's too late."

He ignored her, and lowered his mouth to my throat, warm lips on my skin, his tongue moving against the bite as he tried to suck out the venom.

"Roan!" Elrine shouted, nearly hysterical. "You'll only poison yourself! What the fuck are you doing?"

He raised his head, spat aside the poison and lowered his mouth to my neck again, the feel of his lips sending a pulse of heat through my body. My heart raced out of control, and I couldn't tell if it was the poison's effect, or if it was Roan's proximity. My muscles spasmed suddenly, and a burst of fluid ran up my throat, blocking my air. Some of it leaked down my cheek, the rest choking me, making me cough. That flame that had been burning in my chest since I'd bitten Roan sputtered, nearly dying out.

"Look at her skin," shrieked Elrine. "The poison is spreading. Let her go, Roan. There's no point!"

Roan raised his head again and looked down at me. He grabbed the front of my dress and pulled at it roughly. I heard the tear of fabric, felt his fingers brushing against my skin. The world blurred around me.

Abellio had said that the banshee keen never lies. When they wailed, death was sure to follow.

Strange. I always imagined death as a darkness closing down on me. But when my vision finally failed, it was replaced by endless, milky white.

* * *

A GENTLE, incessant tugging pulled at my chest, over and over. I felt at peace here, sinking deeper into a cool, heavy neverness.

And yet that warm tug pulled at my chest, piercing the calm, a niggling, irritating thing, like an un-snoozable alarm clock, telling me that it's time to get up get up get up. I wanted to swat it away, but that would mean moving, and I just wanted to let my body fall into the never.

The warm tug intensified, and I whimpered. With that one exhaled breath came air, and body, thoughts, and pain. Warm, powerful hands on my chest.

Something warm and delicious pressed against my lips, bringing with it a vision of amber light streaming between oak leaves, sparking the earth with gold.

I coughed and bucked, my body pulling from the cool never. My eyes snapped open as I gasped for breath, the light sharp—too sharp. That persistent, warm tug pulled at my heart, forcing it to keep on beating. I wanted to scream, wanted to flail, wanted to fold into a ball and fade back into the white.

Instead I took another, painful breath. And another.

"She's back," Branwen said. There was something in her voice. Disbelief, perhaps.

"Cassandra, can you hear me?" Roan said, his voice laced with a panic I'd never heard from him. "Blink twice if you can."

As soon as the words were out of his mouth, I tried to remember what he'd said. How many times did I need to blink? And had I already done it, or did I still need to?

"I can hear you," I croaked, my voice like sandpaper. It hurt my throat to talk, and I let out a cough.

Roan let out a long breath, pulling me closer. "Thank the gods."

Slowly, the world swam into focus. I was laying on the brick courtyard, not far from the church. Something moved to my right, and my eyes followed the motion. A mourner, leaving the church. Ignoring us completely.

I swallowed hard. "What happened?"

"The spider poisoned you."

Elrine was giving me a death stare, apparently furious. "And you died."

I looked at her in confusion. It seemed my death had really pissed her off.

Another tug at my chest. I flinched at the tug and noticed Roan's eyes shift at the exact same moment.

"What is that?" I asked.

"What is what?" he asked.

"That sensation... like a tugging. Like something is pulling me—There! It happened again!"

"That would be your bond," Elrine said, her eyes dark with rage.

"Bond?"

"The bond that Roan—"

"We were bound to each other yesterday," Roan said, his voice tense. "I never... severed the connection. That's what pulled you back."

"Pulled me back?"

"From death. My heart beat for both of us."

I shut my eyes. I'd *died?*

"Can you get up?" Roan slid his arm behind my back. "I can lift you if you can't."

"Give me a moment."

Groaning, I pushed up onto my elbows, and as I did, a breeze whispered over my breasts. Roan tugged the ripped front of my dress together, and I held it in place. I looked around to see who might have been enjoying the view.

Apart from the fae, nobody, it seemed. The mourners from the funeral strode past, completely ignoring us. Roan's glamour was powerful as hell.

"Watch where you put your hand," cautioned Roan.

I looked down, and realized that a mound of the white strands lay inches from my fingers. I quickly drew it back.

"You touched it," I said numbly, remembering him scraping it off. "Do you have some sort of... magical protection?"

"No," Roan said. "I'm just used to the feeling."

Christ. A long silence fell over us.

"We should get it out of here," I said at last. "Or it'll poison half the neighborhood."

"No problem," said Branwen, pulling out a lighter. She flicked it, then crouched down, touching the flame to the piles of silk. Instantly, they blazed with a roaring fire, and Branwen jumped back with a shriek. The spider's silk was highly flammable.

I leaned into Roan, feeling that warmth return to my chest. Somehow, he'd brought me back from the other side.

CHAPTER 17

e got back to the mansion, crammed into a sleek Rolls Royce Phantom that Nerius had parked nearby. I sat in the back, and the wind from the open windows rushed over my skin. Roan sat by my side, his body warming mine. Apparently, our bond was still partly keeping me alive, and we had to stay close while he helped to keep my heart beating. That glowing warmth in my chest had returned, pooling around my heart.

We drove south through the city, heading past Savage Gardens on a street called Crutched Friars. God, this city had amazing street names. At last, we came to an arched carriageway—a covered street called French Ordinary Court —and Nerius took a right into a dark, underground parking lot. He parked the car before a whitewashed stone wall in the passageway. "Here we are."

I opened the passenger's door, stepping out. As soon as I did, the world spun, and I nearly collapsed onto the cobblestones. Roan grabbed my waist and steadied me, helping me cross to the wall. With one arm around me, he lifted his hand to the wall, and it shimmered away, revealing a stunning redbrick mansion with turrets and an arched entrance into a courtyard. I glanced upward, at the golden stag's head that gleamed in the sunlight above the door.

Elrine walked past us, pretty much sneering, her eyes pure ice. *What the hell, woman?* If I had to guess, she was pissed that Roan had put his own life in danger by sucking the venom from my neck. She was clearly protective of him.

With Roan's arm around my back, we walked through the courtyard to one of the oak doors. From there, Roan led us through the dark-walled halls into a room hung with ancient tapestries. Through warped windowpanes, milky light streamed onto carved oak chairs and a round table.

I sat beside Roan, squinting in the bright light. Dust motes hung suspended in the air. Abellio took a few extra moments to fetch me a glass of water. An eerie silence hung over the room, and I had the sense that all the fae were upset about something—Elrine especially. But I had no idea what.

Once I'd taken a few sips of water, Roan turned to me. "What exactly happened back there?"

"I found the keys to the locked room. I found my way there through a reflection, unlocked the door." I shuddered at the memory. "The whole place was full of bodies coated in that stuff. The spider's silk. The bodies were in various states of decay. Lord Balor was there." I knew what was most important to them. "He had no information about your spy. He asked me to kill him. I had no way to get him out."

"Did you?" asked Roan.

"Yes."

Elrine gritted her teeth. "If you were as good as you said, you'd have found a way to get Lord Balor out alive. Maybe get out yourself in a way that didn't involve Roan endangering his life."

Roan waved a dismissive hand. "Not now."

I crossed my arms, trying to ignore Elrine's hostility.

"Lord Balor said something about a bloodline of dread, that he knows about two people who possess a certain power. He said it only works for terror, the most ancient human emotion." I frowned, not entirely sure if that was true, but I'd leave it for now. "He said that most of the bloodline of dread had been abolished, but now two remain who can manipulate fae terror. I guess that's me and... someone I'm related to. Maybe the Rix's brother."

Nerius glared at me. "Nonsense. And then, what? You killed him?"

"He was dying in agony. I had to act quickly."

Nerius pushed back in his chair, his face reddening. "You can't seriously believe this drivel? A bloodline of dread? We would have heard of it."

"It bears consideration," Roan said. "Let's not forget she managed to kill three banshees, something I'm not sure you could do."

Nerius's expression darkened. "If she was working with them, that would explain everything as well. I never saw any proof that those banshees were dead, like she said. And as it happens, she just murdered one of our allies."

Roan eyed him, his eyes flickering. "Do you really think I wouldn't know it? Even *now*?"

The temperature in the room dropped sharply, and Elrine's lips flattened into a thin line. A heavy silence reigned over the room, and I stared at Roan. What did he mean by that? *Even now?* Why was now any different?

Something had happened that I didn't understand, but seeing as everyone was ready to rip my throat out, I kept my mouth shut. Elrine looked like she was two seconds from leaping over the table and slamming my head into the oak. Mistress of Dread or not, I could not take that woman in a fight right now.

Nerius finally lowered his eyes. "I trust your heart."

And that was definitely unexpected.

Abellio drummed his fingertips on the table. "Hello? It's almost like no one listens to me anymore. I already cleared her."

Elrine leaned back, crossing her arms. "But what does that change? Even if she does possess this magic, there are stronger beings than her. And who's to say she won't join the Court of Terror again? She belongs under the sigil of the Drowned Man. It's in her blood, Roan. You of all people should be disgusted by this."

Roan merely stared at her.

Branwen reached down, picking up my handbag from the floor. She plopped it on the table, and I realized for the first time she'd been carrying it for me. "Let's move on, shall we? Cassandra and I found something in the safe." She pulled out the three rolled parchments, placing them in the center of the table.

Roan picked the first one up, unrolling it to read the contents.

"What is in there?" Nerius was trying to peer over the top, though no one touched the rest of the parchments. Apparently there was an order to how things were done around here, and Roan took precedence.

"We definitely have a traitor." Anger laced Roan's voice, and he began to read out loud. "'I have met with our associate tonight after he showed up in bird form. He escorted me to a hidden trail in the Hawkwood Forest. My guide informed me that Elder Fae and traitors use this path. The trail ended abruptly in the river, which seemed too wild to cross. But my guide made me follow him across the river, and then I could see that it was nothing but clever glamour, hiding the path. The location is in a bend of the river, with dozens of sharp-looking rocks. The water breaks upon their jagged peaks with a roar. Both river banks are covered in dense foliage, old oak trees, and nettles. To get there…'" He scanned the page. "There are very detailed instructions."

"A bird form," Branwen echoed, touching her finger to her lips. "So. A shifter."

"Maybe." Roan uncurled the next parchment, reading it over. "Listen to this one. 'Our associate showed up again tonight, in the guise of a young woman. We flew through the City of London until we arrived at a small warehouse. It is my belief that this warehouse should contain something of interest. The address to the warehouse is 103 Savage Gardens.'" He raised his green eyes, snarling, "The address of the cache the king's men raided."

"So… " Abellio chewed at the tip of his fountain pen. "A woman who shifts to a bird?"

"Well, it says a *guise* of a young woman," Branwen pointed out. "As if that weren't her usual form."

Elrine remained silent, and I could practically feel her anger pulsing across the room.

Ignoring her, I peered at the parchment. The contents didn't entirely make sense. "Why would he take them to the locations? Why not simply tell them where to find them?"

No one answered, and Roan unrolled the third parchment. This one looked different—thicker, and the seal had already been broken.

Roan opened it, reading, "'It has come to my knowledge that there's a pixie who poses a serious threat to our kingdom in the human City of London. Among other crimes, the mongrel is suspected in being involved in the death of the estimable Rix, assaulting Grendel of Balor Court, burning down the manor of Siofra of Weala Broc, and attacking seven of the king's guests in a royal gathering. She is dangerous, like a rabid bitch. She may be known by either the human name Cassandra Liddell, or the designation the Mistress of Dread or the Queen of Terror. She is to be killed or captured without delay, using your best assassins. She has a..." He cleared his throat. "There's a general description here. Quite detailed. It's not important."

"Really?" I raised an eyebrow. "Please share."

Elrine spoke for the first time, her voice venomous. "Enlighten us."

"Just... height. That kind of thing."

"You said it was detailed." I peered over the parchment, glancing at the runes.

Roan sighed and resumed reading. "She has a pink, wanton mane of hair, and a young, nubile body which she uses to distract the honest fae around her like a bitch in heat. She dresses as a harlot would, exposing her breasts and flaunting them. Her pixie emotions inspire shameful lusts in all those she comes in contact with. She is a bit shorter than the average fae, a corrupted runt who should have been slaughtered at birth."

My face reddened. "I do *not* flaunt my breasts. And can hair even *be* wanton?"

"Sounds accurate," said Elrine acidly. "A bitch in heat."

"Elrine," barked Roan.

She glared at him, her nostrils flaring with rage. Okay, she *really* hated me.

"I told you I was the Mistress of Dread," I said, cringing slightly at the petulant *I told you so.* "But the rest is inaccurate. I didn't burn Siofra's manor. That was Roan's friend. And Grendel and the Rix attacked me first." I cleared my throat. "I did do all the killing and assaulting, I guess."

Roan rolled up the parchment. "King Ogmios used the house of Arawn in an attempt to efficiently and silently dispatch the Mistress of Dread. He is, quite simply, terrified of you."

"Can I see that letter?" I asked.

Roan handed it to me and I held it, staring at the curvy

runes. They were beautiful… and completely undecipherable, as far as I was concerned. I rolled it again, completing the wax seal—a lone cypress tree. I shivered with recognition, running my fingers over it. "I've seen this before."

"It's the private seal of King Ogmios," Roan said. "He seals all his royal missives with it."

"Only he has it?"

"Yes."

I swallowed hard. When I'd touched the London Stone, I'd seen another person's memories, flashes of his life. And in those memories, I'd seen this very seal. I had glimpsed moments from the king's life. Somehow, touching the Stone let me see fragments of his memories.

CHAPTER 18

*A*fter reading the three missives a few more times, we moved on to the papers I had photographed on my phone. It was dreary work—I flipped between each image, and Roan scanned the document, reading it aloud. Several times he accidentally touched the screen, shifting the image around or closing it, at which point he would thrust the phone back at me, muttering in frustration about human technology.

I transcribed a list of the notes in English. Some were just logistical memos—supplies bought and stored, a shipment of swords that had arrived, an increase of pay to the high officers. Others were reports or instructions—a request for a troop of guards to escort an envoy to the court of Balor, a report mentioning a Seelie spy who had escaped incarceration, a demand for additional skilled archers as many had been killed during the attack on the Elder Fae. Nothing mentioned the Stone, or the Mistress of Dread, or anything that seemed relevant.

I spent the afternoon helping Branwen cook. After dinner, I wandered through the halls and found Roan in the training room, shirtless and practicing with a sword. I let my gaze roam over the muscles of his chest as they flexed, and the savage tattoos that snaked around his body.

As I crossed into the room, my pulse began to race, heart speeding up—almost as if I were the one doing the workout. That strange flame burned brighter. What exactly *was* this bond connecting us? Everyone else seemed to know, and I wanted some answers.

He paused in his training and turned to look at me, a faint sheen of sweat shimmering on his powerful body. He smiled slyly, and I bristled in annoyance. He could sense the flicker of desire, and I clamped down on it. *Pure ice.*

"You should learn to let go," he said, returning to cutting his blade gracefully into the air—as if he needed practice. "Whatever you feel is a natural reaction. Lust and dread, life and death—they're dancing partners. You must know that."

I did know that. Baby booms often followed bloody wars, and during the bubonic plague, people had screwed like rabbits when they weren't busy succumbing to their buboes. The scent of death filled people with the need to feel alive. "Terror and Lust." I smiled. "Sounds like us. Speaking of us— that bond between us... the thing you did. What exactly was that? I felt it like a warm glow in my chest. I still feel it. It feels... golden. I don't know. I can't explain it."

"It's a connection between souls. It allowed me to see some of your memories so I could make sure you were telling me the truth."

I took a deep breath. "It's more than that, Roan. It's keeping me alive. Elrine hinted that your heart is working for both of us. Is that true? I felt it when I was walking in here, like my heart was speeding up along with yours."

Another wicked smile crossed his sensual lips. "I can think of another reason that might happen."

My cheeks warmed, pulse racing. Was he flirting with

me? Something had changed in him ever since he did that bonding thing. "So what exactly is this bond? And how long does it last?"

"Cassandra, magic can't always be explained with words. Some things just *are*. It's a connection. It's keeping you alive. It lets us share some emotions, some memories. That's it."

"Can you sever it?"

This made him pause. "It would kill you right now."

"And what about once I get better?"

He stopped slicing his sword and turned to me. His expression was hard to read; was that sadness? "Of course I would sever it. If that's what you want."

I blinked. "Well, I don't understand what it is, and I don't like things that I can't understand."

"Of course."

A heavy silence fell over the room, and I decided to change the subject. "I think the London Stone is important."

"Important how?"

I shook my head. "I don't know. It just felt... powerful. I went there, searching for my mother. I heard her screaming, like she was trapped in the Stone. It was like there were thousands of terrified souls trapped in there, and it exuded power. At least, to someone like me. A terror leech. But here's the weirdest thing. I saw someone's memories. And I'm pretty sure it was the king's."

He narrowed his eyes. "Anything we can use? A weakness in his defenses?"

I shook my head, trying to think clearly through the haze of whiskey-soaked memories. "There was a sacrifice, I think. Almost like he was terrorizing people to feed their fear to the Stone. Like it's a... like a weapon. I had a sense that it was a living part of the city, the ancient part of the city's mind, where terror lives."

Roan scrubbed a hand over his mouth. "If the Stone

connected you to the king, it may have alerted him to your presence. If it linked your minds, this might be how he knows about the Mistress of Dread in the first place. That's probably what triggered the assassination attempt. Whatever your powers can do, he believes you are a great threat." He studied me carefully. "We need to understand your powers better. When we finally launch an attack on the king's keep, we'll need all we can get. Once we weed out our spy, we'll have surprise on our side. And we have some raw power."

I let my gaze roam over his body for a moment. "Yep. I've seen that."

"But the king has legions of powerful fae. Perhaps if we can use your powers of dread, it would tip the scale."

"Of course. That's exactly what I want to do, to use my powers to destroy the king. I just need to learn how. It's not like the reflection magic; it doesn't just happen when I need it. It only happened that one time, after they killed Gabriel. I just need to learn to focus it, right?"

He crossed to the weapon rack, carefully resting his sword in an empty spot. "This sort of magic is more powerful than reflection magic. You'll need to learn how to unleash it, and that means you'll need to inhabit your true nature." He shoved his hands in his pockets, walking slowly back to me. Sunlight from the windows gilded his body and sparkled in his forest-green eyes. "Powerful magic is not about focusing. It's about releasing something inside you. You don't focus when you need to breathe, or to blink. These things happen because that's what your body wants."

I wrinkled my nose. "I'm not sure I can put that advice to use. I don't know how to develop a skill like that."

He crossed to me, his gaze moving slowly up and down my body. "You need to let go. You're holding yourself too tightly." He stepped closer to me, the heat radiating from his body. He reached out, tracing his fingertips gently over my collarbone as though he were exploring it, memorizing me.

His touch left a trail of hot tingles over my skin, and my breath sped up, pulse racing. This close, I could see the stunning contrast of the gold flecks in his eyes with his black eyelashes, and the dark, graceful sweep of his eyebrows. The streaming sunlight seemed to ignite his golden hair, giving him a halo.

His fingers moved up higher along my throat, brushing lightly over the place where he'd once bitten me. "Your body is full of years of memories and emotions that you've always contained, and never faced. They are battering to be let out. And constantly trying to *understand* everything is just wasted effort."

I swallowed, trying to ignore the heat building in my belly. "Right, so... I need my prefrontal cortex to become less active, and let my limbic system and occipital—"

"What?" He dropped his hand. "I don't know, but it sounds like you're still trying to understand it. Look, I need to train you."

"And how do you propose we practice?"

Roan cocked his head. "I think I have an idea."

* * *

ROAN HAD INSISTED that I spend some time resting before we could train. I'd tried to explain that I wasn't tired, but he flat-out disagreed with me. Apparently, his body had been picking up the slack for both of us. So I'd trudged back to my room, thrown myself down on the bed, and had fallen asleep within minutes. After three hours, he'd roused me to return.

I trudged back to the training room to find a handsome fae standing in the doorway. With his striking feline eyes and

159

brown skin, I instantly recognized him as Morcant—one of the fae who'd helped us rescue Scarlett.

"Cassandra," he said. "It's good to see you."

"You too," I said hesitantly. "Are you here to help me train?"

His eyes were completely unreadable, but his mouth quirked with amusement. "No. I just brought the targets." He nodded inside the room.

When I peered inside, my breath hitched. Kneeling on the floor were two fae—a male and a female. The male had glittering lines of blue scales that ran down his cheeks to his neck, stark against his snow-white skin. The female's skin was a pale gold, her eyes dark as a starless night sky. Rags hung off their bruised and emaciated bodies, and their hands were tied in front of them.

"What the hell is this?" I asked.

"Prisoners," Roan said. "You can try and use your dread power on them."

I shook my head. He wanted me to torture prisoners? They might pull that in the CIA, but that wasn't my style. "I can't do that. Have you been starving them?"

"What do you mean, you can't?" Roan arched an eyebrow. "They have plenty of fear, I can guarantee that."

"If it helps," Morcant added, "they volunteered. They get an extra ration of food for participating."

I stared. Both of them gazed straight ahead, their eyes blank. The man's lips trembled. Roan was right—I could feed off this fear for weeks.

"There are ethical problems with this," I muttered.

"They'll feel no physical pain," Roan said. "It's no different from a nightmare. Certainly better than the drowning techniques your human friends—"

"Okay, okay." I held up my hands. "What did they do, anyway?"

"Two of the king's assassins."

Anger simmered in my chest, burning away the guilt. Just like the assassins who'd slaughtered Gabriel in the street.

I crossed to them, peering down at them. I could see their fear plainly etched across their features, but I couldn't connect with their fear as easily as I would with humans. I couldn't feel that powerful sense of terror washing over me, like when the banshees had attacked.

I loosed a sigh. "I can't feel anything."

Roan crossed to me, and I felt that warmth in my chest glow brighter. "Empty your mind. Don't let thoughts drown your senses, your experiences. These two work for the king who had your friend killed. The same king who taught his right-hand man to torture women for pleasure and fear. Think of all the suffering that the Rix and Siofra and Ogmios inflicted over the past months. These two are part of it. Let your anger ignite your powers."

I stared at the prisoners, trying to stoke the embers of fury. And yet—they just looked so pathetic, their shoulder blades jutting out. "I feel nothing."

Morcant huffed a laugh. "Mistress of Dread. Right. I'm going to look for Elrine. See how she's doing. Enjoy your session." He turned, gliding gracefully from the room.

"Never mind the prisoners," Roan said. "I want you to close your eyes."

I closed them, uncomfortably aware of the prisoners in the room, looking at me.

"Imagine a place you love," Roan said. "A place you feel safe. Where you once felt happy."

His voice was soft and soothing, like a gentle caress. I found myself slowly relaxing, my mind conjuring the apartment I'd shared with Scarlett after college. The sofa with the coffee stain. The old TV that had a green splotch in the corner, no matter what it was showing. The books scattered everywhere, the table you had to take apart to get to the washing machine in the cramped kitchen. For some reason, I'd slept beautifully in that old shithole.

"Good," Roan said, his voice getting softer. He was standing closer now, his scent enveloping me. "Can you see it clearly?"

"Yes." I could almost feel the soft sofa beneath me.

"Good. Now I want you to imagine Ogmios burning it to the ground."

My eyes snapped open. I'd thought it was a relaxation exercise. "What?"

"You're not imagining, Cassandra. I want anger. I want darkness. I want the predator in you, fighting for her life." The temperature in the room dropped, and his eyes flickered to gold. "Let go of control, Cassandra. Do you remember how the banshee looked after she slaughtered your friend? That glimmer in her eyes? That was *pleasure*, Cassandra—a thrill at your grief. The way Gabriel looked, his eyes wide open, his life stolen from him."

My stomach churned. How did Roan know all this?

Of course. He'd seen it all in my mind because of our soul-bond.

I backed away, shaking my head. "Stop that. Those memories are not yours. You have no right."

But Roan just stepped closer, his eyes boring into me. "Remember Grendel, his slimy fingers pawing at your body. How many women do you think he attacked before you met him? How many since? That's the culture King Ogmios has created. A culture where men view women as their possessions. How did those bodies look, the ones the Rix tore apart in London? That's the king's legacy, Cassandra, all of it."

"Roan, you need to shut your mouth. You have no right to trawl through my mind like that."

He paced forward, our bodies almost touching, eyes

162

blazing gold, and he brushed his knuckles over my cheeks, sending a shiver rippling through my body. "And what of the time a young Weala Broc assassin showed up at your house and slaughtered your parents, while you hid under the bed? Do you remember *that,* Cassandra? Or did you hide it away with all your other unpleasant memories, doing your best to forget it, to distract yourself? Your parents, murdered in the next room, while you fed off their fear, not knowing why you felt this dark thrill."

He'd invaded my mind and started smashing the walls of ice I'd built for years. Tears rolled down my cheeks. The room faded away, all I could see was him, viciously tearing into me, stripping me bare.

He cupped my face. "Of course, *they* weren't your parents at all, were they? They had another, innocent baby girl. And she was taken without their knowledge, and they got you instead—"

A furious wail ripped from my throat, shutting out his words, and in that moment time slowed... slowed... slowed...

In the depths of my mind, screams rose, deafening my own. And then I could see them—dark tendrils of fear, surrounding me. Not just the two prisoners. But Roan's. And others, all around me. Curling, and twisting all around me, undulating like ink pooling through water, all within my grasp. With fury blazing, I arched my back, letting the fear fall into me like light into a black hole.

And then, I threw it back.

My eyes flicked open. Roan stared at me, his eyes wide open, fists clenched. The two prisoners were lying on the floor, one whimpering, the other's mouth ajar in a silent scream. Somewhere, from distant rooms, screams pierced the air. Branwen. Abellio. Nerius cursing in a trembling voice.

Deafened by their fear, I toppled to my knees, hands on my ears, trying to block them, but they were *inside* my skull.

Roan's powerful arms wrapped around me. "Cassandra, are you—?"

I shoved him away. I stumbled to my feet and stared at him, furious. "Leave me alone."

Still seething with rage, I pushed past him and fled the room.

CHAPTER 19

I stared in the mirror, my heart slamming against my ribs.

Siofra gazed back at me, her eyes dead, scalp peeking through her thinned hair. "Hello, Changeling."

My scream woke me up, and I grasped at the air, trying to push her way.

Heart pounding, I flung off my covers, rising. It was still night outside, and I'd spent most of the day pacing my room, trying to come to terms with the chaos Roan had wrought in my brain.

My throat felt parched, and a lingering sense of dread hung in the air. Probably all that fae-terror I'd flung about the place earlier. The air felt heavy tonight, thick with secrets. A thick fog roiled in the London streets outside, and rain hammered the windows. And yet despite the damp air, my throat was parched.

I pulled open the door to the hall, my body covered in a cold sweat, and crossed through the hall to the curving, stone stairwell. In bare feet, I padded over to the kitchen and found a pitcher of water standing on the old oak table. As a breeze filtered into the room, rippling over my skin, I poured myself a glass.

I crossed back into the hall, sipping the cool water, when something caught my attention outside. I paused, peering out one of the windows. In the courtyard, moonlight silvered the mist. Through the silvery fog, I caught a glimpse of a figure sitting on a stone bench beneath a yew. By the breadth of his shoulders, I knew it was Roan. What was he doing out there in the rain, in the middle of the night?

I pushed through the door into the rain, and as I drew closer, I could make out that he was bare chested, the scars on his back just barely visible in the dim light among his tattoos. The rain dampened my hair, my white nightgown.

At the sound of my footfalls, he turned his head, and the sadness I saw in his green eyes pierced me to the marrow. Not only was he sitting out here in the rain, but he was wearing only his underwear. Something was definitely wrong.

I resisted the strange urge to sit in his lap and throw my arms around his neck, instead sitting next to him. "Are you okay?"

He'd plucked a sprig of wild strawberry leaves from the garden, and he twirled it between his fingers. It looked identical to the one he had tattooed on his chest. "Just bad dreams," he said. He'd been sitting in the rain long enough that the rain had formed his eyelashes into little peaks, and rainwater poured over the muscled planes of his chest in tiny rivulets.

I hugged myself, shivering. I wouldn't have expected Roan to become so unsettled by nightmares. "I'm quite familiar with those. Anything you care to share?"

"Wings. Severed wings." His voice broke as he spoke, and he trailed off. He cleared his throat. "I think something happened after you used your powers today. I don't feel the same."

A lump rose in my throat, and I swallowed hard. I'd seen severed wings before—when Siofra had taunted him with his own memories of Trinovantum. I took a deep breath. "When our souls bonded, I saw a beautiful woman with gossamer wings. She was important to you."

"She was my mother." His voice sounded far away, laced with pain. "She used to sing me to sleep every night. Her voice was beautiful. Even in prison, she sang to us every night. And when the king wanted to punish me... he forced me to watch her execution. I will never forget what he did to her." He'd crushed the strawberry stem between his fingers.

My heart ached for him, and I stood, grabbing his face in my hands. I kissed his forehead, tasting the rain, and he slumped into me, resting his head against my heart. I stroked his damp hair, and he wrapped his arms around my waist, holding on to me as if I could save him from drowning.

"Come inside with me, Roan," I said. "You're drenched."

He pulled his head from my body, eyes lingering for a moment over my rain-soaked nightgown—which I now realized had gone completely transparent. Roan's eyes flickered gold for a moment. Suddenly self-conscious, I crossed my arms in front of my chest.

His expression cleared, raindrops streaking his face. "You should go in. I still need to clear my head."

I knew that feeling, that isolation so deep it cut to the bone—the feeling that walking into your empty room would mean your own death. Or maybe he just didn't want to have to face his memories again. For just a moment, I considered asking him if he wanted to stay in my room. In fact, the urge was almost overwhelming, but I didn't know what was going on with him and Elrine. They seemed to have a powerful bond of their own.

Steeling my nerve, I took a deep breath, ignoring the rain that spattered on my skin. "Are you and Elrine lovers?"

A line formed between his eyebrows. "Elrine? No."

"Does she know that?"

His lips curled slyly. "I'm fascinated that you're so interested in this." Without another word, his powerful hands were around my waist, and he pulled me into his lap. His gaze raked down my body, his expression purely carnal as it roamed over my transparent gown, my breasts peaked in the chilly rain. Instantly, I felt him harden against me.

Once his gold-flecked eyes met mine again, my pulse began racing out of control. Roan Taranis, Lord of the Fae Court of Lust, had focused the full force of his attention on me. All at once, warmth flooded me, and I fought the urge to strip off my nightgown. We were, after all, sitting in the middle of the courtyard in the pouring rain.

Still, Roan didn't seem to care where we were. Slowly, he slipped his hand between my knees, pulling my legs just slightly apart. His fingers traced lazy circles inside my thigh, his touch lighting me up. My back began to arch.

"Tell me exactly why that interests you, Cassandra." His deep voice snaked around my skin like a velvety caress.

"Just curious," I said, my breath hitching in my throat. "It's nothing to do with me." I slid one of my arms around his shoulders, my back arching just a bit more as he teased my thigh with his fingers.

"Lies." He leaned in, his breath warming my neck. "Tell me what you want from me, Cassandra."

As he swirled his fingers over my rain-soaked skin, teasing me, I let my legs fall further apart, my mind begging him, *Higher. Please. Please.* A searing ache built in my core, and the strap of my nightgown fell off my shoulder, rainwater pouring down my skin. What would he do if I just stripped off my panties and straddled him? What if I just let myself go?

"Tell me, Cassandra," he whispered. "What do you want?"

His fingers traced another idle swirl, nearly distracting me from the fact that I felt exposed out here in the courtyard. "Shouldn't we go inside?"

That wicked smile crossed his lips again. "Go inside for what, Cassandra? You haven't told me."

My chest flushed, and I couldn't think straight. My thoughts now came in bursts, words like *fingers, touch,* and *wet,* but I couldn't piece a single coherent thought together.

"Um," I said. "Just… inside. Me. I mean… What?"

I nearly moaned at the feel of his fingers moving higher up my thigh. He was taking his time, toying with me. He enjoyed my desperation, the fact that I was on the verge of begging him to fuck me right here.

I arched my neck, and he brushed a kiss over my throat, his lips warm on my skin. That was all it took for me to stop caring about going inside. "Tell me what you want, Cassandra."

"You," I breathed.

"Good." He lifted his face, then pressed his lips against mine, rewarding my admission with a kiss. I opened my lips, and his tongue brushed against mine, sending heat streaming into my belly. I groaned into his mouth, and felt his fingers flex on my thigh for just a moment as he struggled to keep control of himself, and yet still he kept his fingers just below the line of my panties. The kiss deepened, my mouth moving against his until he nipped at my lower lip.

The sensation drove me insane, and he pulled away from the kiss. Slowly, his gaze raked over the curve of my breast, a low growl rising from his throat. His fingers traced another circle between my thighs, and my legs opened wider, a silent invitation. My nightgown had now ridden all the way up my thighs. Gently, Roan brushed his knuckles over the front of my panties, and I gasped.

Okay. I wasn't above begging if that's what he needed. "Roan. Please."

"Mmmm. I like that you know how to ask nicely."

My memory sparked with the fantasies that had danced in my mind when I'd drunk the nectar, the intense desire to feel his mouth on me. I let the strap of my nightgown fall lower, exposing my breast. Rainwater streamed down my skin, but I no longer cared at all that we were outside. I just wanted him. As if hearing my thoughts, Roan lowered his mouth to my breast. His tongue flicked over my nipple, hot waves of pleasure imbuing my body as it swirled over my peaked breast. *Imagine what his tongue could do elsewhere...*

My pulse racing, I grasped at the back of his head, lacing my fingers into his hair. His mouth was just where I wanted it, but I was mentally begging him to move his hand higher up my thighs. I began to rock my hips on him, urging him to touch me.

"Roan," I said again. "*Please.*"

He pulled his mouth off my breast, and raised his face to mine, letting his lips hover above mine. "Please what?"

"I need you."

"Mmmm. Here?" He slipped his fingers into my panties, snarling with pleasure at the feel of my wetness. And yet still, he was holding back, his touch infuriatingly light. He was driving me crazy on purpose, enjoying the hold he had on me. I moved my hips against him, letting him feel my arousal, and his control started to slip. His eyes blazing, he ripped through my panties. I yielded fully to him, letting my legs fall open, my nightgown riding up, and he plunged his finger into me.

I arched my back, moaning, and he kissed me again, his tongue moving against mine. As his fingers dipped into me, I undulated my hips against his hand, the world falling away until nothing existed but the feel of his fingers plunging between my legs. Liquid heat drenched my body as he kissed me and stroked me, harder, faster, dipping in a second finger. I rocked against his hand until I began to shudder against his fingers, tightening around him.

Roan growled, thumb brushing against me until a powerful wave of pleasure ripped through me. My body clenched tight around him, and I gasped with release. I loosed a long, slow breath. My body trembling, I rested my head on his shoulder, and for reasons I couldn't explain, a tear rolled down my cheek. Roan's body glowed with a powerful golden light.

"Cassandra," he whispered into my neck, and he pulled his fingers from me.

I pushed down the hem of my dress and wrapped my arms around his neck. His heart beat rhythmically against me, and he leaned in to kiss my forehead.

Then, he nuzzled my neck, whispering into my ear, "I'll be able to sleep just fine now."

For the first time in ages, a genuine smile curled my lips.

"Am I better at curing your nightmares than Abellio, then?"

"Mmmm. I think you have a superior technique. The others might let him root around in their minds, but I won't let him near my memories."

"You let *me* near your memories."

His powerful arms encircled me. "You're different. You're Cassandra."

CHAPTER 20

We crossed back to the house, Roan's hand in mine, my dress clinging to my skin. But as soon as we crossed through the doorway into the darkened hall, my breath caught in my throat. A figure loomed in the shadows. When she stepped into the light, silvery moonlight washed over Elrine's cherry-red hair, her pale skin.

She folded her arms, eyes narrowed. "Enjoying yourselves?"

Awwwwkward. I let go of Roan's hand. Had she been watching us? Were they a couple? What the hell? "I'll just…" I cleared my throat. "I'll just go up to my room."

Elrine took a step closer, her eyes locked on Roan's. "I'd say that's a good idea. Letting Cassandra go to her own room —wouldn't you, Roan? You know what happens if you sleep together, don't you?"

The tone of her voice suggested that it might involve castration. Now I was getting annoyed. What, exactly, was the deal with these two? If Roan and Elrine were together, what had just happened between us?

I put my hands on my hips. "Am I getting in the middle of

something, by any chance?"

Roan met my gaze. "No," he said firmly. "You aren't. But Elrine's right. You should go to your room to get some sleep."

"Whatever." Feeling like I'd just been dismissed, I stalked off.

Maybe I wasn't getting in the middle of anything, but Elrine and Roan has secrets they didn't want to share with me, and that stung more than anything.

* * *

I WOKE IN THE MORNING, tangled in my bedsheets. Pale light glowed through the ancient windowpanes into the room, the clean white bedsheets, the stone walls.

I'd slept soundly—a pure, nightmare-less sleep for the first time in ages. But when I woke in the morning, already confusion clouded my mind. Had Roan merely been feeding off my lust last night? After all, that's how he drew his power. And with his hand between my legs, I'd certainly given him enough to feed from. He and Elrine seemed to have a bond forged by centuries of closeness.

The storm hadn't yet abated, and rain still hammered the windows. In my nightgown, I rose from my bed. After a few minutes of rifling around the clothes I'd borrowed, I pulled on a black dress and a pair of underwear. A strange sort of tension hung over the mansion today, as if the terror I'd instilled yesterday still lingered in the air.

In the hall, the sound of faint voices drew me downstairs to the dining room, along with the scent of roasted meat. My stomach rumbled fiercely. What the hell time was it, anyway?

I found them sitting sullenly over a dinner of meat pies and mashed potatoes, the gravy curling with steam. Branwen sat with her head in her hands, staring at her dinner, her eyes puffy and red. Nerius glared at me, his lip curled. Abellio had a dazed look, his blue eyes open wide. And Elrine—Elrine sort of looked like she wanted to rip my ribs out and beat me to death with them. Only Roan looked happy to see me, his body still faintly glowing. A place had been set to his right, with a pie waiting for me. Dinner. Apparently, I'd slept the whole day.

Roan arched an eyebrow. "I was just debating waking you, but when I peered in, you looked so peaceful."

The look Elrine shot him made my stomach flip. Then, she leveled her icy gaze on me. "Cassandra. How wonderful you could join us. Are you planning on inflicting your lovely powers on us again, Mistress of Dread?"

I swallowed hard, pulling out the chair next to Roan. "Sorry," I mumbled. "I understand you all got caught in the crossfire. I don't quite have control yet."

Elrine stabbed her fork into her pie, the movement alarmingly violent. "As I understand it, you and Roan were the only ones who got any sleep last night. And we all know why that was."

My cheeks warmed. *Let's not make this a group discussion.*

I opened my mouth to speak, but Roan cut me off. "Enough. Yesterday was a clear demonstration of Cassandra's powers. We need to keep developing them, to train more—"

Elrine slammed her fork into the table. "Like hell you will! I'm not subjecting myself to *that* again."

Branwen cleared her throat. "Roan, the nightmares I had last night... if Abellio hadn't helped me get past them, I would have lost my mind."

Roan looked at them both, and then said, "From now on, we'll find another place to train. Somewhere secluded, and away from other fae. But we have to keep going. The king fears her because she's terrifying."

"She *is* terrifying." Abellio swirled his glass of nectar. "To all of us. A lesser man than myself would have spent the day pissing himself yesterday. You can't seriously be thinking of continuing with these dread powers, are you? Her abilities are far too erratic. She'll disable us all during combat. We should plan the attack ahead, discounting them."

Nerius leaned over the table, his dark eyes intense. "Absurd. She may be a Weala Broc fae and a fortal, but she is a deadly weapon. And weapons should be used. She needs to be trained, and then we can use her."

Branwen raised a hand. "Agreed. She's fucking terrifying. Let's focus that terror on the king's troops."

I cut into my pie. "I don't suppose anyone cares what the deadly weapon thinks?"

"No," said Elrine with finality.

"Go on," said Roan.

"I think there's more to this."

"Meaning?" Nerius asked.

"The London Stone connects to both the king and my powers."

Nerius glowered. "It's just a big fucking rock."

I pinched the bridge of my nose. "I don't know exactly how, but I just know that it's important. It ignited my ability somehow. We need to study it more. *I* need to study it more."

Roan frowned at me over his glass of nectar. "Last time you touched it, it nearly overwhelmed you. Are you sure you want to try it again?"

I nodded. "That Stone has power, and we need to harness it to our use."

"To *your* use, you mean," Elrine said. "Since you'll be the one who touches it. We just need to wait and hope for the best."

I shook my head. "No. We need to take the initiative. It's powerful and we need to get it away from the king. We need to steal the London Stone."

* * *

I SAT with the truck's passenger's window lowered, letting the cool breeze blow on my face as Nerius drove through London's empty streets. Branwen, Roan, and Abellio sat behind us, and I peered up at the cloudy night sky, not a star in sight.

The rain had stopped, thankfully, and the air had a freshness to it that lifted my spirits. At just after four a.m., a heavy silence hung over the city. Even the drunks were sleeping by now.

It had taken Nerius a few hours to rent the truck, a brand new brown Nissan Navara. Five of us had crammed in the truck, with Elrine left behind because A) there weren't enough seats, and B) she kind of seemed like she wanted to murder me.

The Nissan's engine hummed satisfyingly as we drove past Bank Station, moving closer to our goal. Mentally, I ran through the plan. I had been worried that the Stone's weight could be a problem. It was, to use Nerius's apt description, a big fucking rock. But it was limestone, which didn't weigh as much as other rocks. And anyway, I had the faint impression that Roan could lift several thousand tons of rock all at once.

After checking online for the rock's measurements, and calculating somewhat pessimistically, I estimated the Stone's weight to be no more than four hundred pounds. No problem.

On Cannon Street, Nerius parked the truck by the curbside, only a few feet from the Stone's display case. I could hardly see it in the darkness behind the metal bars, but we'd brought some tools that could cut through the grate. It would be noisy, but would get the job done.

I pulled open the passenger door and stepped down, crossing to the rock. From the back seat, Branwen pulled out a leather bag with her lock picks. She walked over to the shop's door and crouched, fiddling with the lock while the rest stood watch, prepared to sound the alert if anyone passed by.

I took out a small mirror and gazed into it, letting it click with my mind. I leapt, the reflection washing over my skin like cool liquid.

I stepped from a reflection in one of the store's mirrors. The room seemed darker tonight, the light dimmed by a moonless sky outside. Already, I felt the Stone calling to me, its dark power trying to draw me closer. In the dark, I could just about make out the white cloth covering the glass. Still broken apparently. It begged me to touch it, only for a second. Gritting my teeth, I approached the counter instead, and began looking for a second set of keys. If I could find them and unlock the door to the shop, our job would already be half done.

From outside, I could hear the faint scraping of Branwen's tools on the lock, then a curse. She'd warned us beforehand that she wasn't sure that she could pick the lock, that she wasn't very good with the new human padlocks.

I opened a drawer and rummaged inside, groping around blindly in the darkness. I rifled past what felt like receipts, a few rubber bands, a stapler. No keys.

I felt under the cash register, checked the shelves on the walls, and had just begun to scour the floor, when a shadowy movement turned my head.

I raised my eyes, then dove to the floor as a fist swung for my head. A loud crash echoed off the walls, and I rolled aside and kicked at the figure in the darkness, feeling my foot connect, hearing a grunt of pain. Adrenaline surging, I jumped to my feet, pulling the stiletto free from my belt.

A huge, roaring figure crashed into me, knocking me to the floor. Metal glinted as he swung for me, and a sharp pain lanced the side of my neck. My eyes were now adjusting to the dark, and I rammed the stiletto upward, sinking it into my assailant's body. Grunting in pain, he pulled back, wrenching the knife free from my grasp. I was now empty-handed.

As I stepped away from the looming figure, the sharp report of gunfire pierced the silence, then a scream of pain. Roan's feral roar. My heart skipped a beat. What the hell was happening?

As my assailant stepped closer into a faint stream of light, I realized for the first time what he'd cut my neck with—a long, curved sword. He glared at me with purple eyes, baring sharp teeth, and plucked the knife from his body as if he were merely pulling out a splinter.

I scrambled back, my hand fumbling for a weapon, closing on something hard. He swung the sword at me and I parried it clumsily with the object in my hand—a goddamn tennis racket. He jerked his arm and the racket twisted in my hand. I tried to feel for his fear, but my own terror was too overwhelming. Again and again he swung his sword, backing me into a corner, the blade whistling past my body.

Then, his purple eyes widened, and he let out a gurgle. He toppled to the floor, clutching his chest. Behind him stood a dark figure holding the stiletto. My own shadow.

"Thanks," I said breathlessly. My shadow, controlled by Branwen, gave me a quick nod. I took my knife from it, then felt the ripple over my skin as it merged back to my body.

From outside, Roan's voice boomed. "Cassandra! It was a trap, let's go!"

My heart slammed against my ribs, panic rising. The king had known that we would come, and had been prepared. I tightened my fingers around my knife in frustration. We'd never get the Stone out of here. Not with the king's people watching it.

"Cassandra!" Roan roared.

There was only one chance. I rushed to the display case, yanking off the white cloth. Carefully, I slid my arm into the jagged hole. I stood on my tiptoes until I could reach the rock, waiting for the rush of power, the screams and memories.

Nothing.

Its power rushed dimly under the surface, and I could almost hear a faint cry through the rough limestone, but it felt distant. Closing my eyes, I searched for the Stone's core, tried to picture the screaming, the visions I'd seen.

Still nothing.

With a slam, the store's door burst open, and two large fae rushed in, faint light streaming behind them. One raised his hand, pointing a large gun at me. I dove for the ground, and gunshots rang out, just missing me. I crawled behind the counter, and more shots slammed into the wooden surface. I could only hope it was thick enough to provide cover. My fingers shaking, I fumbled through my purse for another mirror and pulled one out, nearly dropping it. At last, I snapped the compact mirror open, let my mind bond with it, and jumped, sighing with relief as the reflection washed over my skin.

The world flickered as I appeared outside by our truck. I had jumped through the side mirror. Roan stood a few feet from me, antlers glimmering on his head, his sword in hand, swinging it in huge arcs. Four large fae surrounded him, closing in. Growling, Roan sliced his sword clean through one's neck. As blood sprayed into the air, another fae pulled a gun.

"Roan, gun!" I screamed.

Roan's blade was already swinging for him, and he brought it down into the fae's arm, cutting it off at the elbow. The fae shrieked, blood pouring from his ragged stump. I looked around me, panicking. Abellio fought off two banshees with a long, sharp rapier, back to back with Branwen, who was crouching, stiletto knives in hand. Her hands darted fast as she slashed at a large winged woman. That's when I noticed Nerius lying on the ground in a puddle of blood, a few feet away. My chest tightened in fear.

In the distance, I could see lights. Cars. They drove up to us, stopping with a screech, and their passengers burst out of the doors. Blades drawn, eyes flickering in the darkness, some holding guns. More fae, all intent on killing us. I had to do something now. I had to stop it, and I couldn't get to my dread powers.

Frantically, I scrambled into the driver's seat of the truck and turned the key in the ignition. The truck roared into life and I hit the gas pedal. The vehicle lurched onto the curb, and I twisted the steering wheel, swerving and smashing straight into the winged woman Branwen fought.

"Get Nerius!" I shouted at her.

The two fae from the shop burst through the door, one of them raising his gun. He pulled the trigger and I ducked. The bullet shattered the truck's window, but his second shot went wide. The fae were amateurs, unused to guns. They let the recoil jolt their hands, and aimed badly.

The passenger door behind me opened and Branwen dragged Nerius inside. I shifted into reverse and kicked the door beside me open. "Abellio!"

He dove inside headfirst as I hit the gas. The truck shot backwards, just as a few additional shots were fired. Roan ran toward us, eight fae on his trail. I shifted gears again into drive, and the truck roared forward. Roan leapt into the cargo bed as we swerved into the street, zig-zagging away.

CHAPTER 21

I clutched the steering wheel grimly, knuckles whitening as the truck accelerated, hurtling down Cannon Street. Behind me, Nerius grunted in pain, and Branwen talked to him soothingly.

"How is he doing?" I asked.

"He's been shot in the stomach," Branwen said, her voice cracking. "Iron bullet. Those fuckers! Fae using iron against other fae!"

I gritted my teeth. "Is there an exit wound?"

"I... I don't think so."

"The bullet is probably still in him. Once we get back to the mansion, we can take it out."

"Get us there!" she shrieked. "Fast!"

I glanced at the rear window. Two pairs of taillights followed close behind on our tail. "We have to lose them first, or they'll know exactly where to find us."

I swerved left on the first crossroad. The truck rocked a bit, and I momentarily lost control, smashing the side mirror into a traffic sign. In the back, I heard Roan curse. After a

181

few seconds I saw the two cars in pursuit taking the turn without a hitch. Gaining on us.

"Damn it," I muttered.

One of them pulled ahead, inching closer. A white-haired fae pushed his torso out of the window and aimed a gun at us. I instinctively ducked as the report of gunshots rang out.

"Everyone stay low!" I shouted, zig-zagging left and right. A screech, and a loud thump rang out. Looking back to the cargo bed, I glimpsed a large white bird transforming into a woman. She lunged at Roan and slashed his face with her talons.

"Cassandra!" Abellio shouted.

I looked up and swerved, just missing a van coming our way, honking as it whizzed past on Fenchurch Street.

"Ah, gods on earth," Nerius groaned in the back.

"We're nearly there," Branwen told him.

We weren't nearly there. Glancing at the rear-view mirror, I saw Roan holding a limp banshee in one hand, her neck at a weird angle. He raised her body and threw it at the car behind us. The car swerved, the banshee's body tumbling into the road.

The car in pursuit accelerated, coming at us from the right. It rammed into us, knocking us off course, and I nearly crashed us into a traffic light. I could see the white-haired fae behind the wheel, his mouth stretched in a wide grin. I felt for all the reflections in that car, and instantaneously flooded them with a bright light. He screamed, momentarily blinded, and I twisted the steering wheel, feeling our truck shudder as it hit their car. They swerved out of control, rammed against the curb, and crashed into a building.

I let out a breath, but just then, the truck began rocking. Something else had landed on the cargo bed. Of course it had. I glanced in the rearview mirror, catching a glimpse of the winged woman Branwen had been fighting. She was huge, almost eight feet tall and covered in feathers, and she swiped for Roan's face with her talons.

The other car was gaining at us again as we neared a corner in the road. I glanced in the rearview mirror, finding Roan grappling with the winged creature, one hand around her throat.

"Roan, hang on!" I screamed, hoping he could hear. I slowed a bit as I took the turn, but it was still too fast, and I could feel the truck tipping, two wheels rising in the air. Behind us, Roan and the creature slammed down in a tangle of limbs. The truck shuddered as it righted itself. The car behind us took the corner, the wheels squealing, without even slowing down. The fae might be new to guns, but some of them definitely knew how to drive.

We were hurtling towards a smooth mass of darkness, lights reflecting on it softly. The Thames. I glanced at the mirror. The car was closing in on us, and I saw the distinct gleam of gunmetal out the window. The fae aimed the gun at us.

"Abellio, grab the wheel!" I barked.

"What?"

"Grab the wheel! Hold us steady!"

His blue eyes wild, he grabbed the wheel. Looking forward, I bit my lip in concentration. Time slowed to a crawl.

Thirty feet.

Behind, on the cargo bed, I saw Roan's fist rising and falling, pummeling the winged creature into a pulp.

Twenty feet.

The engine roared as we flew past the buildings toward London Bridge, hurtling across the Thames.

Ten feet.

I focused on the rear-view mirror, feeling for the reflection. It flickered.

Now.

I lunged up, plunging my hand through the mirror, following with my body. My upper half emerged from the mirror of the car chasing us, and for a fraction of a second, my eyes locked with the eyes of the driver, his mouth lax in shock.

I grabbed his steering wheel and jolted it aside. As I felt the car swerve, I pulled back, leaving the mirror and falling back into the driver's seat. Behind me, I saw the car careen over the bridge's stone wall.

Roan stood up and threw the lifeless body of the winged creature onto the pavement.

Our truck hurtled onward, free of pursuit.

* * *

WITH NERIUS'S body limp in Roan's arms, we stormed back into the mansion. In the hall, Roan laid him on the floor. He was bleeding profusely from the bullet wound in his stomach, his face pale, his eyelids flickering as he barely maintained consciousness.

"Elrine!" Roan roared. "Get over here!"

I knelt by Nerius, and raised my eyes to meet Branwen's. "Give me your knife."

She wordlessly gave me her stiletto, and I registered the panic in her dark eyes.

"Whiskey," I said. "Fast."

Branwen hurried away as I sliced Nerius's shirt open. The bullet had hit him in the side. As far as I could tell, it hadn't hit any vital organs, but I wasn't a doctor, and I wasn't even sure how much fae anatomy mirrored humans. The gun had been fired from close range, burn marks darkening his skin. Probably the only reason the fae had managed to hit him in the first place.

Branwen returned with a bottle of whiskey, and I poured some on the blade.

"Sorry, this'll hurt." I poured some on the wound as well. Nerius hissed, teeth clenched tight.

"What happened?" Elrine's voice sounded sharp behind me.

"Nerius got shot," Abellio said. "With iron."

"I'll get my kit." She fled from the room in a blur.

Gingerly, I spread the wound with my fingers. Nerius let out a moan, and then slumped as unconsciousness finally took hold. At least that would make my job easier.

Now, I could see the bullet lodged in his flesh. I was about to try and pry it out with the stiletto, when Elrine joined my side, a bag in hand.

"Move," she said.

She pulled out a pair of tweezers and clamps. She handed the clamps to me.

"Hold the wound open with these," she said.

I inserted the clamps into the wound gently and pulled it open, ignoring my welling nausea. Blackening blood oozed from the wound.

"I need more light here," Elrine muttered

"My phone is in my bag," I said.

Branwen pulled it out and tapped the screen. It glowed with a faint light and she held it close to the wound.

"Okay, let's get this fucker out," Elrine said. She slid the tweezers into the wound. After a few seconds, the phone screen went dark, and Elrine cursed. Branwen hurriedly tapped it, and tipped the screen back to set its ghostly light on the wound. Finally, Elrine pulled the slug out. Her revulsion was apparent as she handled the iron bullet, her mouth twisting as she held it away from her body. She let it drop on the floor, far from us. Then she rummaged in her bag and took out some bandages, which she pressed to the wound.

"Hold that tight."

Branwen grabbed the bandages from her, pressing them down on the wound. Her face had gone nearly as pale as her twin's. "Will he be okay?"

"He's a tough bastard." Elrine wiped the back of her hand across her forehead. "I think he'll be fine." She let out a long breath. "Where's the Stone?"

Roan shook his head. "It was an ambush. The Stone is still there."

CHAPTER 22

Through the morning and afternoon, Branwen sat by her brother's bed at all times, while Elrine and I alternated checking on him, cleaning his wound and changing the dressing.

He lay unconscious for most of the time, occasionally waking up for several moments, during which he would grit his teeth at the pain, muttering curses. Branwen had joined Elrine in shooting me death stares. At one point, she snapped at me that if it hadn't been for my obsession with the damn Stone, this would never have happened.

I cooked the dinner myself that night, alone in the kitchen, though no one came to the table. I dropped the pies off in people's rooms, finding Roan's empty. At last, I crossed back into my room, eating by myself at a rough wood desk in the corner.

Well, my Stone plan had certainly backfired, and it hadn't even been worth it. I'd felt nothing when I'd touched it, and one of our own had ended up seriously injured. Worse, I was pretty sure no one trusted me anymore, other than Roan.

As I finished my dinner, I noticed a small wooden

drawer in the desk. I pushed my plate aside, then pulled open the drawer. Inside, I found small wooden figurines. One by one, I picked them up, turning them around in my fingers. A woman with a spear, and what looked like a feathered dress, a raven on her shoulder; a cloaked man with a skull-like face; a woman with tree branches that curved sensually around her body; a powerful man with rays of sun gleaming from behind his head. And a final carving—the most exquisite—a muscular man with stag antlers, like Roan's. Among the carvings, one lay broken—a winged woman whose arms reached for the skies. She lay, cleaved in two.

A sudden warmth spread through my chest, that flame that still burned inside my ribs. I blinked, exhaustion over-taking my body. Without thinking about it, I crossed to the bed, still gripping the tiny, horned figure. I crawled into bed, collapsing onto the sheets.

I dreamed of thickly wooded forests, air heavy with the scent of soil, and the wind rustling the leaves. It felt like I had slept for no more than fifteen minutes when a hand shook me. Blinking, I opened my eyes, staring at Roan. Pouring in from the widow, the moonlight formed a halo around his head.

A frown creased his brow, and his gaze darted to the little wooden figurine clutched in my fingers. He sat on the bed next to me, gently pulling it from my hand. He studied it carefully, handling it with reverence. "Where did you find this?"

"In the drawer," I mumbled, my voice thick with sleep. "I found him with the other carvings. What are they?"

"Gods. I used to play with them as a boy. My father carved them for me. I'd wondered what happened to these." He ran his fingertips along the finely-carved horns. "This was one of my favorites."

He handed the horned man back to me, then rose to cross to the desk, pulling open the drawer.

"This was my room once. I'd forgotten about those figures."

Rubbing my eyes, I sat up in bed. I watched as Roan pulled out the broken figurine, the woman, his features darkening.

"Was that another favorite?" I asked.

He stared down at the two broken halves, and an intense look of pain flashed in his eyes. "I remember breaking it when I was angry at my mother." In the next moment, his expression had cleared again, as if he'd mastered himself. "I think I was a nightmare as a child."

"I think that's all children." I looked down at the horned figurine in my hands. "I don't know why I took it into bed."

He flashed me one of his wicked smiles, suddenly flirtatious. "The closet thing you could get to me. You can keep it." He sat on my bed again.

"So, Roan. Are you ever going to tell me what Elrine meant when she threatened some kind of dire consequences if we slept in the same bed?"

He looked away. "She's just looking out for me, that's all. She's very protective of me."

"Ah. And she doesn't trust you with a terror leech. I get it."

It didn't explain why Roan had agreed with her, or why we'd slept in our own beds since then. Obviously, he'd merely been feeding from my lust. I didn't need him to spell it out by asking directly.

I clenched my jaw, trying to ignore my growing irritation with him. "What are you doing in here? Did you come in just to check up on me?"

"No. I have plans for us. You'll need to dress warmly. There's a chill in the air tonight."

"What are we doing, exactly?"

"Training. I found a place where we can be secluded, away from the other fae."

I sighed. This was the last thing I wanted to do, but without the London Stone, we had nothing else to go on. "Fine. I'll get dressed." I narrowed my eyes. "Will you turn around?"

A wicked grin curled his lips. "Suddenly shy now, are we?"

"Just protecting you from my terror fae wiles." Did I sound bitter when I said that? Whatever. Roan was flirtatious one minute, distant the next. I was pretty sure I'd never understand the interior world of the fae.

"I'll wait by the front door." He crossed to the door, closing it gently behind him.

I tucked away the little figurine and pulled off my nightgown. While Roan waited outside, I dressed myself in a pair of leggings and a long-sleeved cotton shirt.

I found him by the front door, huddled in the shadows. Together, we slipped out of the glamoured building into the darkened parking lot known as French Ordinary Court. Moving quietly, we crossed to the Nissan parked into the corner, its exterior battered. The cool night air kissed my skin, and I shivered.

I still had the keys, and I unlocked the truck. "Should I drive?"

"Yes."

I climbed into the driver's seat, turning the ignition.

Roan took his seat next to me. "There's a place called Temple Church. Do you know how to get there?"

"Yeah," I said. Gabriel had taken me there, a week after we'd killed the Rix, and we'd eaten sandwiches in a quiet, grassy garden among the church buildings. A pang of sorrow swelled in my chest, but I buried it under the ice.

As I pulled out onto Savage Gardens, Roan glanced at me.

"You shouldn't do that. You need to face your sadness. In order to develop your powers, you'll need to learn to unveil."

"Unveil."

"You nearly did it already."

I nodded. "When I bit you. I still don't really understand why I did that, you know."

"Instinct. Anyway, if you want to unveil, you can't run away from yourself."

I shot him a sharp look. "What makes you think I'm running away? I didn't say anything."

"I could feel it."

"You face your sadness head on, I suppose?" I ventured. "Like a soldier battering the shit out of his enemy with a broadsword."

"That's one way to put it."

"It's not how I operate." If I'd spent my life dwelling on my parents' deaths, I'd never have been able to function.

"It's how you'll need to operate if you want to harness your power."

"Are you going to dredge up my worst memories again, Roan? You know, that's not really how therapy works. You can't completely take someone apart, throw their trauma at them, and fail to put them together again."

"But it's not therapy, Cassandra. It's war." He glanced at me. "I'll do my best to help put you back together again."

"Thanks."

I gritted my teeth, trying to imagine myself unveiling. He was right—it had nearly happened when I'd bit him. My claws had begun to grow, my teeth lengthened. When I thought about it, the feeling of losing control had sort of terrified me. I wasn't a fae like Roan was.

"Do I really need to unveil?"

"It's the only way to make you safe among the fae. When fae unveil, our power increases tenfold. We become tuned into the world around us. Faster and stronger, aware of every sound and smell around us, every movement."

"It sounds overwhelming. No wonder you spend so much time alone in the woods."

"When I unveil, I become my true self. You need to learn to do the same if you're going to continue to live among us."

I heaved a breath, listening to the hum of the engine as we drove down Fenchurch street.

I looked out the window as we drove, hardly able to remember what the streets looked like in daylight anymore. At night, the city had a strange beauty to it. It glowed with pearly streetlights, the passersby on the streets walking at the casual pace of people looking for a good time. I glanced at the time. Half past midnight.

"What made you choose Temple Church?"

"It is a sacred place. Sacred places have power. Also, the church grounds will be completely empty at this time of night."

"And… where are the prisoners coming from?"

"No prisoners."

"Then who will I train on?"

"You will train on me."

"I don't think so. It messed you up last time. What did I just say to you? You can't rip someone's mind apart and then fail to put them back together. That's not how it works."

"I will be fine."

I shook my head in frustration. Stupid macho attitude. "Roan, my dread power… when I used it on those banshees, they were *paralyzed* by fear. If I accidentally dredged up something you're not ready to deal with—"

"You don't need to… amplify my fear. All you need is to feel it. This will be our first step. Then, you learn to unveil."

Empathy. I could do that. "Okay. Fine. We'll take it one step at a time."

I pulled through a gate into a parking lot, ancient stone buildings on either side of us. We stepped out of the car and crossed the cobblestone ground, moving through the grounds of Temple Church, past the church itself—the round, medieval temple. Outside the church stood a pillar carved with two Templar knights at the top, marking the place where the Great Fire had ended, according to Gabriel.

Roan led me on through the grounds, to a stony court-yard surrounded by brick buildings. A pool of water with a fountain burbled in the middle of it all. An ancient, gnarled tree snaked over the fountain, its leaves rustling in the wind. Roan stopped by the fountain's edge, turning to face me.

I pointed to one of the brick buildings. "I take it there are no fae in there?"

He shook his head. "None."

A chilly breeze whispered over my skin, and I hugged myself. "And what happens now?"

"You need to face your true self," he said. "Until you accomplish that, you won't be able to reliably use your powers."

I cocked a hip. "And what if my true self involves a lot of repression? Because I'm quite comfortable with that state of being."

"You're limiting yourself. Did you stop studying after you first learned to read, because you had learned enough? Did you become complacent?"

"No. I just don't understand exactly what it is you want me to do. I don't know what 'face your true self' means."

"Humans sometimes say that they are angels trapped within the bodies of beasts, godlike sparks stuck in a cursed, beastly body. Two opposing forces at war with each other."

"I never met anyone who said that."

Roan ignored me. "But the fae are different. We become gods through embracing our bestial drives and desires. We are not gods trapped in the bodies of animals. We are bestial gods of the forests and rivers, the earth and sky. When we embrace our true selves, we are powerful."

I fought my natural instinct to intellectualize all of this. I was pretty sure quoting Freud wasn't "embracing my bestial self."

But because I'm me, I failed pretty fast. "Right," I said. "So I need to embrace my id. Right? Primal drives and desires, let the superego chill out a bit?"

"Tune out any distraction around you, the never-ending thoughts about the past you cannot change, or events in the future that you have no control over. Empty your mind completely, except for what you see, what you smell, what you hear, and what you *feel*. And your most basic needs. A fae who is free can unveil."

"I have no idea how to unveil at will."

"You are fae. Every fae can unveil."

I nodded. He seemed to know what he was doing, and I just needed to trust him.

For the next four hours, Roan led me through a series of exercises. He had me close my eyes and describe the scent of the night air, the feel of the wind over my skin, the feel of his fingers tracing over my hipbone, over my ribs. *That* particular exercise had been distracting enough for both of us that we had to stop, and we moved on to the much less pleasant task of him asking me to do pushups to exhaust me.

As I breathed hard, arms still trembling from effort, I thought of the moment Gabriel died, of his open vacant eyes, of my failure to—

"No!" Roan roared. "Do not analyze your memories, or imagine what you could have done differently. There is a wound in your soul, and you need to accept the pain. There is a hole inside of you. You need to confront your hole."

My arms were shaking with fatigue, and in my exhaustion, I seemed to regress about a decade. "'Confront my hole?' I'm sorry, but that just sounds wrong."

Roan snarled, unimpressed.

I tried over and over to *accept the pain,* to *confront my hole* the way Roan wanted me to, but he could somehow sense my thoughts—probably through our connection—and seemed dissatisfied.

By the time we climbed back into the car, the sun tinged the sky with streaks of honey and periwinkle, and my body felt wrecked. I started the engine.

"We have a lot of work to do with you," Roan said grimly.

I said nothing as I steered the car onto the road.

* * *

By the third night of our training at Temple Church, I'd still failed to unveil, and I began to doubt Roan's declaration that every fae could do it.

I lay on the stone ground, trying to focus on my heartbeat, listening to the burbling of the fountain. Even if I hadn't managed to unveil, things were looking up for Nerius. He'd woken for a few hours today, and he'd managed to eat some fruit. Branwen was still pissed—

Roan's fingertips brushed over my shoulders. "You are unfocused, Cassandra."

I sat up, blinking. "Right. Sorry."

Roan sat on the stony ground by my side. "Your weak human side is getting in the way."

"You know what I like about you? You always know how to make me feel better." We lapsed into silence, listening to the sound of running water, and then I said, "We need a new plan to get to the London Stone."

"Forget the London Stone. The king is waiting for us to return to it."

"I feel like that's the key to my power. You're asking me to be in tune with my true self, and I felt it there. My bloodline is connected to the Stone. I just need to figure out how to tap into that power again."

"What do you mean, 'figure out?' I thought you said you only needed to touch it?"

I shook my head. "I tried. When we were ambushed, I figured I could just touch it, get that instant connection, that it was better than nothing."

Roan's jaw clenched. "And what happened?" he finally asked.

"I couldn't... connect. It wasn't like last time. I couldn't hear the screams, couldn't see the king's memories. I felt the Stone's power, but it was submerged deep under the surface. I couldn't hear my mother's voice, like I did before. I have no idea why, but maybe next time it will work."

"There will be no next time, Cassandra. There are two dozen guards on the Stone now, day and night."

I chewed my lip. "I'm certain it's the best way to get to the king."

"Are you sure it's the king you're after?"

I stared at him. "Of course. What else?"

"You're lost and adrift. You feel painfully alone. You heard your mother's voice there, and you're desperate for a family."

Tear stung my eyes, and my breathing sped up. I was getting seriously frustrated with Roan's intrusive ability to see into my soul.

For a few moments, I listened only to the sound of my own breathing, until I stood, blinking away my tears. "I'm ready to continue my training."

* * *

OVER THE NEXT WEEK, my days begun to form a strange

routine. I'd go to bed just after dawn, when the sun reddened the sky and my body pulsed with exhaustion. I slept with the little horned figurine beneath my pillow. Each morning, I dreamed of the wind whispering through oak leaves, and the strange music of the forest singing through my blood. I'd wake in the late morning, finding Roan already gone. Off on some rebel business that he told no one about. He still hadn't identified the spy, and he wasn't taking any chances. On the plus side, he apparently trusted me enough to return my gun to me.

Strangely, the person I spent most of the time with during the day was Nerius. Day after day, I sat by his bedside. I read him books from my cell phone—romances, mostly, about virgins and brawny Scottish men. Apparently, that was what Nerius liked to read, and when we got to the sexy parts, he'd fold his hands behind his head and arch his eyebrows suggestively at me.

He was still rude as hell, but when he wasn't spurring me on to read smut to him, he was teaching me to read fae runes. As the week went on, his insults morphed into inappropriate sexual innuendos, which didn't bother me too much. After a while, I began to suspect that he was getting slightly addicted to my pixie emotions, because he seemed unusually pleased every time I walked into his room.

When I wasn't in Nerius's room, I was sparring with Branwen. She gave me two stilettos, teaching me some basic moves. I wasn't even close to moving as fast as her, but I was improving, mixing my hand-to-hand combat knowledge with Branwen's moves.

I also fashioned myself two small mirror bracelets that I began to sport at all times. That way, I could jump away in a second's notice. With my gun, my stilettos, and the mirrored bracelets, I felt pretty well-prepared should King Ogmios's assassins turn up again.

Roan began to ask me to search the reflections for locations, or fae that I had met. Twice we drove a mile away from the House of Sorrow, and I linked us to some of the rooms there. We'd watch the goings on inside the complex, with Roan cursing at my inability to transfer sound.

I didn't make any perceivable progress on the Mistress of Dread front. It seemed Cassandra's 'true self' had no intention of appearing.

* * *

I STOOD BY THE FOUNTAIN, my muscles burning with fatigue. After two days of silence and Roan being completely absent from the mansion, he'd woken me again at midnight, his hands soft on my shoulders.

By the fountain's side, I felt the faint spray of water over my skin. I was supposed to be connecting to my bestial side, focusing on the sensation of water against my skin. Instead, I opened my eyes, gazing up into his deep emerald pools. "What have you been doing during the day?"

He looked away, as if deciding what he could share with me. After a moment, he spoke. "I've heard more and more talk about armies amassing. Not just the king's Unseelie army, but the Seelie, too."

"Who exactly are the Seelie?"

"They're the fae who drove us from our ancestral home, Cleopolis. You've felt the power of the underground Walbrook River, haven't you?"

I nodded. When I walked over the buried river, I felt a thrill of power.

"Once, humans worshiped us as gods. The Weala Broc—your line—were worshiped at the river. Then the Seelie invaded Cleopolis, driving us out, slaughtering thousands of

Unseelie. We were forced to flee to Trinovantum, where we pushed the Elder Fae from their forest lands."

I nodded, my attention rapt.

"Two thousand years, we've lived in exile. Ogmios, who was but a child when the Seelie attacked, grew to be one of the most powerful fae amongst the Unseelie. He managed to wrangle control from the Council and crowned himself king. That's when he started to change us, to demand we act more like the Seelie. For two thousand years, he's suppressed the Unseelie."

I bit my lip. "And now, after two thousand years, the Seelie are back in the picture?"

"According to my sources, several skirmishes have erupted alongside the borders between Trinovantum and Cleopolis. King Ogmios has been slowly sending his armies further and further from the keep. Our chance to launch a surprise attack might be soon, if we can do it without our spy betraying us."

"How big is the rebel army, exactly?"

His expression became guarded again. "We're here to train, Cassandra. We've made little progress. This feels like another distraction. You run from yourself." He ran a hand through his hair. "You keep yourself busy with noise and chatter."

Chatter. For just a moment, I thought of Odin, the raven who'd rambled on about romance books, quoting all the dirty parts. He'd been a beautiful distraction. What had happened to Odin? He and Nerius would get along beautifully—

"Cassandra," said Roan. "You need to face yourself."

"I know. I'm sorry." And that's when the image of Gabriel seared itself into my brain—the lifeless hazel eyes, the ravaged throat. A wave of sorrow slammed into me, and I dropped to the fountain's edge, letting the tears flow down my cheeks. With my head in my hands, I heard Roan's footfalls move away from me as he left me alone in the dark. I'd never felt so alone in my life, the isolation nearly ripping my mind apart. Pure emptiness welled in my chest, gnawing at my ribs.

I wasn't sure how much time had passed when I felt Roan's arm around me, pulling me close.

I looked up at him through my tears. "Should I try unveiling again?"

Roan shook his head. "It's nearly dawn. We should leave."

I blinked. "Nearly dawn? We just started."

"You've been crying for more than two hours, Cassandra."

My breath halted for a long moment. *Two hours?* "You know, you could have given me a shoulder to cry on."

"It would have defeated the purpose of being alone with yourself."

I wiped the back of my hand across my cheek. "That was part of my training?"

"Of course."

* * *

"Good morning, goddess. *Squawk!*"

I blinked in confusion, bolting upright in bed. Roan sat on a small chair in my room, with Odin, the raven, on his shoulder.

I rubbed my eyes. "What is going on?"

"My nipples tingle with delight. Squawk! Nevermore."

My jaw dropped. "You found Odin?"

Roan's lips quirked in a smile. "Yes. You'd mentioned once that he was in an animal shelter. I found it. The proprietor seemed to be relieved when I took him."

"Dreaming dreams no mortal ever dared to dream before. Lick my nevermore. *Squawk!*"

"You saw him in my thoughts, didn't you?"

"Yes."

"So… what, is this a new part of my training? To see if I'm able to concentrate with more distractions?"

"No." Roan shifted uncomfortably and got up. Odin squawked in outrage and flew from his shoulder to the side of my bed, hurtling erotic quotes in anger. "This is your raven. I thought it would make you… happy."

I stared at him, shocked. He turned to leave the room, closing the door behind him.

"Once upon a midnight *throbbing cock.*"

I grinned. I couldn't wait to introduce him to Nerius.

CHAPTER 23

I was sitting in a soft leather chair in the library, paging through a book about the great Seelie invasion, laboriously deciphering the runes, when Branwen pushed through the door into the library.

"There you are," she said. "I just looked for you in your room. Everyone's gathering in the dining room. There's something going on."

The book thunked hollowly as I shut it, and I slid it back into a dusty shelf. I followed Branwen into the dining room, where Roan, Elrine, and Abellio sat around the table. I pulled out a chair next to Branwen, unnerved by the somber feeling in the air.

After a few moments of silence, Nerius slowly shuffled into the room. He winced as he sat down.

Roan cleared his throat. "We've heard from our man inside. King Ogmios is launching an attack on the Seelie in four days. His fortress will be largely undefended."

A heavy silence fell over the room as this sank in. Branwen and Abellio exchanged worried looks, and my stomach clenched. I'd gotten nowhere with harnessing my powers or learning to unveil.

Roan leaned back his chair, surveying the room. "This obviously means that we have run out of time. To make things worse, it seems our spy was captured just after delivering this message. We've failed to make contact with him since, and it's safe to assume that he's being tortured to extract every bit of information he has."

Elrine paled, and I could guess why. She'd been in the king's dungeons, and had experienced their methods of torture.

Branwen pushed her dark hair out of her eyes. "Does the spy know about us? Does he know about this place?"

Roan shook his head. "No. I made sure he knew only what was necessary, and most of what he knows is false."

"So we're attacking, right?" Nerius asked. "An assault on the keep?"

Roan nodded. "Most of the king's armies have already been deployed, and the keep is nearly empty. There are two troops that will probably march to the borders tomorrow, and we can strike after that."

Abellio drummed his fingertips on the table. "And the traitor? He could give away our plan."

"He doesn't know our plan yet," Roan said. "Because only I know it. Tomorrow evening, four of our leading generals will come here, and we'll discuss the attack. You will all be deployed as lookouts to make sure no one gets near the mansion while this is happening."

I understood at once the real reason for this. Roan wanted all of us away from the meeting, so none of us would know the attack plans. I wondered how he planned to handle Nerius' limited maneuverability.

"What about the Seelie?" Nerius asked. "Assuming we manage to remove the king, we'll create a power vacuum.

The Seelie might use that as an excuse to launch an attack of their own."

"They definitely will." Roan agreed. "If we manage to do this, we will do our best to contain the information until we have full control over the military and the Council. If things go according to plan, by the time the Seelie find out that the king is gone, someone else will be ruling in his stead."

Who was this 'someone'? In all the time I'd been here, no one had ever talked about that openly. Did Roan plan to take control? Or did the rebels have anyone else in mind? I had to wonder how the unaligned fae felt about continuing to live under the control of nobles.

Roan stood. "After the war council, I'll let you know your roles in the attack. Good night."

As we rose, chairs scraped over the stone floor. I hurried out the door after Roan, catching up with him in the hall. I touched his arm. "Roan."

"Cassandra, I'm afraid we won't be able to train together tonight. No time."

"That's fine." I had my own plans for tonight. "Listen, I don't know if I'll be able to use my dread powers in the attack. I still can't access them at will."

"You won't," he said matter-of-factly. "Your human side has stunted your powers. This will take months to fix, and we don't have that."

"You do have a way with words," I muttered.

He turned to face me. "I will need your reflection magic during the assault, Cassandra." Unexpectedly, he brushed a finger down my cheek before pulling his hand away again, his face hardening. "You're an integral part of this now. Part of us. But I want to keep you away from the heart of the battle. I need to keep you safe, Cassandra."

As Roan walked away, I felt a strange surge of warmth, that flame burning in my chest. A light in the darkness.

* * *

GRIPPING A PLASTIC BAG, I walked into my room, shutting the door behind me and locking it.

Odin hopped onto the desk, quirking his head. "Squawk! O, human love! thou spirit given, on Earth, of all we hope in Heaven!"

"That's beautiful, Odin. You can be so romantic."

"Spread your legs! Squawk! Nevermore."

I sighed, sitting down by my table, and traced a finger down Odin's feathers. He shut his eyes, chirping quietly with contentment.

"Tonight, we're on a stakeout," I told him. "We'll need some sustenance."

I pulled a box of raisins from my bag and poured out a few on the wooden desk, scattering them in front of him. Immediately, he began pecking at them, while I pulled a thermos from the bag, full of strong black coffee. For the stakeout I had planned, I'd need the coffee. On the desk, I laid out four bags of chips: one bag of Doritos, one Cheesy Wotsits, one prawn cocktail, and one bag of salt-and-vinegar flavored Walkers, because I was trying to sample more of the local culture. From prior stakeout experiences, I knew that less than four bags simply wouldn't cut it.

"Squawk! Come, let the burial rite be read."

Ignoring the raven, I rummaged in one of the drawers, and removed four mirrors I'd stored there a week ago. I set them in front of me, propped up against the wall.

Maybe the ambush in the London Stone had just been a clever decision by the king. Maybe he'd realized that the Stone was powerful enough to warrant attention from the rebels, or my contact with him through the Stone had tipped him off.

But the way that fae had waited inside the store, how

they'd come prepared with cars to chase us—it felt like they'd known our plan beforehand. And unless Roan had told any of the other cells, which I doubted, only six people knew about that plan. The six residents of the mansion.

That meant the spy was probably right under this roof.

I reached for the leftmost mirror, searching for Nerius first. The reflection flickered and he appeared, sitting, looking straight back at me. He was staring out the window, while I watched him through the window's reflection. Apparently, he was on watch duty, sitting in a tall oaken chair. These past two days, he'd done more watch duties, since he couldn't do much else. It was the easiest way for him to contribute.

Next, I scanned for Elrine. She combed her hair in front of a full body mirror, wearing a transparent nightgown, her beauty breathtaking. Something turned her head and she crossed to the door, opening it. Roan stood there, talking to her, and she leaned into him. A sharp pang of jealousy pierced my chest, and I grappled to force it away. He *had* said she wasn't his girlfriend, right? I desperately wanted to know what they were talking about.

Focus, Cassandra.

Elrine turned back to the mirror, a smile curling her perfect lips, her nipples showing through her nightgown.

Odin let out a long whistle.

"Stop that," I said. "Be professional."

"Squawk! Her legs were long and smooth, and between them—"

I flicked him, and he let out an outraged squawk, hopping back.

I moved on to the third mirror—the one for Branwen. She lay in bed, staring at the ceiling, seemingly lost in thought. The mirror in her room displayed the entire bed.

Lastly, I merged with a reflection in Abellio's room, finding him already asleep in his room.

If there was a spy in the mansion, he would probably act tonight. Though none of us would be in the war council tomorrow, the spy would almost certainly contact his handler tonight and inform him that an impending attack was looming, and that the meeting was taking place. The king's forces could sweep in tomorrow and take out Roan and the other generals in one swift and efficient strike. The thought made my heart clench with dread. It would be a crippling blow to the rebels, one they probably would never recover from.

I poured myself a cup of coffee and sipped from it. Odin let out a chirp.

"It's *mine*. Eat your raisins."

In the parchments we'd found in the safe, the report had mentioned direct contact with the spy. They didn't use magic or something technological to transfer the information. If I was right, one of the four fae would leave the mansion tonight to pass on the information.

From the desk, I pulled out the two copies I'd made of the parchment missives and read them slowly, occasionally glancing back at the mirrors to see if anyone had moved. Something in the parchments felt weirdly familiar, but I couldn't put my finger on it.

I sipped my coffee, staring at the mirrors. Elrine went to sleep half an hour later, her arms above her head like some beautiful version of Ophelia floating in the water. Branwen blew out the candles in her room and shut her eyes. Nerius occasionally rose to shuffle around to a different part of the mansion, and the mirror flickered as I followed him from different reflections. When he passed by my room, I did my best to contain my emotions tightly, so he wouldn't notice my alertness.

I tore open the Doritos, chomping through them. Then, I ate my way through the prawn cocktail crisps, regretting my failure to bring a glass of water.

The hours ticked slowly on, and I downed three more cups of coffee, my heart rate rising with the caffeine. I tried not to think too much about my fears for the upcoming attack, but I couldn't shake the feeling that our best chance was the London Stone. I just couldn't quite explain why. Somehow, the attack felt like a bad move, something we were being forced into.

Just as I was tearing into the salt and vinegar crisps, something caught my attention. Branwen sat up in bed, barely visible in the faint moonlight. I glanced at the time—just before three a.m. What was she doing up at this hour?

As she dressed herself, my pulse raced, a mixture of excitement and painful disappointment. I liked Branwen, and deep down, I'd been hoping the spy would be one of the other fae.

I watched her pull on a tall pair of boots. Then she bent over, checking her reflection in the mirror. I felt my heart thump as her dark, almond-shaped eyes stared right at me. She smoothed her hair, then put on a shock of bright red lipstick. She was getting dressed to meet someone, and I wondered if that was how they had gotten her. Had she been lured into a romantic relationship with someone in the king's army? Someone who had slowly convinced her that their cause was wrong, or that it was bound to fail, perhaps promising her a noble title once this was over?

I'd seen the jealousy etched across her face when Roan and Elrine had gotten too close. Had a broken heart led her to the dark side, or a chip on her shoulder about being a 'gutter fae'?

She crossed to her door and listened intently before opening it. Then, she walked silently down the corridor. I made a split-second decision and used the other mirrors to focus on reflections around Branwen. I couldn't lose her now.

Intently focused on the mirror, I watched her creep to the door to the garden and unlock it, furtively looking around her.

She moved in the mirrors, quickly scaling a tall apple tree in the garden to hop over the wall. The wall was designed to keep people out, but someone from inside could easily sneak out unnoticed using this route. From the side mirror of a car in French Ordinary Court, I watched her leap out of the glamour, appearing to spring forth from the side of a brick wall one story up. She landed on her feet, nimble as a cat.

If I stopped her now, she could claim she was out for a walk, nervous about the upcoming attack. Would Roan believe her? Probably not, but I decided not to take the chance. I had to catch her doing something significant.

As she crossed into Savage Gardens, I shifted the reflections, watching her from several windows.

I took a deep breath, and then searched for other mirrors in the house. I merged the windows and mirrors in the mansion with these four. Now everyone in the mansion could have a view of what was about to happen.

It was time to move on to the next phase of my plan.

Branwen suddenly tensed, and so did I. On Savage Gardens, a figure leaned against the wall, cloaked in shadows. I saw her smile, her face beaming as she approached the figure. The silhouette moved into the light, and my heart slammed against my ribs.

It was a banshee from the Court of Sorrow.

I'd seen enough. I had to act fast before Branwen told her everything. I grabbed my gun from the desk, and plunged into the mirror.

CHAPTER 24

I leapt from a large window to the chilly street and into the glare of a streetlight. Branwen stood with her back to me, but the banshee spotted me as I materialized, and her eyes widened. I quickly raised my hand, pointing my gun at the banshee. I recognized her as the young banshee I'd seen sitting by the fire in the underground complex. She moved faster than I expected, slipping into the shadows, where I couldn't see her. I nearly shot after her, but in the darkness, it would only mean wasting one of my precious few bullets, and I didn't want any unnecessary noise.

Branwen leaped forward after her, and I shouted, "Branwen, stop!"

She whirled to face me, shock hitting her face when she registered the gun pointed at her chest. "Cassandra? There was a banshee down there. She's going to get away. We need to go after her."

"You need to stay still," I said, my fingers clutching the gun tightly. "If you move, I'll have to shoot, and I don't want to do that."

"What are you talking about?" Hysteria tinged her voice.

"Stop aiming that iron weapon at me! Have you lost your mind?"

"Knives on the ground. Now."

"Cassandra, lower that fucking gun." Her eyelids began to flutter.

"No. Here's a better idea. You slowly remove all your hidden knives and then come with me—"

A strong hand grabbed my right wrist and twisted it, hard. I fired, but the shot went wide. I elbowed my assailant, and whirled to face him. A huge figure swung for me. I realized it was my shadow just as its hand connected with my cheek, my face blazing with pain. I had been standing quite a distance from the streetlight, and consequentially, my shadow was eight feet tall.

I kicked at its knee, but it didn't even budge. One of its hands closed on the gun, the other gripping me by the throat. It jerked my weapon away, and the fingers around my throat tightened. I struggled, lungs burning, my vision blurring as I tried to breathe in. *Air.* I tried to pull the dark ethereal fingers apart, tried to kick my attacker, but it was useless. Panic rose in my chest, and I bucked and writhed in desperation, the world around me dimming. *Air.* I glanced at the mirror on my wrist, trying to feel the reflection, but all I could feel was my desperate need for air.

I grabbed the shadow's body and jerked myself to the left. We both rolled sideways, the fingers around my throat slipping.

I sucked in a ragged breath, reality shifting back into focus. Ten feet away from me, Branwen stood motionless, her eyelids fluttering. I couldn't win against my shadow. I had to get her.

I bent my knee and kicked the shadow hard. Then I rolled and bounded to my feet. My shadow was already charging at me when I flicked my hand and leapt into the reflection on my wrist.

I landed a few yards away, plunging out of the side mirror of a car on the opposite side of the street. My shadow whirled around, searching for me. I pulled a stiletto from the sheath on my belt, and estimated my distance to Branwen.

Quietly, I crept alongside the row of cars, keeping my head low until I was right across from Branwen. Then I leaped over the hood of the car, dashing for her.

My shadow froze, and Branwen swiveled into a crouch, stilettos in both her hands, baring her teeth in anger. "I don't know what's going on, Cassandra, but you need to stop."

"I saw you sneaking to meet the banshee, Branwen. Give it up. It's over."

"That's a lie, I never—"

"*Everyone* saw it, Branwen. As soon as you sneaked out, I began to transfer the images to the mirrors around the house. Nerius was on watch, and he saw it. I'm sure he woke up everyone else. They all know. They're all watching *right now.*"

Her mouth hung open, her arms lowering to her sides. "What have you done?" she finally asked in a frail tone.

"What have *I* done? You were sneaking out to meet our enemies."

"You fortal whore!" she screamed. "What have you done?"

Her eyelids began fluttering again, and I noticed my shadow begin to move. I bolted just as it lunged forward. I reached Branwen in three steps and punched her hard. She flew backward and slumped on the floor, out cold.

Out of her control, the shadow slithered back to my body, latching on to my feet. I stared at Branwen, then bent to pull the stilettos from her clenched hands.

I felt his powerful presence behind me before I heard him

approach. I turned around, my body exhausted. There was no sense of victory, only a hollow feeling of sadness.

"You saw it?" I asked Roan.

"Most of it." He stared at Branwen's unconscious form. "Nerius woke us all up as soon as the reflection materialized on the window."

"Now what?"

"We'll take her to our holding cell. She'll be interrogated. We need to know how she was turned." He ran a hand over his mouth, shadows sliding though his eyes. "She was loyal once."

* * *

As I RETURNED with Roan to the mansion, all the adrenaline burned from my body. By the time I walked through the glamoured front door, all I wanted to do was crawl into bed and sleep. With Branwen lying unconscious in his arms, Roan slunk through the shadows of the courtyard, heading for the holding cell. I crossed into one of the halls. Within moments, the sound of oncoming footsteps greeted me, and Abellio and Elrine stood before me.

Elrine crossed her arms, staring at me. "What happened? Is Branwen…" She seemed unable to end the sentence.

"Roan took her to the holding cell." I blinked blearily. "We caught her meeting a banshee, one of the women from the underground Court of Sorrow."

Abellio's deep blue eyes shone in the candlelight. "Why did she do this?"

I shook my head. "I don't know. Maybe we'll know more tomorrow."

Elrine narrowed her eyes. "How did you know to watch her in particular?"

I shrugged. I wasn't about to talk about how I had

watched them all without their knowledge, or that I'd seen her giving Roan a view of her nipples. Definitely not now. I crossed to the stairwell, heading for my room. I left Elrine and Abellio behind me, talking in hushed tones.

When I reached the door, I hesitated. My body begged for rest, but I knew there was one more thing I had to do before I could sleep. I crept down the hall to Branwen's bedroom and turned the doorknob.

In the guttering candlelight, Nerius stood inside, staring at something.

"Oh," I said. "I'm sorry, I didn't know... I'll leave you alone."

"It's okay." His voice sounded ragged. "You can come in and snoop around. I assume that's why you're here?"

I hesitated. "Yeah. I hoped there would be something... anything that would give us some more information."

He wiped his eye with the back of his hand. "Not really. She destroyed it."

I frowned and moved inside, joining him by the small oak table.

"I didn't believe it," he whispered. "Even when I saw... when I woke everyone up. I actually thought she was being attacked by that banshee, you know? I woke Roan first so he could go and help her. And then you appeared, and the banshee fled, and she attacked you... and still I thought there was some explanation for it all."

"I'm sorry."

He gazed at a small bowl on the table with a snuffed, half-melted candle in it. Around the candle lay scattered pieces of parchment. A burnt letter.

"She was the *good* one. The one who always tried to do the right thing. I was the shitty, violent, bad-mouthed brother. She was the one everyone liked. And she always believed in this rebellion. I just can't understand why she would..."

He opened his palm, showing me the tiny scrap of paper that had ripped his world apart.

"I found this by the candle. She didn't destroy it properly."

I picked it from his hand carefully. Several runes were still readable. *Tonight... outside... secret...*

"I saw her burning it." He shook his head in disbelief. "Earlier in the evening, I'd come in to say goodnight, and I saw her burning something. She flushed when she saw me. And when I asked what it was, she said it was nothing, just a stupid love poem she wrote. She used to do that, you know? Write poems. But this isn't her handwriting. I should have known."

"You couldn't have known," I said sadly. "You believed in your own sister. Everyone else did, too."

"Yeah." Without another word, he turned, tromping away.

I looked at the table, and then began to pace the room, looking for anything else out of the ordinary. Her stiletto collection lay in her dresser, amidst her clothing. I glanced at the mirror through which I'd watched her, my own reflection looking haggard and worn.

I noticed something on the bed, peering out from below the blanket. I snatched back the bedsheets, finding an envelope. I picked it up, and looked at it. It was empty, with no writing on it. I noticed a faint smell of wood anemone and grass. I frowned at its familiarity. Was that her handler's scent, the banshee she had sneaked out to meet?

I found nothing else in the room, and after ransacking it, I left it empty.

CHAPTER 25

The next day, a thick sense of grief hung over the mansion. Nerius stayed in his room, his door shut, refusing food. Elrine and I hardly spoke to each other, both of us cocooned in our bubbles of misery. I had no idea where Roan and Abellio were, but I could only guess they were involved in interrogating Branwen. Even Odin had fallen quiet, hardly squawking the occasional Poe quote.

It was dusk before Roan returned, and his voice boomed through the mansion, summoning us to meet him in the library. When I pushed through the door, I found him standing in the center of the dusty, candlelit room, grimly leaning against a bookshelf. "The war council will begin in an hour," he said. "I want the four of you on lookout by the time it starts."

"Why?" Elrine asked. "We caught the spy. What else is there to worry about?"

Roan met my gaze. "Branwen could have passed on information to the banshee before Cassandra got to her."

I nodded. "I don't think she managed to say anything, but it's best to make sure."

"How do you want us deployed?" Abellio asked, chewing at his fountain pen.

"Elrine and Cassandra should take the roof. Cassandra, I want your eyes on the north. Monitor every street within five hundred yards to the north. Can you do that?"

"With mirrors, sure."

"Good. Abellio and Nerius, I want you monitoring the garden wall to the south of the mansion. Make sure no one comes that way."

"We can't keep a lookout as good as Cassandra," Abellio said.

Candlelight danced over the planes of Roan's face. "Our cell is not the only one keeping watch tonight. The rest of the perimeter is handled by different cells."

It was a good reminder that we weren't in this alone. There were plenty more rebels on our side.

Roan started toward the door, before turning back to us. "Don't leave your post until the council is over. We're a day away from victory. Let's not make any mistakes now."

* * *

THANKFULLY, a cloudless canopy of stars hung over us. Rain would have made it into a miserable night. Elrine and I dressed in sweaters and sat on the roof of the mansion, on lookout duty. On the tiled roof, I laid out eight mirrors, each reflecting the starry night sky. As the breeze rippled over my skin, I felt for their reflections, searching for a good vantage point. Slowly, the mirrors flickered to visions of the London streets.

"Does that cover all the positions we need to watch?" Elrine asked.

"I think so."

She nodded. "Looks good."

We sat in silence, our gazes alternating between the mirrors and our view of the dark street below.

After a few minutes, Elrine pointed at one of the mirrors. "Look. What's that?"

I stared at the mirror pointing to Crosswall. It looked as if a black hole of darkness was slowly swallowing the street. Passersby seemed oblivious to the incoming dark void, simply moving aside to avoid it as it rolled in the center of the street, a cloud of writhing smoke.

I swallowed at the eerily familiar sight. "I actually think he's one of ours. He helped us save you and Scarlett, remember?"

"Vaguely," Elrine said hesitantly. "I was mostly out of it that night. But I think I remember… he was there, but wasn't. I was feverish. I thought I was hallucinating."

"His name is Drustan. I'm betting there's a car in the midst of that darkness." A memory of riding in a car within the void flickered in my mind, and I glanced at the stars, strangely reassured by their silvery light. "I'll make sure."

I pulled out my phone, dialing Roan. It took him a minute to answer, and I could hear him fumbling with his phone. He still wasn't used to modern technology.

"Yes?" His deep voice rumbled through my bones.

"Any chance Drustan is somewhere around here, driving with his car?"

"Yes. He's nearby."

"Thanks." I hung up the phone, shoving it back in my pocket.

After a minute, the roiling darkness pulsed onto Savage Gardens. From the way the humans reacted on the streets below, it was clear they didn't see it the same way we did. To them, it was just something to avoid. As Drustan's darkness moved closer, the light dimmed around us, the stars blackening. I couldn't tear my gaze away, feeling as if I were watching a void devouring our world. Then it began fading, and I realized I'd been holding my breath.

I peered down at the street and the Porsche, now parked on Savage Gardens. The doors opened, and four fae stepped out. I recognized Morcant—the fae with cat-like eyes—and Odette, the willowy rebel banshee. Both of these lethal fae had helped us attack Siofra's mansion. The shape made of darkness I recognized as Drustan. The fourth one, with his chin-length hair, looked familiar as well, but I had trouble placing him. He wore a silver boar pin on a green robe.

Elrine let out a long, shaky breath. "King Ebor."

"Oh, right," I muttered. King Ebor and I probably weren't on the best of terms. Last time we had met, I had stabbed him with a knife.

The four generals crossed beyond the mansion's glamoured façade, and I heard the door shut behind them. I could almost feel the tingling sense of raw power exuding from below.

"What do you think they're talking about?" I asked.

Elrine glared at me. "You're the one who's supposed to have a soul-bond with Roan. Why don't you tell me?"

"I know you're upset about that. I don't really understand why."

"You don't understand a lot of things. But know this—I've known Roan since we were children. I was there for him when he got out of prison. He was broken, and I helped to put him back together. I was there for him in the Hawkwood Forest when no one else was. If you break him again, Cassandra, I will end you."

Okay, then.

An oppressive silence fell over us, and I resumed staring at the mirrors.

* * *

THE WAR COUNCIL went on for hours as night settled around us, and I wasn't sure which was icier—the cold of the roof's tiles, or Elrine's attitude. I used my coffee thermos to warm my frozen hands, occasionally sipping from it to wake myself. It was after two when the mansion's door opened, and the four fae generals slipped out, beyond the glamour again. They all looked at Drustan, and for a moment I heard the faint and unsettling flutter of wings. Then, the world darkened, swallowing the street below us in a cloudy void.

The darkness crept away until it disappeared from sight. Only then did I sever the connection to the eight mirrors. I loosed a relieved breath, suddenly drained from the effort of maintaining this vigil. It was the second night that I'd summoned the reflections for hours on end, and my body was starting to hunger for power. If this went on any longer, I'd have to seek out some terrified humans to feed from.

Without speaking, we packed up the mirrors, crawling back over the tiled rooftop to the window we'd snuck out from.

Exhausted, I stumbled through the hall, Elrine close behind me. We found Roan sitting alone at the round table, lantern light dancing over his skin. He sat with his arms folded, staring at the table.

I pulled out a chair and sat, relieved to be in from the chilly night. Elrine sat across from Roan, glaring at him. As we waited, Abellio crossed into the room, then Nerius, pale and wincing as he walked.

When everyone had taken a seat, Roan raised his gaze. "We attack tomorrow."

My stomach clenched.

"Our spies report that only one of the legions have been sent to the borders," He continued. "So the king still has one legion, as well as the keep's usual guards, and the king's own elite guardsmen."

"How many do we have?" Nerius asked.

"Not enough for a frontal attack," Roan said. "But there's another way."

"Ulthor's pass?" Abellio whispered.

Roan nodded, then glanced at me. "During the last rebellion five centuries ago, my father and his forces created an underground tunnel. They used it to breach the fortress."

"But the moat has been flooded and destroyed," Nerius said.

"The king has used a dam to flood it, yes. But for the past several weeks, we've had a group of selkies working their way through the underground river, shifting rubble to clear the tunnel of debris. They've managed to reach the bowels of the keep. Only one or two blockades remain. We paid a hefty price for that passage. Seven of them died during their work, of sudden avalanches and mud slides. I plan to ensure their deaths have meaning."

Abellio twirled his silver ring around his finger. "From what I understand, it's always been a narrow tunnel. If the king's forces hear us approaching, they could trap us inside and slaughter us."

I leaned back in my chair. "I'm having a hard time picturing this. Is there a map or anything?"

Nerius snatched the bottle of nectar from the table. "It's quite simple." Slowly, he dripped the viscous liquid onto the table, forming a round shape that gleamed in the candlelight. "Here is the lake of Lir. The Acciona River flows from the fortress, into the lake." He poured out the nectar in a long line from the circular lake. It looked… inappropriate.

"You're drawing a cock and balls," I pointed out.

He arched an eyebrow at me. "You have a very dirty mind, pixie." At the end of the penis—the river, rather—he used the nectar to draw a large blob. "The river flows under the fortress, but outside the fortress walls, it flows aboveground toward the lake. Ulthor's Passage is an underground tunnel below the fortress, that's been flooded with river water for centuries." He pointed further back on the shaft. "The dam is here."

I nodded. "Near the ball—the *lake*. Got it."

Roan folded his hands. "And that's where we need to attack. Here's the plan. I will lead a large frontal attack on the keep. The majority of the rebel forces will be with me and Elrine, as well as Drustan and Odette. It will be a formidable battle, but one the king is likely to win, and it's not our real attack. While the king's forces are distracted by us, King Ebor will lead a small group of Elder Fae to destroy the dam. It's usually well-guarded, but we believe most of the guards were sent to fight the Seelie. Then, Abellio will join Morcant and a small group of rebels. With the underground tunnel clear of water, they will cross into the fortress." He set his eyes at me. "This whole attack falls apart if one guard manages to escape from Ebor's attack, or if for some reason the tunnel can't be breached. You keep eyes on all of us. You have to let us know if anything goes wrong. We'll have people with mirrors everywhere."

Elrine straightened. "Seems a lot of effort to breach the fortress when Cassandra could just break in with her reflection power. Isn't that what she does?"

Roan stared at her. "We're not sending her in on her own. Her pixie emotions would draw every guard in the fortress. She'd be dead within moments."

Elrine shrugged as if this didn't seem like a major concern.

"And the blockades that remain in the tunnel?" I asked.

"Morcant will be leading a small force into the underground passage," Roan added. "He'll destroy them using his fire power."

At Siofra's house, I'd seen what the cat-eyed fae could do with his explosive powers, and had little doubt in his ability.

Roan focused his gaze on Abellio. "Once you're inside, we'll need you to open the front gates to let us in. We will be waiting for that moment, but the longer you take, the higher the casualties." He turned to me. "Cassandra, this is going to be a war zone, and fae battle is something you're not prepared for. As soon as the dam is breached, I need you to leap out of Trinovantum. Wait for us here."

I bristled. "What? I'm not leaving you all in the middle of battle."

His eyes flashed with gold. "In order to fight among the fae, you need to unveil. As fae, when we unveil, we become faster, stronger, more powerful. Without that ability, you're vulnerable. You'd be like a mouse among the wolves, and your safety would distract me until I'd no longer be able to function the way I need to. Until you can unveil, you'll never be safe among the fae."

Elrine decided to rub salt into the wound. "Truer words were never spoken. You don't belong here."

"That's not what I meant." Roan's voice was ice cold.

Irritations simmered, and I leaned over the table, meeting his gaze. "What if Abellio and Morcant encounter some unforeseen problem inside the tunnel? Or if you need them to change course? No cellular towers in Trinovantum. You'll need me as a go-between."

Nerius frowned. "The pixie has a point."

Roan gritted his teeth, his expression hardening.

"I won't flee as soon as things get dicey, Roan. Not when I'm needed. Ogmios killed Gabriel, and I intend to make him pay."

Roan stared at me for a long time, the wheels turning in his mind. Could he feel my resolve through our bond? He could obviously see the benefit of what I suggested, even if he was reluctant to bring me into battle.

I touched his arm. "Roan. I need to do this. I *need* this."

He nodded. "Fine. And after this battle, you need to return back to your own world. Agreed?"

His words cut me to the core, but I nodded mutely.

Elrine met Roan's gaze. "And what about your power, Roan? What if we need it?"

He shook his head. "No, Elrine. We won't need it. You know why."

But I didn't know the story, of course. A heavy silence fell over the room.

At last, Abellio let out a long breath, pushing away from the table. "We should rest now. Tonight, we sleep. Tomorrow, we face our deaths."

His words sent an icy shiver of dread snaking up my spine.

CHAPTER 26

In the depths of one of Trinovantum's forests, a swallow chirped above my head, oblivious to the pervasive undercurrent of tension that wound around the small rebel group. The scent of fear tinged the air, and my heart beat hard in my chest like a war drum. Slowly, ruddy rays of sunlight began piercing the iron-gray clouds, gilding the horizon as the sun set.

Seventeen of us hid in the grove, a few hundred yards from the keep. Morcant stood to my left, Abellio to my right, but I didn't recognize anyone else. Several looked feline, their features similar to Morcant's, even if they weren't quite as big. Three had bull horns, and one wore only a loincloth over his silvery skin. Our guide was a willowy selkie—a tall man with shimmering sea-green skin and half-lidded eyes. Apart from Morcant, all the fae were armed, including me.

In my belt, I'd tucked my two stilettos and my gun. A pair of binoculars hung from my neck, and mirrors adorned my wrists, both of them flickering.

On my right wrist, I glimpsed Roan standing before a large force of fae. I didn't have the whole perspective, but I thought there might be a hundred armed rebel soldiers. Roan faced the horde, standing on a tree stump. He waved his sword in the air, speaking animatedly.

In the crowd, I spotted Elrine's cherry-red hair, and I caught a glimpse of the crossbow over her back. From one corner of the horde, darkness roiled, staining the air. I couldn't find Odette, the rebel banshee in the group. Maybe she was the one holding the mirror.

On my left wrist, I had a view of Ebor's group, nearly covered by foliage in another oak grove. They hid not far from the Lake of Lir, ready to attack the dam.

I raised my eyes to the fortress, the stone now stained violet and coral in the dying sunlight. It was an immense structure, the walls towering hundreds of feet over the rocky earth, the turrets and battlements lined with archers.

Peering through my binoculars, I watched the forces on the battlements thicken, and soldiers rolled smoking cauldrons to the edges of the wall.

My stomach lurched. Boiling tar and oil probably filled those cauldrons, ready to burn the skin from our bodies. I tried not to think about it too hard.

Although the king had noticed the attack forces outside the fortress, it seemed he wasn't worried about an extended siege. One of his cohorts was only a day's march away. If the rebels surrounded the fortress, he could easily call his cohort back. That left us with two options—either attack, or slink off home.

Something glinted in my right mirror, and I peered down at Roan raising his sword. The rebel horde before him raised their weapons, waving them in the air, the mouths wide in furious battle cries. *It's time.*

My pulse began to race, and a primal battle cry pierced my own mind, my body singing with a mixture of excitement and fear. To my horror, my legs began to shake, and I could only hope that no one else would notice. I tightened my fingers into fists, trying to calm my own nerves.

The horde began to move, some of them dragging battle rams. Drustan's darkness curled into the air, and I caught a few glimpses of winged fae flying within the swirls of darkness, bows in their hands. They would keep the archers busy, allowing the battering rams to move closer to the gate. Others carried ladders, to scale the walls.

All for show, of course. The real attack force was us, even if my body was now shaking so hard it could have made the earth tremble.

The sound of blaring horns rumbled through my bones, and the ancient cry of war shook. *It's time.*

On my left wrist, movement flickered. Hearing the battle horns, King Ebor motioned his men forward, his sword in the air.

"Ebor is moving," I said quietly, working to keep my voice steady.

Morcant nodded, his cat-eyes gleaming in the rosy light. "Drustan's cloud of darkness is about to unleash hell on the fortress."

The darkness spread across the sky in smoky whorls, already enveloping the battlements. Some covered their eyes, or curled in fright. Other blindly nocked arrows and shot them into the air, unable to see their targets. Deadly missiles were raining from within the darkness—our own winged archers. Already, a few guards on the battlements were falling, arrows protruding from their bodies.

And yet, it wasn't enough. The darkness only covered a small segment of the wall, and as the rebel horde moved closer, the rest of the king's archers rained arrows onto the forces below. Roan's soldiers held shields above their heads as they charged forward.

In the reflection on my other wrist, Ebor's forces were

reaching the dam, still shrouded by the forest's foliage. Whoever held the mirror moved it around so I could get a good look at everything. Eight guards stood before a small wooden dam, only six feet high. The guards' bodies looked tense, but from where they stood, they wouldn't be able to see the Elder Fae moving through the forest.

Just at the edge of the treeline, the Elder Fae unslung their bows, loosing a volley of arrows into the air.

Four guards fell instantly, arrows in their hearts. Three took cover, and a golden-skinned fae raised his hand. From his palm, a wave of fire rushed at the Elder Fae, foliage bursting into flame around them. When I raised my gaze from my position, I locked my gaze on the plume of black smoke curling from the woods.

"They'll be fine." A hint of worry tinged Morcant's voice as he watched the smoke.

In the reflection, Ebor charged from the forest—in his boar form. I tilted the mirror so Morcant could watch, too, silently cursing myself for failing to bring a larger one. A wave of flame hit the boar, but the beast didn't even slow down, crashing straight into the fiery fae, goring him. Ebor dragged his opponent down to the earth. The rest of the oncoming Elder Fae hammered the remaining two guards with arrows. Two guards... someone was missing.

I frowned, scanning the scene. "There was one more. A little one with blue skin."

"Another guard?" Morcant asked.

"There were eight guards. I see seven dead. Where is the eighth?"

"Damn it," Morcant muttered. "If that one manages to get away..."

He didn't finish, but the consequence was obvious. He could alert the king that the dam was under attack, which would immediately betray our plan.

"Can you find him?" Morcant asked.

I quested for the other reflections in the vicinity, leaping blindly from one to another, panic rising. "No, there's nothing... hang on!"

From the surface of a small pool, I had a sudden view of the blue-skinned fae. He crept along beside the river, trailing blood from an arrow lodged in his arm. "There!" I said.

"Tell Ebor!" barked Morcant.

"No time," I said. I pulled out a pocket mirror. Taking a deep breath, I merged with the river's reflection, and plunged in.

My torso submerged on the water's surface, the freezing water knocking the breath out of me. With the shock of the icy water, my body froze, and I struggled to kick my legs, reaching for the gun in my belt. My heart slammed against my ribs.

The wounded fae whirled around at the sound of the rippling water, his eyes widening. Kicking to keep myself afloat, I aimed the gun at him, firing four times. My hands were shaking uncontrollably from the cold, but one shot hit him in his belly. That was all I needed. He crumpled to the ground just as I sank back under the icy surface. I kicked hard, emerging into the air again, and managed to bond with the broken reflection in the water for long enough to jump back through the mirror on Morcant's belt. I tumbled to the ground at his feet, dirt clinging to my icy body. I coughed and spluttered, teeth chattering.

"What happened?" Morcant asked.

"He's dead." I coughed.

"And the dam?"

Shivering, I stood, raising my bracelet. Ebor's men assaulted the little wooden dam with their enormous axes. In my other reflection, Roan held a shield above Elrine's head as she nocked an arrow. In the background, boiling tar poured onto one of the rebels, and he burst into flame. My stomach flipped at the carnage.

The Elder Fae weren't moving fast enough for me, and I gritted my teeth as they swung their axes into the wood. "Come on."

Just then, the dam broke. The flood of water took one of the Elder Fae by surprise, and he was carried with the current. The rest managed to rush to the rocky banks.

"Look," Morcant pointed.

The tunnel's water level had already begun dropping, clearing the way through Ulthor's Passage.

* * *

WE WADED into the icy water, the river freezing me up to my waist. The watery underground passage was narrow—barely enough for two to walk side by side. Morcant and the selkies led the way.

In the dim light, dank air enveloped us. Up ahead, the faint glow of magical glowing orbs led the way, and I pushed ahead until I had just enough light to follow the reflections in my mirrors. I kept glancing at my wrists, checking the advancement of the main assault, breathing a sigh of relief every time I saw Roan unharmed.

We trudged on, half-frozen by the water, our labored breathing echoing off the crumbling walls. The underground river seemed to go on forever, the water still up to our waists. So *this* is how people ended up with trench foot.

As we walked, the cold began to numb my muscles, and my teeth chattered uncontrollably. At one point, Abellio turned to give me an encouraging smile. Of all of us, he seemed like the only one who relished this trek, his eyes shimmering in excitement.

As we walked, I caught a glimpse of Elrine, blood

streaking her face, her features contorted in pain. Then Odette, aiming a silvery bow into air, her mouth wide in a banshee death scream. The rebels had managed to position several ladders on the walls, but all of them had been repelled, rebels flung to their deaths. Drustan's writhing darkness seemed to be causing the worst damage to the defenses, but its tendrils had begun to recede. He was getting tired.

Then Morcant cursed, and I looked up to see the enormous blockade standing in our way—a wall of enormous boulders.

The selkie guide shook his head. "This wasn't here before. Where in the gods' names has this come from?"

Had the ceiling collapsed?

"Stand back." Morcant held out his hands to the sides. "I'll start clearing this away."

As we shuffled backward, sloshing in the icy water, dread crawled up my gut. Something was very wrong. Morcant raised his hands, and fiery white light shot from them, hitting the rocks. They crumbled—revealing more rocks. And large barrels, and discarded furniture.

This blockade had been *built* by someone. And that meant the king knew we were coming.

A strange sound echoed in the tunnel—a terrible, keening wail, quickly joined by another. And another.

All at once, the tight space around us echoed with wails that pierced me to the marrow.

The screams of banshees.

My heart was ready to burst free from my chest, and our own men began to scream in pain. One suddenly disappeared, dragged underwater, flailing. I yanked a flashlight from my pocket. Casting my beam back on the water, I glimpsed movement—a scaly creature swimming between us, slashing with her claws. Some of the rebels began to thrust their swords into the water. One hit something, and a head rose from the river—a scaly, green-skinned woman, her eyes vacant and her hair a tangle of river-weeds.

"Nymphs," Morcant snarled.

The banshee's screams grew louder, deafening now. From the other end of the tunnel, they were moving closer—a whole troop of them. Twenty, maybe more. I dropped my flashlight, then pulled my gun and one of my stilettos free from the belt.

"Move!" Morcant screamed.

Oh shit. Explosions coming.

Along with the other rebels, I flattened myself to the rocky tunnel wall. Morcant raised his hands, pointing them at the incoming banshees. Bright rays of light blinded me, and one banshee fell, no longer screaming, but the rest moved on like phantoms. Cold fear burned through my nerve endings. I aimed my gun, using the line of sight to take several shots at the wailing women. Another floundered and fell; a third lurched backward as my bullet hit her in the shoulder.

And the water around us churned.

Something snaked by my foot and I reflexively jumped back, swinging my stiletto down. It sunk deep into the meat of one of the nymphs and she raised her head, her eyes burning with fury. She wrenched free, taking my stiletto with her. I shot at her, pulling another knife with my free hand. I had no idea if I'd managed to hit her under the murky water.

"It was a trap!" Morcant roared by my ear. His face morphed, now nearly completely feline, canines bared. "Tell Roan!"

Half our crew were now trapped between the rubble blockade and the incoming banshees. Morcant grappled with a banshee, his hands glowing bright as he wrapped them around her neck.

Screaming in frustration, I pulled out a mirror, letting my mind bond with it as I stared at Roan, blood-soaked in battle. As the cool mirror washed over my skin, I felt a sharp stab of pain just below my ribs.

* * *

THICK SMOKE and the cloying smell of blood instantly replaced the smells of claustrophobic tunnel, and I tumbled to the ground. Darkness had fallen, and screaming fae surrounded me, some shooting bows, others charging forward with a battering ram. An arrow sank into the ground inches away from me. For a moment, the shock of the battle raging around me stole my breath.

"What are you doing here?" Roan stood above me, eyes gleaming cold, antlers high above his head. He dragged me up, blood streaking his body. "What's happening? Why isn't the gate open?"

"It was a trap!" I shouted above the clash of swords. "They knew we were coming!" We'd missed something. Branwen had been locked up, unable to pass on information... and yet somehow, the information had been leaked.

An enormous fae charged Roan, gripping an axe, and Roan whirled. He cut his blade through the fae's neck, blood soaking him. The fae's head splashed into the water, his body crumpling, and Roan turned to me. "Where's Morcant?"

I shook my head. "He was in the tunnel. He's trapped. They're all trapped."

I forced myself to focus, looking around me, gripping my gun. The attack was in chaos. Our troops were breaking up, the ground littered with dead and wounded fae. Wine-dark blood stained the earth, seeping into the soil.

233

"We have to retreat, Roan!"

He looked around us, his raw rage icing the air. He grabbed a battle horn tied around his neck, and raised it to his lips. When he blew it, my eardrums nearly ruptured. The sound of the horn echoed across the battlefield. Three short bursts.

Immediately, the fae charging with the ram dropped it, shields still over their heads. They began to retreat. Others turned from the walls, stopping to help the wounded up. I glanced at the sky, where Drustan's darkness still enveloped the battlements.

"Drustan will buy us time to retreat," Roan said. "Come on. Hurry!"

I turned from the fortress, but as I took a step to run, I stumbled to my knees, my head swimming. My side burned with a sharp pain.

Roan gripped me under my shoulder, helping to pull me up. "What is it?"

"I think I'm hurt." A cloud of darkness whirled in my skull, and I gripped my side. I raised my hand, finding it streaked with blood.

Roan slipped his arm around my waist. "I'll help you. We have to get out of here."

I leaned on him and we moved away from the fortress, moving further from the range of the arrows as he pulled me along. Roan's musky scent engulfed me.

"Did Abellio make it?" Roan asked.

"I don't know. We got separated. Where's Elrine?"

"I lost sight of her. I last saw her when…" Roan's voice faded away.

When I looked up, a fresh wave of fear slammed me in the chest. About two hundred yards away from us, a line of fae rode for us on enormous horses, all heavily armored. The moonlight washed over them, casting them in an eerie blue light. The sight stopped the rebels in their tracks

"Who are they?" I breathed.

"That must be the king's cohort." Roan's voice sounded hollow. "The one he sent to the border last night."

Fatigue smoldered in my muscles. Looking around me, I felt doom closing in on me. Injured, with no horses, no wings. The king's troops were swooping in for a massacre.

"Everyone, into the forest!" Roan roared. "Run!"

Panic crackled the air around me, and the rebel horde turned for the trees. I stumbled, leaning into Roan. We just had to make it to the edge of the forest, where the horses would struggle to follow us.

I fought past the pain that splintered my ribs, rushing for the forest. But even if we ran at full speed, we'd never make it. The horses were closing in on us, their hooves making the earth tremble. There was no way we'd survive. Gripped with pain, my knees buckled. I wasn't leaning on Roan anymore. Where was he? I stumbled, wheezing as I ran, my muscles screaming.

I glanced over my shoulder.

And there was Roan, running *away* from the forest, heading directly for the king's troops. He lifted his sword above his head, charging—completely alone. He was running to his death.

My world tilted. What the hell was he doing? I froze, clutching my bleeding ribs, staring in horror. The oncoming death horde was less than fifty yards from him, eyes gleaming in the dark. Forty feet now.

Something ancient and dark vibrated over the turbulent landscape. Wind whipped around me, pushing me forward, and darkness gathered above Roan's head, blotting out the moon.

The darkness of a storm. Roan's storm.

I stumbled closer to him, grasping my gun. I needed to get to him—I didn't know what I would do, just that I was gripped by an overwhelming desire to protect him.

"Roan!" I shouted, stumbling toward him. This was madness, utter and complete madness, and yet I had to press on.

The horses were nearly upon him when lightning struck. Some tumbled to the ground; others reared to their hind feet. Another bolt seared the sky, thunder cracking the air. The wind whipped over my skin, a hurricane gale, and it knocked me to my knees. Dirt and debris whipped over my skin, whirling around Roan. He stood in the eye of the storm, sword raised, and I tried to fire at the troops surrounding him. I had no idea where my bullets were going.

A sharp crack of lightning speared the sky, touching down in the king's troops. The soldiers fled, horses panicking—but not all of them.

"Roan!" I screamed over the wind, rushing forward. Maybe I could reach him.

A group of full-plated riders galloped at him, and he swung for them, his sword whistling in the air. Lightning cracked the sky, blinding me, and I felt something sever. That flame—the warmth I'd felt in my chest—snuffed out, and darkness welled from within. My connection to Roan was gone.

And the shadows pulled me under.

CHAPTER 27

I lay on a damp, bumpy floor, pain fracturing my ribs. Complete and utter darkness enveloped me, and I reached up to grasp the blindfold covering my eyes, but I found nothing there.

Either I'd gone blind, or the earth had swallowed me up.

"Roan?" I whispered.

My voice sounded strange in my ear, cracked and weak, and it echoed around me, as if reverberating from nearby walls. What had happened? I remembered seeing Roan running at the cavalry, and then the dying of the flame in my chest—that connection between us. Panic threatened to engulf me. Had he died? *Please, no.*

"Anybody there?" I asked, desperate now, my voice trembling.

Only the sound of dripping water answered me. I pushed myself up onto my elbows, my side pulsing with pain. I felt around me, my fingers tracing the ground—damp, curved stone. I traced one of the stones. I bit my lip, and felt it over and over until I realized what this was. Cobblestones. I was lying on a cobblestone floor. To one side, I could feel a rough stone wall formed from rectangular blocks. A thin layer of sludge covered the grouting between the blocks.

I tried to stand up, but a wave of dizziness hit me hard. I sucked in deep breaths, trying to manage my pain until the dizziness passed. I crawled on my knees, moving along the floor, but hit a wall almost instantly.

I needed to figure out the counters of this room. I kept circling the floor, tracing the wall until my fingers brushed against metal—a smooth surface, three feet wide. A door. I traced my hands over its surface, feeling for a handle or even hinges, but there was nothing. I shoved at the door, unable to budge it an inch, then slammed my fist into it. A *thud* echoed over the room, and beyond that, nothing happened. I kept crawling and feeling around me until certainty sank into my mind; a heavy, poisonous knowledge. I was in a cell in the king's dungeons. I couldn't imagine a scenario in which this would end well for me.

I slumped to the floor, despair clawing at the back of my skull.

On the plus side, I probably wasn't blind—just sitting in complete darkness, somewhere under the earth. No light—no reflections. I was completely trapped in here.

I forced myself to my hands and knees, trying to block out the stabbing pain in my ribs, and crawled over the floor to see if I could find any tools at my disposal. As I scrambled around the cell, I tried to feel that warmth in my chest, my connection to Roan.

Nothing. *Please, Roan. Please let me know you're okay.* I couldn't lose him.

After fifteen minutes of desperate fumbling in the darkness, I gave in to the certainty that I had nothing. They'd stripped off my bracelets, armor, weapons, and shoes, and I now wore only tattered, drenched leather leggings and a water-logged shirt. I was in a cramped square cell, about six feet across. When I managed to stand up, leaning against the wall, my head cracked against the ceiling. It was only four feet from the ground, which meant I couldn't stand. They'd probably designed it this way on purpose to elicit a sense of claustrophobia. And it worked, making me feel that the walls were closing in, that I'd be buried alive among the dark and vicious things that crawled underground. I curled up on the floor, breathing fast and heavy, shivering.

I had no food bowl, no water. A tiny hole in one of the corners was probably supposed to be a toilet.

Roan. Where are you? Are you there?

I slowed my breathing, trying to marshal the rising panic, to think clearly. What the fuck had happened? I'd been running to Roan, my gun drawn. The king's cavalry had closed in around him, a storm roiling overhead, and then I'd felt my connection to him sever. I had probably lost consciousness from blood loss, and the king's guard must have found the 'Mistress of Dread.' Right now, I was probably buried in a dungeon in the bowels of the fortress.

My heart was ready to shatter into a million pieces. How had everything gotten so fucked?

The king had known. He had known everything. Someone else—besides Branwen—had been spying. A traitor among the rebels had served us to the king on a silver platter. That was the only answer that made sense. But who?

I wasn't sure how much time had passed when the sound of footfalls echoed off the walls. A guard, maybe, coming to deliver food? I could use this. The moment the door opened, I'd have a glimmer of light. I would lunge at the guard, and use the reflection in his eye to jump away. Get back to London. Maybe try to find Nerius, see if he knew what was going on. Assuming he wasn't the one who'd betrayed us.

Just on the other side of the metal, the footsteps stopped, and the sound of a clicking lock echoed off the stone. I positioned myself against the wall, ready to pounce when the door opened.

"Wait," said a deep voice. "The torch."

"This an absolute bloody nuisance, you know that?" another grumbled.

"We have our orders."

A moment of silence, and then I heard one of them say, "I can hardly see the door now."

"Neither will she. That's the whole point. No light, no escape."

A cool draft chilled my skin as the door opened, but that was it. My stomach sank. *No light, no escape.*

"Food," a gruff voice said.

Something clinked against the floor, and I tried to gather the strength to lunge for one of the guards, but pain fragmented my chest. I could hardly stand. A few moments of blinding agony later, and the door shut, the lock clicking. With each footfall down the hall, a little more of my hope disappeared.

I blindly felt around the floor until my fingers brushed against a clay cup and a piece of dry bread. I drank the water in the cup, letting the final drops splash onto my tongue. I wasn't hungry enough to eat the bread, so I decided to save it for when hunger ate at my gut.

I closed my eyes, desperately searching for that warm flame. *Roan. Where are you?* Only a sharp, gnawing emptiness greeted me, and a wave of grief threatened to wash over me, but I couldn't fall apart now. If I wanted to survive this, I needed to keep a clear head. I let my mind ice over, glacially cold. *Think, Cassandra. Concentrate.*

My fingers tightened into fists. They hadn't killed me, which meant they needed me for something. At some point, they'd make a mistake, and time was on my side. At some point, anyone could get complacent. Putting out the torch and igniting it later in the pitch black is a hassle. Eventually, they might decide to leave it. All I needed was *one* reflection.

A disturbing squeaking sound pierced the silence, and it took me a moment to realize what it was. I grasped blindly for the bread, but it was already gone—stolen by a goddamned rat. I cursed, slumping back against the dank wall. Nothing to do but wait for the next meal.

For now, I needed to figure out who our traitor was. I breathed in, letting my mind roam back over everything I'd seen; the visions from the rock, the parchments. I thought over the events of the past days, taking apart each moment, looking at it from different angles.

Clarity comes in the strangest moments. Alone in the darkness, I suddenly knew why the missives we found in that safe felt so strangely familiar. Slowly, the seed of an idea took root, and a new theory began to bloom.

Branwen had never been the traitor. She had been framed.

CHAPTER 28

*B*y the time the guards showed up with food again,
I was starving enough to tear through the dry
bread immediately. Listening to them talk as they moved
past my door, I learned with a sinking sense of dread that
they'd found a way to manage the torch hassle. They just
didn't bring me food often, skipping my door every
other meal.

After eating, I spent what I thought was a few hours
sleeping on the rough, bumpy floor, and the time began
to pass in a disorienting blur of sleeping and staring
into the darkness. When I slept, I dreamed of food—
Branwen's meat pies, a vat of creamy macaroni and
cheese. After what I thought might have been a few
days, I began to dream of food when I was awake, too. I
could feel myself losing weight, my ribs jutting from
my body.

In the middle of a particularly delicious dream about
bacon double-cheeseburgers, the door swung open, and a
cool draft rushed over my skin. I woke with a start, and
wiped the drool off my chin.

I crawled on the floor toward the bread, my stomach rumbling.

As I groped in the dark, a boot slammed me in the side of the skull, sending me sprawling back, too weak to even cry out. Tears stung my eyes, but I stifled a cry. I wouldn't give them the satisfaction.

"Hello, Cassandra." A familiar, soothing voice echoed around the room, and my heart tightened. I'd been putting together the pieces, and this only confirmed it.

"How nice of you to visit," I said through gritted teeth. "I'd tell you to pull up a chair, but I don't have any."

I heard him crouch. "You reek like an animal. Worse than an animal."

"You're enjoying this, aren't you, Abellio?"

"You don't sound surprised that I'm here."

"I've had time to think," I rasped. I wanted to buy some time, gather my strength. I needed an opportunity. "You weren't as careful as you thought you were. Do you know what gave you away?"

"What?" he asked. His voice was flat, bored. Not good. I had to keep him interested.

"Those letters we found at the safe. There were strange details in them. The nettles near the secret path. They weren't there when I walked along the path."

He sighed. "It does sound strange."

"Right? And why would the traitor risk himself by meeting face to face every time? And why would he take the handler to the actual locations? So many unnecessary risks." I wondered if my body could move fast enough now that I'd spent a few days recovering.

"Why indeed?"

I sidled even closer. "Stinging nettles that didn't belong there. They symbolize pain. To someone who fears nature and wants to control it, they symbolize the wildness and cruelty of the natural world. The person writing these missives had inserted symbolic images into events. He also mentioned spontaneously flying. And meeting a person who looked different every time, but he *knew* who that person was. I've seen those things before."

"Really? Where?" He was now intrigued. Good.

"During my studies of psychology. These were dream journals, weren't they? You were meeting your handler in his dreams. Wearing different faces, flying with him across a dreamscape. Showing him what he needed to see."

"That's right." A hint of surprise tinged his voice. "How clever of you."

"On the first night I met you, you said you hardly slept at night. And yet, you went to sleep immediately on the night Branwen snuck out, and did the same on the night just before our attack. You had to sleep to meet your handler."

"Yes, Cassandra. Right on all counts. But as interesting as it is to hear you tell me things I already know—"

"And I figured out how you framed Branwen, too. She had asked you to help her with her nightmares, right? When you entered her dreams, you learned things. You found out she's in love with Elrine. I'd thought it was Roan. But it wasn't him at all, was it?"

"Yes," Abellio said. "A gutter fae in love with a noble. It would be sweet if it weren't so pathetic."

"You wrote Branwen a note, setting up a hidden rendezvous that night. You put some of Elrine's perfume on the envelope. And she burned that note so no one would know."

"I actually wrote her that she should burn it," Abellio said. "I didn't want to take any chances."

"And then you quickly went to sleep, arranging for a banshee to meet Branwen, framing her. I just don't understand why she didn't tell her interrogators about the letter. She could have cleared this up."

He loosed a long sigh. "Who, exactly, do you think interrogated her? I'm the fae lie detector. I shook my head sadly and regretfully at her tearful lies."

I gritted my teeth. "How did you know I'd follow her that night?"

"I hoped that *someone* would. It seemed like a good night for the spy to make his move, to contact the king with news of the upcoming battle and the war council."

"Right… Then why didn't the king just arrest Roan and the generals during the war council? Why go through that elaborate charade?"

"Because, you grotesque fortal whore, we didn't want to *stop* the rebellion," he sneered. "We wanted to *decimate* it. To crush the rebel army so completely and viciously that no one would ever rise against the king again."

A sharp pang of panic pierced my chest. *Roan.* What had happened to him? Was there any way he was still alive? I took a deep breath, trying not to give in to the fear. "Right." My body tensed. Was I close enough? I had one chance to do this. "Why are you here, Abellio?"

"To talk to my sister one last time."

Fear slammed me in the gut. "Your *what?*"

He laughed. An angry, venomous chuckle. "So clever, but you didn't figure *that* out?"

"You're the Rix's son?" I stammered. "That's why you betrayed us?"

"The Rix?" He huffed a dismissive laugh. "You honestly think you're the Rix's daughter? What gave you that idea?"

My mind reeled. If the Rix wasn't my father, who was?

"The changeling…" I stuttered, my mind reeling. "Whose daughter am I? What happened to my mother? I heard her screaming." My own voice sounded nearly hysterical.

"Sorry, Cassandra, you're babbling, and I'm bored. Goodbye, sister—"

I lunged for him, clawing at his face. He shrieked in pain, and I could feel a slick of blood under my nails.

Then he rammed his fist into my cheek, and I was knocked sprawling onto the floor. He took a step forward, and slammed me in the stomach with his foot, knocking the air from my lungs.

"You'll regret that, bitch," he snarled. "You'll beg for forgiveness when I'm done with you."

He walked out of the cell and slammed the door shut. I lay on the floor, fighting for breath, terrified to move. Tears ran down my cheeks. His words slithered in my brain, grasping for purchase. The patronizing way he spoke about the Rix. And yet, my twin changeling was in the Rix's home. Why? Was he told to take her in? A terrifying idea bloomed in my mind.

And my fingers tightened around Abellio's silver fountain pen.

* * *

IT WAS a few hours before I heard the boots outside my cell, and a lick of fear snaked up my spine. I'd attacked Abellio, and he'd promised pain in return.

My mind whirled with possibilities. Abellio's fountain pen, if it was the same one from before, could be used as a reflection. If they were careless, and opened the door with light, I'd disappear before they knew it. If I failed somehow or didn't have the energy, I'd lose my one pathetic chance to get out of here when they ripped it from my hand.

Swallowing hard, I decided to risk it. I crept closer to the door, wincing as the bruises from Abellio's kicks pulsed at the sudden movement. The footfalls stopped at the door, and the lock clicked. My heart thrummed in my chest.

"Lights," I heard Abellio warn.

Damn damn damn. I tossed the pen to the corner of the room, praying they'd never notice it.

The door swung open, and it sounded like the footfalls of several men shuffling in. Rough hands grabbed my hair and pulled me up. I scrambled to my feet, gritting my teeth to avoid screaming in pain. A fist sank into my stomach and I folded in two, winded and coughing. Before I could catch my breath, a cloth sack wrapped around my face, and someone tied it around my neck with a coarse rope. The sack smelled of sweat and blood. It had been used for this purpose before, and the smell made me gag. I tried to control my breathing. Throwing up in this thing wouldn't help.

Rough hands shoved me from my cell, then wrenched my hands behind my back, tying my wrists tightly. Then someone grabbed the rope around my neck and pulled. I stumbled forward.

"The mongrel's leash," said a voice. He gave it a sharp tug, and I fell to my knees.

Laughter echoed off the walls. Four voices—one of them Abellio's. Someone jerked the rope around my neck—the leash, as they'd called it—and I stumbled forward, stomach lurching.

Roan. Where are you? Please, Roan!

I walked as fast as I could, desperate to keep up. With my hands tied behind my back, every fall would be painful. Someone kicked me from behind and I slammed against the wall. More laughter, echoing in my skull. Fury was building in my chest, and I wanted to rip Abellio's fucking heart out, the way I'd seen Roan do when he fought.

They shoved me around for several minutes more until suddenly, we stopped.

"Close the door," Abellio said.

The sound of a slamming door echoed around the room, and a pair of hands pushed me down, onto a wooden chair. Someone grabbed my leg and I kicked at them, too weak to really fight.

Desperate, I searched for their fear, trying to recall Roan's instructions. Empty my mind. Find my true nature, my primal, bestial side. There was nothing.

Something slammed into the side of my face. The shock drove everything away but the pounding pain.

"I could do that all day," one of them said.

"Just standing here is intoxicating," another said, his voice thick.

They were getting high on my fear—Weala Broc fae. Just like me.

One of them slapped my right ear, and it began ringing. They laughed again, the laughter changing, verging on hysterics.

"Pull her head back," Abellio said.

Someone grabbed my head, pulled it backwards to face up.

"Drink up, my lovely sister," came Abellio's soothing voice.

A sudden shock of cold water engulfed me. He was pouring water on the sack that covered my face. I coughed and spluttered, then inhaled—

There was no air. The wet cloth had become clogged with water, and when I tried to breathe in, it clung to my mouth and nostrils. My throat spasmed, my body bucking and writing. *Air. Air.* Desperate for a single breath, my body convulsed. Another shock of water hit me as they poured more water on top of me.

Someone screamed, blubbered, begged. It was me. I was

trying to make them stop with the little air I had left, my self-control now lost to me.

Weala Broc—Court of Terror. Skulls under water, screams at the river bank. The Drowned Man.

The water stopped pouring, and I gasped for breath, the cloth latched to my face. My lungs burned, and the world was fading away, the laughter around me getting further...

Someone lifted the sack from my mouth, keeping it firmly still over my nose and eyes. I inhaled desperately, relieved. One breath. Two. Three.

The sack came down again. More water. I struggled, sobbing. No air. No air. *The Drowned Man. The Drowned Man is me.*

I didn't know how long they kept this up. It felt like hours, but it might have been only minutes. Pouring water, letting me suffocate, then giving me some desperate breaths before starting again, and again.

At last, when my mouth was free from the sack, I heard a vehement whisper in my ear. The deep, soothing voice of my brother. "Tell me you're sorry for scratching me."

"I'm sorry," I gasped. "I'm sorry I scratched you."

"Beg for my forgiveness."

No. There was no way I would... When I got free I would deliver him a painful death.

I felt the wet cloth lowering to my face again, and my legs kicked out uncontrollably.

"Please forgive me!" I shouted.

The laughter of four men echoed over the room.

"Look at how her clothes cling to her," one said, his gravelly voice so rough, it sounded like stones rubbing together. "We could take her. Now. We could take turns."

The laughter stopped almost instantly, and a dark silence fell over the room.

"In the king's keep?" one of them finally said—Abellio, I thought. "Do you have a death wish?"

There was a small forced chuckle, thick with fear. "I was kidding, of course. I wouldn't touch her pixie body. Not even... never. I would never do that."

The seconds ticked. I breathed in and out. I'd kill him. I'd fucking kill him, take his life from him slowly and painfully.

Roan. Are you there?

"Take her back to her cell," Abellio finally said, the mirth gone. "I got what I wanted from her."

They didn't untie my hands when they pushed me into my cell. They ripped the hood off me, then shoved me. I crashed into the floor, slamming my head. The world faded.

CHAPTER 29

J don't know how long it took me to wriggle free from the ropes, but it was long enough that I'd fallen asleep twice, and the guards had brought me bread twice. I'd crouched over it, gnawing away at it, with my hands tied behind my back. I no longer cared how I smelled or looked. Right now, my only goal was survival. If I could survive, I could still get revenge. I could still try to save Roan, just as long as...

I pushed the dark thoughts away. I couldn't consider the possibility that he'd died. I needed to cling on to the belief that he was alive.

As the hours dragged on, I used Abellio's fountain pen to slowly pry away at the knot, my shoulders aching. At last, I loosened it enough that I could tear my arms free, scraping a large swath of skin against the rough rope. My body was in bad shape—battered and exhausted, and without access to human fear, I healed very slowly.

Time began to blur. In constant darkness, I had no idea how long I've been in that cell. I tried keeping track of the number of times I fell asleep, but eventually I lost count, my mind fuzzy and confused from hunger and weakness. Some-times, before I fell asleep, my body burned with fever, my skin cold to the touch, and I lay on the floor shaking, trying to feel Roan's presence. The fever broke, but the isolation remained. I couldn't feel him.

As time drifted on, people began visiting me. It started with Scarlett. For a while, the conversation was fun and light, and we talked about that time she'd accidentally sexted her professor, but the mood quickly shifted. She started lecturing me about my decision to stay in London—of course it wasn't going to turn out well! What had I been thinking?

Before I knew what was happening, I found myself yelling at her, tears spilling down my cheeks. Then, she'd disappeared into the darkness again, like a wraith.

Then Gabriel showed up, his neck bleeding, eyes wide. I begged for his forgiveness, but he said nothing. The visit from my parents unsettled me the most. They merely stared at me as I cried, silently judging me. Roan showed up, wounded, shackled, bleeding, his eyes burning gold, antlers gleaming on his head. I talked for both of us, rambling on about the flame in my chest, how I needed to feel it alight again, how I needed to smell his skin, to feel his heart beating beneath my palm. I told him we belonged together, that I wanted to entwine my body with his, like the roots of two adjacent willow trees. He didn't respond.

When all my visitors had left me in the shadows, I had nothing left but the fountain pen. Slowly, I dug into the stone wall, scraping it with the pen. I'd found a small hole in the sludgy grouting, and managed to widen it by twisting the pen in it, and then scratching it over and over and over, my fingers raw and sore between the cinder blocks. After a while, I made a small dent into the grouting, half an inch deep, wide enough to stick my finger into. In a few months, I'd dig a deep enough tunnel for my finger to escape through.

I laughed at that idea hysterically, tears pouring down my cheeks, then laughed some more. When Scarlett showed up for a visit, I told her my hilarious joke about the escape of my finger, and we both laughed.

Food was scarce, but I found a good way to improve my situation.

Whenever I got a piece of bread, I'd put some of it on the floor and wait, motionless. Sometimes, Gabriel would start to speak, to offer me something better to eat, but I always shushed him. It was important to be as still as a rock. When the rat showed up, I'd grab it and smash it against the wall. Then, I had a little meat to add to my diet. Sometimes, I used rat bones to dig my tunnels, but they broke too easily. The fountain pen was better for that.

My dreams tormented me. Not because they were nightmares, but because I dreamed I was free again, that Gabriel was still alive, and we were walking in the sun-dappled gardens of Temple Church, sipping lattes. Or I'd dream that I was lying in Roan's arms beneath a willow tree, enveloped in his golden glow. When I woke again, the horror of reality assaulted me anew, and I'd remember where I was. I'd sob for hours, until Gabriel or Scarlett came to cheer me up. When Roan showed up, he never cheered me up. He'd just bleed on the floor.

Scrape scrape scrape. The pen scraped at the wall, my finger going in almost to the knuckle. When my fingers finally escaped, they would go find Abellio and poke him repeatedly. That would be my revenge. I laughed. Scarlett laughed.

Then the tears poured down my cheeks again, and I couldn't remember why.

* * *

ONE OF MY visitors used the door, which was strange,

because usually only the guards used the door. I hid the pen, like I always did when the door opened. There were rules in the cell. If the door opened, you hid the pen. Bread brought rats, and to catch them you had to be quiet. You peed in the hole in the corner, because otherwise it got messy. Life here was simple.

The figure knelt in the darkness, and I had the impression of a broad outline.

"Hello." My voice sounded dry and hoarse, but I wanted to be friendly. I liked the company.

"Hello, Cassandra." The sharpness in his voice made my mouth go dry. Sharp like my fountain pen. It sounded slightly muffled, too, and it took me a moment to realize he was probably covering his nose because of the smell in here. I couldn't smell a thing anymore, but the guards always mentioned it.

I considered offering my guest some rat meat, but thought better of it. "Who're you?"

"My name is Ogmios."

"Oh." The name sharpened my dull mind. Ogmios. The king. The enemy. "What do you want?" I slunk back against the wall.

"To see you."

I cleared my throat. "Well, it's a bit difficult here. It's dark, and several of my visitors have been dead. But if you light a torch, you'll be able to see me."

"Already broken?" he asked, almost to himself. "After just two months?"

Two months. I grabbed that tidbit with all the strength I had. Knowing how long I had been there sharpened my mind further. It was like seeing the horizon after floating in a void, a thin line in the distance to orient myself.

"Are you here to kill me?" I asked hollowly. "To execute me for my crimes?"

"Perhaps. I haven't decided yet. It's certainly a... temptation."

There was something there. The way he said it. The old Cassandra would have been able to make sense of it, but this Cassandra had become engulfed in shadows.

"I'm dangerous," I hissed from my corner. "The Mistress of Dread. That's me. I'm a threat to your life."

He let out a thin laugh that chilled my blood—a bitter, mirthless chuckle. "I doubt you're a risk to anyone at the moment. And to kill you now would be too soon. I want your death to have an impact."

It was time to prod the beast. "Tell me, King," I croaked. "Am I your greatest shame?"

"Silence!" He roared.

Bingo.

"Who was she?" I asked. "My mother? I heard her screams, trapped in the Stone. How did you know her? Did she seduce you?"

His fist slammed into the side of my skull. The blow dizzied me, and my mind whirled. *The bloodline of dread.* And I, its heir.

"Mad mongrel," the king said in disgust. "I intend to finish with you soon. A public execution for both of you will quash any remnants of opposition."

Both of you. Both of you. Both of you. My heart sped up, pulse racing as a spark of hope ignited in my chest.

Roan was alive.

I shut my eyes, replacing darkness with darkness. Hope kindled in my heart like a candle flame, and the king shifted.

"I can feel it, you know," he snapped, fury lacing his voice. "Your emotions leak from you like water from a broken vase. Disgusting abomination. A terrible mistake. Let me tell you where your whore-lover is. There is another cell, much like this one. And he sits there in the darkness, shackled in iron to the wall, surrounded by iron. And I promise you this. Whatever horrors you think you are suffering, his have been worse."

I let my mind ice over, refusing to give in to the rage.

The king let out a small breath.

I shook, trying to contain myself. And yet, the presence of the old Cassandra simmered under the surface of my mind, whispering, still in control. Telling me what I needed to know.

She told me that women terrified this fae. *Why?* To men like him, women are the cruelty of nature, wild creatures in need of taming. I'd seen it in his mind—the apple orchard, a fruit hanging from a bough, red and tempting until the skin blackened and rotted before my eyes. He feared his own desires, wouldn't let himself enjoy too much. Enjoyment meant a lack of control, submitting to base desires, giving in to the beast. He didn't just hate women. He hated himself.

Right now, he enjoyed his control over a female pixie, but enjoyment meant the need for restraint. Too much pleasure meant he'd lose the leash on himself, indulge in pleasure. And nothing would shame him more.

Let's see what happened when he felt a real thrill... I flooded my mind with images of Abellio torturing me, of Roan bleeding as they raked him with iron blades. Of both of us burning to death before a crowd of fae. I had been standing on the brink of insanity for too long, and the terror nearly swept me away, but I clung fiercely. And the king let out an exhilarated sigh of pleasure, nearly a moan.

And then I instantly took control of my thoughts, letting the ice encase my emotions, a glacial river. Icy mastery over myself. And I smiled in the darkness. I was in control.

"Enjoying yourself, *Your Majesty*? Did I take away your pleasure?"

He snarled, lunging for me, grabbing my throat and

pressing tight until he regained his composure. Pushing me away in disgust, he stood up abruptly. I had an instant of satisfaction when he forgot how low the ceiling was, smacking his head on the stone. Then he left, slamming the door behind him.

My finger traced my neck as I smiled faintly. The king had given me my control back.

* * *

SPURRED on by the knowledge that Roan was alive, that I could still find him, I spent every waking moment scraping at the hole in the wall. I didn't know how long this bubble of clarity would last, but I had to take advantage of it. The fountain pen was wearing away. When, one day, I felt a sudden crack, my heart skipped a beat. I'd finally broken it, destroying what little hope I had left. I pulled it back and felt the tip.

It wasn't broken.

I stuck it through the wall and felt around. Nothing blocked it. I had drilled a deep hole through the wall.

I set to widening it, twisting the pen inside the wall over and over. The wider the better. I needed it as wide as possible for my plan to work. And I needed it *fast*. For all I knew, maybe the guards would notice the hole I'd made from the other side. They'd transfer me to a different cell, and I'd have to start again.

I couldn't let that happen.

Scrape scrape. Dust fell from the wall as the hole widened. *Scrape scrape scrape.* Darkness in my cell, and darkness outside it. But beyond this hole was a hallway. And that meant hope. *Scrape scrape.*

And then I heard it. Footsteps. The guards coming. And

for the first time in more than two months, I saw something nearly impossible.

A glimmer of light, far away, but still dazzling to my eyes. I nearly shrieked with excitement.

The torch flames cast a warm glow over the hall, faint so far away, but still brilliant as the sun. Colors delighted my eyes—sweet, heavenly light. The walls were cast in a pink-orange hue that danced along the stone.

Light meant reflection. Light meant escape.

A grin curled my lips, and I quickly raised the silver pen to the hole, letting the soft torchlight reflect on it.

And my heart constricted.

All the sheen had been scraped off the pen. Days—weeks?—of using it to scrape the walls had dulled and dented it, leaving only a dark, misshapen rod. I wanted to weep, my mind on the verge of snapping completely.

"Let's skip her cell today," one of the guards said. "I want to get home. My wife has been poorly."

"We skipped it yesterday," the other guard reminded him. "We don't want her to starve."

"Fine," the first one muttered.

The light from the peephole instantly vanished as they extinguished the torches. I stared at the useless hole in disbelief. The door opened, and I heard the scrape of the clay cup on the floor. Then the door closed.

After a moment, the orange light of the torches penetrated the hole again. It began to move further away.

"How old is your wife?"

"One hundred and thirteen."

"Cradle robber!"

The light began to fade. Suddenly panicking, I rushed to the cup, lifting it, seeing the outline of its shape for the first time. It was made of rough clay. No reflection.

I tipped the water toward the hole, tilting it just enough,

my hands shaking with desperation. Precious drops spilled on the floor. *Come on... come on...*

A glimmer of orange light flashed over the dark surface of the water, and I felt what I hadn't felt for months—a reflection bonding with my mind. I searched for another reflection, and leapt.

CHAPTER 30

I moved slowly, trapped between reflections.

Another reflection glimmered faintly. Far? Near? Distance had no meaning here. It was... away. And I was moving closer to it, but it felt slow. Too slow.

Confusion swirled in my mind, but I could still vaguely grasp what was going on. Kept away from human emotions for two months, my magic had dried up like rat bones in the sun. What should have been an effortless jump took my last drops of power, and I wasn't sure I could push on.

The world between reflections stretched out infinitely in all directions, horizonless and empty. I tried to clear my mind. It couldn't be that I'd broken free from my cell only to end up trapped here, alone for eternity.

No. Not alone. Something flickered in the distance.

A furious face, eyes bright with rage. She was coming for me. She knew this world much better than I did, knew how to move in it. All I could do was float, watching helplessly as Siofra came closer, a menacing smile on her lips.

Frantic, I reached out of the other reflection, and Siofra tried to grab for me as I leapt, her fingers brushing against my ankle, but I was already gone, the clean reflection washing over my skin as I fell—into another cell.

I crawled from a pool of rainwater beneath a small, square, barred window. Sunlight shone through it, and I covered my eyes, the light too bright.

"Cassandra?" A rough whisper.

I rolled away from the window and opened my eyes into tiny slits, my clothing damp.

Roan sat on the floor before me. He was the first one I had thought about when jumping, and I'd searched for him immediately. Thanks to the reflection in the puddle, I'd found him.

He was shackled to a wall, naked. Red wounds slashed across his body, blood seeping from his skin. He still looked beautiful, but his cheekbones were sharper, his skin paler. He squinted at me, his green eyes perplexed. I knew what was happening. He thought he was hallucinating, just like I had. I tried not to gape at the blood crusted over his body.

"Roan!" I crawled to him. "What have they done to you?"

His eyes cleared, as the realization hit him that I was real. "*Me?* What have they done to you?"

I stared at him, then at myself. Scraps of fetid rags hung over my body. The puddle water formed a sludge over the caked dirt and blood on my body, hardly an inch of skin visible through the grime. I couldn't smell myself, but I knew I'd been living among dead rats and filth. My elbows and knees protruded from holes in my clothes.

"Abellio." I couldn't get the rest of the sentence out, couldn't form a coherent thought.

"I know." Sadness gleamed in Roan's eyes. "He's been paying me visits."

I took a deep breath, my eyes burning in the light. "I think he might be the king's son," I blurted. "I'm not sure, but I think he could be." I couldn't bring myself to tell him the rest.

261

That I could be the king's daughter, too. Not just a terror leech. The daughter of the man who'd killed his family, who'd taken everything from him. Devourer of fear, eater of rats—heir of the bloodline of dread.

Roan's eyes widened. "The king has no heirs."

"He could be a secret bastard." *And I might be, too.* "Forget it. It doesn't matter." My eyes lingered over Roan. He looked like a dream, so beautiful I could hardly believe he was real. Maybe it was the fact that he was naked, or the rainwater he'd had by his side—or just a perk of being a lust fae—but Roan still looked and smelled amazing.

Roan's expression suddenly cleared, his green eyes keenly alert as though he'd just woken from a dream. "You have to get out of here." His eyes widened, flashing with panic. "I thought you'd left. I saw you running with the others, and when I couldn't feel you any more..." His voice grew guttural, ragged with desperation. "When I couldn't feel you, I had to believe you'd escaped. I thought you were in London."

I shook my head. "I saw you running for them. You were alone. I couldn't leave you."

He stared at me, his eyes shining, hungry. I thought I saw pain flickering there, and he reached for me, but the chains stopped his movement. He broke my gaze, staring again at his shackles as if awaking from a dream. "You have to go, Cassandra," he said sharply. "They come for me every day at this time. They interrogate me, whenever the shadows grow long like this. They'll be here any minute."

Every day at this time. I'd been tortured only once, and it had snapped my mind. They were coming for him every day. Too much. Too much to process. I curled into the corner, shaking.

"Cassandra, what are you doing? Get up!"

"In a minute." My breath came in short, sharp breaths,

and I tried to calm myself. That overwhelming need to protect him tugged at me again, rooting me in place.

"If they find you here… Please leave! This is your chance, Cassandra. This is your one chance."

I squinted in the light, struggling against the sensory overload. "Leave? Where to?"

"Anywhere! Out of here!"

"I can't do that," I said slowly. "I don't have any power left."

He paled. "You have to try. You should never have stayed for me, Cassandra."

I shook my head. "If I get stuck between worlds, we're both screwed."

"You must try! You should never have returned for me. You should have left London long ago. You belong in the human world. It's not safe for you among the fae."

"Okay, stop arguing!" I held up a hand. "Let's get out together. First, why are you chained to the wall?"

He blinked. "I am a prisoner. Do you remember what happened?" He spoke slowly, as if to a child.

"Of course I do." I looked at the shackles closely. "I mean… can't you rip through them? You're stronger than any living being I've ever seen."

He raised his wrists, showing me the raw skin, the ravaged wounds where the iron had bit into him. "You think I haven't been trying?"

I wasn't letting this go. "You're Roan Taranis, Lord of the Court of Lust. I've seen you tear a man's heart from his chest more than once. You can rip the shackles from the wall." I was excited, the sunlight and the physical contact with another person making me giddy.

"These shackles are made of iron, Cassandra. They've been weakening me, poisoning my blood."

"Maybe I can help." I tried to piece together my thoughts,

but they were swirling in my brain like panicked rats. No! Not like rats! Like... something else. There was more to life than rats, and I just needed to remember.

"If you can't leave through the reflection, you should wait by the door," Roan said. "They won't be expecting you. Just get the one with the keys, and throw them to me."

"It would be easier if we fought them together," I reasoned.

His eyes were pleading with me. "Cassandra—"

"Shut up for a second."

I stared at him. He drew strength from human lust, and he'd been starved down here with no human contact, just like I'd been. All he needed was a bit of strength. The Roan Taranis I knew wouldn't let shackles hold him down—iron or not.

I closed my eyes, moving just close enough to breathe in his scent—the moss and oaks. I thought of us sitting out in the rain on that stone bench. His hand moving slowly up my leg, his sensual kiss warming me, his tongue gently sweeping in. I envisioned the raw desire that had claimed my body. The feel of his fingers stroking me, caressing me. Warmth rippled over my skin, and when I opened my eyes, I saw the spark in his green eyes.

I couldn't go near him—I knew I smelled too bad, looked too repulsive. But if I thought of him clearly enough, he could feed from my lust from here.

Closing my eyes again, I envisioned myself clean, wearing a white dress and my favorite cherry-colored lip gloss, my hair spilling over my shoulders. In my mind's eye, this Cassandra—the other Cassandra—crossed to him, tracing a finger over his body, the physical contact blazing over her skin like electricity. She was hungry for him. Her fingers ran down his powerful chest, lower over his stomach, and he sucked in a breath.

Clean Cassandra breathed huskily, shivering with excitement, letting her clean hair fall over his shoulders. She lifted her dress, wrapping her legs around him. She was in control. With him shackled, she could do anything she wanted to him. She could lick his neck... taste the salt on his body, the hint of rainwater. She could run her fingertips over his abdomen, tracing lower until he gasped, kiss his neck until he moaned. She could writhe against him, grinding her hips into him, until ecstasy glistened over her skin...

A *crack* echoed across the room, a low growl rumbling in his throat. My eyes snapped open—Roan had torn one of his hands free, his body glowing with golden light. It was working. I closed my eyes again, just beginning to envision his mouth kissing the inside of Clean Cassandra's legs, his warm lips moving higher and higher to the apex of her thighs, when—another *snap*. Free from the wall, he moved for me, eyes burning with lust, horns appearing on his head. Instantly, the flame in my chest ignited, blazing hot.

But I scuttled back. I was the wrong Cassandra. I was the one covered in filth.

Confusion flickered across his features, but the clicking of the door interrupted us, and my heart skipped a beat. *No.*

The cell door swung open, and two guardsmen stood in the doorway, staring.

Then I realized they didn't stand a chance, not with Roan freed from his tethers, imbued with the power of my lust.

He was on them like a flash, impaling the first one with his horns. Blood sprayed over the room, and in blur of golden light, Roan was already lunging for the other guard, grabbing him by the throat. He twisted the man's neck, snapping it like a twig. He shook the now limp body in rage, and then smashed it to the floor. Then he turned to me, his eyes flickering gold, blood streaking his features. From the floor, I stared up at him.

"Let's go," he growled, holding out a hand to me.

"Okay," I said in a throaty whisper. "Is it okay if I lean on you? I'm not feeling myself."

He leaned down, helping me up. "I think that would be fine."

* * *

TAKING the keys from one of the guards, Roan unlocked the iron shackles from his wrists. It took only a minute for Roan to strip one of the guards and pull the man's clothing over his own naked body. The uniform was about half the size it needed to be, but Roan managed to squeeze his body into it with only a few tears in the fabric. Moreover, he now had a sword.

Already, with the lust I'd thrown his way, his wrists were beginning to heal and the wounds in his chest were closing over. As soon as he pulled the iron from his wrists, he stood taller.

Every time I looked at him, I was struck by his beauty, the uniform sculpted to his body. Despite my fatigue and the filth covering my skin, I couldn't stop staring at him, envisioning how his lips had felt against mine. And there it was— the twin souls, horror and lust. So close to death, my body craved life. And Roan was life.

As we walked down the torchlit hallway, I glanced at his muscled form, and I knew he was feeding from my body's reaction to him. I could feel the magical bond between us, dampened for so long, starting to thrum with power. It gave me just enough strength to move, leaning into him as I walked.

As he propped me up, we walked past dozens of locked cell doors, finally reaching a stairway. I stared up at the door at the top of the stairs.

"The dungeons' only entrance is through the guardroom," Roan said. "There will be king's guards waiting up there."

"How many?" I asked.

He shook his head, body glowing with amber. "It doesn't matter. They'll all die."

Quietly, we began climbing the stairs, and the sound of voices filtered through the door. A cold lick of fear snaked up my spine, my mind burning with the memory of my cell, the isolation so sharp it pierced my bones. My stomach tightened. I couldn't go back there, to the damp and the rats, the dulling pen.

My body shook, and I froze, squeezing his arm. "I can't," I whispered.

Roan pulled me closer. "You don't have to do anything. Just wait behind me."

My heart slammed against my ribs. What would Abellio do to me this time once he learned I tried to escape?

Gently, Roan stroked my arm. "They'll start wondering about the two men I killed in a few minutes. It has to be now. It will be okay. Trust me."

I nodded mutely, and we climbed a few more stairs. Laughter carried into the stairwell from the other side of the door. The sound sank into my heart, and my mind raced, memories flooding my mind.

The four fae laughing around me as I struggled to breathe, a sack on my head.

I let out a gasp, frozen, paralyzed.

We could take her. Now. We could take turns.

I clenched my teeth, tears in my eyes, a bitter taste in my mouth.

Tell me you're sorry for scratching me. Beg for my forgiveness.

My body tensed up, and I realized my nails were digging into Roan's arm. But something changed, my fear now driven out by pure, icy rage.

My fight or flight response resolved in a sudden, enraged, *Fight*.

I burst through the door, finding eight of them around a card table, and they all froze as the door opened. A ginger guard reached for the sword when time slowed to a trickle.

Their fae fear unfolded before me, the tendrils of dark dread that flowed around the room like strands of silk in the wind.

White hot fury erupted in my mind. They'd tried to break me. They'd tried to break Roan. *No one touches my man.* I'd make them wish they'd never been born. I latched onto the threads, feeding on them, letting the power thrum through my body. Fae fear, human fear—it didn't really matter. Not to me. I was the Mistress of Dread, and I'd come right out of their worst nightmares.

Energy pulsing in me, I summoned all the fear in the room, drawing it into me, growing stronger. As a dark smile curled my lips, I transformed their fear into terror. Then, with a sharp arch of my back, I flung out my arms, slamming it back at them in streams of dark magic.

Eyes widened, fear exploding all over the room. I had paralyzed them with dread, and now I would rip their fucking hearts from their bodies.

Roan gripped my arm, fixing me with a hard gaze. His sword was already drawn, his hand shaking. In a golden blur, he rushed past me, his sword cutting into one fae after another. He grabbed a winged guard by the throat, slamming his head over and over into the wall until the man's skull shattered.

As time accelerated, chaos erupted around me, a cacophony of roars and smashes, panicked screams. And one of them was a voice I recognized, a voice that would forever remain seared into the darkest parts of my brain.

The one with the gravelly voice. The one who'd said, "We could take turns."

He crawled over the floor, scrambling for his sword and screaming, his voice tinged with hysteria. As he reached for the sword, I stepped down hard on his wrist, questing for his fear.

It was there, pulsing and strong. I drew it from him, the strands of terror that sang in my blood. Then I flung it back at him, his screams of horror a music to my ears. I flooded away his sanity with his worst nightmares. His eyes rolled back, and he slumped on the floor, pants stained with urine. Over and over, I lashed him with his fears, until his mouth simply opened in a silent scream. A mind dismantled, completely destroyed by dread.

My body shaking, I stepped back, heart hammering like a war drum. He gibbered incoherently on the floor, shivering. He would never recover.

I swiveled and looked at Roan, rage quaking my body. "I want Abellio!"

"Not now." Roan's eyes glinted with cold fire.

"Now!"

Real fear sparked in Roan's eyes, but he was trying to master it. I'd struck him in the crossfire with my dread powers. "No. Get yourself under control, Cassandra."

Slowing my breath, I surveyed the stone room. It looked like it had been hit by a hurricane of death.

"Now what?" I asked.

"Now we get the hell out of here."

Before heading for the door, I scrambled over to one of the prone guards and pulled a ring of keys from his unconscious body.

CHAPTER 31

*O*utside the room, I jammed a key into the keyhole, locking the door behind us. I had no idea how much time we had until someone raised the alarm, but Roan had been right. We needed to move fast, and I'd just have to slaughter my darling brother later. I couldn't handle the thought of being caught again, of being locked back in the dark cell, with the rats and the filth. Of my own mind betraying me.

As my pulse raced, I scanned the dark stone hall, searching for signs of movement, but I saw only the wavering of torchlight, dancing shadows over the flagstones.

I took a step forward, and Roan caught my arm. "Wait. I need to glamour you."

I looked down at myself, newly repulsed by my appearance—the bony elbows protruding from my threadbare clothes, the layers of filth coating my clothes, my skin. *I'd rather die than go back there.* I tried to master my fear, nodding. "Right. Go ahead."

Roan touched my cheek, and I flinched. Didn't he know how *wrong* I'd become?

"Cassandra," he said quietly.

"Just go ahead. Glamour me."

His magic whispered over my skin, gentle strokes of tingling power, like a soft embrace. When I looked down at myself again, I saw the body of a guard, dressed in leather. He'd even given me a trim, ginger beard. *Better than I looked before.*

We took off, moving quietly through one hall after another—some darkened tunnels, some sunlit corridors with brightly embroidered tapestries lining the walls. As we moved through the fortress, my heart constricted, certain that at any moment the alarms would sound, and an army of guards would descend on us. If Abellio found out that I'd escaped, if he captured me again...

I tried to let my mind ice over, to cover the thoughts in ice. At least Roan seemed to know the way, and I simply kept up my pace with him.

And yet, even as my heart slammed against my ribs, no alarms sounded. The king's fortress was designed to keep people out—not to keep anyone in. Its primary function had never been to serve as a prison. Once Roan glamoured the both of us as guards, no one looked twice at us. To anyone passing us, they'd simply see an enormous blond guard and his ginger-haired pal.

Somehow, that knowledge didn't stop the rampant memories searing my brain—the feel of rat bones against my fingers, the muffled voices outside the putrid bag on my head.

As we strode through the castle, the real issue turned out to be my pixie emotions.

"I am not powerful enough to mask your feelings," Roan said through gritted teeth. We crossed into a white stone hall, the sunlight blazing from high, arched windows. "Get your feelings under control!"

I couldn't control anything. The sunlight seemed blinding, completely overwhelming. One minute I felt exalted at the light and color; the next, it seemed to pierce my skull, my brain dulled by months of sensory deprivation.

Worse, I couldn't seem to dull my fear. If we were caught, I'd be sent back to my cell, and Abellio would bring down his psychopathic torture gang. As soon as I thought of my half-brother, another emotion threatened to drown me: rage.

My ability to ice over my mind had been completely destroyed in that dank, black hole. My filters no longer worked, and the neurons in my amygdala blazed at full capacity.

I tried to move faster. *I can't let Abellio get his hands on me again. I can't let them get Roan again.*

"Where are we going?" I whispered to Roan.

"The main gate, through the courtyard," he said under his breath.

Of course. Apart from the river under the castle, it was the only way out of the fortress. As we pushed through an oak door into the cobbled, sun-drenched courtyard, fear stole my breath. Blinding light gleamed off the stone walls surrounding us, piercing my eyes into my brain. This close to escape, I felt like something awful would happen at any moment, that I'd be back in the black hole, losing my mind...

I slowed my breathing, trying to master my fear as my eyes adjusted to the light outside. *Focus, Cassandra.*

At the far side of the courtyard, six guards flanked the arched gateway, each of them gripping spears. Two archers stood on the stony walls, arrows ready to shoot anyone acting suspiciously. Through the open gate, a steady stream of fae moved in and out. With the glamour shielding us, we could blend in—as long as my emotions didn't betray me. *Don't think about the black hole. Don't think about the darkness, the rats, the man with the gravelly voice.*

I stared at the cobblestones, concentrating on the droplets of rain that shimmered over the stones. It must have rained recently, before the blazing sun had come out. *Think of nothing but stones and rain.* Gray, boring stones. Stones beneath my fingers, the wearing down of the pen, a creature scurrying over the floor...

Thud, thud, thud.

The sound of my own heart deafened me. Surely all the fae noticed it thundering over the courtyard, echoing off the cobblestones?

I took a tentative step, trying to act normal. *Just focus on what you see, Cassandra. A quantitative analysis.*

I scanned the fae milling in the courtyard. *Three traders, a mother with her three children, so that's a total of seven. Seven times seven is forty-nine. Forty-nine times seven... three hundred and something... add to that six guards and two archers who could catch us...*

Just as I took another step, slowing my breathing, the sound of alarm bells pealed over the courtyard, echoing off the stones, off the interior of my skull.

I sucked in a sharp breath, dread climbing up my throat. *We were so close.*

The guards shifted their stances, forming a barrier in front of the gate, their pikes ready to impale anyone who stepped out of line. One of them slowly turned his face to look at me, and I could instantly tell that he felt my pixie fear, even with Roan trying to mask it. He had a rat-like appearance, with a long-thin face. "Nobody move!"

Rage began simmering in my blood. I knew that voice.

Drink up, bitch.

The man next to him shifted his stance. "Go get the captain. I think we have escaped prisoners here."

Him, too. I knew that voice, too.

The mongrel's leash. I could do that all day.

Molten lava erupted in my skull, burning away all other thoughts. But as we were trapped in here, maybe I could use my rage.

"Cassandra…" said Roan.

Slowly, they all began to aim their pikes on me.

"I've got this," I whispered.

Around us, the crowds began to point and stare. My fury was attracting attention. It didn't matter. I had the guards right where I wanted them now, and I wanted them to feel the terror I'd felt.

Time crawled slowly, thin tendrils of fear creeping closer through the air like silk from a spider's web. Not much fear —yet. But it was enough. I took it. I arched my back, letting it flow into me. And when I'd pulled the fear into my chest, I churned their unease into foreboding, then simmered it into fear. At last, I turned up the heat, boiling it into full blown terror.

I spread my arms, flinging the terror at the guards, the men who'd tortured me, mocked me, and humiliated me. I brought them to their knees, eyes wide. The guard to my right clutched his heart, sliding to the ground, eyes wide, dead. A heart attack. The others fell to their knees, blubbering, whimpering. One of the archers on the wall fainted and toppled down. People around us screamed and shouted.

"Now," said Roan.

With the guards incapacitated, we ran for the gate, my body still slowed by weakness. My muscles struggled as I tried to hurry, stumbling closer to the guards. Roan had drawn his sword, and from the corner of my eye, I caught the arc of blood, the flash of steel. He'd cut down the two guards blocking our path, and we pushed through the gate, my body aching.

Our feet pounded over the grass in a frantic attempt to escape. Ten feet from the gate, I heard the unmistakable twang of a bow string releasing. It went wide and missed us by inches, clanking on the ground. The wind picked up, shrieking around us. On the horizon, storm clouds darkened the sky, roiling like oil in a cauldron.

Roan ran behind me—probably trying to make sure I didn't fall behind. Was he shielding me? Each footstep sent a sharp ache racing up my bones. I was slowing him down. I might be glamoured like a guard, but it was my own weakened body underneath the illusion.

More arrows rained around us, but the wind knocked them off their trajectory, shifting them to the right.

My breath grew ragged in my lungs, and I breathed in the dirt whirling through the air in the impending storm. Roan shifted from behind me. Now the wind gusted at my back, driving me onward with powerful gusts. My speed increased.

As we ran for the tree line, a hundred years away, lighting cracked the sky, touching down in the nearby forest. A few fat drops of rain fell from the clouds, and thunder rumbled the drops nearly horizontal as the wind blew them. But underneath the thunder was another sound—one like hooves pounding the earth.

"Horses!" I gasped, trying to shout above the gale. "They're chasing us!"

Adrenaline ignited. *They'll take you back, to the black hole and the rats, the fetid sack over your head, the mongrel leash.*

The storm clouds unleashed a heavy rain, and cold droplets hammered against my skin.

A powerful gust knocked me over, and I fell to my knees. As I scrambled to my feet, Roan scooped me up in his powerful arms. As soon as he did, the glamour faded from my body, and I looked like Cassandra again—Cassandra the filthy, the bony, eater of rats.

Roan broke into a sprint, clutching me tight to his chest.

"You'll never outrun them like that!" I yelled. "Leave me here! Get out of here on your own!"

"I'm just getting away from the fortress. I don't want to hurt any innocent fae."

What the hell is he talking about?

The storm whipped at his hair—long now, and pale blond, snaking around his head in the wind. A flash of lightning gleamed off his antlers, his pointed ears. At that moment, as I stared up at him from his powerful arms, he looked like a vengeful storm god, about to cast his wrath around him. Roan Taranis, storm-kissed.

My teeth chattered as his speedy gait jostled my body. So close now, nearly at the forest line.

I craned my neck, peering over his shoulder. An icy tendril of fear coiled through me. Nine horsemen thundered toward us, a few hundred yards away, their enormous horses kicking up dirt and grass.

"They're here," I whispered.

Roan whirled, then gently lowered me to the wet grass. "No matter what, don't move, Cassandra!"

He widened his stance, pulling his sword from his scabbard as the cavalry raced toward us, a hundred yards away now. Lighting ignited the sky, touching down just in front of the horsemen. Two horses reared on their hind legs, throwing off their riders. The panicked horses bolted.

Lighting struck again, searing the earth just by the horsemen.

I suddenly realized that I could hardly feel the wind, though all around us branches, dirt and rocks spun into the air, hitting the riders and their frightened horses. We were standing exactly in the eye of the storm.

Was this why Roan had told me not to move?

A powerful bolt struck a horseman, and he and his mount tumbled to the ground, the air filling with the scent of burning flesh. The thunderclap that followed boomed in my eardrums, and I clamped my hands over my ears.

All around us, lighting struck again and again, the world a chaotic maelstrom of fire and rain, until, at last, no riders remained

Slowly, the storm around us abated, the wind dying down.

Roan fell to his knees, spent.

I knelt down, pulling at his arm. "We need to go."

"Give me a moment, Cass. I need to rest," he mumbled.

He had never called me Cass. No one did, except for Scarlett.

"Look!" I pointed. Twenty yards from us stood a riderless horse. "We can use that."

That made Roan rise to his feet, moving toward the horse as I followed close behind. The black horse didn't budge, eyeing Roan warily.

When we reached it, Roan carefully grabbed for its harness, uttering soothing words in a language I didn't understand. When the horse's breathing had slowed, Roan turned and reached for me, lifting me onto the horse.

In the next moment, he was behind me, his arms encircling me, body warming mine.

He nudged the horse, pulling on the reins, and we took off at a gallop toward a winding forest path.

As the horse's hooves hammered the earth and the wind whipped at my hair on our way to the Trinovantum portal, for the first time, I embraced the hope that I was truly free.

* * *

I'D NEVER REALIZED I could miss the din and chaos of the city so badly. As soon as we'd returned to the city and heard the honking of cars, I'd cried with relief, leaning into Roan's chest. And God bless him, he never mentioned how bad I smelled; he just scooped me up and carried me to the nearest hotel. We couldn't go back to his mansion—not when Abellio knew how to find it—so Roan ferried me to an old Victorian hotel in the city.

If they'd actually seen how we looked, Roan carrying me in his arms, covered in the ragged filth of two months in a hole, they would have turned us away immediately.

Luckily for us, Roan was able to glamour the both of us and charm the woman behind the counter. When she'd asked if we wanted one room or two, I blurted, *"Two."* I didn't like Roan seeing me like this any more than he needed to. So two keycards it was, and the woman simply batted her eyelashes at Roan, asking if we wanted breakfast in the morning. Was she kidding? I wanted breakfast *now.*

In the elevator, Roan held me in his arms, closing his eyes as he leaned against the mirrors. After so much time desperately searching for reflections around me, the vastness of the mirrors in the elevator seemed like a stunning luxury.

On the fourth floor, Roan carried me to my room, gently putting me down before the door, and then he crossed to his own room.

The first thing I did when I walked into my hotel room was to snatch the box of matches that lay on the bedside table. Then I stumbled to the bathroom and shut the door behind me. I stripped off the piss-stained, mud-soaked tatters that had been clinging to my body for months and I dropped them in the sink—pants, underwear, shirt. Stark naked, I struck a match, then held it to the pile of rags. The match went out. I went to the minibar, and took out all the bottles that were at least forty proof. I poured them one after the other on the humid, moldy rags, the air in the bathroom becoming dizzying. I lit three matches together and tossed them into the sink, and a large flame rose upwards. I stood back, watching them burn, the smell overpowering. Fortunately, there was no smoke alarm in the bathroom. I had no plan for what to wear now that I'd burned my only clothes, but I'd rather go naked than leave those things in existence.

While the rags burned, I crossed barefoot to the shower, my body shaking, ready to give in. But I couldn't sleep or rest until I'd cleaned myself, and I turned the shower up as hot as it would go, letting the room fill with steam. Holding on to the towel rack for support, I stepped, trembling, into the shower. The scalding water washed over me, and I grabbed the soap, scrubbing at my chest, my arms, the back of my neck, between my legs. I poured out an enormous dollop of shampoo into my hand, working up a thick lather in my hair, then grabbed the soap again, clawing at the creamy bar with my fingernails to clear the crusted dirt from under them. Mud and grit swirled into the bottom of the tub along with the soap suds. When I couldn't stand anymore, I sat on the lip of the tub and lifted my feet, scrubbing at them with the soap, wearing it down. My mind flashed with the image of the silver pen, worn down to a dull nub. I scoured the pads of my feet, grinding down the soap with all the force I could muster—scraping, wearing it down. When the last of the dirt had swirled down the drain and the soap had turned into a thin sliver in my palm, I turned off the shower.

Stepping out of the tub, I stumbled to the sink and turned on the water, dousing the last of the flames. I glanced at the bathmat beneath my feet, lured downward by its softness. I practically fell to the floor, curling in a ball. For reasons I couldn't quite explain, tears rolled down my cheeks, and I sniffled into the bathmat.

Hadn't I spent enough time alone already?

I reached up to the towel rack, snatching off a fluffy white towel. Slowly, nearly ready to collapse, I pulled myself to my feet and wrapped the towel around me.

Leaning against the walls for support, I shuffled to the door. Slowly, painfully, I made it to Roan's door and knocked. It took a few moments for him to open the door.

He was shirtless, water droplets glistening over the muscled planes of his body. "Are you okay?"

"I want to stay with you."

Without another word, he opened the door wider, and I shuffled into his room. I collapsed onto his bed, my eyes already closing. And as sleep began to claim my mind, images rose from the back of my skull—images of a silver pen, worn down to a nub, rat bones snapping in grout. As I drifted off, the towel wrapped around my damp body, I became vaguely aware of a masculine presence enveloping me, powerful arms curling around my body. Then my visions shifted, and I dreamed of sunlight filtering between the oak leaves.

CHAPTER 32

As we walked in the tall grasses of Hampstead Heath, the sun edged out from behind a cloud. Rays of sunlight shone through a hawthorn's leaves, which were just starting to redden in the September air. The grass sparkled with remnants of the night's dewdrops. My eyes filled with tears as I looked around me, taking in the calm beauty. Fresh air, sunlight, the smell of wet earth, vivid colors. I had once taken these things for granted.

Never again.

"This is it." Roan squinted in the sunlight. "This is the meeting place. I should have chosen a different one. We're too visible here."

"I can think of worse places to be," I whispered.

When I had woken up that morning, Roan was gone. He'd returned half an hour later with some fresh croissants and a cup of coffee for me, as well as clothing for both of us. When I had asked him where he got the cash, he muttered something incomprehensible, and said that we had to go, that he had sent a message to whomever remained of the rebels to meet us in Hampstead Heath.

Most shockingly of all, along with the new underwear, pants, and shirts, he'd included a tube of cherry-red lip gloss. Roan explained that I'd been talking about it in my sleep, and he'd gone out on a little early-morning shopping trip. The idea of Roan Taranis walking into a department store to select just the right shade of lip gloss brought a smile to my face that wasn't going away any time soon.

I took a seat on the grass beneath the tree, running my fingers across the soft blades, then gently stroking the damp earth. The dew dampened the seat of my jeans, and it felt glorious. Everything about being outside thrilled me. "This would be a lovely place for a picnic."

Roan sat next to me, and his lips quirked slightly. Sunlight ignited his tousled hair, electrifying the strands of gold. "A picnic."

"Cheese, wine, bread." My stomach rumbled, and I smiled at the thought. "Chocolate. We need chocolate." When I glanced at Roan, I caught him studying me carefully. "What?"

A faint smile played about his lips. "Nothing."

I leaned back on my hands, the dew wetting my palms. "Have you spoken to Elrine?"

He shook his head. "I haven't found her yet. I don't know who we're meeting or where to find the other rebels."

I frowned. "How did you arrange this meeting, then?"

"I had some help."

"Care to elaborate?"

His brow furrowed, and he looked extremely uncomfortable. He muttered something under his breath.

"Who?" I leaned closer, trying to hear him.

"Alvin helped me," he said at last.

"Alvin *Taranis*?" I asked, bemused.

"Yes."

"Your relative?"

"*Distant* relative."

"And you trusted him to set up this meeting?"

"Not at all," Roan said sharply. "But I had no choice. I couldn't find anyone else. Alvin has no love for the king. Ogmios killed his entire family, too."

"Right." I shivered, the name *Ogmios* casting a shadow on this beautiful day.

"I was hoping he'd find Drustan. Maybe Odette. We need the rebellion's leaders."

I surveyed the park, searching for signs of Drustan's darkness. When I saw nothing moving in the tall grasses, I shut my eyes, letting the gentle warmth of the early September sun bake my skin. Unusually warm for this time of year, and it felt sublime.

"Good morning, Goddess. Squawk!"

My eyes snapped open, and I raised my eyes. The raven perched on a branch above us, quirking his head.

"Odin!"

"My nipples tingle with delight! Squawk!" He flapped his wings and took off over the grass, his black shadow rippling in the green expanse. I jumped to my feet, and took off after him.

Running. Running in the sunlight, no walls around me, the slight breeze blowing against my face. A perfect moment.

It wouldn't last long, I knew. Soon, we'd meet the rebels. We would talk about war and death and betrayal, and danger lurking ahead. But for now, I didn't care. I focused on the *now*, enjoying the open air, relishing the simple chase. Laughter bubbled in my chest.

Odin led me to a line of trees, cutting a lazy arc through the air. He flapped his wings, curving slowly down, heading for a man's shoulder. A hulking man with a beautiful face, marked by a scar over his olive skin, glared at the raven.

"Nerius!" I breathed.

He smiled at me just as Roan caught up to me, his long shadow moving over the grass.

Without saying anything, Nerius nodded at the line of trees, leading us onto a path. From the trees, a kestrel called. We followed the fae warrior, my eyes dazzled by the light piercing the canopy of birch and oak leaves, flecking the ground with gold.

Within a grove of oaks, Elrine and Branwen waited for us, leaning on tree trunks. Elrine's face lit up with a huge smile as she saw Roan, and she ran into his embrace. She buried her head in his shoulders, gripping him for dear life. "Roan. I'm so happy you're okay."

Branwen didn't move, or smile. Her dark eyes met mine, and she said nothing.

"Where are the rest?" Roan asked, pulling back from Elrine.

"There are no *rest*." Branwen's voice was ice-cold. "We could get in touch with no one. They've gone deep underground."

"No one contacted you?" Roan frowned.

Branwen folded her arms. "I believe the general consensus was that it was best to stay away from the cell that had a spy in its midst."

Elrine's eyes glistened. "The rebellion is dead. It's over. The remaining survivors went into hiding with the Elder Fae, deep in Hawkwood Forest. I managed to find Nerius by tracking him to his hideout."

"What happened to my home?" Roan asked.

Elrine seemed reluctant to pull away from him, her arm still around his waist. "Abellio gave them the location. The king gave it to Grendel."

A muscle twitched in Roan's jaw. "What's the news of the war with the Seelie?"

"The invasion has started," Elrine said. "Heavy casualties on both sides. I think Ogmios underestimated their strength. But just for now, the Unseelie have the advantage. The king is using enormous amounts of the energy he had managed to store over the years. Human terror that he's drawing on somehow."

"Store it?" Roan asked. "How?"

I straightened. "The London Stone."

Nerius scrubbed at his jaw. "As far as we can tell, Cassandra is right. Ogmios has been storing fear in the Stone for centuries. Lately he's accelerated this process, spreading fear throughout London. He amplifies it and feeds from it."

The Rix and his serial killings. Siofra and her attacks on London—the dancing plague and the floods. All designed to spread fear. King Ogmios had harvested all that fear, storing it in the Stone. I hadn't been entirely certain before, but this confirmed it. I was the king's daughter. It all fit—and it mirrored my powers precisely. The bloodline of dread, and I, its heir.

Roan ran a hand thorough his golden hair. "We have to get to Hawkwood Forest, find the rest of the rebels. The king won't be prepared for another attack, not while he's fighting the Seelie. We'll—"

"No!" I practically shouted it.

Everyone turned to stare at me, the single word piercing Roan's speech.

"We need to get me to the London Stone," I said. "I'll use it against the king. It's the key."

Nerius shook his head. "Last time you touched it, nothing happened."

"I think I know why. I can make it work."

"It doesn't matter," Nerius said. "The London Stone is gone. Ogmios took it. He has it hidden somewhere."

"That's okay," I said. "I know how to find it."

* * *

THE MAN behind the desk at the hostel glared at me, scratching his beard. The fluorescent light flickered above him. "I'm sorry, miss, I have no idea what you are referring to."

"A golden compass. Not too big. I left it in room eleven a couple of months ago." I was certain I'd left it behind with my other things when I'd left in a rush for Trinovantum. I gripped my handbag tighter. I'd filled it with hand mirrors, and had everything I needed at this point. Except the compass.

The man tapped his stubby fingers on the counter, then he wagged a finger at me. "I remember you. You left the room in a terrible state. I should be billing you for damages."

A throat cleared behind me. Roan stood by my side, towering over me. The receptionist seemed to wither as he stared upward at his face.

Roan leaned on the counter. "She's merely asking for her belongings," Roan said. "You should accommodate her."

The man cleared his throat. "I really wouldn't hang on to a compass."

Roan leaned forward and grasped the metal desk bell from the counter. He clenched his fist, twisting the bell as if it were made of paper.

The man jumped back. "Oh! *That* compass! I have it right here." He crouched down, rummaging below the desk. A few seconds later, he slammed it down on the countertop. "There you go. I think it's broken. It doesn't point to the north."

"Thank you." I plucked it from the countertop. "Wonderful service. I'll be sure to recommend this place to my friends."

"I'd prefer you didn't," the man muttered to our backs as we strode outside.

We walked out onto the narrow London street, and I nodded down the road. As I walked, I glanced at the compass, which pointed north. "Let's go that way."

As we moved along the sidewalk, I kept my eyes locked on the compass. After walking several yards, the needle shifted slightly, and I loosed a sigh of relief.

Roan peered over my shoulder. "We just walk in the direction the compass is showing us?"

"That's right."

"What if the king shipped the Stone to another land?"

I tried to avoid passersby as I stared at it. "He didn't. The Stone is still in London."

Roan's enormous form cast a shadow over the compass as he looked on. "How do you know it's in London?"

"Because the needle just moved. So it means the Stone is close because..." I hesitated. "Because of math." I didn't feel like explaining about vector intersection just then.

Roan walked by my side along London's winding city streets, moving northwest along the sidewalks. After a while, I began to suspect I knew where we were going. I recognized the sleek, modern apartment buildings just up ahead.

"The compass seems to be taking us to Cripplegate. Barbican. The Stone is probably in the banshees' compound under the church."

Roan squinted in the sunlight. "That makes sense. A good hiding place, with many soldiers from the house of Arawn."

As we moved closer to the church, striding over the brick, I stared at the compass. The needle pointed unerringly to the large terrace beside the church. Then all of a sudden it wavered, flipping around and pointing back. I stopped.

"Hang on," I said. I slowly took two steps backward. The needle wavered again, and then spun wildly in a circle. "We're standing right above it."

We both looked down at the brick ground. Somewhere below us, the London Stone waited.

"Can you get into the compound?" asked Roan. "You just need to touch it. Is that right?"

"Yeah. Last time I connected to the king, the connection maintained for over a week. I'll find it, jump in, touch it, and leave."

Roan frowned. "And you're sure this is worth the risk?"

"Completely sure," I said with more confidence than I felt.

I unzipped my handbag, pulling out a small hand mirror. As I gazed into it, I let my mind bond with the glass, then I scanned for reflections below.

Instantly, I realized my options had become more limited since the last time we'd visited. Learning from their mistakes, the Arawn fae had removed most of the mirrors. Still, they'd left behind metal candle holders, small puddles of water, the well-polished wood. People don't realize how many things cast reflections.

I scanned the compound's reflections, shifting quickly from one to another—past the images of blank walls, of banshees bathing, of rooms full of guards. I searched each room for the London Stone. I found it nowhere, until, with a sinking feeling, I realized where they'd hidden it. I lowered the mirror.

"There's a lot more security inside the complex," I said. "About twice as much as before. They have six fae watching the front door, and more patrols. Guards in the study as well. They definitely bolstered their defenses since last time."

Roan crossed his arms. "Did you find the Stone?"

"I couldn't find it, but there are nine guards stationed in the atrium that leads to the spider's lair. Last time there were none. And the spider's lair has no reflections in it."

"Jumping in, touching the Stone, and getting out is out of

the question. We need ten or twenty more fae on our side before you can go in there."

I shook my head. "Soon enough, the king will realize that we're going for the Stone, now that we've escaped," I said. "If we wait, he might even add more protection to it, or move it to his keep in Trinovantum. We have to do it now. Can your... storm powers work inside?"

"No. Weather tends to stay outdoors. And I don't think I can summon another storm so soon after the last one."

"Okay." I took a deep breath, unwilling to let this go. "What if you create a distraction? The guards might leave their post around the Stone."

"If the London Stone is really in there, they won't leave their post."

"Okay. So they won't." I was determined to make this work. "You create a distraction to avoid anyone coming to their aid, and I jump in, take them out, and get into that room."

"Take them out?" Roan repeated, deadpan. "Take out nine guards. I'm starting to worry that your mind was destroyed in that prison."

Yes, it was. "Branwen could help me."

He arched an eyebrow. "With Branwen controlling your shadow, you can take out nine guards?"

"Yes. Just as soon as I get control over my dread powers."

"Your powers are unstable," Roan said gently. "They might not work, and leave you to die at the hands of the Arawn Fae. It would take months of training—"

"I've already had months of training. Months with nothing but myself, in total isolation. I faced everything within me. All the walls in my mind are broken. I can do this, now. You've seen it happen when we escaped the keep."

"For a fae to gain complete control over her powers, she needs to unveil."

I hadn't really managed that yet, but the kernel of a plan took root in my mind, and I started to perceive what Roan wanted me to do. He wanted me to embrace my fae side, once and for all.

CHAPTER 33

J'd asked Roan to meet me at Temple Church, and I showed up a few minutes early. September had begun to cool the air, and I'd worn a long dress that fell to my ankles, and wrapped a thick woolen sweater around myself.

I had a plan, though I wasn't entirely convinced it would work. The one time I'd come close to unveiling had been with Roan. I'd been broken, and I'd lost my inhibitions. I'd jumped on him, and bit him in the neck, and the claws and teeth had come right out. Roan wanted me to tune in to the world around me, to let go of my worry and guilt, to shed my self-consciousness. I needed to simply tune in to the natural world around me, to bond with it.

And when *else* had I done that before? Not when I was angry, or near death. It had been when I was enjoying myself —drinking the nectar, touching Roan.

Maybe just a tiny sip of it before Roan arrived would help things along. I just hadn't told him about it. For some reason, I knew he wouldn't approve. He'd been kind but distant, unwilling to let me too close to him.

I had a vague idea of what might happen if I drank the nectar around him.

I leaned over the fountain, peering at the moonlit water. I stared into the reflection until my mind clicked with it. Then, I linked it to Roan's dining room, where a crystal decanter stood on the table—the one Nerius had used to draw the penis. It was still there. I reached into the water, plucking out the decanter. I held it to my lips, tasting the delicious sweetness—one sip, two. I forced myself to stop after that. Reluctantly, I shoved the decanter back into the watery reflection.

As I pulled my hand from the fountain, I felt aware of the water dripping over my skin. My mind flashed with impressions of the stone and brick around me—a Shakespearean play performed in one of the nearby buildings, the bard himself in attendance four hundred years ago; the roses that grew around him then, the white and red signifying the warring armies of kings, their scent intoxicating. Beauty and blood, love and terror.

And here I prophesy: this brawl today, / Grown to this faction in the Temple Garden, / Shall send between the red rose and the white / A thousand souls to death and deadly night.

Love and terror. I stroked my fingers through the water, feeling it wash over my skin. I needed to stay in the present, to let the beautiful *now* engulf me. Moonlight dazzled over the water. I kicked off my shoes, trailing my feet into the fountain's cool water. I glanced up at the night sky, stunned by the beauty of the starry vault, the gleaming heavenly fires. They called to the flame in my chest. I pulled off my sweater, tossing it to the flagstones by the side of the fountain.

I noticed another thing I really didn't need right now: a bra. I reached behind my back, unhooked it, and slipped it out from under my dress, dropping it on the stone. My dress skimmed over my bare breasts.

From the tree overhead, a jackdaw chirped. I lifted my dress higher, letting the water soak my skin. Splashes from the running water cooled my skin, and brought with it the song of the river gods, the ancient ballads of the Thames. I dipped lower in the fountain, sitting in it completely until I'd submerged myself up to my shoulders. This is where I belonged...

The sound of footfalls sparked excitement in me, and I turned to see Roan walking across the flagstones, silvered in the moonlight. Pale light washed over the perfect counters of his face, and the sight thrilled me. *A god... he looks like a god, one come to bless me with his presence.* Ecstasy bubbled in my chest, and I couldn't form the words to tell him how perfect he was. Here we were, love and terror, come together in the Temple Garden. We belonged together.

I was overcome by a sudden desperation to see his true form. Slowly, I rose from the fountain, and the chill of the September air rushed over my skin.

His golden eyes gleamed in the darkness, penetrating me to my very core. His body looked strangely alert. "What are you doing in the fountain?"

Slowly, my eyes roamed over his perfect body, his inviting black shirt that fit his torso so perfectly. I couldn't quite remember how to speak, so I simply stepped from the fountain, letting the water drip down my skin, down my cleavage. As I moved closer to him, his eyes dipped to my breasts, peaked from the cool water.

Loosing a breath, he reached for my waist, then stopped himself, his fingers tightening. A muscle twitched in his jaw, and his body went rigid with tension. "What are you doing?" he asked again, a ragged edge to his voice, a voice that licked up my spine.

I took a deep breath, close enough now that I could smell him, could feel the warmth radiating from his body. My nerves were sparking on overdrive, all of my senses heightened. *Imagine how his body would feel, moving under mine, his hands palming my breasts... terror conquering love, love conquering terror.* I licked my lips, and his penetrating gaze caught the movement.

My body heating, I traced my fingertips over his collarbone. Shuddering, he took a deep breath. His gaze dropped to my breasts again, as if he were losing a battle with himself. I wanted to feel his hands brushing over my nipples, then his mouth. I could pull his clothing off, one piece at a time, to run my tongue over his skin.

I traced my fingertips lower on his chest, brushing just over the waist of his trousers. I slipped them under the hem of his shirt, feeling his powerful body, and he gasped.

At last, I remembered how to form a coherent sentence. "I need to learn to unveil," I said.

He grabbed my wrist. "What's going on? How did you get nectar?"

I didn't answer. Words weren't going to work in this situation. I pulled my wrist from his grasp, then cupped his face. Sighing, he closed his eyes, brushing his face against my hand as if he were giving in, just for a moment. Even as he fought against it, a fire ignited between us.

I edged closer, and one word rang in my skull. *Mine.* I had the sudden revelation that Roan was mine, and we weren't going to achieve anything until he understood this.

I felt my breasts grow heavy, my body seeming to swell. The dress felt too restrictive around me. I wrapped my arms around his neck, letting the strap of my dress fall lower, exposing the top of my breasts to the night air. As he stared into my eyes, I let the strap fall completely off. I stood on my tiptoes, brushing my body against his as I moved up against him. I pulled his face to mine for a kiss, pressing my hips into him. For just a moment, he fought against his desire, his body tense.

And then, his control slipped. His powerful arms were around me. He kissed me back, the slow brush of his tongue sending my body racing with need. His kiss was pure pleasure and pure devastation, a kiss that shattered me and put me back together again. Beauty and blood, love and terror. My knees went weak, heat pulsing between my legs. How could I get him to touch me where I needed it? I felt my thighs clenching, his powerful arms flexing around me.

He pulled away from the kiss. Our breath mingled, and he stared into my eyes. "What are you doing, Cassandra?" His deep voice licked up my spine, soft as a caress.

Don't let him speak. His mouth needed to be doing something else—licking the fountain water from my skin, kissing my neck, my thighs, my breasts.

I thought I knew how to silence him. As heat pulsed through my body, I pulled the straps of my dress off my shoulders, letting the entire dress fall to the flagstones. I stood before him in only my tiny, sky-blue lace panties. I slid my fingers into the hem of my panties, threatening to pull them off. For a moment, his jaw slackened, eyes flaring with sunlight. Then, his gaze slowly raked over my body, memorizing every curve. He sucked in a sharp breath, his antlers shimmering on his head, eyes gleaming gold. With a snarl, his canines flashed, claws lengthening.

That was it. He wouldn't be talking anymore. I reached under the hem of his shirt, pulling it off him, then stood on my toes again, my breasts brushing against his tattooed torso. I curved my hips into him.

His hands stroked down my bare body, cupping my ass, and I ground my hips into him. Pulling him closer, I licked his neck, sucking the place where I'd once bitten him.

He moaned, fingers tightening on my ass.

I wanted him on the ground. I pulled away from his neck. Gently, I began pushing him to the garden—the one that bloomed with the ghosts of red and white roses. He'd unveiled, and no longer cared about whyever the hell he wasn't supposed to kiss me. A wicked smile curled his lips, and he backed up into the soil and plants, the smell of the earth enveloping us. I reached for his shoulders, gently nudging him into the ground.

He looked up at me, his gaze hungry, carnal. I slid into his lap and wrapped my legs around his waist. I glanced at his neck again, and stared at the rhythmic pulse of the vein beneath his skin, the primal rhythm strangely in sync with my heart. The beat drew me in, hypnotizing. As he arched his neck, I let my tongue flick over his skin, sucking and licking, my hips rocking against him until I became more frenzied, desperate for him. He'd hardened completely against me. He tilted his head back further, and I rocked against him.

I met his gaze, my mouth just inches from his.

"Cassandra," he said, his voice a guttural growl, ragged with need.

At the sound of my name on his lips, a euphoric warmth burned in my ribs, and I brushed my thumb over his full lower lip.

He gripped my waist, his thumbs tracing circles over the hollows of my hipbones. God, it felt amazing, my world narrowing to those slow, circular strokes, each one heating my body more. I moved in his lap, pressing my hips harder into him.

He let out a low growl, the sound making my toes curl with pleasure, and his fingers tightened on my hips. His thumbs pressed lower, and my back arched.

He stroked his fingers down the front of my chest, tracing over my breasts, and an overwhelming wave of pleasure washed over me, pulling me under until I couldn't remember my name. Visions flashed in my mind, of oaks and sunlight, the soil of the forest.

The next thing I knew, I was on my back in the dirt, pulling off my sky-blue panties. I needed him *now.*

I let my legs fall open, staring up at him with anticipation. Roan's gaze dipped between my thighs, his body practically vibrating with the effort to restrain himself. He leaned in, his arms on either side of my head. He kissed my throat, teeth grazing my skin. I began to groan beneath him, and I grasped for his belt, frantically unhooking it. I needed him naked, needed this to move faster. And yet he moved glacially slow, his kisses slowly tracing down my body. His mouth was on my breast now, sucking, licking.

I arched my back, trying to pull him closer, but he held back, taking his time to brush one kiss after another further down my body. His mouth moved lower, over my hipbones, and I threaded my fingers into his hair, desperate for him now. Fragments of words whirled in my mind... *touch... fingers... wet...*

At last, he parted my legs, hooking them over his shoulders. Slowly, gently, he kissed the inside of my thighs, his glorious lips on my bare skin. I gripped his hair. I wanted his tongue on me, I wanted...

He started to kiss me between my legs, his tongue flicking over the apex between my thighs. Soaring with pleasure, I moved against him. My body blazed with fiery heat, and I groaned, hips bucking. When his tongue moved inside me, I cried out, digging my fingers into the earth. With each movement of his tongue my body soared higher, until a powerful climax ripped through me and my thighs clenched around him.

"Roan," I whispered. He kissed my thighs again, tasting my skin, his body glowing with pure, golden light. Unspeakable power. I felt limp, trembling.

And yet, I wasn't there yet. I still hadn't unveiled. I needed more of him, needed all of him. I could tell he still held back, keeping some kind of leash on himself.

Then I knew what I needed to do. I'd dreamed it, long ago when I'd first met him. Dreamed that I was running through the woods, stripping off my clothes. It had been a *hunt,* and I'd been his prey.

I turned over, something compelling me onto all fours. Instantly, a growl rumbled over the garden from Roan's throat. His fingertips slowly stroked down my back, his touch sending hot shivers over my skin. He cupped between my legs, and I moved against his hand.

"Cassandra," he groaned.

I arched my back further, opening my legs, desperate for him. He growled, his legs sliding between my knees, and I bent lower, arms stretching over the garden's plants. Gripping my hips, he held me in place. Finally, with a feral groan, he plunged into me until he filled me completely. Pleasure gripped my mind. As my body adjusted to him, he moved slowly, and I could think of nothing else but his slow thrust. My fingers dug into the dirt as he began to move faster. Fragments of ideas spun inside my skull like autumn leaves in a storm... *fill me... claim... mate... mine... hunt...*

A primal rush flooded my body, and it was no longer my fingernails tearing into the earth—it was my claws, my canines piercing my lower lip. Roan moved faster, one hand on my neck. Then, his mouth replaced his hand, his tongue flicking against my skin. A hint of teeth, a gentle bite as he stroked hard between my legs. I felt myself meld with him, with the earth, until at last, pleasure shattered me into a million pieces. My body tightened around him, and I moaned. Roan growled as he came hard, his mouth on my neck, body glowing against mine. Panting heavily, he pulled me against him, his arms enveloping me.

He whispered into my ear, "You unveiled." As I caught my breath, leaning against his bare body, he pushed my damp hair from my face. "And there's my Cassandra."

Slowly, I rose and peered into the reflection of one of the darkened windows. There, I saw myself unveiled, my canines glinting in the moonlight, my hands clawed—and two pointed ears protruding from my pink hair.

There she was—Cassandra unveiled.

CHAPTER 34

*A*s I sat in the cafe across from Branwen, my pulse raced. I stared into a hand mirror, the reflection displaying the door to the spider's lair. Now, *eleven* guards milled in the hallway. Was this added security because they were worried we might try something? Or did the guards just have nothing better to do?

I looked up from the mirror, meeting Branwen's gaze. She sat across from me at a formica cafe table, sipping from her mug calmly, completely ignoring me. She wasn't in the mood to chat with the woman who had spied on her and accused her of treachery. I couldn't blame her.

Still staring at the mirror, I said, for the third time that morning, "I'm sorry, Branwen."

Branwen didn't answer, and silence fell over us again.

As I sat at the table, nervousness tightened my gut. Roan, Elrine, and Nerius had entered the church more than twenty minutes ago, and I had no idea what was going on. I was about to search for the palace's entry hall, see if they had attacked, when the first banshee's wail keened distantly through the air. The hair rose on the back of my neck. The cry was muffled, far away, but instantly recognizable. The attack had started.

Branwen rose. "It's time."

I stood, my muscles tensed. "Do you have my back?"

She simply stared at me, eyes dark and cold.

Okay. Not particularly reassuring, but I've got no one else to work with here.

I looked down at the mirror, trying not to think of the last time I'd gone into a reflection, when Siofra had come after me. I'd have to move quickly.

I took a deep breath, my mind merging with the reflection, clicking with it. Then, I jumped, and the cold reflection washed over my skin. I leapt through into the palace halls— just in front of the surprised guards in the atrium. Two recovered almost immediately, lunging forward, swords raised.

I let my mind go blank, searching for the beast within, that focus, the *now.*

But I was underground, in a cramped hallway. Cramped like my cell, hemmed in by utter isolation, the place where nothing moves, and nothing happens and my ribs pierce my skin, no no, *no no no no*—

The guard closest to me swung his sword. It clashed into something with a loud clang. A stiletto blade.

My shadow stood in a crouch by me, holding two stilettos. It whirled, and the stiletto sank into the guard's neck. The second one charged at my shadow, roaring. I shifted down the hallway, running.

Branwen had bought me the time I needed to get a hold of myself. I whirled, staring at the incoming men, feeling a sudden exhilaration. This was it. I might die here, but if I did, it meant something. And I would die moving.

An ancient dark power blazed, and I moved faster away from the guards, like an arrow soaring on the wind.

Wolf claws lengthened from my fingertips, and I felt my canines extending. I whirled, desperate to tear into fae flesh. As the guard reached me, I grabbed the nearest one, slamming him against the wall. I tore his neck, blood on my tongue. His screams echoed off the stone wall.

In the distance, a banshee wailed. Someone was going to die.

I let out a roar and shifted to face the others. Three more were coming for me. My shadow was losing ground, fighting a fae with a huge battle axe. Beyond us, two fae loaded crossbows.

I arched my back, and time slowed to a trickle.

Dark tendrils of fear coiled around me—the strongest one coming from the fae I'd bitten. The fear of death. I absorbed it into me, along with the rest. I combined them, churning the fear into a stronger, nightmarish terror.

Mistress of Dread.

Flinging back my arms, I reflected the terror at all the guards around me.

The fae with the battle axe fumbled, dropping his weapon. The rest paused in their tracks, bodies trembling violently. Someone wept; two more shrieked, eyes wide with terror.

Then, the shadow and I moved.

Stilettos and claws swinging, slashing, piercing, cutting into flesh. Some died screaming. Others were silent, robbed of the air in their lungs, unable to utter a sound. Two tried to get away, get help, and died with blades in their backs.

The blood fury flowed in me, and I thought of nothing but the power of the moment, a pure predator.

Within moments, it was all over. Some were dead, others close to death or unconscious, no longer a threat. I hurried to the door, trying the doorknob of the atrium. Unlocked.

There was no need to lock a door guarded by eleven male fae, after all.

It opened with a loud screech.

* * *

As I STEPPED into the dark interrogation room, the door screeched closed behind me. Moving quietly into the room, I pulled a small flashlight from my pocket. My footsteps echoed off the stone walls.

I cast the beam around the room, taking in the layers of web that covered the floor and the walls. The beam darted over Lord Balor, his eyeless corpse gaping at me. Bile climbed up my throat, and I shuddered, moving the beam around the room, searching for the Stone.

"The pixie has returned." A low whisper from the corner of the room send a shudder snaking up my spine.

Tensing, I whirled to point the beam of light at the sound. A spidery form moved from the shadows. She stared at me, her insect-like eyes glinting in the beam of my light.

"I'm thrilled," she hissed. "The taste I got from you the last time was… exquisite."

I licked my canine teeth. Behind her loomed the dark, squat form of the London Stone. I could almost feel the power pulsing from it, luring me closer.

The old woman prowled closer on eight spindly legs. Then, she lunged for me, a strand of silk spinning from her mouth. My shadow darted forward, slamming her in the chest with her boot.

"Shadows don't despair." I bared my sharp teeth in a predatory snarl.

It was my turn. I unfurled my senses, searching for the tendril of fear.

I found nothing.

She moved forward, quick as a snake, her limbs clacking on the stone floor. Her tail whipped out, striking the shadow, knocking it over. The interrogator spat another web strand at me, and I leapt away, rolling on the floor, the web missing me by inches. She scuttled toward me, her tail in the air. I scrambled back, my hand brushing against the strand of silk.

Immediately, sorrow pulled me under. It was a lost cause. She was stronger, faster. She had no fear. I should kill myself before she wrapped me in her sticky web.

As she took another step closer, my shadow stepped between us, buying me precious seconds. Summoning every shed of willpower I had, I scraped away the silk from my hand, rubbing it onto the stone floor. And as I did, the despair dissipated.

"You shouldn't have come, Mistress of Dread." Her ancient voice dripped with contempt. "I fear nothing. I'm older than the city itself."

"Everyone fears something." I pulled a lighter from my pocket. When I flicked it, a tiny flame sparked, entrancing me. I raised my hand, holding the dancing flame directly above a stream of silk. "If you strike me, this drops. Your web burns easily, doesn't it? I've seen it."

She laughed, her voice raspy. "Will you set this entire room ablaze? You'll burn with me, little pixie. You'll die."

"That's fine. I could use a rest." I lowered the flame further.

She twitched, a flicker in her eyes. Fear. I quested again, and time slowed to a crawl. It was there. A tiny coil of dark fear.

That was all I needed.

I tilted back my neck, pulling the coil of fear into me. Deep within my ribs, it pulsed like a tiny heart, growing larger. Her fear twisted and turned, singing of infernos and fiery death. It sang of blackening skin, of hair set ablaze.

Death waited beyond, even for her. And then, with a sharp arch of my back, I flung it back at her.

Her body trembled, her feet making a strange clacking sound on the floor. Her face, more insect than woman, wore a twisted mask of horror, paralyzed with terror.

I shifted, raising a claw, marking her bare throat, vulnerable, soft. I took a step forward, then froze.

Her tail still moved, swinging left and right, the venomous tip raised high. The terror in her brain did nothing to make it stop, as if it moved of its own accord, a reflex that would lash and sting if I got too close.

I dodged to the side, out of her tail's reach. Apart from the twitching tail, she didn't react, her mouth agape in horror. Moving at a safe distance from her tail, I ran straight for the London Stone.

As I got closer to the Stone, its cries rang in the back of my skull, beckoning me closer. And there, keening high above the rest, my mother's voice shrieking in the din.

My hands morphed into pixie hands, the fingers pale. I ran my fingertips over the Stone's rough surface, feeling the power that pulsed dully underneath. But nothing happened. The Stone remained shut.

The first time I'd touched it, the magic had overwhelmed me, but the conditions hadn't been the same. When I'd first touched it, my hand had been bleeding from the broken the glass of the display case. And when I touched the Stone, my bloody hand had ignited it.

The bloodline of dread.

I pulled the stiletto knife from my belt, gripped the blade with my right hand, and swiped it in one swift movement, wincing as the blood ran down my palm, my wrist. Then I opened my fist wide and slapped it hard on the rock.

Screams rose around me like a maelstrom of agony. Hundreds of voices, wailing in horror and fear and pain, me among them, screaming as well, a voice in the crowd. A river of torment, rushing endlessly.

In the London Stone.

I had no name, no body, nothing to call mine.

You are Cassandra Liddell, terror leech, pixie, Mistress of Dread, former FBI agent.

All I could do was blend into the din, add my voice to the torment.

You are looking for King Ogmios. Your father.

Over the onslaught of wails, my mother's voice keened above the rest.

Her own scream of fear, stored here by Ogmios. I could feel the king here, too—another presence in this sea of dread. His spirit coiled around me, icy wisps of dark magic. I tilted back my head, letting his presence flow into me, linking us. When I'd pulled his spirit into mine, I knew it was time to leave.

Only, I couldn't. The voices drew me closer, beckoning me into the chaos, the inexorable lure of mass fear. A terrified crowd has power. Fear breeds strength, in its own horrific way, and I wanted to merge with them. To scream with them. I let myself sink into the dread, opened my mouth to wail.

But something pulled me away, yanking on my arm. I struggled against it, trying to stay here, where I belonged.

And then suddenly, I was back in the interrogator's cave, my shadow dragging me away from the Stone, and pointing emphatically behind me.

The interrogator was turning to face me, her face twisted with hatred.

"You will suffer!" she shrieked, still trembling.

I reeled, still in shock from the thrill of the terror I'd felt, but that fear had also fed me, too. The interrogator scuttled closer, her tail high above her head.

I pulled the small lighter out. When I clicked it, the tiny flame sparked again. I tossed it into the webs. As the interrogator's horrified eyes followed the arc of the flame, I twisted my wrist and stared into the reflection on my bracelet.

A hot, searing flame licked at my skin as I leapt away.

CHAPTER 35

Touching the Stone had unleashed the screams of terror in my skull all over again.

In my clean, crisp hotel room, I lay in the bed and shut my eyes, trying to tune out the noise. I'd wanted to be alone. I momentarily considered opening the hotel's minibar, drowning the screams away, but I quickly shoved the idea away. Never again.

Instead, I searched for my mental connection with King Ogmios.

There, under the roiling surface of my mind, was an alien presence, a web of memories and thoughts that didn't belong to me, that I could hardly understand.

I prodded gently against the web, the dark strands of memories. As soon as I touched a strand, I was immediately overcome by a stream of images and feelings so powerful they knocked the breath from me. Quickly, I backed away, my heart thrumming hard.

Ogmios was a very old fae. He'd lived for centuries. Diving into his memories would be like trying to dive into the Atlantic Ocean, and I'd drown within seconds.

No. If I wanted anything from his mind, I'd have to fish it out. Carefully.

I hesitated. Where should I start? I had no idea how to scan the web of memories for his precise weaknesses.

I would start with myself—his greatest shame.

Closing my eyes, I conjured in my mind the day when Ogmios had come to visit me, when he'd balked at the wretched smell. And I used this image to prod his memories, a strand of memories glowing hot among the web.

I wanted to see her, but it was too dark. My own instructions, of course. I knew what the abomination could do with just a flicker of light. The tiniest reflection, and she would be gone. No, I would leave her in the darkness. It was enough to feel her pixie emotions—broken, scared, desperate. I felt the exquisite fear in her, and for a moment was tempted to taste it, enjoy it, revel in it, but resisted the temptation. I would not lose control to this... mistake.

"Already broken?" I asked her. "After just two months?"

I pulled away, my throat clenching. His poisonous thoughts revolted me, fed on hatred and anger. After a moment to gather my thoughts, I moved closer to the memory again. It was linked to others, and one beckoned me —the brightest, the strongest.

Reaching out with my mind, I touched the strand.

* * *

A MAN DRESSED in sky blue velvet stood on the tile floor before me, over the stunning mosaic of a skull beneath the water. His hands were shaking, and the sight of his terror filled me with a dark pleasure. I leaned over my desk, trying to hide my smile. Sunlight streamed in from tall windows, igniting his ginger hair.

"I am very sorry, Your Majesty," he stammered. "But the

human woman insisted that you owe her a debt. Should I have her thrown to the cells?"

I stared coldly at the simpering servant. Worthless. All of them worthless—except for one. "A debt?" I let him hear the rage in my voice. "To a human animal? A filthy beast? How could you even consider such a thing? That you trouble me with this matter right before the council meeting amazes me."

"Of course, Your Majesty." He bowed even lower, his forehead touching the tip of the skull mosaic. "I will take care of her at once."

"No. You will take care of nothing. You will go to the captain of guards and inform him that you should be given thirty lashes for being useless. And on your way out, send in the human animal. I will take care of her myself."

The servant practically tripped on his cloak in his rush to get out. Had I been too lenient with my punishment?

My gaze flicked to the bowl of apples in the corner of my desk. Two days old, no longer as succulent and tempting as they were before. All untouched, of course. I should have them replaced with new ones.

When the door swung open, a young woman entered, clutching a bundle of cloth. Her fear slammed into me, a hot thrill. I nearly shut my eyes in relish, but I struggled with the temptation. Her terror had a familiar taste.

It was *her*.

My misstep a year ago, after the memorial to my parents. A repugnant weakness. Her body had been young, soft and inviting... and she had caught me at my weakest moment. Harlot. Animal.

The bundle of cloth suddenly moved, emitting a slight sound. The woman held it closer, murmuring to it. A babe.

"What do you want, whore?" Ice laced my voice.

"Your Majesty, ten months ago, we met at the rune-stone ceremony. You were—"

"I remember you. I remember that night. Didn't take much for you to open your legs, did it?" The beast might have been beautiful, but her morals revolted me.

She was one of the few humans who still worshiped the fae as gods, the way it was meant to be. She and her animal friends had summoned us to the rhinestones, had worshiped us. And then, she'd seduced me with her sheer dress, her breasts on display like a whore, tempting me.

"After the ceremony in May, I became pregnant. I had a daughter. This is her. If you could allow me to live here—"

"My child? Impossible!" Icy fingers of rage gripped my heart. I couldn't have given life to such an abomination... Unthinkable.

"It must be yours, my king. There was no one else."

"I am not *your* majesty, beast. Harlot. You are not fae, and never will be." My fists clenched in anger. "Come closer."

She stepped towards me, her blond hair cascading down her back. Beautiful, yes, but not fae. A forbidden fruit.

I rose from behind my desk, desire and fury pounding in my body. I wanted to cut her throat right there. I wanted to rip her clothes off and fuck her as she squealed like a beast on the cold tile floor.

I did none of those things. I was in control, not the weak fae I had been in the intoxicating atmosphere of the human fertility ceremony. I approached her and stared down at the babe.

My own deep blue eyes stared back at me, eyes blue as the ancient Weala Broc river. She was a mongrel, I could feel it, even though her emotions were still simple, the emotions of a young babe. An abomination with my blood.

Her mother lifted her. "Her name is—"

"I don't care what her name is, whore."

"Your Majesty. We need money. A few gold coins like the one you gave me that night would be more than enough—"

Of course. Gold. What more would a greedy animal want? "Wait outside. I will take care of it."

"Of course." She smiled at me, backing away.

I waited until she left, trembling with fury. How could I have been so weak?

I considered having her killed instantly, but something stayed my hand. I turned to the bowl of fruit, took one apple in hand, and smelled it, my mouth watering even though it was already dying.

I stared at it and then clenched my fist, crushing the fruit into pulp. I was stronger than temptation now. I would keep this reminder of my weakness alive. It would help me stay strong.

I crossed to the back wall, where a silver chain connected to a bell. I pulled on it, summoning the Rix.

As I waited, I crossed over the tiles, cleaning my hand with an embroidered handkerchief. After a few moments, the Rix appeared, bowing deeply in respect. The one man I could trust.

"There is a human woman outside," I said. "With a babe. A pixie babe. An indiscretion of one of our fae lords."

He showed no shock at this, no emotion at all. "Yes, Your Majesty."

"Take the woman to the cells." I considered for a moment. No reason to let good things go to waste. "I will feed her fear to the Stone later."

"And the baby?"

"Take her to the changeling midwife. Have her placed somewhere... far away. In the human realm."

"What do I do with the human changeling we receive in her stead?"

I couldn't care less. "Kill her, sell her, keep her as a slave—do as you please."

"Yes, Your Majesty." He turned and left. I stared at his back grimly, thinking of my own whip. I would atone again tonight, and never make such a mistake again.

* * *

I PULLED BACK from the memory, bile in my throat. It *had* been my mother's scream I'd heard. The king had fed her terror into the Stone.

My fingers tightened into fists. Perhaps a few months ago, I would have crumpled up and fallen apart.

Not anymore. I knew who I was. I knew what I needed to do, what I needed to focus on next.

I let that part of the web die, envisioning it rotting within my mind. I spared only the memory of the king feeding my mother's fear into the Stone. I reached for the strand of memory, and touched it.

So many memories related to the Stone, branching out in the web of his thoughts.

One was the oldest, and the strongest, and I pulled it to me.

* * *

I WANDERED the dirty streets of Lundenwic, hungry for fear. My body had become weak, drained of magic, slowly wasting away. Ever since the Romans had abandoned Londinium, the remaining Seelie could hardly feed, and few remembered to worship us.

Perhaps we should emigrate north, but abandoning our conquered lands to the Seelie was too much to bear. No. We had to bide our time, wait until the moment was right. Or die

C.N. CRAWFORD & ALEX RIVERS

—here, by the Weala Broc River, where humans had once worshiped us.

On a filthy dirt street, I passed by a woman washing clothes in a tub of dirty water, her face lined with grime. I looked around, scanning the crude wooden houses around us. Completely alone.

No man to chase me away with an iron spear. Only the woman and me. I stalked closer, and she raised her eyes, warily, and I could already feel the sharp tingle of fear. I snarled at her, letting my canines shimmer just for a moment. She screamed in horror, and scrambled back, but I was beyond caring, shutting my eyes, letting the fear fill my body.

And then a man ran out of the house. Large, wide, holding an iron blade.

I turned to run, the woman's fear giving me speed I didn't have before. I sprinted through the streets, hiding outside Londinium's stone wall.

Breathing hard, I suddenly felt a sharp tug, something beckoning me—strangely familiar, like my mother was calling me home. I followed the sensation, deeper into Londinium.

A tall stone stood in the midst of an empty terrace. And it thrummed with power.

I came closer, my steps hesitant, afraid. But the closer I came, the more certain I was that this thing would not hurt me. That it, in fact, *belonged* to me, to the Weala Broc bloodline. I lay my hand on it, overwhelmed by the immense power held within.

A terror reservoir.

It whispered in my ears, telling me of its past, of the screams of Londinium when Boudicca had burned it to the ground. I knew it was even older than we were. Older than the fae. It was here long before. And it offered me power. All

I needed to give it in return was fear. Not just human fear, but fae fear as well. For the stone, they were one and the same. I would deliver sacrifices, and it would give me power to take back our lands from the Seelie.

A deal sealed in blood.

I picked up a shard of clay from the floor, and cut my hand with it, my pulse racing. Then I took a step forward and touched the stone, smearing it with my blood.

* * *

I PULLED BACK from the memory quickly, before I had to share Ogmios' bonding with the Stone.

My breath shuddered, my fists clenching the bedsheets. Nausea climbed up my throat, and sweat dampened my body. Now, my hand throbbed in pain, almost as if it echoed the pain from all those centuries ago.

His corrupted mind bloomed in mine like a tumor. His emotions were too intense, too desperate, too acidic. I was losing myself. Still, I had to know more, had to understand my enemy.

A knock on the door echoed in the room. "Cassandra?" Roan's voice.

"Go away!" My voice sounded strangled, strange.

He immediately opened the door, the disrespectful wretch. Hatred simmered in my chest.

"Are you all right?" he asked. "You've been here for more than three hours and—"

I glared at him, rage searing my mind. Roan, from the house of Taranis. The house of whores, of filthy traitors more beast than fae.

"I told you to go away, you carnal parasite!" I roared at him. "Get out before I flay you with an iron blade like I flayed your treasonous father!"

His eyes widened, and he seemed to freeze.

I gritted my teeth. "Not now, Roan, please. Ogmios… I need just a bit more time. Almost there."

Roan reached for me. "He is corrupting you."

"Stay where you are!" I roared. I wanted to lunge at him and tear his throat out. I could feel my claws materializing…

No. It was Ogmios. Not me. I forced the craving away.

"Just… a bit more," I managed. "I'm almost there."

He hesitated, then gave me a sharp nod, fury glinting in his eyes. He crossed the threshold, slamming the door behind him.

I was following a strand in the web of memories, and I could feel the answer just beyond the next curve, to an older memory, one that pulsed with emotion.

I tugged the strand closer, and it swallowed me.

* * *

OUTSIDE THE PALACE, just fifty yards from our beautiful orchard, Father stared down at me from atop his horse. "You can do it. You are big enough to mount a horse on your own."

Tears of frustration pricked my eyes. Father's horse was enormous, angry. Once, when I'd pet him, he'd bitten me. I still carried the scar.

My father's blue eyes were unrelenting. If I didn't ride on my own, he'd leave me behind with my mother.

Marshaling my resolve, I turned back to the dark horse. I clenched my jaw and ran up to the horse, gripping his mane as I jumped. I hoisted myself up, flinging a leg over his back. And then, suddenly, I was on top of him, looking at the world from above. I had ridden this horse many times before, but it now almost felt as if I sat taller.

My father's face cracked in a proud smile. "Well done, Ogmios."

His words warmed me, and I lowered my eyes to hide my blush.

"We should leave," he said. "The scouts reported a large group coming our way. It's probably nothing, but we should always be vigilant in case the Seelie invade."

I nodded. A leader should be on his guard.

"Arausio," my mother's soft voice purred behind us. "My lord."

We both glanced back. Flanked by two guards, she stood outside the gleaming palace walls, dressed in white. Her body shimmered with the orange glow that always followed her, eyes sparkling with a pale violet.

"I need to go," Father called to her. "We will be back in two days. Three at the most."

She crossed her arms, pouting. "You're leaving without kissing me goodbye?"

"A kiss with you never ends at that," my father said, pleasure tinging his voice.

My mother turned away and stepped through the palace gate, and my father stared after her.

After a moment, he said, "Wait here, Ogmios. I will only be a minute."

I knew from experience that was a lie, but I watched helplessly as he got off the horse, and followed my mother through the gate.

I waited for a minute, and one more. My stomach rumbled, and I sighed. I wouldn't have time to eat once we began riding. I glanced at the apple orchard. The apples were at their best now, their red color gleaming in the sunlight. My mouth watered as I imagined the sweet, juicy bite. But Father had told me to wait.

Of course, he said it would only be one minute, and it clearly wasn't. I was old enough to know what he and

Mother were doing. I would just hop down, eat an apple or two, and get two for the road.

The jump from the horse scared me, but I managed it. I hurried to the orchard, the sweet smells drawing me closer. The bees hummed around me as I approached the closest tree, searching for the perfect apple. Then I noticed one, a bit deeper into the orchard, on a smaller tree. I bowed my head under a large branch and walked between the shady trees, closing in on the perfect piece of fruit. It had been ready to drop, and I plucked it easily. I smelled it, shutting my eyes at the sweet scent, then took a large bite. Perhaps it was the hunger talking, or my previous moment of glory on the horse, but it tasted like the sweetest apple I had ever eaten.

The sudden shout of a guard took me by surprise. I had been daydreaming, munching on the apple, imagining myself riding Father's horse on my own. I hadn't even noticed the time pass. I turned around and hurried to the tree line, where I stopped.

There were dozens of them on horseback. Glowing with beauty, their hair pale, bodies adorned in leaves. They streamed through the arched gate into the palace, gripping pikes. The Seelie. I had rarely seen them before, and certainly not beyond our borders. My body froze, and I simply stared from the line of the trees, my fist tightening around the apple in my hand.

It seemed that time slowed to a crawl, until I heard my mother's scream from inside the palace walls.

I stared as a Seelie ran from our home, carrying my mother. She was limp, and bloody, and the Seelie tossed her body on the ground like a discarded apple core. She crumpled without resisting, drenched in blood, eyes open and vacant.

I couldn't move, my heart frozen. On horseback, another Seelie galloped from our palace, sheathing a large sword.

Then his eyes met mine, and his mouth twitched cruelly. My hand crept to the knife on my belt. I would charge him, slit his throat, and get my mother out of there. My father would charge out of the house and help me fight the invaders off. We would make them pay.

The Seelie warrior took a sudden step in my direction.

I bolted into the orchard, heart beating, and the Seelie's laughter echoed in my ears as I gave in to my own cowardice.

* * *

I PULLED BACK from the memory, still feeling the branches of the orchard trees snapping against my face as I fled the laughing Seelie, consumed by self-hatred and fear.

I took deep breaths, trying to carefully detach who I was from the emotions and thoughts of the Unseelie King. I wanted to know more, but maybe Roan had been right. Ogmios was slowly corrupting me. The fae was old and powerful, and with every memory I delved into, his web of thought seemed to grow larger in my mind. I could already sense his memories growing in power.

But this was a two-way street.

If I could sense his thoughts merging in mine, maybe he could feel mine, too.

I carefully quested in my mind, scanning the web of his thoughts. I didn't want his memories anymore. I needed to see him *now.*

...I watch the battlefield from atop the hill. The Seelie are slowly losing ground, and I smile. We've managed to breach their defenses in three different places along the borders. Their army will not be able to spread itself so thinly for long. A week, maybe two, and we'll push in. Perhaps in two months I'll be able to walk on my parents' land again.

I clenched my fists, shielding my mind, reminding myself

who I was. Cassandra, not Ogmios. Then, I plucked an image out of my own memories—a single, clear image. And I flung it at the king's web of thoughts.

The Seelie archers were skilled, better than mine. I resolved to train a separate cavalry unit to charge at the enemy's archers. Thicker armor, they wouldn't need the flexibility of the—

A strange image popped in my mind. A dark-skinned human man with hazel eyes and a talking raven on his shoulder, standing in the London streets. I blinked in surprise, losing my thread of thought. What a bizarre thing to think about during a battle. A human beast. I shook my head. It was time to send the auxiliary troops in. I raised the battle horn to my lips.

I let a smile spread on my face. Gently, I got off the bed, a sudden wave of dizziness assaulting me. How long had I been lying here?

"Roan?"

He opened the door almost immediately, concern etched across his features.

"I think I can get him," I said faintly. "I can get the king."

CHAPTER 36

*A*s king, I'd made a promise to reclaim our lands. And now, I'd fulfill it.

Through the flapping canvas entrance, a cool breeze filtered into the tent. I let myself enjoy its gentle caress—the feeling of victory. It was the breeze of our own land. And it carried with it a faint waft of smoke and blood, the scent of war.

I tried to stay focused, tuning into the general as he spoke "...Thirty-five wounded. Three have to be sent back. They will not be able to fight any longer. However, the Seelie forces suffered the loss of a crucial defense outpost, and their casualties number more than a hundred. We caught nineteen prisoners..."

I let my eyes roam over the war council. They all sat straight in their chairs, listening with rapt attention to their general. There was a glass of water and a fruit bowl by each and every one of them, all untouched.

Why? Aren't they hungry after the battle? An intrusive thought. I had no idea where it came from.

My mind jumped to the last time someone had taken a

fruit from the bowl. Had he thought I wouldn't notice? Or had he assumed I was too drunken with victory to care? How he had screamed as the whip flayed his back. I would not tolerate weakness in my commanders. I gritted my teeth, forcing myself to listen to the general.

"… A second line of defense several miles inland, but beyond that, I believe our progress would be easier. Our men will be ready to move on in three days…"

The smell of the fruit in your bowl is amazing. Its sweet flesh would be sublime. Can you imagine the feeling of the juice on your tongue, dripping down your fingers?

Mutinous thoughts.

"…And I believe that with the troops coming from the north we can take the largest outpost by surprise, securing a crucial advantage…"

Think of the taste of that red apple's juicy meat, your canines sinking into its skin, the nectar dripping down your throat.

"…We think we can get additional materials for siege ladders from the current… uh… from the current outpost that…" He blinked, appearing confused.

"Yes, general?" I asked testily.

He looked at me. Several eyes glanced at me as well. I realized I held an apple in my hand, only inches from my mouth. Angrily, I crushed it in my fist, letting them watch the pulp roll down my palm.

"You were saying?" I gritted out.

"Of course." He hurriedly cleared his throat. "As I was saying, we can find additional materials in the…"

I stopped listening, my heart beating angrily. How dared they question my strength! Did they think I would bite that apple in front of them all? I was just testing myself!

I flung the pulp's remnants on the ground, the delicious scent of fruit engulfing me.

* * *

I MARCHED DOWN THE CAMP, the darkness of evening slowly creeping around us. Campfires blazed among the darkness, and I could smell the scent of sizzling meat. My stomach grumbled, and I decided to eat a small slice of meat tonight. I deserved that, after my victorious day.

As I walked, a raven-haired serving maid crossed the path in front of me, her body and face covered. I stopped and looked at her severely, making sure that no skin showed. Lusts rose high after a battle, and I would have none of my men corrupted by temptation. They were not as strong as I was, and I couldn't expect from them the same amount of—

Imagine her body underneath all those fabrics. Imagine her nipples puckering under your hands.

The same... the same amount of self-control...

Imagine how she'd moan as her legs opened for you. How warm she would feel in your bed.

Blood drained from my head, racing to all the wrong places, and I gaped at the filthy harlot.

"I should have you branded, whore!" I screamed, spittle flying from my mouth. "I should have your nose cut from your face!"

Her terrified eyes met mine, and she scuttled away into the darkness. Wouldn't be so tempting with a mutilated face, would she?

Enraged, I marched on. I would go to sleep hungry. I would not let victory crowd my determination.

* * *

THE MORNING TRUMPETS woke me up from a long night of vivid dreams. Naked women writhing in front of me, licking my body, offering me fruit and wine. I laughed with them, drinking with abandon, fucking them senseless. The night stretched for hours. Twice I awoke, and atoned for my licentious dreams. Whenever I shut my eyes, they materialized again, tempting me with their flesh.

I was dazed, exhausted, my back burning from the night's atonement, flesh raw and bleeding. My stomach grumbled. That was the cause of my dreams. I had been too hard with myself, and my body had confused its basic needs, mistaking hunger for lust. I should have allowed myself a small meal. Perhaps some dry bread and salted meat. I shook my head. I would go to the kitchen later, and get myself some rations to satisfy my hunger.

I pulled on my clothes, glancing at the bowl of fruit by my bed

Do you see those grapes? So large and green. Succulent. Imagine one cracking between your teeth.

Then I went and washed my face in the icy water from the basin. I sat in a chair to pull on my boots.

Try one. Just one. You deserve it. Such an amazing victory yesterday. Let yourself enjoy it.

I shoved those thoughts from my mind, focusing on the upcoming day. I would be present at the prisoners' interrogation. I'd feed on fear. Perhaps ask some questions of my—

A sharp, sweet taste in my mouth took me by surprise, and I looked down at my hand. I held a cluster of grapes, and the sinful juice ran down my chin.

I roared in anger and shame, throwing the grapes on the ground. Weakness! It had been so long since… since I…

Try another one. It tasted so good.

Where were these thoughts coming from? Surely, they weren't my own.

I scrambled to my trunk, flung it open, and pulled out the flail. I began lashing myself over and over, ripping through the clothes on my back, tearing into the open wounds, the pain driving any shred of temptation away.

Finally, breathing hard, I let the flail drop, its strands glistening with blood. My back burned as if someone had spread live coals on it. I let the pain cleanse me, make me stronger. I—

It would feel so good to feel a woman's hands soothing you. Can you imagine it?

I shook my head, trying to banish those thoughts. What was happening to me? I stumbled back to the basin, and washed my face with icy water again. I lifted my eyes to the small mirror above it, watching my haggard face, my eyes red-rimmed, my shoulders bloody from the lashing.

I should have all the unmarried fae women killed.

And then the reflection flickered, and instead I saw a young woman looking at me, a smile on her face, her blond hair cascading down bare shoulders. Cassandra's mother.

I yelled, and hit the mirror, flinging it on the floor, where it shattered into pieces.

And to my horror, a mocking laugh rang in my mind.

* * *

I WAS FALLING APART. Two days. Two days of endless images of food, and wine, and naked whores, dancing in front of me. The days were bad enough, but I worked tirelessly, inspecting our progress, dispensing orders to my commanders, poring over battle plans and maps. I kept away from temptations, removed the fruit bowls, tried to fill my stomach with bread and water. I whipped myself until I bled through my clothes.

The nights were horrifying. An endless orchestra of debauchery and lewdness. My brain was being poisoned. By that... by that...

Mistress of Dread. Terror leech. Pixie. Your own mistake. Your greatest shame. Your daughter.

By that abomination! How was she doing it?

Maybe it isn't her at all. Maybe it's you. Maybe you're getting weaker.

Was I getting weaker? Could it be? No! Impossible!

"Your Majesty? Is everything all right?"

I whirled and stared at the fae. One of my commanders. He stared at me strangely. I realized I was standing, gazing at nothing, like a stupid cow. His eyes dropped to my shirt, at the blood that had stained it all over.

"I'm fine!" I said sharply, and followed his stare. It wasn't just the blood. I'd buttoned my shirt crookedly. I had begun dressing in the morning with no mirror. Whenever I glimpsed a reflection, Cassandra's mother appeared in it.

"Get out of my sight!" I roared at the man, and he fled. My fists clenched. I needed to crush something. I needed to kill. I needed...

What you need are warm thighs to spread. A mouth to kiss.

A tear of frustration materialized in my eye as the images swamped me, and I heard her laughter. Again.

* * *

"We have a six-hour march ahead of us..."

In the humid, stuffy tent, I could hardly breathe. I tried to unfasten my cloak. Get some air. There was no air. My general talked on calmly as if everything was normal.

"Our scouts will move ahead of us to make sure that..."

Another wave of images hit me. A naked woman, her breasts glistening, licking her lips, her hand between her thighs...

"Enough!" I shouted, thumping on the table.

All eyes turned to stare at me. A peal of laughter bloomed

in my mind. The abomination, the mistake. How was she doing this? How?

The London Stone.

The realization hit me like a stormy wave, and I dropped down into my chair, closing my eyes. I suddenly recalled a report on my table, yesterday. A freak fire where the Stone had been kept. The Stone had been unharmed, but some of the Arawn fae had lost their lives. At the time, I had dismissed the report as unimportant. After all, the Stone was safe; that was all that mattered. But now I put the pieces together.

It was her. She'd been there. She had touched the Stone, and we now shared a connection.

I ignored the commanders' searching stares, and focused inward. Searched my soul, my memories, my—

There.

There it was, a strange thing, one that hadn't been there before. A small web of consciousness, such that only a short-lived animal would create. I touched it with my mind, and recoiled in disgust at the emotions and images that suddenly filled my thoughts. Shameless lusts, wantonly behavior, weakness... How could this creature have come from my loins?

I needed to find her, to rip her head from her body. I was no fool. This was what she wanted. She thought she could bait me into a trap.

We would see.

But first, I had to search her mind, as distasteful as the task was, and find out where she hid. This connection worked both ways. If she could invade my thoughts, I could invade hers. I focused on the web, mentally prodding at it, and I tried to catch a glimpse.

An image instantly flickered into my mind. I was

watching the world through her eyes—a wooden house, surrounded by lush, green countryside.

I stood up, pushing my chair backward. "I am leaving. I am taking your fastest cavalry troop with me."

"Your Majesty, we're preparing to march on the outpost in—"

"You will march without me! And without one troop! Can't you take one measly outpost without me holding your hand?"

The general blinked. "Of course, Your Majesty. The troop will be ready within an hour."

I left the tent, letting the flap flutter behind me, my fists clenching. Right now, most of all, I needed loyalty. There were few men in this camp I trusted completely. I would need to use *him*.

I found him in the outer rim of the camp, playing dice with several officers, and his blue eyes met mine.

My face twisted with disgust. My second moment of weakness, in the flesh. The dreamer, the bedbug, named after the fae god of apples and sin. At least his whore mother had covered up his true heritage, and only my bastard son knew the truth.

"You," I barked. "Abellio!"

He quickly scrambled to his feet. "Your Majesty?"

"Saddle up. We're leaving."

"Yes, Your Majesty."

Obedience and loyalty. Unlike his sister, the abomination, he had these two qualities going for him. Of course, he wasn't half-beast. "And get our esteemed prisoner. Tie him to a horse."

He blinked in surprise and nodded.

I allowed myself a small smile of satisfaction. "We'll need him, too."

* * *

THE RUMBLING of the horses made my heart beat faster as I spurred on my own mount to go faster. The sooner we slaughtered the fortal, the sooner I could go back to my moment of victory.

Moment of defeat, you mean. You're going to lose. Best enjoy the little time you have left. Maybe stop at the next village, find a woman—

I blocked the thoughts away, grimacing. She thought she could waylay me with temptation? When I got my hands around her she would feel what I do to whores and harlots. I'd maim her before I killed her.

As we thundered closer to the portal, I searched for more and more glimpses from her eyes. I could see her talking to her companions. Only four. Taranis was the biggest, his face so similar to Ulthor's, his traitorous father. The second, a woman, I identified easily. She was the lowest of the lot, the real scum. I had her locked in a prison once, but she'd escaped. The other two were filthy gutter fae, and I dismissed them in my mind. Of course a Taranis would consort with criminals and peasants. I'd make him watch as I mutilated his precious whore.

Four fae and one abomination, trying to lure me into a trap.

I was going to enjoy slaughtering them.

I surveyed my bodyguards, and my cavalry.

Hawkwood Forest lay ahead of us, the portal only miles away. I smiled, spurred on by the promise of vengeance.

* * *

WE CROSSED the field of yellow, blooming rapeseed, miles and miles to the northwest of London. It had taken us eight

329

hours to find this gods-forsaken place. As we'd moved through the city and countryside, glamour had shielded us from the humans, forcing them instinctively to move away from our horses. But it had been worth it.

In the past eight hours, I had been constantly connected to her, drawn to her by our connection. And as I moved closer, our connection grew. I could see her watching through the window, waiting, could feel her anticipation, her excitement. She was beckoning me closer. Into a trap. They were waiting for us with guns full of iron bullets. I had seen her training them to shoot. They hid in that house, waiting for us to get close enough to the structure, and they'd open fire on us. I would be their target, I knew.

In the field of rapeseed, we paused by a sycamore, a few hundred yards from the decrepit house. I avoided looking straight at the crooked white structure where they hid. If she watched through my eyes, I didn't want her to know my exact location.

I dismounted and looked at Abellio. "Bring me the prisoner."

He nodded, and led a black horse forward, strapped with a dark form. I could not see it exactly, yet I knew he was there. Shackled in iron, starved and beaten, too weak to struggle. But still there.

"I need you to do something for me," I said.

He didn't reply.

"I need you to drown that place in darkness. Do it now, or you will suffer."

He did not speak; a strange sound like the fluttering of wings rose around me, and his words echoed in my mind like a thought, echoing off my skull. *No, I will do no tasks for you. My suffering means nothing.*

I wasn't surprised. As one of the generals of the rebellion, he wouldn't be so easy to break. I wasn't about to waste time with threats. I had one offer, and he'd accept.

"If you do this one thing, I will give you a clean death. Tonight. I give you my word."

Tension curled through the air. *Tonight?*

"Yes, if you do it right. You drown that place in darkness. No shred of light, not even a glimmer. No…" I let a small smile show. "Reflections."

Very well.

We all waited, hardly breathing. Darkness bloomed, seeping into the structure. Quickly, I whirled to Abellio.

"Now!" I barked. "Burn it! Kill anyone who tries to leave!"

He set out at a fast gallop, torch in hand, the cavalry following him. All had flasks of oil. All held burning torches. I watched them ride forward, and then looked inside, watching from *her* eyes. As they moved closer to the white house, I saw Cassandra run to the window, and I felt her delicious fear.

With my eyes closed, I tuned in to her sensations. Through Cassandra's eyes, I watched as she turned to the other fae, shouting something. Was she realizing her mistake? A cloud of darkness was descending over the wooden house. They couldn't see their targets, couldn't shoot.

While I watched from a safe distance, my soldiers surrounded the house submerged in darkness, dousing it with oil. And after they'd flung oil over the building's exterior, they dropped their torches.

On a windy day like today, the flames rose fast.

Cassandra shouted at the other fae, demanding that they flee. I felt the fear in her blood as they smelled the smoke. The fae bolted for a door, Taranis hesitating just for a moment. She motioned him away. She had a different way to flee. She fumbled in her purse, then suddenly raised her eyes, staring at the growing darkness. It had an oily feel to it as it roiled around her, covering everything, a black void. She pulled a mirror from her purse, her hands trembling. She looked at the reflection just as the darkness closed on the mirror. And the reflection vanished from sight.

I'd make Taranis look at her charred corpse before he died.

She panicked, then; heart beating, she began to run to the door. The smoke was thick, the fire heating the room. But she couldn't see the flames. Couldn't see anything in the billowing smoke, in the darkness created by the fae. At any moment, she'd walk into a wall of fire.

Now, following her, I couldn't see through her eyes anymore. But I could feel the smoke entering her lungs, making her cough and gag. Could feel as she accidentally ran into flames she couldn't see, burning her face and hands. Could feel as her hair caught the flames. That pink, whorish hair igniting in cleansing flames.

Hundreds of yards away, in the clear air by the sycamore, I felt her agony. The flames burned me, too, but I clung to her, feeling everything she felt as she rolled on the ground, screaming in torment, blinded, burning, dying.

And suddenly, it all stopped. My eyes snapped open, and I heaved a sigh of relief, breathing the fresh country air, only faintly tinged with smoke from this distance. The sun pierced the sycamore branches, and I stared at the beautiful flames that claimed the house, that burned my daughter's body.

My muscles relaxed, and I let myself smile. I was finally rid of my mistake. I should have killed her when she was a little baby.

You really should have, Your Majesty. You can't surprise someone who can hear your every thought.

My jaw dropped, and something gurgled behind me.

Turning around, I stared in shock as one of my guards fell off his horse, his throat slit. By his side stood that worthless carnal parasite, Taranis. And just behind him was my daughter, her pink hair whipping in the smoky wind, blades in both her hands.

CHAPTER 37

*D*izziness washed over me as I finally unlatched myself from the king's thoughts. My head throbbed—a result of the last three days of abuse. I'd hardly slept as I'd constantly maintained my vigil in the king's mind, carefully setting up the trap. The final day had been the hardest, conjuring images and feeding them to the king's mind, making him think I'd been in the countryside house.

In the field of yellow blossoms, I stumbled back, vaguely aware of the battle around me—the guards spurred on to action by Roan's attack, Elrine's arrow in a soldier's neck, the clashing of swords.

Weakened, I closed my eyes, sinking away from the action, blocking out the cries, the din of weapons clanging. I knew that, by now, the Elder Fae were descending, ambushing Abellio and the cavalry.

The trap had snapped shut.

As I moved away from the action, Ogmios whirled, locking eyes with me, features contorted with rage. I flashed him a mocking smile, knowing that his anger weakened his sense of control. I hoped that he couldn't see the tiredness in my eyes, how I could barely stand. The stilettos in my hands were a joke—I didn't have the strength to plunge them through a chunk of butter, never mind a fae warrior.

One of the king's warriors suddenly turned, charging for me. I scrambled back, helpless, lifting my stilettos in a pathetic defense against his huge blade. But as I braced for his attack, a cloud of darkness enveloped him, and he screamed in fear. Drustan had joined the battle. I lunged forward, my blade cutting the warrior's hand. Nothing serious, but in his blindness, the sudden pain terrified him. Pain is much more frightening when you don't know where it's coming from. Abellio had taught me that. The warrior scrambled back, and Branwen lunged forward to slide one of her blades across his neck. In battle, she'd unveiled, and her eyes shone like cat's eyes, dark wings sprouting from her back.

Shakily, I took another step backward in the rapeseed, and then felt a tingle at the back of my neck—the power building. I looked around frantically, and noticed that the king was staring into the air, as if focusing on something invisible.

"No," I blurted. "Stop the—"

Time slowed to a crawl, but this time, it wasn't my doing.

The King of Dread smiled as dark tendrils of fear coiled around us. He plucked them as easily as a child picking flowers. He had been doing this for centuries, and had the terror of thousands of souls to feed his power.

As he drew all the fear into him, he unveiled, growing larger. He flashed a predatory grin, sharpened teeth, as fur covered his body.

And then I knew what a skilled dread fae could do. The fear became a storm of terror within him. A hurricane of nightmares.

He unleashed it like a tidal wave, slamming everyone in

sight, his men as well as ours. The fae around me crumpled, minds numbed with fear, turning their muscles into liquid.

Then, time resumed its course as silence fell around us.

The king looked surprised as he noticed I was still standing. He cocked his head. "Well. They don't call you the Mistress of Dread for nothing." He pulled a long, beautiful sword from the scabbard on his back.

I crouched, raising my stiletto, staring at him. I felt the rush of power as I unveiled, my teeth lengthening, claws growing from my fingertips.

He dismounted, and crossed to me, his features calm. Sunlight glinted off my stiletto, and I widened my stance, my eyes locked on his.

"The least I could ask from my daughter is obedience," he snarled. "But I guess that's too much to ask of an abomination such as you."

"I am not your daughter."

"You are. Your mother brought you to me when you were a babe, and—"

"My mother was Martha Liddell. My father was Horace Liddell. All *you* ever were was a weak sperm donor."

He gritted his teeth, and I threw one of my blades at him.

It missed him by almost a foot, thudding to the ground behind him. He laughed cruelly, and then stepped forward, his blade swinging in lightning speed.

Then, I jumped through the reflection in the blade in my hand, materializing behind him through the other blade. With speed only a burst of adrenaline could give me, I snatched the stiletto from the ground and thrust forward, sinking it into the back of his shoulder.

He screamed and whirled, slamming his fist into my face. I fell on the ground, all my strength gone, the left side of my face throbbing. Face twisted in fury, he raised his sword.

At that moment, a dark shadow lunged forward. Roan.

His resistance to the dread magic had been sharpened by my practicing on him. His sword was lightning fast. The king whirled, trying to parry, but his arm was wounded and clumsy.

Roan's blade sunk into Ogmios' chest. With a loud snarl, he gored his antlers into the king's throat.

The king fell to the ground, silent as the life faded from his eyes.

CHAPTER 38

I walked down the gravel path, ignoring the fine rain that pattered my skin, dampened my hair. The raindrops masked the tears I knew would come soon.

Gabriel's remains lay in a small graveyard encircled by stone, his burial plot marked by fresh dirt, and a stark stone engraved with his name.

Gabriel Stewart

1981 - 2017

To his left stood the grave of Lorena Stewart, who'd died three years ago. Instantly, I regretted not bringing another bouquet for her.

I laid the sheaf of white lilies on Gabriel's grave, amongst three other bouquets. It felt almost as if I was acting out a ceremony that meant nothing. My friendship with Gabriel did not have anything to do with flowers. If I had really wanted to leave something that signified my bond with him, it would have been a Starbucks coffee cup. But leaving a plastic cup on the grave would have been crude, so I went with traditional flowers.

I thought of him as I wanted to remember him—fixing eggs in his tidy kitchen, playing his old jazz band. Trying to keep me away from a murder victim, because he didn't want me to be traumatized. Listening to me as I explained I was a pixie, his face serious and rapt, without a shred of disbelief. Giving me his coat during a cold stakeout, as we waited for a serial killer to show up. Helping me on a mad dash to save Scarlett's life. Over and over, risking his career and life to help me.

Always there. Always caring, listening, trying to help.

I smiled as I recalled his persistence in calling the fae "demons." How he had insisted on entering a fae club with me because he didn't trust Roan to keep me safe. A twenty-first century knight in shining armor.

His loss gnawed at my chest, a void.

The guilt was gone, transformed into sorrow. Looking back, I knew I'd made mistakes, but Gabriel's death hadn't really been my fault. The people who were to blame were all dead. I had made sure of that.

I didn't talk to the grave, pretending I was having a conversation with a dead man. I knew it helped some people, but not me.

I was just glad to keep a piece of him in my memories, a gleaming strand of Gabriel's essence.

* * *

I CROSSED through the hall in Roan's mansion, squinting at the sunlight that slanted in from his windows. Daylight still felt like a shock to my eyes, but I was endlessly grateful to be back in Roan's palace of windows and light. Since we'd killed Ogmios, we'd been able to return here. The place had almost started to feel like home in a strange way.

As I walked, I looked down at the little figurine in my hands—the woman who'd been cleaved in half. I'd carefully glued her back together and let it set and dry. I smiled as I looked down at it, imagining a tiny, furious Roan Taranis hurling it at the floor in fit of temper.

In the past day, I'd started to feel different. Lighter, almost, as if something heavy had lifted from my chest. I could no longer feel my dread powers, or sense the fear in other fae, but it felt like a ton of rocks had been lifted from my chest.

Pausing at the library doors, I pulled open the heavy, carved oak.

There, I found Roan sitting in one of the leather library chairs, under the ivory light of the oculus illuminating his hair like a golden crown. Already, my pulse raced at the sight of him. As I crossed the room, he met my gaze.

"You've been in here for hours," I said, oddly tempted to crawl into his lap. "I brought you a present."

A smile played over his lips. "Did you?"

I held out the figurine in the palm of my hand, watching as his jaw dropped, his features slightly awestruck. Carefully, he pulled her from my hand. "You fixed it."

"I thought you might want to keep it."

"You never fail to surprise me, Cassandra."

Blushing, I dropped down into the worn leather armchair next to him. "That's not the only reason I came to see you. I don't suppose you have news about the envoy to the Seelie?"

"The envoy made contact." He still traced his fingertips over the figurine. "The Seelie are willing to listen. They heard that Ogmios is dead. We told them that the Council wanted to end this war before we shed any more blood. Negotiations are underway."

"You think they'll agree?"

"They were losing the war," Roan said. "They've suffered great losses. I doubt they'll risk anymore."

I stared into the light at the fine dust motes circling in the streaming rays, trying to pick through the possibilities. In the old days, Trinovantum had been ruled by the Council—six elected representatives from each Unseelie kingdom. Would the days of the old republic return, or would another tyrant fill the vacuum?

"Any idea what Abellio is doing, or is he still missing?" I asked. When the rebels and the king's cavalry troop had recovered from the king's wave of dread, Abellio was already gone. Maybe, since he was also from the bloodline of dread, he was immune to its powers, too, and had taken advantage of the distraction to escape.

"Elrine is searching for him with some additional hunters. They'll find him."

I stiffened, suddenly overcome by a memory of Abellio laughing as I struggled to breathe.

A range of emotions played over Roan's features. He could feel what I felt, but he was unwilling to reach for me, to pull me close. "What will you do now? Keep searching?"

"Searching for what?"

"You've been constantly digging at your past. Perhaps, now that you know who your mother was, you could find some blood relatives."

"No. I know who I am. I'm Cassandra Liddell. My parents were Horace and Martha. That's all there is to it." I couldn't bring myself to tell him that I was also the biological daughter of the man who'd slaughtered his family, who'd imprisoned and tortured him over and over. Roan believed in the importance of bloodlines more than I did. He'd never look at me the same way again.

"Will you return to the United States?"

"I don't know yet," I murmured. "Do you have any opinion? Do you want me to stay here?" My pulse raced as I waited for him to answer, and my cheeks warmed as an awkward silence fell over the room.

He took a deep breath. "This is what I really wanted to speak to you about."

I swallowed hard. Did he want me to leave? "About what, exactly?"

"We're bonded, you and me. Some fae, if they're lucky, find their soulmates."

My breath quickened. "Alvin told me about that concept. I don't believe in it."

"It's the reason I was reluctant to mate with you."

My heart began to race. "What do you mean?"

"We're soulmates. In Trinovantum, when Siofra was tormenting us, she provoked me to unveil. Then, something compelled me to bite your neck. That's when I first began to suspect the truth. And when you came here to my home after Gabriel died, you felt it, too. You bit my neck, connecting our minds and souls. It meant I was able to see some of your memories, and bring you back from the dead when the spider killed you. That was the full meaning of the ceremony that bonded us."

My breath caught in my lungs. "Which you failed to explain in advance."

"I did try."

"Not very hard."

"You must feel it, right?" He leaned forward, still clutching the figurine. "It's why you stayed behind in Trinovantum, when you should have run from the king's troops. You felt compelled to protect me."

"Not because of magic."

"What was it?"

342

I swallowed hard. Love? Surely I didn't know him well enough to love him? The truth was, I could feel our bond, but I didn't understand it. "I don't understand what it all means. What is a mating bond? Some kind of predestined decision from the gods that we have no control over?"

"It's a *gift* from the gods, bestowed only to a few. You said fear was the most ancient human emotion. The most powerful. I don't think that's true."

My mouth had gone dry. "A gift. I still don't understand. If we're mates, why do you keep pulling away from me? What did Elrine mean when she stopped you from coming to my room that night?"

"Mating is how soulmates pledge eternal commitment."

Irritation flared. "It's not a pledge if I didn't know what it meant."

"I know."

I felt my heart beating as anger blossomed in me. What was he trying to tell me? That we were destined to be together? "I don't know a fraction of the things about you that Elrine knows. In the real world, you are closer to her than you are to me. She's obviously in love with you, and she actually knows things about you. Maybe *she* should be your mate." I didn't *want* her to be his mate, but the words were tumbling out anyway. "She's known you and cared for you for centuries."

His gaze went cold. "You want me to be with Elrine?"

"That is how normal relationships work. You spend time together. You get to know each other. You tell people things about yourself. You don't just bite each other's necks and fuck in the bushes and then you're eternally committed whether you like it or not. Especially when you've been hiding things from me. Like the whole commitment pledge thing, which I entered into without knowing."

"I tried to tell you. You were unrelenting."

I rose from my chair, fury warming my cheeks. "Elrine knew, didn't she? *She* knew we were mates, even though I didn't." I whirled to face him. "And who else knew, by the way?"

He shrugged, almost imperceptibly. "Everyone raised in the fae realm would understand the meaning of the bond that brought you back and kept you alive despite the interrogator's venom."

I folded my arms. "So all the residents of the mansion knew, and I was in the dark. Why didn't you say anything?"

"I thought you should return home. You couldn't live among the fae without knowing how to unveil. You were vulnerable and needed to live among the humans. And more than that, I didn't want a mate."

Anger flared. "Well that's charming, isn't it? 'You're my mate, but by the way, I never wanted you. We're just stuck together because we screwed in the bushes.' Whoops!"

He closed his eyes, as if marshaling his patience. "This is coming out all wrong." When he met my gaze, his green eyes shone in the pale light. He pulled down the front of his shirt, exposing his tattoo—the wild strawberry plant with three leaves. "For years, my mother and sister and I were imprisoned. We looked after each other, the three of us. Or rather, they looked after me. I was the youngest." He covered the tattoo again. "Until one day, when I made a mistake I'll never forget, and the king punished me for it. I watched my mother die. I watched my sister die. The king used my love to torment me. My love for them made me vulnerable."

My heart ached, and I could feel my anger abating. I almost wanted to wrap my arms around him. "I'm sorry."

"As my mate, you'd be an easy target. The king would have wanted to punish me by hurting you."

I stared at him. The king had tormented him, exploiting

his love to control him. If Roan knew the truth about me, what would he see when he looked into my blue eyes? The Court of the Drowned Man. The man who'd ripped his world apart, imprisoned him for years, tried to crush his soul.

If soulmates were indeed real, the gods had played a cruel joke on Roan by gifting him with me.

"I still don't know you," I said hollowly. "And you don't know me."

Before he could answer, a knock boomed from the oak door. Roan crossed to it, grabbing a sword that rested against the door frame. Sword in hand, he called out, "Yes?"

"Sir? There's word from the Council." A muffled voice pierced the door.

Roan pulled open the door. An abashed messenger handed him a rolled parchment, before scurrying off into the hallway. Roan shut the door and unrolled the parchment, reading it, his expression darkening.

"What is it?" I asked.

"The Seelie are attacking. Our forces were caught unaware. They're invading Trinovantum."

A chill stroked up my spine.

Roan stiffened. "There was also an attack on the house of Arawn in London." He raised his eyes to meet mine. Gritting his teeth in anger, he crumpled up the parchment. "The Unseelie suffered a lot of casualties. The banshees would have probably fought with us against the Seelie, but most are dead now."

My stomach churned. Focusing inward, I searched for the connection with the Stone, for the screams and that dark tug.

Nothing.

"It was never about the banshees," I said, feeling empty. "It was about the London Stone. The Seelie have done some-thing to it. Possibly destroyed it."

And along with the Stone, my dread powers had disappeared.

* * *

THANK you so much for reading. To find out about our next releases, please sign up to our mailing list.

—Alex Rivers and C.N. Crawford.

ACKNOWLEDGMENTS

We'd like to thank Alex's lovely wife Liora for her amazing notes and letting us know when people are acting creepy.

Our cover designer, Clarissa did another fantastic job.

And finally, we'd like to thank our wonderful editors, Elayne and Izzy.

ABOUT THE AUTHOR

Alex Rivers is the co-author of the Dark Fae FBI Series. In the past, he's been a journalist, a game developer, and the CEO of the company Loadingames. He is married to a woman who diligently forces him to live his dream, and is the father of an angel, a pixie, and a gremlin. He has two voracious hounds that wag their tail quite menacingly at anyone who comes near his home.

Alex has been imagining himself fighting demons and vampires since forever. Writing about it is even better, because he doesn't get bitten, or tormented in hell, or even just muddy. In fact, he does it in his slippers.

Alex also writes crime thrillers under the pen name Mike Omer.

You can contact Alex by sending him an email to alex@strangerealm.com.

C. N. Crawford is sometimes two people—a married couple named Christine and Nick. But for the Dark Fae FBI series, it's just Christine. Christine grew up in New England and has a lifelong interest in local folklore—with a particular fondness for creepy old cemeteries. She is a psychologist who spent eight years in London obsessively learning about its history, and misses it every day.

Please join us here to talk about books, fantasy, and writing   updates! https://www.facebook.com/groups/cncrawford/

ALSO BY C.N. CRAWFORD

The Demons of Fire and Night Series

Book 1: Infernal Magic

Book 2: Nocturnal Magic

Book 3: Primeval Magic

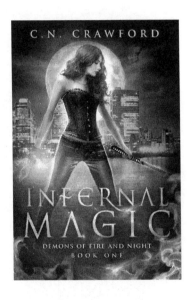

The Vampire's Mage Series

Book 1: *Magic Hunter*

Book 1.1: *Shadow Mage*

Book 2: *Witch Hunter*

Book 3: *Blood Hunter*

Book 4: *Divine Hunter*

Made in the USA
San Bernardino, CA
18 August 2018